"Sire," he said, "tomorrow Your Grace will be seated here, on a chair, as throne. But . . . not on the stone. The Coronation Stone."

"No," Charles agreed, but without sounding in any way concerned. "That is in London. One day, let us hope . . ."

The other coughed, and glanced round his companions, who all were watching him heedfully. "*A* stone is in London, yes, Your Grace. The stone which has sat in Westminster Abbey for three hundred and fifty years. But that is not the true Stone of Destiny, we believe, the *Lia Fail*."

The monarch frowned. "What mean you? It is the stone under the Coronation Chair. On which my father was crowned. The man Cromwell has not taken *that*, has he?"

"No, no, that stone, no doubt, is still there. But . . . that is, as we understand it, only a lump of sandstone from this Scone's quarry. A shapeless mass. Whereas the true stone is . . . otherwise."

He had aroused real interest, however doubting, in those royal eyes now. "Otherwise? I do not understand."

Honours Even

Nigel Tranter

CORONET BOOKS
Hodder and Stoughton

Copyright © 1995 by Nigel Tranter

The right of Nigel Tranter to be identified as the Author of
the Work has been asserted by him in accordance with the
Copyright, Designs and Patents Act 1988.

First published in Great Britain in 1995 by Hodder & Stoughton
a division of Hodder Headline PLC
First published in paperback in 1996 by Hodder and Stoughton
A Coronet paperback

10 9 8 7 6 5 4 3 2 1

A CIP catalogue record for this book is available from the British Library

ISBN 0 340 62584 8

Printed and bound in Great Britain by
Cox & Wyman Ltd, Reading, Berkshire

Hodder and Stoughton
A division of Hodder Headline PLC
338 Euston Road
London NW1 3BH

Principal Characters in order of appearance

James Ramsay: Younger son of the Laird of Bamff, Perthshire.

Sir Gilbert Ramsay: Father of above.

William Keith, Earl Marischal: Great Scots noble and soldier.

Rev. Andrew Cant: Prominent Covenanting divine.

Archibald Campbell, Marquis of Argyll: Chief of that clan.

Sir David Ogilvy of Clova: Brother of the Earl of Airlie.

John Campbell, Earl of Loudoun: Chancellor of Scotland.

King Charles the Second: Newly succeeded to the throne.

George Villiers, Duke of Buckingham: English favourite.

Charles Maitland, Earl of Lauderdale: Great Scots noble.

Lord Lewis Gordon: Rightful Marquis of Huntly.

Lady Mary Keith: Daughter of the Earl Marischal.

Jean Ramsay: Sister of James.

Mariota Ogilvy: Daughter of Sir David.

James Ogilvy, Earl of Airlie: Great Scots noble.

Ludovic Lindsay, Earl of Crawford: A Scottish commander of note.

General David Leslie: Notable Scots soldier.

Lieutenant-General George Monck: Cromwell's deputy in Scotland.

Lieutenant-General Lambert: Another English commander.

Christian Ogilvy: Daughter of Sir David Ogilvy of Clova.

Alexander Leslie, Earl of Leven: Scottish commander-in-chief.

Andrew, Lord Gray: Scots noble.

Sir William Dick of Braid: Former Lord Provost of Edinburgh.

Lady Anne Dick: Wife of above.

George Ogilvie of Barras: Keeper of Dunnottar Castle.

Rev. James Grainger: Parish minister of Kinneff.

David, Lord Ogilvy: Son of the Earl of Airlie.

Archibald Campbell, Lord Lorne: Soldier son of the Marquis of Argyll.

Donald MacGregor of Glengyle: Proscribed clan chieftain. Father of Rob Roy.

Sir John Keith of Kintore: Brother of the Earl Marischal.

Janet Ogilvie: Wife of Ogilvie of Barras.

Christian Grainger: Wife of the Rev. James Grainger.

Major-General Morgan: Welsh officer of Monck's army.

William Cunninghame, Earl of Glencairn: Great Scots noble and commander.

John Middleton of that Ilk: New commander of royal forces in Scotland.

1

Jamie Ramsay glanced sidelong at his father to see how he was taking the talk around them. Sir Gilbert was frowning, as well he might, his son considered. The divines seemed to him to be vying with each other in their harsh and strident assertions and claims, Argyll and the other lords not seeking to tone them down, as they ought to be doing in Jamie's opinion. This was no way to welcome the new monarch, surely. This should be a great day for all, for Scotland – perhaps even for Commonwealth England also.

He transferred his gaze seawards. Out there, still fully a mile off in Spey Bay, the single ship was tacking a way in against quite a strong westerly wind; they had been watching it doing so for the last half-hour at least, and it would undoubtedly be as much again before it made the river-mouth and jetty. It was a strange place to receive a king, and one who had never before so much as set foot on the soil of his ancient realm. It occurred to Jamie that Mary Queen of Scots, Charles's great-grandmother, had at least done better than this when she arrived back in Scotland at the age of eighteen, from France. She had been suitably and officially welcomed at Leith, port of Edinburgh, her capital, and conveyed in style up to her palace of Holyroodhouse – to a grim reign admittedly, and eventual dire death. Jamie often all but wept over Mary, being somewhat romantically minded, although of course her religion was against her, as a good, or goodish Protestant, he had to concede. Charles was no Catholic, at least. He was twenty years old, Jamie Ramsay two years younger.

His older brother, Thomas, standing at the other side of their father, was speaking, having almost to shout to be heard against the upraised voices of the proclaiming divines used to thunderous preaching. "Is it not strange that he comes with only the one ship? You would think that there would have been an escort, a squadron even, to protect him from Cromwell's wretched navy. But there is no sign of other than just this one."

"One vessel can be safer than any squadron," Sir Gilbert said. "It can sail unnoticed, as a group could not. It will have come from The Hague, by an easterly route, to avoid the English patrols. And if any of them saw her, flying the Dutch flag, they would assume her to be but a merchanter."

"It is all wrong that the King of Scots should have to come to his own land so," Jamie asserted – and not for the first time. "In secret. Hiding, almost. And from his own subjects, if not his own *people*. For he is King of England, too."

"He will not wish to go the way of his father!" Sir Gilbert said dryly. Charles the First had been executed, by order of the English parliament, some sixteen months before.

Even stronger upraised voices to their right turned the Ramsays' heads, like those of others waiting there. An altercation had broken out between a group of black-robed clerics – they all but outnumbered the lords and lairds present, if not the common folk, who stood well back – and the Earl Marischal, no less, and they were actually shouting him down. It was changed days for Scotland when ministers of religion could shout down an earl, especially the hereditary Marshal of the realm; but these days, with the great Montrose dead, executed, the Covenant divines all but ruled the land, aided and abetted by Archibald Campbell, Marquis of Argyll, for his own purposes.

It was the Reverend Andrew Cant, of St Andrews, who was dominating the discussion, if that it could be called, a very senior Covenant churchman, even though once he had been an Episcopalian.

"I say that this is Christ's kingdom before it is Charles Stewart's! As such he must have reception. You, my lord, represent the second, we the first!"

The other clerics uttered vehement agreement.

William Keith, seventh Earl Marischal – who was in fact kin

2

to the Ramsays by marriage – a handsome man who had been a Covenant forces commander, shook his head. "As Marischal, it is my simple duty to receive His Grace first, Master Cant. Lacking the presence of his lieutenant-general and viceroy!" That, with a brief side glance at Argyll, an oblique reference to the late Marquis of Montrose, whom Argyll had had executed. There was no love lost between these two noblemen. "Then you may have your say."

"No! The Kirk takes precedence!" That was the Reverend Robert Blair, of Aberdeen, another stalwart of the Church Militant, who actually claimed prophetic powers and direct communication with heaven. "You are but an earthly vassal of an earthly monarch. We speak in the name of the Most High!"

"Who made you so?"

Argyll intervened, softly. It was strange that Archibald Campbell, chief of that name and clan, MacCailean Mor himself, should have such a soft and sibilant Highland voice in view of his reputation: sibilant but sufficiently penetrating, and positive enough to be heeded, even by divines. Whether he was looking at Cant, Blair or the earl was hard to tell, for he had a notable cast in one eye which could confuse his hearers, and which nowise enhanced foxy, narrow-chinned features. This was the real ruler of Scotland.

"I suggest that my Lord Marischal goes on to the ship first," he said. "And that when His Grace sets foot on land, the Kirk greets him first. Only then, we others." That was typical Argyll.

It had its effect, none challenging.

Jamie Ramsay was turning to his father, to whisper in the sudden hush, when another voice spoke up, and loudly, and another Campbell at that, John, first Earl of Loudoun.

"His Grace is not well versed in conditions here," he pointed out. "He will require much . . . instruction. But, I suggest, not all at this first meeting!" Loudoun, one of Argyll's protégées naturally, had proved quite an effective general for the Covenant – Argyll was no warrior and preferred others to do the fighting for him – and was now in fact Chancellor of the realm, that is, in effect, chief minister of state. He was in a position to know the new king's condition, for he had gone, not long before, to The Hague, with two other earls, Lanark and Lauderdale, to persuade the young monarch to come to his ancient kingdom of Scotland from exile in the Netherlands. Loudoun had come home thereafter, leaving the other two to bring Charles in person. No doubt they were in that ship out there.

"He will be instructed!" the Reverend David Dickson declared briefly but with authority. He was almost as senior in the Kirk as were Cant and Blair.

The approaching vessel was now much nearer, protected from the offshore wind by the loom of the land, sufficiently so for all to see the Dutch flag of William of Orange flying from its masthead. Jamie felt that there ought to be cannon fired in salutation for this auspicious occasion; but there were none such at or near Garmouth, where great Spey reached salt water, in north-eastern Moray, which had been chosen, presumably by Argyll, as a suitably remote spot to receive the new monarch. Sir Gilbert Ramsay had opined that this was not only to avoid English naval attack, informed by spies as Cromwell surely would be, but to ensure that the populace of such as Edinburgh, Glasgow, Dundee or Aberdeen did not welcome Charles too heartily and kindly, and give that young man erroneous notions as to his position and power – or the lack of it – in his Scotland.

It occurred to Jamie, for one, that it was strange that Garmouth, a mere fishing village, had been selected, only a mile or two from St Ninian's church at Bellie, a little further up Spey, where not so long before James Graham of Montrose had buried his fourteen-year-old son, the Lord Graham, a lad worn out by the campaigning in which he had been so determined to take part, and when Montrose had proclaimed that he hoped to rejoin the boy before so very long – a strange prophecy from the man who had, for a brief spell, conquered Scotland for Charles. Could he have guessed, somehow, that despite all his brilliant victories, Argyll and the Covenant would win in the end? If it was indeed the end?

4

As the ship neared, the welcoming party moved down to the jetty. They could discern a group standing in the bows. Jamie thought that he could distinguish two slighter and younger figures amongst the others. Was one their liege-lord?

He felt like cheering, but nobody else seemed to be so inclined. Grapnels were thrown to the jetty-timbers, and slowly the vessel was warped in. All could see which was Charles Stewart now, the youngest man there, long, dark hair curling down to his shoulders, not handsome as his father had been but large-eyed and heavy-lidded with a long nose and somewhat sallow complexion, as had been his grandfather, James the Sixth and First.

A gangway was run out from the ship.

Promptly the Earl Marischal strode over, to board, and behind him the other notables surged, the divines well to the fore.

As Charles came forward, flanked by Lanark and Lauderdale, with the other younger man close behind, the Marischal sank down on one knee to take the monarch's hand between his two palms in the gesture of fealty.

Jamie did raise a cheer now, and after a moment Thomas hesitantly joined him. Nobody else did.

After a word or two, Charles turned to introduce the over-dressed and dandified fair-haired man behind, and all heard him say George, Duke of Buckingham. Then he beckoned forward another solid and bearded man of so very different type, no doubt the captain of the ship. Then the group moved forward to the gangway.

And now they were faced with what amounted to a challenge. For the Kirk ministers had pushed on to the gangway itself, fronted by Cant, Blair and Dickson and, since it was only wide enough for three abreast, they completely blocked it. There was no getting down on knees, now, only stern, unsmiling faces.

Charles stared, blinking those large, liquid-seeming eyes. His had been a strange life and upbringing hitherto for a prince and a monarch; but this was probably the strangest experience yet.

"Sire, we greet you, in the name of Almighty God, the

5

Father, the Son and the Holy Spirit. Amen!" Andrew Cant announced, at his most sonorous and authoritative. "By God's grace and permission you come to this ancient land where your forefathers have reigned for a thousand years. It is our duty, as representing the Covenanted Kirk, to require of you, before you set foot on its sacred soil, that you take the Covenant."

An absolute silence fell on all there, not even a gasping, only suddenly held breaths as everywhere men all but gaped.

"Take the Covenant! Take the Covenant!" the divines reiterated in chorus.

Charles's great eyes widened as he looked from them to his companions and back again. "Take . . . ?"

"Aye, Your Grace. Although you are *not* Your Grace yet! Take the Covenant. The National and the Solemn League Covenant, between Almighty God and His Kirk," Cant said forcefully. "Accept and swear to it. As we all have done."

The young monarch stood silent. He would certainly have heard of the Covenant, but as certainly would know little of what it meant.

Strangely the silence was broken by laughter of a sort, a tittering. It came from the ridiculously dressed Buckingham, with his painted face and ribboned ringlets. George Villiers, second Duke, was aged twenty, two years older than Charles.

"Ha, Charles, by God, here is a play-acting, no? Better than anything we have viewed at The Hague, I vow. Better even than any I have penned! Bow before them! I – "

The Earl of Lauderdale coughed and raised a hand to urge the younger man to stop. He was looking as appalled as his somewhat heavy features allowed, whether at the divines' demand or at Buckingham's remarks it was hard to say, possibly both.

The duke was not finished, however. Son of the previous two kings' favourite, he was an accomplished poet, playwright, and known as the most wicked and depraved man in all Europe, with a great influence over the younger Charles. He was not used to being waved down.

"These are . . . clerks?" he enquired silkily.

6

Cant pointed at him. "Silence!" he cried. "We are God's appointed representatives in this land. How dare you to speak! *We* address and inform the king-to-be. For he is not yet crowned." That was only a little-disguised warning. He turned back to Charles. "Your Grace, it is necessary that you take the Covenant before you set foot on the soil of this Scotland."

Charles looked from Lauderdale to Lanark for guidance. Neither earl looked happy, the former frowning, the latter's cadaverous features unhelpful. Lanark shook his head, but not decisively. Lauderdale nodded, but looked away, which was of scant assistance to their twenty-year-old liege-lord.

It was the Earl Marischal who spoke, from behind the royal group. "This is absurd! Intolerable!" he exclaimed. "To speak to His Grace so. Make way, I say, for His Grace to land."

"No!" That was the Reverend Blair. "This is the moment of truth! Do we worship the King of Heaven? Or the would-be King of Scots!"

"We are not worshipping here, sirs. We are welcoming King Charles back to his own land and kingdom."

"Only if he takes the Covenant," the Reverend Dickson insisted.

"Swears to accept and abide by the Covenant's provisions," Blair amplified.

The other ministers at their backs shouted agreement.

Again it was that unlikely peacemaker, Argyll, who intervened. "Sire, it would be best, wise, to agree," he said carefully. "It must aid your royal cause. You need the Kirk. I am Argyll."

Charles, who up till now had spoken only that one word "take . . . ?" found his voice. "You . . . *you* are Argyll! Who had Montrose beheaded!"

"The Estates of the Realm did, Sire. And the General Assembly of the Kirk. In their wisdom. He betrayed the faith he once supported. The first hand to sign the Covenant. But that is by with. Agree the Covenant, Your Grace, and be welcomed to your realm."

"What is it? To what should I agree?"

7

Cant it was who answered him. "Three main provisions. You swear to renounce Popery. To maintain the Reformed Religion in its Presbyterian form. And to adhere to it all your days, banning all episcopacy and bishops."

"But . . ." Charles wagged those long curls in bewildered objection. "How can I do that? It is against all that, that . . ."

"It is necessary."

"Necessary for what?" There was a spark of spirit there.

"Necessary for your coronation, Charles Stewart! Until you are crowned at Scone you are not the king. And only the Church of this land can give you coronation – the Kirk!"

So there it was, the secret of the divines' power and Argyll's support for them.

The lapping wavelets against the jetty timbers made all the sound.

Buckingham tinkled another laugh. "The masque unfolds! Even the man Shakespeare did not rise to such heights of pretence, Charles. It was worth our journey to hear this!"

No one else was taking the situation thus lightly. The Campbell Earl of Loudoun spoke up.

"Sire, the form of it is none so grievous. Your Grace's one word will suffice, I think. Then all can be done suitably and in order. We all here seek to welcome you to your ancient kingdom. *All*."

Despite the emphasis, the divines stood still, completely blocking the gangway. Clearly they were not going to move, and nobody there, as clearly, was going to try to move them by force, although Jamie Ramsay for one, seething with anger and shame, would have wished it.

Lauderdale and Lanark eyed each other, and nodded. The former spoke.

"I advise that you take the Covenant, Sire," he said. "Montrose, after all, was its first signatory, those years back."

"But reneged." That was Argyll.

Helplessly the young monarch shrugged. He had come many hundreds of miles for this day, at major risk. The Marischal

8

would have cleared the gangway had he had the means, as no doubt he would conceive it his duty; but here were no forces to marshal. And any physical struggle, pushing and striking, would be unseemly to a degree. The Kirk stood firm.

"Do you, Charles Stewart, take the Covenant?" Cant demanded then. "Swear to uphold and maintain it?"

The young man drew a deep breath. "Yes," he said flatly.

"Good! That is well. Your Grace has taken the Covenant. Your coronation may now be proceeded with. At Scone." He had, with his companions, won the day. He turned, and gestured for them to clear the gangway.

There were probably more sighs of relief than mutterings of offence.

Urged on now by Lauderdale and Lanark, Charles moved forward at last, if less than assuredly, Buckingham sauntering elegantly behind. The royal foot came down, for the first time, on the earth of the longest line of monarchs in all Christendom, but this one made no sort of token of it. He no doubt had had enough of tokens. Argyll was the first to come to take the royal hand between his own – but not on bended knee.

It was no very large party which had awaited the King's arrival, deliberately limited as to numbers so that there should be no unsuitably enthusiastic welcome from non-Covenant supporters; and the small port of Garmouth, little more than a fishing village, was no place to raise a crowd. There were perhaps thirty there other than the villagers. Sir Gilbert Ramsay and his sons were present only because of their Ogilvy connection. James Ogilvy, second Earl of Airlie, had campaigned with Montrose, and suffered direly for it, being captured, imprisoned and excommunicated. One brother, Sir Thomas, had been slain in battle; but the other brother, Sir David, had been fortunate to escape and was here present, representing the earl. And Sir Gilbert Ramsay was his cousin and friend, and had been the earl's aide. So they had come on this especial occasion more or less as representing the great and loyal family of Ogilvy rather than merely as Ramsays. Theirs was no very great house, although they had been settled at Bamff, on the Perth–Angus borders, for over four hundred years.

Not all the company was lining up to kiss the royal hand; certainly no divines were. And Jamie, a mere eighteen-year-old second son, was uncertain as to whether *he* was entitled to do so, eager as he was. But his father joined the line and did not sign to his sons not to follow, so he and Thomas dared.

Somebody else was looking doubtful, a youngish man of good looks and hot eyes – and those eyes made the doubts seem the stranger. But he had reason to doubt, with a glance at Argyll and the ministers. For he was a Catholic, and all there knew it, the Lord Lewis Gordon. Indeed he should have been Marquis of Huntly, his father and elder brother both having paid the supreme penalty for their religion and support of Montrose, and the title was forfeited meantime. But this was very much Gordon country, and the Gordons could still field a couple of thousand fighting men at short notice; so he had risked being present to greet his liege-lord. He had been a successful, if not always disciplined, captain of cavalry. Jamie, who had been introduced to him by his father, noting the hesitation, and sympathising, gestured for Lord Lewis to join the line in front of himself, and the other, nodding, did so.

Waiting his turn to kneel, Jamie inspected the young man he was there to greet and pay allegiance to. Seen close at hand, Charles Stewart had an interesting face, not strong nor handsome but prominent as to features, refined save for that overlong nose, with a twist to the mouth which might bespeak humour but equally disdain, and a gleam in the eyes. It was those eyes which really made the impression, however, not hot like the Gordons', but deep-seeming as they were large, scarcely soulful but holding a quality of, as it were, slumbering intensity. Jamie had never seen eyes quite like these; it was said that James the Sixth had similar, derived possibly, it was whispered, from David Rizzio, Mary Queen of Scots' talented Italian secretary, who might have been her son's father.

When it was Jamie's turn to kneel and take the royal hand between his, Charles was scarcely using those eyes to best effect, not to the kneeler at any rate. He was, indeed, looking all but bored with the proceedings, glancing away from the line of fealty-givers. Jamie would dearly have liked to express his sympathy with the ordeal with which the new monarch had been confronted, and his shame over it all, but recognised that this was not the time nor himself a suitable mouthpiece. He merely murmured his own name and added "God save Your Grace", even so wondering whether there had not already been a sufficiency of God's name brought into the occasion. But at least he held the king's hand in his own, the great-grandson of Mary Queen of Scots whose memory he doted on, and swore to be his man so long as he had breath.

When all this was over, the clergy, impatient with it all, led the way to the waiting horses, the local village folk falling back respectfully to give them passage. It was only then that most there learned that they were bound for Bog of Gight Castle, a Gordon stronghold nearby, for the night. This would be why the Lord Lewis's presence there had been tolerated. It was the nearest, indeed only, major house to Garmouth, such as was required; and he would be allowed to provide comfort and hospitality for all.

It was rather comic, Jamie thought, to reach those horses and find them watched over by a troop of Gordon men-at-arms, with extra mounts thoughtfully provided by the Lord Lewis for the voyagers. Presumably the Covenant enthusiasts perceived themselves as quite safe in these hands, owing to the royal presence. All mounted, Lord Lewis assisting Charles to mount the best horse and then leading the way due southwards up-river.

The Spey was broad here and slow-flowing through bogland and sandy shallows, with many sub-channels and islanded banks, so very different in character from its wild Highland genesis, indeed from most of its one-hundred-and-seven-mile course. But the ground did begin to rise a little as they moved up the river's east side into wooded slopes. The Ramsays rode well to the rear of the column with Sir David Ogilvy, a fine-looking man of middle years. His kinswoman Isabel had been Sir Gilbert Ramsay's mother, and the Ramsays had other Ogilvy blood and connections. Well out of earshot of Argyll and the clergy, they went over the day's doings, thus far, and deplored most of it. But they all recognised how carefully all had to tread, at this juncture, for it had been touch and go whether the ruling Covenant faction would in fact allow Charles to come to assume his late father's throne; and equally uncertain that these young men would agree to come. It had taken the embassage of the three earls, Loudoun, Lauderdale and Lanark, much persuading to achieve it. The backgrounds of those three were significant: Loudoun, representing his Campbell chief, Argyll, who it seemed wanted the royal presence purely to enable him to rule Scotland as he would without too much interference by the divines; Lauderdale, a confirmed and hard Covenanter; and Lanark, a Hamilton, royalist but not a militant one, who had not actively supported Montrose. Scotland was a divided nation indeed that summer of 1650.

After three miles, they passd the small church of St Ninian's on a rise above the river, where Montrose had buried his son. Only some there eyed it with anything like Jamie's intensity. If Mary Queen of Scots had been his heroine, James Graham of Montrose had been his hero, from childhood. That both had died under the executioner's axe greatly affected that young man's thinking.

Soon they were riding through the village of Fochabers, a small burgh-of-barony, really the castleton of the large Bog of Gight Castle, their destination. No doubt the Gordon men-at-arms who escorted them lived here. Montrose's son had in fact died in this castle before being buried in that kirkyard. The Lord Gordon, Lord Lewis's elder brother, now dead like their father, had acted host then, a lieutenant of Montrose. It was a strange place for the Covenant ministers and Argyll to be going for hospitality, these who had taken and all but destroyed the main Gordon seat of Strathbogie, at Huntly in Aberdeenshire.

It was a great and imposing stronghold, when they came in sight of it, despite its odd name, and giving still odder style to the Gordon chiefs, who were prouder to be known, in North Country fashion, as Gudeman o' the Bog and Cock o' the North than as Marquis of Huntly and Earl of Aboyne. The bog referred to the surrounding marshland, deliberately undrained, so that it provided a vast and impassable moat, crossable only by hidden and twisting causeways, keeping the castle out of range of any possible cannon-fire, and difficult for cavalry to approach save by the said causeways, in single file, as good a defensive site as any rock-top fortress in the land. What Charles Stewart thought of it, raised in London, France and Holland, was not to be known.

The present Gudeman o' the Bog had certainly not let his anti-Covenant sympathies restrict his provision for the occasion. There was ample and excellent accommodation for all, servants in plenty to attend them, and what amounted to a banquet laid on in the great hall, even with pipers, singers, harpists and entertainers. This last was almost certainly deliberately prolonged, for of course the Calvinist divines frowned on music, dancing and the like as devices of Satan. As a result practically all of them walked out – but after they had partaken of the fare – whether to go and chant psalms or merely to rain down curses on their host, who could tell? At any rate, Charles seemed to appreciate it all, drinking deeply, even though Buckingham looked scornful at such primitive and barbaric entertainment, however colourful.

Later, in one of the angle-towers across the courtyard, which had been allotted to the Earl Marischal, the Hay Earl of Kinnoull and Sir David Ogilvy, this group, with the Ramsays, discussed the future – or such of it as they could learn or guess at. The Marischal had managed to discover something of the proposed programme from Loudoun the Chancellor. On the morrow they would ride by Elgin, where they all had spent the previous night, and where Charles would be shown the mighty ruined cathedral, magnificent even yet in its remains, destroyed by the Reformers as proof of their devotion to correct doctrine, and their power. Then they would head on for Aberdeen, nearly eighty miles, to halt at what was left of Huntly on the way. Dunnottar Castle, the Marischal's main seat, a score of miles south of Aberdeen, would house the company before the next leg of their long journey to Perth, where they would stop preparatory to the coronation ceremony at Scone, three miles distant up Tay. After that, who knew? Charles, once actually crowned king, might begin to show and exercise his new authority.

All in that tower greatly felt for their young liege-lord and were eager to aid and support him, where they could, in the taking over of his kingdom. But the Kirk? And Argyll? And that Buckingham! None of them liked the look or sound of him. And apparently, as Charles's personal friend and adviser, his influence could be great, and the reverse of beneficial.

Jamie Ramsay went to bed that night in no very somnolent frame of mind. What lay ahead of them all?

2

The city of Aberdeen, situated between the mouths of the two great rivers of Dee and Don, gleamed silvery before the royal cavalcade, its defensive walls, built of the local almost white granite, reflecting the June sun. It could look grey indeed of a wet or misty day such as the North Sea so frequently threw at it; but today it was at its most brilliant, suitably to welcome its king. It was a long time since it had had a monarchial visit.

Whether Charles looked forward to entering his first Scottish city was hard to say. He was not being very forthcoming, set-faced, those eyes hooded, apt to confine his remarks to George Villiers on this journey, despite Argyll's rather surprising efforts to engage him in conversation, and still more surprising cultivation of Buckingham, whom he obviously saw as a useful ally. Who could blame Charles, lectured and hectored all but incessantly as he was by the representatives of the Kirk, who seemed to be more or less practising their sermons on the young man, enough to offput even the most seriously minded. The divines were clearly not content that he had taken their Covenant, and were intent on driving the lesson home. After all, there were rumours that he inclined towards Catholicism. His mother, daughter of a King of France, had been a Papist; and his brother, James, Duke of York, was a notorious Catholic. So they had reason to be heedful. Perhaps Aberdeen could be made to convey to him something of the realities of his situation, even though it had in the past had a wretchedly Episcopalian and bishop-conscious bias, the fault of its university and the so-called Aberdeen Doctors, undoubtedly.

The Reverend Cant, who was senior minister of the city, and the Earl Marischal who, with his Keiths, had a powerful influence in Aberdeen, had ridden on in advance to inform – and perhaps warn – the city fathers; Cant at least to ensure that the correct messages were conveyed to the royal visitor.

Coming down Donside, the company would have approached the North Gate. But the divines insisted that they work round to the main South Gate. There, presently, they saw a party coming out to greet them, no very large party. But then, this was all at short notice.

The Marischal and Cant led forward a portly and distinctly flustered individual, handsome gold chain of office somewhat askew about neck and chest, to be presented to Charles as the provost of His Grace's loyal city of Aberdeen. Behind him were such of the bailies as could be found in time, the chancellor of the university with his bedellus or mace-bearer, and the principal of Marischal College, this founded by the earl's grandfather some fifty years before.

Charles did not dismount, so the provost had to make a rather breathless speech of welcome gazing upwards, interrupted by one of his bailies who poked him in the back to hand over the large ceremonial keys of the city, their cushion forgotten in the rush, quite heavy obviously. Reaching up with these, the provost almost dropped them, to his further agitation. He was, after all, a fish merchant to trade, and this his first experience in receiving a king.

Buckingham laughed aloud and clapped beringed hands as Charles bent over to touch the keys, as symbol that he accepted the dutiful allegiance of the city.

Thereafter they rode on for the open South Gate and, since the royal party was mounted and the civic party was not, and the former made no attempt to delay for the latter, the odd situation developed whereby the visitors arrived at the gate well in advance of their hosts, although the Reverend Andrew Cant, perceiving this infelicitous circumstance, made haste to remount his own horse and hasten after the others, leaving the Marischal to accompany the civic worthies back.

Cant's concern became the more understandable when, in time to rein up beside Charles at the great gateway, he was able to grasp the royal arm and point upwards to

16

the gatehouse parapet, on which sundry gruesome objects projected on spikes: skulls, rag-covered bones and the like.

"Yonder, Your Grace – second from the left," he directed. "The right arm of the renegade and miscreant Montrose!"

The monarch looked up at the sorry thin and twisted relic of the man who had died for his cause and whom he had made no attempt to save, and looked away again quickly, wordless. Clearly this was why the entry was being made here at the South Gate.

They rode on into the narrow streets of Aberdeen, more than Jamie Ramsay set-faced.

Cant leading, and not waiting for any of the welcoming dignitaries, the royal party was taken on a mounted tour of the city, the minister pointing out his own great church of St Nicholas first, naturally, this in the middle of what he called the new city. Apparently there was an old city also, to the north, near to the Don's mouth rather than the Dee's, which he spoke of in no very favourable terms as where were established the university, Marischal College, St Machar's former cathedral and other unfortunate monuments to past errors. The town, within its walls, was built on four eminences, none very high but sufficiently so for viewers to gain an impression of the layout, Castle and Port Hills the most prominent. On the latter the visitors were rejoined by the panting provost and some of his bailies, who announced that a repast would be available at the town-house, beside the tolbooth, given an hour's time. Also reaching them here was another cleric, a young, dark-avised man, whom the divines greeted more warmly and who was thereupon presented to Charles as the Reverend Donald Cargill, minister of the reformed St Machar's down in the old city.

The tour resumed, with this Cargill joining it, riding pillion behind one of his colleagues.

Jamie was interested to see Aberdeen, whatever his feelings about the procedure in general. It was by this time the third largest city in Scotland and its second greatest port. It was while riding down through the dock area that Charles Stewart showed his first real sign of animation when Buckingham, who

17

evidently had a keen as well as a fleering eye, pointed out a ship moored at one of the quays, the Dutch flag flapping above it, recognising it as the frigate which had brought them to Speymouth. And there, standing at the quay-head, was the thickset and bearded captain of the ship, whom the monarch actually dismounted to speak to. Evidently he had formed a regard for this Netherlander, who at close sight proved to be younger than at first seemed, and apparently named Cornelius van Tromp.

As they waited, Jamie asked his father why this? Why had the Dutch ship had to come to remote Speymouth, and they all go to meet it there, when it could have come in here, to Aberdeen port, as it had now done? Sir Gilbert said that he supposed that it was all arranged so as to avoid possible interception by Cromwell's navy vessels, which patrolled the Scots coastline, as well as the English, in arrogant fashion. They would be looking out for Charles undoubtedly, and might well watch Aberdeen, where they would scarcely consider Speymouth's fishing haven. And once the royal traveller was disembarked, there was nothing to prevent the Dutchmen coming in here; the Netherlands and England were not at war meantime, however much they might disagree over the monarchial situation.

They rode on for the town-house, for the promised repast, van Tromp making his own way on foot.

It was nothing like so fine a provision set out as Lord Lewis had made for them at Bog of Gight, but this was understandable given the unanticipated nature of the visit. There was no lack, at least, fish being very much to the fore.

Accommodation for the night was found for them in various senior citizens' houses. Deliberately, no doubt, Charles himself, Buckingham and van Tromp were installed in a prosperous merchant's establishment directly opposite the tolbooth and town-house, this probably not so much for convenience or quality as for the fact that Montrose's hand, cut off from the gateway parapet arm, was nailed to the tolbooth's door. The Ramsays were left to find house-room down near the docks, but not before they, and all, were given no uncertain orders to attend divine service at St Nicholas Kirk in the morning – for next day was the Sabbath – and at an early hour, for another celebration had to be fitted in at the Reverend Cargill's St Machar's before noonday. If this seemed to be overdoing it – and why such timing? – the Earl Marischal, before he left them that night, explained. The Covenant leadership was concerned not to let Charles stay for any length of time in Aberdeen lest the population begin to show its loyalty and regard, and give him wrongous notions as to his authority and subsequent power. So they were to leave the city by midday on their continued journey southwards. Fortunately, perhaps, it would not be a very long march tomorrow, for they were only going as far as his, the Marischal's, castle of Dunnottar, where he was to have the privilege of entertaining all. At least his friends would have more suitable and comfortable quarters for their next night.

So on the morrow it was an early start for the worshippers, however reluctant some of them might be. Actually Charles was late in reaching St Nicholas, but Andrew Cant was not going to wait for any mere earthly monarch in his approaches to the Heavenly One. So the king and his two companions had to take something of a back pew in the crowded church, Buckingham making no attempt to do so quietly or reverently, to fierce glares from the pulpit.

In fact, almost the entire service was conducted from that pulpit, for the then Presbyterian was a preaching Kirk, with greater emphasis on the Word than on petition, supplication, confession, adoration and congregational participation. The sermon not only took precedence, it dominated. And Cant's sermon that Sunday was a feat indeed, of instruction, admonition, assertion, condemnation, threat – and endurance, for all concerned. None there was left in any doubt as to their duty, responsibility, need for repentance of their undoubted sins and the certainty of hell's fire for those who failed to adopt and support the Covenant's righteous creed. Much of the preacher's notable eloquence was clearly directed at Charles Stewart.

Especial emphasis was placed on elementals, for the royal benefit. Daily living was to be strictly disciplined. Such shameful frivolities as cards, play-acting, dancing and the like were an abomination. Walking abroad on the Sabbath was forbidden, a sin. Unseemly and decorative dressing was obnoxious – with an actual pointing finger at Buckingham. Women to be plainly clad and covered from the neck down to the ankles. The wearing of crucifixes round necks, male or female, was an insult to the Crucified One. Kneeling in prayer was Popish. And so on.

There was particular accusation and warning for Aberdeen itself, a wayward city in the past, inclining towards the sin of bishop-worship. God had shown His anger at it by sending the plague here three years before, when no fewer than seventeen hundred and sixty had died, one-fifth of the population – let all mind it. Witchcraft, warlockry, spell-casting and sorcery had flourished in this unholy atmosphere, and it had been necessary to burn twenty-two women and one man, on Castle Hill, some years before. There would be more burning if any further demonology was reported. A General Assembly of the Kirk had been held here back in 1605, and only nine faithful ministers had attended, to the shame of the nation. Aberdeen had rejected the Covenant until long after the other burghs and towns had seen the light. Let this graceless city beware – Almighty God was not to be mocked!

When at length this especial sort of worship was over, it was a bemused and all but numbed congregation which escaped out into the streets, but not to stroll, talk or linger, of course. Home to their houses with them; that is, save for those ordered to attend the second service at St Machar's in the old city, which to be sure included the royal party. That old city particularly needed God's word, even more than this new. The orders for the folk to go and shut themselves in their homes would conveniently prevent them from possibly lining the streets to view and wave to the new monarch.

Outside the church, Buckingham was urging his friend not to go any further with this farce, enough being more than enough; but Argyll strongly advised otherwise. Until he was actually crowned, Charles needed the ministers, he depended on them, must not offend them. They held his future in their hands.

So it was down to St Machar's for a further instalment of

instruction, Jamie Ramsay demanding of his father where the God of love, kindness and forgiveness came into all this?

The Reverend Donald Cargill's conducting of his service was not dissimilar – it could not be, with his senior divines present – but he did go in for more of the need for prayer and supplication, with repentance and humble obedience. He reserved his fiercest assault however for episcopacy and the deplorable prayer book, and leanings thereto still evident here in the university and Marischal College. However, he had not much time, for Cant had rather overstepped the allotted span, and the noontide hour set for departure was approaching. So this congregation was in some measure spared, to major relief.

At least, the Earl Marischal promised them, there would be no sermonising at Dunnottar, even though, it appeared, the clergy were coming to lodge there also.

Probably all were as glad to get out of Aberdeen as were its citizens to see them go, handsome city as it was. They rode due south again, just up from a rugged coastline, past the fishing havens of Crawpeel, Findon, Skateraw and Muchalls, where a fine new Burnett castle had recently risen on the foundations of an old one, and so to the quite large township of Stonehaven, or Stanehive as the Marischal called it, a score of miles but easy riding. This last was very much a Keith community, with Keith estates of Cowie, Fetteresso, Auquhiries and Benholm surrounding it, with their farms and castletons. But impressive as these might be, they paled into insignificance when, climbing out of the town by a steep road above heightening cliffs, suddenly the visitors viewed Dunnottar before them, an extraordinary sight indeed. An enormous stack of rock, not far off two hundred feet high, rose out of the sea, linked to the precipitous shore by only a precarious narrow and uneven strip of land, the sides everywhere all but sheer. And on top of this soared the towers and battlements of a fortress, Jamie counting no fewer than eleven different buildings, from great square keep and parapeted ranges to what actually looked like a church. Those who had not seen Dunnottar before stared, silent. Even Buckingham had no comment to make.

The Marischal led them down the steep descent almost to sea-level and the start of the narrow land-bridge. Here, at a small bay beneath the cliffs, was a range of cot-houses and stabling, the castleton; and here all must dismount, for apparently there was no way by which horses could mount to the rock-top stronghold. Servitors would bring up their baggage hereafter. Some comment did now develop, some grumbling, as all perceived the quality of the climb ahead of them. Smiling grimly at the divines, William Keith led the way, unfurling a flag from his saddle-bag, strangely, this bearing the Keith arms, presumably for identification.

At first it was just steep climbing. Then about one hundred feet up it developed into steps and stairs, this why horses could not mount it. Halfway up what was narrowing into a deep rock cleft, they came to a gateway in walling fully thirty feet high, defended by outworks, shot-holes gaping menacingly at them. The Keith banner's use was now evident, for the great barred gate opened creakingly for them. Behind these was a massive iron portcullis, with men-at-arms hoisting it up with cranks to let them past, the winding chains clanking. These saluted only their lord. Beyond was another flight of steps for the panting climbers.

Another masonry barrier blocked the cleft ahead of them, with a gun-looped gatehouse. The gate here opened for them also, more sentinels eyeing them expressionless. There was a guardroom just inside, out of which the captain of the guard came to welcome the earl, ignoring the rest. Now the ascent turned at sharp right-angles, with more steps, all defended by arrow-slits and shot-holes. This led up to a tunnel bored through the naked rock, fully twenty-five feet of it, narrow and easily defended by a couple of swordsmen, a door at the end. Too breathless to make adequate remarks and comments, the visitors had negotiated this when they were confronted by still another tunnel, steeply ascending. Mounting this, at last they were out on to the summit area of the rock, Charles clearly dumbfounded, but too short of breath to say so.

Sir Gilbert managed a word or two. "You are . . . well protected . . . here, my lord! I . . . have never . . . seen the like."

"My forebears had to be," he was told. "They were excommunicated for some years by the then Pope for building a castle on the site of yonder ancient church. A prey for any who would earn the papal blessing!"

That at least went down well with the Covenant clergy.

The rock-top was more extensive than had appeared from below, almost four acres of it, they were told, so that there was ample room for the eleven buildings. The visitors were astonished to see an actual bowling-green there, and a graveyard with tombstones beside the churchlike edifice.

They were met outside the main keep of the castle by George Keith of Benholm, the earl's brother, who was entitled to call himself the Master. Warned in advance of their coming, he greeted Charles suitably, and welcomed all. Refreshments awaited them in his great hall upstairs, he announced.

That last climb up the winding turnpike stair seemed to tax Buckingham in especial, for clearly he was not in fittest condition. The visitors collapsed into chairs and on benches, and they were served with restorative wines and whisky by a woman and four young girls. The Marischal introduced these as the Lady Margaret Hay, his brother's wife, daughter of the Earl of Kinnoull here present with them; and the girls his own four daughters. Sadly, his wife had died two years previously giving birth to their only son, who had survived only the one year.

Digesting this with their wines and oatcakes, Charles made sympathetic noises, although George Villiers found sufficient breath to remark, *sotto voce*, that it was small wonder that they had died, imprisoned in this extraordinary and dreadful place.

Lady Margaret, who seemed efficient as well as pleasant, although scarcely beautiful, after greeting her father, announced the allotment of chambers and beds for the party, quite a formidable undertaking for over thirty of them, even with the considerable accommodation. When they were ready, they would be taken to their quarters. A repast would follow, in an hour or so's time, here in this hall.

Servants escorted the groups to their lodgings in the various many ranges of buildings dotted over the summit area. The Ramsays were taken by the eldest of the Marischal's daughters, however, to an angle-tower perched on a spur of the cliff-top, not the most convenient location perhaps but undoubtedly in the most dramatic situation with dizzy-making views. Their guide, Lady Mary Keith, was a lively fifteen-year-old, whom Jamie found attractive, and whom, amongst all the older folk, she clearly approved of also.

She took him to the window of the small circular tower bedchamber allotted to him, and opening the wooden shuttering below the glass panels, leaned out, beckoning him to do likewise.

It was worth doing so – and not only because of the vista, but because the fairly narrow window-space between the flanking stone seats meant that two bodies had to be exceedingly close to each other, indeed squeezed together, so that Jamie's arm went protectively round the girl for, after all, it proved to be an awesome drop. The view out to sea was, of course, farflung and tremendous, with the cliff-girt coastline on either side, picked out in the evening light, colourful and challenging, north and south. But it was straight down where the girl pointed, to where it could be seen now that this spur in fact overhung the rest of the precipice face considerably, so that they seemed to be situated high in space, the wrinkled sea surging far below and the waves breaking out of sight because of the overhang, although their spray was visible, an eerie sensation. A more secluded and secret-seeming roost would be hard to imagine, detached from all else. The Lady Mary revealed that this was in fact her own room, but that she had been temporarily dispossessed to go bed down with her younger sisters. She said this with an eloquent giggle, which drew an extra and appreciative squeeze from the young man.

They were in no hurry to return to the rest of the party.

The meal that night was more than adequate. Jamie wondered how all the provision was brought up to this skied fortress in quantity? There seemed, of course, to be ample manpower to carry it, back-breaking and exhausting as this must be.

Later he discovered that his brother preferred to come and

share his bedchamber with him rather than use the dull one he had been allotted. Jamie was rather ashamed to find himself wishing for alternative company.

In the morning, it transpired that the company was not proceeding on its way until the morrow, this to give both men and horses a rest before the long and taxing ride to Perth, over fifty miles across part of the backbone of Scotland. So all were left to their own devices, although the Marischal did offer sport on his bowling-green, not only of bowls but skittles and even archery, all frowned upon as sheer time-wasting frivolity by the divines, who preferred to sit in the sun and discuss more vital matters, such as election and grace, and the punishment of evil-doers. For his part, Jamie managed, without too much difficulty, to find the Lady Mary and suggest that they might look round the castle and its sights. He restrained himself from saying preferably alone, but the girl seemed to take that for granted anyway; and without drawing too much attention to themselves, they slipped off on their own.

She took him first along outside one of the ranges, of bakehouse and brewhouse, to climb down to a ledge on the north-east face of the rock, which she called her eagle's nest, and which entailed the somewhat hair-raising descent of a skeletal track which even a goat might have found unnerving; this Mary Keith appeared to have a head for heights, perhaps not to be wondered at reared where she had been. Here she pointed out to him the fulmars, kittiwakes, guillemots and puffins roosting and nesting on still narrower ledges and protrusions of the cliff-face. Here they sat for a little, legs dangling over the edge, and Jamie felt entitled, indeed incumbent on him, to encircle his companion with that protective arm just in case she suffered an attack of vertigo. Thereafter, to his further surprise, she took him still lower down the precipice, by what could scarcely be called a track, rather a stepladder using natural breaks and crevices in the stone for footholds, fortunately provided with a long rope to grip.

This zigzag and tortuous descent brought them eventually to quite a long ledge, only some thirty feet above the waves,

25

which Mary said was her fishing place. Here she could cast baited lines down, and catch flounders and the like. Reels of hooked cord lay stored on the ledge.

Jamie perceived this to be an excellent way of passing the day in selected company, and proposed a fishing session there and then. Mary proved to be nothing loth, but pointed out that they would require bait. Lug-worms were the flounders' favourite; but that meant going and digging for them in sand, and there was no sand on Dunnottar's rock. The nearest was down at the little shore and boat-strand below the castleton. They would have to go there and dig for them.

This programme nowise displeased that young man – so long as they could do it on their own. Unfortunately there was no way of reaching the castleton's little bay from this rock save by climbing back up to the castle itself and then finding their way down through all the defensive approaches, tunnels and gateways. This would take time; but it was not so much that which concerned Jamie as the avoiding of his brother and any other idlers up there who might well feel inclined to join them. He was not an unsociable character, but on this occasion he felt that two was sufficient company.

Mary pondered this, and came up with a brilliant idea. If she went up alone, avoided her sisters and aunt – not that the Lady Margaret was difficult – collected some food to sustain their fishing vigil, then made her way down alone to the castleton where the girls had a small rowing-boat of their own for coastal expeditions, and rowed this round here to below this ledge. It was quite possible to climb down to the water's edge if one was careful, using the rope – often she had to do it if lines got caught or entangled – and she could collect him there and they could go and dig for lug-worms. Or, better still, she could dig the worms on her own, and return. It would not take her so very long.

Admittedly this all seemed a long and complicated process to catch a few flatfish; but that was not the sole object of the exercise, and Jamie found no fault, only regretting that his role seemed to be a less than active one. Mary, obviously something of a tomboy, however feminine a one, laughed and said that his

26

time would come. Fishing, of course. Meantime he could go to sleep in the sun, on that ledge, if he felt bored. He could accompany her to the castleton if he wished, but they might well collect companions on the way.

He preferred to remain where he was. She commenced her ascent, advising him that it would be decent not to watch her climbing up, high-kilted as her skirts already were.

He reassured her, moderately.

So he settled down to wait – although a call and wave from the girl from her eagle's nest point did have him looking up, but not at close range – and indeed presently he did fall asleep in the warmth of the June sun reflected from the bare rock-face, he having already discarded his doublet and opened his shirt. It occurred to him that this was scarcely what he had anticipated when his father had suggested that he and his brother might like to accompany him and Sir David Ogilvy on their mission to welcome their new king to Scotland.

Thus it did not seem so long after all before the creak of oars opened his eyes, and there was the Lady Mary, sleeves rolled up, rowing her boat round a bend of the rock, pulling strongly. Unnecessarily, probably, for she was obviously expert, he climbed carefully down to assist her to land, and to tie the boat to that useful cliff rope. Laughingly, accusing him of being asleep, she said that he might have fallen off the ledge into the sea. Could he swim? That would have wakened him up! She handed him up a small pail of lug-worms she had dug; and in the doing so, he was interested to see that she also had been feeling the heat, with her rowing and digging, and had opened the neck of her silken blouse, as he had done with hs shirt, so that the cleft of quite full and shapely breasts was entirely visible.

Climbing up to their ledge again, it seemed something of a comedown to have to engage in the distinctly unromantic business of threading messy and easily burst lug-worms on to hooks.

Thereafter, Jamie had to be shown the serious process of fishing for flounders, something he had had no occasion to learn at Bamff Castle in the hills of the Perth–Angus border. Lead

27

weights were attached to the ends of the lines some eighteen inches below the hooks, and these carefully lowered into the water, heed to be taken to see that they were not swept aside by the surging tide nor caught in seaweed. When the weights could be felt to touch the sandy bottom, they had to be raised again a foot or so, and there held, the line over a forefinger so that the slight tug of a fish taking the bait could be felt and a jerk given to ensure that the hook bit and the bait were not just sucked off; then the line pulled up. All this instruction entailed fairly close association, which compensated for the slimy worms and brown-stained fingers, however, and Jamie proved a willing if occasionally preoccupied pupil.

The lines lowered, he was pleased with himself when, after only a minute or two, he felt the first bite over that finger, jerked hard, too hard, and lost his catch by tugging bait and hook out of the fish's mouth – to head-shaking from his instructress. But even as she scolded, Mary too got a bite, and twitching her line moderately, felt the fluttering sensation of a firm catch, and was able to draw up a fair-sized flounder, bending almost double this way and that as it came up out of the water, to be expertly despatched by a slap against the rock, Jamie admiring.

The girl got another before her companion achieved his first success, although he had one or two nibbles which came to nothing. His fish was a large one however, which pleased him inordinately.

After that there was a lull, at least in that sort of sport, and, sitting side by side, they talked of this and that, the king and Buckingham, their family life, their likes and dislikes, the follies of brothers and sisters, and much else. But it was not all talk. They sat silent as often, and what with the fish, the lug-worms, and Jamie's discarded doublet, on that narrow shelf, they found it entirely necessary to sit very close together again, indeed soon hand in hand, for their fishing-lines demanded only one forefinger each. But pleasing as this was, the young man felt that he could perhaps make better use of his spare hand, and releasing it, he encircled the girl with his arm. He had a good long arm and the hand on the end of it had to have a resting place. Mary's smooth bare arm was convenient for stroking; but after not very long, with her leaning against him companionably, her bosom became the obvious destination – and that hand not rejected.

He found it a most pleasing sensation to hold and fondle that rounded breast, warm and full, rising and falling gently with its owner's breathing. There was certainly no need to talk now and the fishing became quite neglected. When, presently, Mary turned further towards him, face upturned, it was entirely natural that they should kiss, even though in somewhat breathless fashion at first; and no less natural perhaps than that venturesome hand of his should adapt to her new position by moving onwards, as it were, towards the further breast and, the neck of her blouse being thus conveniently open, to slip within.

There it, and he, found delight, bliss and pleasing challenge for his fingers; and at the same time the kissing improved. Flounder-fishing became sufficiently irrelevant for Jamie's other hand to lose its hold on the line, and this not to be noticed. The girl's breathing deepened satisfactorily.

So they sat, legs over the edge, the seafowl wheeling around them, the waves surging below, and for these two time stood still. They were young, only eighteen and fifteen years, and sought no more than this for satisfaction, whatever stirrings might move within them. Words remained superfluous.

It was in fact an insistent jerking of Mary's line, still coiled round one finger, allied to the sheer hardness of their rock ledge on their bottoms, which eventually not entirely ended their idyll but made for interruption, repositioning and an interval. The girl, laughing now, pulled up a fish, small indeed to have been making such a fuss; and Jamie was surprised to discover that he had one also on his own abandoned line, and twice the size of hers. Unhooking this catch, he would have been happy to resume the embrace but Mary now proved her femininity by halting him and declaring that it was time that they ate the provision which she had brought for them. So it was down to the boat to collect honeyed scones and gooseberries, these last gathered from one of the cottage gardens, both agreeing that it must be the fishing which made them hungry.

Jamie would fairly promptly thereafter have reverted to their exchange of courtesies, but his companion now pointed out that seven flounders would not go very far with the company up above, and would not look a very adequate result from a whole day's fishing. And they had, of course, to return the boat to the castleton strand. So it was back to baiting and hooking, and with subsequent fair success, Jamie not exactly grudging. Nevertheless, they did have another mutual caress, brief but even more satisfactory as to quality, before Mary asserted that it was time to be gone, or *she* for one might have some explaining to do, to her sisters and aunt, even to her father.

So reluctantly they left their ledge and descended to the boat with their now quite respectable catch. Jamie took one oar for the row back to the castleton bay, where he donned his doublet again and the girl buttoned up her blouse and rolled down her sleeves, as became an earl's daughter. Then it was up through all those defences to the rock-top stronghold, Jamie at least unable to recollect when he had had such an enjoyable and rewarding day. The pity that they would be off on the morrow.

He too had some explaining to do to his brother thereafter, the flounder catch hardly satisfying Thomas. Their father made no comment.

That evening in the great hall, the Lady Mary Keith helped her aunt and sisters to entertain their guests, with entire decorum and hardly a glance at her fellow-fisher. The flounders, of course, did not go round more than a chosen few, but she saw that Jamie got one, also his brother and father, and King Charles, although not Buckingham, whom she had confessed that she did not like.

In their bedchamber that night Thomas, who was no fool, asked some searching questions but had to be content with only guarded answers. At twenty-one years, he probably guessed the rest, indeed may well have over-guessed at more than had actually taken place. Jamie did not enquire how the other had passed the day.

The royal party was off early in the morning for its lengthy journey, but not too early for the Keith family to see them off. Jamie was at some pains to contrive a necessarily very brief private parting from Mary, round the back of their angle-tower, using the excuse that he had left something behind in his room. It came to only a kiss and a hug, but the best that could be achieved. He assured her that he would not forget Mary Keith and Dunnottar, ever; and hoped that they would meet again before long – he would *ensure* that they did, he declared.

Then it was down to the castleton and the horses, and away southwards. He thought that he saw someone waving from the topmost keep battlements as they rode up the steep incline to the road, and waved back – but perhaps that was only wishful thinking.

3

It was small wonder that there should be some forethought and concern about the journey to Perth, delayed for that day; for although fifty miles was not excessive for seasoned horsemen, the route, across half the width of Scotland, entailed crossing rivers innumerable, few indeed provided with bridges. It would have been all but impossible to effect in one day had it been winter, or in the spring thaws and floods. It was Argyll and the clergy who were anxious to cover it in one day, this not in any great haste to achieve the coronation at Scone but because suitable places on the way, to put up a large and important company for the night, were inconveniently owned – for this was very much territory hostile to the said Covenant faction ruling Scotland, much of it Graham of Montrose country indeed: the Earl of Strathesk's Kinnaird Castle, his father-in-law; the Maules, Earls of Panmure, at Brechin; and the Lyons, Earls of Kinghorne, at Glamis. None of these houses did the controlling group wish to approach with Charles, whom they considered it important should not gain over-much impression of the faction's unpopularity in parts of the land. Hence the taxing ride.

Basically their route lay up Strathmore, the longest, widest strath in the country, fertile and rich, but watered by the great number of major rivers which drained down off the Highland mountains flanking all the strath to the north, and all requiring to be crossed for this particular journey. To reach it they rode south-westwards from the coast, by Laurencekirk, whereafter they began to reach the wide plain of it, the mighty heather and rock mountains endless on their right, green, lower hill ranges on their left, miles by the score. The Marischal remarked to those he rode beside, including the Ramsays, that it was as

32

well that these Covenant divines were considerably tougher physically than had been their fairly decadent and pampered predecessors, the bishops and abbots of the pre-Reformation days, who could never have faced such a challenge in their fine canopied litters. He wondered about Charles and Buckingham. Would they stand up to the test, however excellent the horses provided?

Charles in fact was, at least at first, interested to view the scenery of his country, the mountain masses especially intriguing him, something that he had never known previously in southern England, the Netherlands and northern France. Told of the sport of hunting and stalking deer therein, he expressed a desire to try it, although Buckingham looked very doubtful. That man, clearly, was not enamoured of what he saw of Scotland, all a deal too harsh and rugged for his tastes.

After fording the rivers of Bervie and North and South Esk, they reached the little cathedral city of Brechin by mid-forenoon, making good time in fine weather conditions; and thereafter, passing Tannadice, came to Forfar, the county town of Angus, in mid-Strathmore, by midday. Here Argyll required the provost to find a sufficient meal for them, and without delay, to that worthy's alarm, butcher as he was. However his monarch's presence spurred him on, and he did manage to produce adequately in the town-house, however peculiar the service.

Then on, by-passing the great Lyon castle of Glamis, to Meigle and Coupar Angus with its great abbey, so called to distinguish it from Cupar in Fife. The abbey, strangely enough built within a former Roman camp, had been much damaged, like so many others, at the Reformation, but still made a sight to see. The clerics explained to Charles how necessary all this destruction of Popery had been – to that young man's hooding of over-expressive eyes. By this time it was late afternoon, and still they had over a dozen miles to go to Perth, more than George Villiers beginning to look weary.

They left Strathmore at last and came into lower Strathtay, a very different and less clearly defined area, but still fertile, with much cattle country. Here they were none so far from the

Ramsay lands of Bamff, at Alyth, and Sir Gilbert was able to point out to the flagging Charles Stewart Dunsinane Hill, on which his extremely remote ancestor, King MacBeth, had had his favourite seat, and where his enemy Malcolm Canmore, or Big Head, had attacked him, his army being able to approach unobserved by the guards under the branches of pine trees, when "Birnam Wood came to Dunsinane". Charles remembered seeing Shakespeare's play about these two monarchs, but was very vague as to details.

After Balbeggie, they actually passed near to Scone, which was of course the ultimate destination for this journey, the coronation place of the Scottish monarchy. But there was no adequate accommodation at Scone for the company; and the Fair City of St John's Town of Perth lay only three miles further, on the bank of Tay near where that great river, the longest in all Scotland, opened into its estuary. Dusk was falling as at last they reached journey's end, Buckingham having to hold on to his saddle-bows to remain upright, despite the fact that there were men almost three times his age present and in better shape.

At least here, in the fine walled town, there were premises and provision awaiting them, for this had been arranged in advance with the local ministers, Perth being strong for the Covenant. They made for Gowrie House, as a suitable and comfortable establishment at the riverside, the scene of the notorious Gowrie Conspiracy of exactly fifty years before, the Earl Marischal informed Charles, as they approached, with a carefully edited version of his grandfather, James the Sixth's, distinctly curious involvement therein, not mentioning that peculiar monarch's verbal assault by the Perth mob with the cry of "Come down, thou son of Signor Davie, come down!" Charles, however, was too tired to be very interested or to demand details.

This, the town-mansion of the former Earls of Gowrie, the Ruthvens, the last one assassinated at the Conspiracy and the title forfeited, now belonged to the Murray family, who had been friends of James the Sixth, like Ruthven Castle itself a few miles away, the name of which they had carefully changed to Huntingtower. This Gowrie town-house was a fine place and spacious, and its Murray owner, the present Earl of Tullibardine, had arranged all for the visitors' reception, and welcomed Charles with a sort of cautious courtesy. The Ramsays were relegated to quarters in the stable block across the courtyard.

Only aching limbs would be apt to prevent all from sleeping well that night.

On the morrow all went out to Scone for a preliminary survey of the scene for the coronation ceremony, with all to be arranged. The celebration place was sacred in Scotland's story from earliest times, for here the ancients had seen it as a symbol of good over evil, where the fresh water of the country's greatest river overcame the salt water of the tidal estuary, and had made it a shrine for their gods, Christianised in due course. Here Kenneth mac Alpin, who united Picts and Scots, had brought the famous Stone of Destiny, the coronation-seat of kings, for safe-keeping after the Norsemen had ravaged Iona, its original resting place. And here the landed men of Scotland had come to pay homage to their new monarchs. Oddly, no king had been crowned here for a considerable time, for James the Sixth had succeeded his abdicated mother, however wrongfully, as a baby, and had been crowned at Stirling Castle; and his son, Charles the First, given an English coronation at Westminster; now Charles the Second was to be made King of Scots, whatever the English Commonwealth and Oliver Cromwell might say.

Perth city was built on the west side of Tay, and Scone was on the east side. There had been a bridge from early times, Agricola having been credited with building the first, of timber. This had been renewed in stone more than once. But it had been almost wholly swept away in a great flood thirty years before, immediately after a General Assembly of the Kirk at Perth – some seeing this as very much God's judgment. And although a new bridge was planned, it had not yet been built, communication across the river having to be by flat-bottomed ferry-boats. Thus the travellers had come over the previous night, the scows built to take horses and cattle.

But now they were informed by the Earl of Tullibardine that a more convenient way of reaching Scone, by large numbers, was to ride up this west bank for almost three miles, to a notable shallowing of the Tay where the River Almond joined it and created shoals and sandbanks. This was the Derders Ford, which the Romans had used between two of their camps. It was less than a mile from Scone Abbey and his, Tullibardine's, palace.

So thither an enlarged cavalcade rode, numbers enhanced by local ministers and dignitaries, by the parkland of the North Inch, where the celebrated and extraordinary judicial clan battle had taken place between the Clans Chattan and Kay before Robert the Third and his queen in 1396. In two miles, by what were called the Woody Islands, they came to the Derders Ford, shallow enough, however broad, for the horsemen to splash across with ease.

The further side led them over level meadowland where many a tournament and sporting event had taken place, to rising ground. Here amongst open woodland, the ruined abbey rose. It had been all but demolished at the Reformation, and a new and palatial house built nearby, this by Sir David Murray, James the Sixth's friend, who had gained the Church lands, and become Lord Scone and Viscount Stormont. His descendant, the Earl of Tullibardine, now acted their host.

Much of the next day's ceremonial would take place in this fine establishment; but the significant detail would be performed further over, at what was known as the Moot Hill. This was a strange feature indeed, actually an artificial mound, no doubt itself set on some slight eminence; but the all but conical hillock rising there was claimed to represent a whole land, the very soil of Scotland. This came about as a result of the traditional and theoretical holding of the entire realm's territory by the monarch, in the first instance. At coronations all who owned land must hold it of the king, and must come and take an oath of fealty, standing on their own soil. To achieve this, in fact, would have entailed the new monarch travelling the length and breadth of Scotland, to every estate and property, quite out of the question. So the gesture was substituted. Every landholder, lord and laird and chief, had to bring with him to the coronation ceremony a bag or pocketful of the earth of his property, to empty this before the newly crowned king, set foot and kneel thereupon and take his oath of allegiance on his own, yet the king's, soil. And so, over the centuries, this earth from all over the land had gradually accumulated and grown into the Moot Hill, flattened at the top for the monarch to sit on his throne.

Charles listened to some account of all this, explained by the Earls Marischal, Kinnoull and Tullibardine, with a sort of detached interest, but no probing questions. A few of the party, excluding the bored Buckingham, climbed that mound with him, Jamie amongst them, fascinated by the aura of the place, for he had never visited Scone before. He, and possibly others, waited for Charles to remark on the Stone of Destiny situation, but no such comment was forthcoming.

The Marischal clearly thought that it ought to be mentioned for, standing there atop the Moot Hill, he broached the subject carefully.

"Sire," he said, "tomorrow Your Grace will be seated here, on a chair, as throne. But . . . not on the stone. The Coronation Stone."

"No," Charles agreed, but without sounding in any way concerned. "That is in London. One day, let us hope . . ."

The other coughed, and glanced round his companions, who all were watching him heedfully. "*A* stone is in London, yes, Your Grace. The stone which has sat in Westminster Abbey for three hundred and fifty years. But that is not the true Stone of Destiny, we believe, the *Lia Fail*."

The monarch frowned. "What mean you? It is the stone under the Coronation Chair. On which my father was crowned. The man Cromwell has not taken *that*, has he?"

"No, no, that stone, no doubt, is still there. But . . . that is, as we understand it, only a lump of sandstone from this Scone's quarry. A shapeless mass. Whereas the true stone is . . . otherwise."

He had aroused real interest, however doubting, in those royal eyes now. "Otherwise? I do not understand."

"You have not heard the story then, Sire? An old story, but interesting indeed. When King Edward of England, known as the Hammer of the Scots, came here invading in 1296, he swore to take the Coronation Stone away, to remove it and all symbols of Scots sovereignty from us, to England, he calling himself Lord Paramount of Scotland. He announced that he would do this, made no secret of it, to take it along with Queen Margaret's Black Rood, her piece of the True Cross of Christ. So the Scots knew of the threat. Including the abbot of this Scone." He paused.

"So . . . ?"

"What would the good abbot do, think you? Leave the stone to be stolen? No – he took it away, to hide it secure. And quarried the lump of sandstone, to leave before the high altar in his abbey, there, instead."

"You mean . . . ?"

"That Edward was deceived, Your Grace. He came for the Stone, found this lump, and took it back with him to England. He had never seen the real Stone, so would not know the difference. But there was a mighty difference! The true *Lia Fail*, on which scores of our monarchs had been crowned, and possibly St Columba's altar, is described by the ancient chroniclers. And very different from any lump of reddish sandstone. Black. Polished. Intricately carved. Ornate. With rounded volutes at its sides for handles. A hollow, it is said, on the top, no doubt for baptismal water when it was an altar. Probably a meteorite, it is thought. These, coming down to earth from above, considered sacred."

"Is this the truth, my lord? Or an old wife's tale!"

"The different chroniclers are at one on it. And the tradition, and these details, have been handed down."

"Well then, where is this true Stone? Is it here? For me?"

"Alas no, Sire. It was hidden from Edward Plantagenet, yes. But the Bruce, he knew of its whereabouts. And on his death-bed ordered Angus Og MacDonald, Lord of the Isles, to take it away for safety to his Hebridean fastnesses. The Bruce was leaving a five-year-old child as heir, and knew that there would be trouble again, with England. He told Angus

38

Og to keep it secure, in his remote Isles, until a worthy successor sat upon his throne! Where the Lord of the Isles took it, who can tell? But it has never been brought back, so far as is known."

Charles wagged his head. "If this is truth, surely someone must know where it is. It should be brought here."

"No doubt, Sire. But . . ." The Marischal shrugged. It was difficult to say that presumably the Lord of the Isles' successors did not think that a worthy successor had yet appeared for Scotland's crown, and there had been ten of them before this Charles Stewart.

Kinnoull, perhaps less than tactfully in the circumstances, recited the ancient jingle.

> The Scots shall hold that realm as native ground,
> If words fail not, where'er this chair is found.

Charles set off down that little hill, set-faced.

Jamie Ramsay, of course, had heard most of all this from childhood. He wondered what effect the account would have on the young man to be crowned on the morrow. No doubt the Marischal had told him of it in order to indicate the importance and priority of the *Scottish* coronation as compared with the English one denied to Charles by the Commonwealth. Yet it might conceivably have a different effect . . .

Thereafter there was much on-the-spot planning of arrangements. Since the abbey was in ruins, the religious observance being all-important for the occasion for many there, if hardly for the central figure, it was decided to hold preliminary worship in Tullibardine's new palace, then walk in procession to the Moot Hill for the actual crowning ceremony and the fealty rendering. If the weather was unkind this would have to be only a token observance, and back to the palace for a continuation of the process, and another winding-up service, to be followed by a banquet provided by Tullibardine. The various parts to be played were allotted and gone over, Charles given his instructions in no uncertain fashion. It transpired that there being no descendant of the ancient Coroners or Crowners

39

available, the Macduff Earls of Fife, the Marquis of Argyll would do the actual crowning, authorised and directed by the three leading divines, Cant, Blair and Dickson. Sundry earls and lords would be permitted to carry the insignia of the regalia, fetched from safe-keeping in Edinburgh Castle.

It was back to Perth, with the distinct impression that this coronation was being held solely by permission of the Presbyterian Kirk of Scotland.

Fortunately the good weather held, important indeed. Word of what was to do had got round the town, and the citizens, however pro-Covenant, were out on the streets in force to cheer on this grandson of the monarch they had shouted at so threateningly at Gowrie House fifty years earlier. Charles, unused to adulation, waved right and left.

It was a much larger company which rode off in the forenoon for the Derders Ford and Scone, everyone from the area who could produce a horse seeming to have joined the procession, magnates and ministers having come in from near and far, invited or otherwise.

When they reached the abbey and Moot Hill it was to find large numbers of the common folk waiting there, in holiday mood, having made their own way on foot.

There were, however, strict limits on those who were permitted to enter the great Murray house for the preliminary service, which the divines at least seemed to look upon as the most important feature of the occasion, and which was held in the lesser hall of the palace, the main one being already set and prepared for the banquet to follow. The seating arrangements were unusual, the massed clergy being allotted one side of the apartment, the remainder the other, with no special provision made for the monarch – who was, after all, only another young member of the Kirk's congregation here – although Tullibardine sat him on a fine chair he brought forward to the front row, and sat beside him, Argyll at the other side, Buckingham, looking displeased, having to share a bench with Sir Gilbert Ramsay and the provost of Perth. Jamie and his brother stood amongst others at the back.

After an introductory exhortation by Andrew Cant, very much in charge today, and a chanted psalm, a lengthy prayer more or less informed the Almighty and all others of what was about to be done, emphasising the unworthiness of most of those present and the need for repentance. Then the vital part, the sermon, a challenging triumph of eloquence, admonition and warning, much of it clearly directed at Charles Stewart, since it dealt with the failures, follies and sins of the late royal-imposed episcopacy, damned as merely a step away from satanic Popery itself. None present was to be left in any doubt as to the duties of a Covenanted monarch, such as this day they were going to enthrone. But set upon an *earthly* throne, under the stern supervision of the heavenly one.

There was much else, for the delivery went on for the best part of an hour, before a premonitory benediction allowed all to emerge into the noonday sunshine, to sighs of relief.

Now it was the duty of the Earl Marischal to assemble the official procession to the Moot Hill. From wooden chests in the palace were brought out the Scottish regalia, the crown on its rather dusty cushion, the two sceptres and the sword of state, all unseen for long. The crown was handed to Argyll by the Lord Lyon King of Arms, one sceptre to the Earl of Loudoun the Chancellor, the other to the Earl of Kinnoull, and the sword to the Earl of Erroll, the High Constable. Then Lyon, with his heralds, led the way, between cheering onlookers, to the beat of a single drum. First strode the ranks of clergy, well ahead of the temporal symbols. Then Erroll bearing high the sword of state, the two earls with the sceptres behind and then Argyll with the crown.

Charles walked alone, looking not exactly nervous, but unsure, all but suspicious. After him came the earls not already involved with the regalia, and behind them the foreign envoys, French, Netherlander and Danish, with Buckingham attaching himself to these, as representing England – however little the Commonwealth parliament would have approved. Lords of the Scots parliament followed, fully a score of them, and finally an assortment of baronets, chiefs, knights, lairds, justiciars, sheriffs and the like – all of whom had taken the Marischal a deal of arranging in their due order, before he took his own place behind the regalia-bearers. The Ramsays tagged along at the back, Sir Gilbert staying with his sons rather than partnering Sir David Ogilvy.

In the event, the head of the ministerial column had reached the Moot Hill before the Ramsays moved off, for there was no great distance involved. Only a small proportion of the procession was to climb the mound, of course, for there was only limited space on top. The three senior divines mounted first, after the Lord Lyon, master of ceremonies, then the regalia-carriers, there to flank the throne-like chair which now sat up there in lieu of the Stone of Destiny. The drummer continued with his rhythmic beating, Jamie considering that it sounded more like a funeral than a proud and historic occasion.

Once the eight of the official group were in position, the earls, who were entitled to surround the throne by ancient tradition, the lesser kings of the Celtic polity, the *Ri* as supporting the *Ard Righ*, the High King – although originally there were only seven of them – climbed up, a round dozen now. There was no room for all on the actual summit, so they had to take up positions on the slope itself, uncomfortable stance as this might be. Some of them glared at those three ministers above.

Then, and only then, did the Marischal bow low before Charles, and taking him by the elbow, led him ceremoniously up past all the others, to seat him on the throne.

Cheers resounded, and the drum stopped beating.

Andrew Cant held up hand for silence. "In the name of Almighty God, we call this assembly of Christ's realm of Scotland to witness the enthronement of His vassal, Charles Stewart, as King of Scots," he cried, at his most sonorous. "Let all heed, note and remember. The said Charles, here seated, has taken the Covenant and duly sworn to maintain it. Only so might he sit on this throne and be crowned, with Holy Kirk's blessing. Heed, I say, and may God bless and keep all here, that they maintain the vows solemnly taken, and to be taken. Proceed!"

Thus, with the Kirk's permission, the state could play its part.

Lyon King of Arms, the senior herald, as representing the ancient High Sennachie, stepped out in front of the throne and bowed. He gestured to the High Constable, Erroll, who bore the great two-handed sword, and lowering it, presented its long hilt to the seated Charles, who touched it briefly, sign that he was, in theory, commander-in-chief of the realm's forces, even though he did not have one man in his army, being dependent on the armed levies of his earls and lords.

Lyon unrolled a scroll then, and began to read in a loud voice. This roll-call of past kings of the most ancient royal line in Christendom, an important feature of the Scots coronation procedure, should have commenced in the vague and misty past, long before written records, as the High Sennachie was wont to do; but that was frowned upon by the present clergy, for these names, if authentic at all, would be of pagan monarchs, and so damned. Instead Lyon started with Fergus mac Erc, of the early fifth century, Christian even if Irish, who came across the Irish Sea to found his kingdom; and on through his Dalriadan ancestors until Kenneth mac Alpin united Scots and Picts of Alba in the ninth century. From then on Lyon named ninety-six monarchs, ending with James the Sixth and First, and Charles the First, lately slain by the English, and father of the present incumbent of the throne. It made a resounding catalogue, such as no other realm could match, even though the reader did stumble a little over some of the curious names of the early kings. Whatever Charles Stewart thought of it all there was no hint from his expression, eyes consistently hooded today. It occurred to Jamie Ramsay, during the recital, to try to count how many of these had died a natural death or even reached middle years – a sobering thought to balance all the flourish.

This over, the anointing with oil by the Abbot of Scone should have followed; but of course there was no Abbot of Scone now, and anyway such Popish practice would be anathema. So the three senior divines came forward and each laid a hand on Charles's bowed head, eyes upturned to heaven. They did not bow.

Lyon then signed to Argyll, who gave him the cushion to hold while he himself took the crown and placed it on the young man's head, straightening it there carefully. He stepped back, head bowed, and then sank on one knee, reaching up his hands to be the first to enclose the monarch's in his in the oath of fealty, he who had executed Charles's lieutenant and viceroy, Montrose.

"My lord King!" he said. That was all, but sufficient.

Lyon signed for the two sceptre-bearers to come forward. The king could hardly handle two, so after he had touched them, they were laid across his knees. Two sceptres represented the two original kingdoms, of Dalriada for the Scots, and Alba of the Picts.

The other earls then lined up to take the oath of fealty, led by the Marischal and the High Constable, each murmuring the required form of words while holding the royal hand within their own. Lyon, after marshalling them in order, went down the hill to ensure that the large remainder of the procession, such as were entitled to do so, climbed up in correct seniority, a lengthy process. None of the ministers took the oath.

When at last it was over, the descent of the mound was rather less orderly, Lyon leading the king down first, but nobody else quite sure of who came next – that is, except for Buckingham, who attached himself to Charles, making loud comments. The Marischal tried to make some order out of it but evidently decided that he could not linger behind, for his place ought to be close to the monarch, and Charles had walked on without pause, heading back to the palace, seeming to consider that enough had been endured for the time being. And he *was* the monarch now, undoubted King of Scots, where before he had been only king-candidate as it were, even if the only possible one. There was a notable difference, although it might be some time before all there fully realised it, even Charles himself.

For their part, the ministers were in no hurry to follow the king, gathering in a large group at the foot of the hill to discuss further procedure, the earls and lords leaving them to it, as though they now felt that *their* grip on affairs was strengthened by having an undoubted head of state restored, Tullibardine, with the banquet responsibility, leading the way.

But if the temporal magnates considered that now all would be changed, they were quickly shown their error. For Lyon was not long in being told to make announcement that before the banquet there would be another service in the lesser hall, a service of thanksgiving and direction for the realm's further progress and the seeking of God's guidance. There was astonishment and objection at this, but when the king was led into the great hall by Andrew Cant himself, none could refuse to follow. Presumably Charles had not yet quite realised his changed position, or else hesitated to demonstrate it too soon.

So the purveying of the Tullibardine hospitality had to be postponed, however ready it all was, and more stern worship, if that was the right term, imposed and inflicted, not dissimilar to the earlier one but this time the sermon preached by Robert Blair. None was left in any doubt but that the Kirk still reigned supreme, and that its General Assembly would meet very shortly to guide the new monarch, parliament and the judiciary as to the better rule of the kingdom. The dismissal benediction thereafter, by David Dickson, was almost curt.

At last those privileged to partake of the quite ambitious and generous meat and drink were allowed to sit down to it, thankfully – even if the Grace before Meat was prolonged and comprehensive. It was noteworthy that the clergy did adequate justice to the provision thereafter.

It was while waiting to be served, in their quite lowly position in the hall, that Jamie Ramsay asked his father why it was that all the earls and lords and barons allowed the Kirk ministers to dominate them in this way, this wielding of temporal power by the clergy as distinct from spiritual guidance which ought to be their role, should it not? Surely the great ones of the land, even his father himself, who sat in parliament as Baron of Bamff, need not bow to the Kirk's rule, as they did? With a wry smile, Sir Gilbert told him that he had, in a way, answered his own question when he referred to the great ones of the land. *Land* was the reason for it all. Land.

45

It all dated from the Reformation. Holy Church, the old Roman Catholic Church, had owned more than half the best land in Scotland, left to it down the centuries by generations of lords and magnates who, as death approached, felt the need for heavenly mercy, judging that prayers should be said for their souls to compensate for some of their deeds in life. Such prayers were an important part of the old Church ritual, at a price. Land was the price. At the Reformation, all this fine land was taken from the bishops, abbots, priors and priests, and allocated amongst the lords who supported the crown – which was why most of them supported the reformers, to get it, rather than from any intense religious conviction. And now there were claims that the Kirk of Scotland, the Reformed and Covenanted Kirk, should have these lands back, or some of them, and the tithes and rentals thereof. When the late King Charles the First had imposed his bishops on Scotland again, Episcopal ones – now swept away in their turn – he had accepted that the said new prelates should regain some of the lost lands. Now the Kirk could demand likewise. So the lords feared to lose much of their wealth if they offended the Kirk. He himself could possibly lose sundry properties in the Alyth area.

Jamie wagged his head. Surely, if the lords were determinedly against it, the ministers could not force them to give up the lands, he argued. They were only parish clergy, after all, without real power or armed men . . .

They had the Assembly, his father reminded, the General Assembly of the Kirk of Scotland. That body, meeting frequently, had much more real power than had parliament. It was united in a way parliament never was, and representatives came from every corner of the realm, able to speak with a vehement and authoritative voice. Whereas parliament was ever split into factions. The lords and members thereof were jealous of each other's powers and influence, earldom against earldom, house against house, clan against clan. They never spoke with one voice as the Kirk did. Many were still Catholic, like the Gordons and the Setons, and many, most, of the Highland clans; some were Episcopalian; and those strongly

46

Covenant would support the divines. No, the Kirk and the Covenant had a firm grip.

Jamie looked over towards the king, and wondered what sort of a realm he had come to reign over; to reign, but, it was to be feared, scarcely to rule.

The banquet over, something of a hiatus developed. What was to happen next? After all the directing and ordering by the Kirk, the ministers now seemed to be detaching themselves from the rest. It appeared that they had other matters on their minds, a General Assembly to be arranged at the soonest, no doubt to decide on other directions for the new monarch and for the realm's good and godly government. Charles himself disappeared, with Buckingham, presently, for some peace and privacy no doubt. Argyll, Loudoun, and one or two of their close associates, went off to confer likewise. And the remainder of the palace company merely hung about, idle now, uncertain. After all, the programme had been to meet the new monarch at a place of safety and then conduct him to Scone for his coronation. That was all now accomplished.

Sir Gilbert went to consult the Earl Marischal. What, if anything, was required of them now? Where was the king going? And when? He and his sons were not part of any court or royal entourage; they had come on this strange venture at Sir David Ogilvy's suggestion, as representing the Ogilvy chief, the Earl of Airlie, to welcome the king. Was there any other task they could usefully perform for Charles?

The Marischal thought not, meantime. He understood that Charles was going to the royal hunting-palace of Falkland, in Fife, no doubt hoping to recover there from an overdose of religion. Whether he would in fact escape the divines there, for a space, was problematical. But they were planning this Assembly for the very near future, and it certainly could not be held at Falkland. So the king might get some peace, and perhaps some sport too. It would be very interesting to see how he behaved now. He was crowned King of Scots, and as such had, at least in theory, great and overriding royal authority, whether, young and inexperienced as he was he fully realised it. That popinjay Buckingham might well urge him to demonstrate his powers in no uncertain fashion. The clergy, and Argyll also, might discover that their situations had changed. If Charles used his authority wisely and firmly, most of the nobility and landed men would probably obey and support him and the Kirk and Covenant be the losers.

The Ramsays, in the circumstances, decided that it was home for them meantime. Bamff House, at Alyth, was barely twenty-five miles away, and it was but mid-afternoon of a July day. They could cover that in less than four hours. The Marischal and the Lord Lyon knew where they were to get in touch with them if they were needed. Sir David Ogilvy agreed that this would be his course also, back to his Lintrathen. His house was only six miles north-east of Alyth. So they would ride together . . .

Obviously there was no call, nor opportunity, to take formal leave of the monarch. With mixed emotions they set off for home.

4

The Ramsays' barony and lairdship of Bamff, although only twenty-five miles from Perth, was remotely placed, all but in a world of its own. Set in the very skirts of the Highland mountains, it was yet near none of the major glens which penetrated these uplands, and served by none of the drove-roads which threaded them. Alyth, its nearest community – it could scarcely be called a town – was only four miles away; but Alyth itself was remote, out on a limb, as it were. Perth folk thought that Coupar Angus, Blairgowrie, Rattray and Kirriemuir were almost in the wilderness; what they thought of Alyth was not hard to guess – if many had even heard of it. Yet Alyth had its claims to fame, important in Pictish times, with its surroundings scattered with stone circles, burial cairns and standing-stones, indicative of much population and sun worship. Here, on the top of Barry Hill, they had established a major fort, important when Perth was not. And to this fort was brought, in the mid-sixth century, the great King Arthur's abducted Queen Guinevere by the usurping Mordred, and held captive until rescued by the gallant Lancelot, the said ruined fort Jamie's favourite haunt since childhood, its views superb and its romantic story his joy. How often had he played Lancelot, and taken the rescued queen to the mysterious Isle of Avalon, which his father declared to be the Isle of Man, in fact.

The Ramsays parted from Sir David Ogilvy at Alyth village itself, he to ride on north-eastwards, climbing steeply over the high pass between the hills of Barry and Loyal, and so down into the great basin of the uplands, hub of many minor rivers, and cradling the Loch of Lintrathen; they to head north-westwards up an extraordinary feature, the Den of

Alyth. This den or dean, as its name implied, is a narrow, deep and twisting gorge or ravine, thickly wooded and extending for no less than three miles into the otherwise treeless Forest of Alyth, its own dark, peat-stained and headlong river which had formed it cascading in falls and cataracts and deep swirling pools. So steep were its sides, so restricted its width, so thick the tree-cover somehow growing out of such apparently hostile terrain, that the sun could only reach the river's winding course briefly of a noontide. So it was a dark and mysterious place, of which stories were told to frighten more than children, a place for the timorous to avoid.

The Ramsays did not avoid it – after all, they had owned it for five centuries – but they did take their way by a climbing and difficult track which flanked the eastern slopes, now soaring, now dipping steeply, the horses having to be sure-footed and to go in single file, a strange access to the barony of Bamff but the only comparatively direct route thereto. Despite all this, Jamie and his brother and sister had always loved the Den of Alyth as very much their own, and peopled it with creatures of their imagination.

Eventually they came out of it into more open country, not exactly treeless here, but the woodland scattered over what amounted to a wide shelf of the hills, with the high bare mountains rising behind. And here, amongst hummocks, stood the lofty old tower-house, the nucleus of which had been erected, probably on an even earlier foundation, by Neis de Ramsay, principal physician to Alexander the Second, in 1232. It was not large, as castles went, to be the seat of so ancient a barony, and on no particularly defensive site. But its approaches were sufficiently protective, and it was strongly built, tall and characterful, its walls whitewashed and provided with shot-holes, its crowstepped-gabled roofs steep over its five storeys. A moat protected it in some measure. Out of sight in a hollow not far off were the cottages of what could scarcely be called a castleton, wherein dwelt the few servitors, cattle-herders and farm-workers of what was, and had to be, a self-supporting little community, even with its own mill. This was home to Jamie Ramsay; and he would not have changed it for any other, even Dunnottar Castle of the Keiths.

His sister Jean welcomed them gladly, a comely, well-built, self-sufficient girl, a year older than Jamie, but even so young to be the mistress of the house, their mother having died years before. She was agog to hear of their adventures, what King Charles was like, was he handsome, and so on, but her brothers had to answer her while she was busily preparing a meal for them in the stone-vaulted basement kitchen with its great arched fireplace, and told not to stand idle while they were telling her, either. They made a close-knit family, Thomas the quiet, studious one, Jamie the active, romantic, and Jean the competent, apt to be the leader in fact. Sir Gilbert, having lost his wife early and not remarrying, had been a good father; but the girl had been acting mother since she reached her teens.

It was good to be home, they agreed, however exciting and dramatic their mission had been. The young people had been brought up to accept their responsibilities and tasks about the house and property, and in dealing with the local folk. Supervision of the cattle-herds was Jamie's main duty, the barony's principal source of wealth; that and stocking up the fires with wood, quite a major task. Thomas, the heir, had to keep in touch with all the tenantry, and as far as possible ensure their well-being and solve problems and grievances – when he could be detached from his books and papers. Jean, with two maids, had her hands full with running the house, the dairy and the beehives which produced honey for sweetening, for honey wine and wax for the candles. Sir Gilbert himself was by no means idle, but was quite often absent these days, troublous times demanding much consultation and decision with neighbouring lairds and lords, especially of course with the great Ogilvy clan which occupied vast lands to east and south, around the glens of Isla, Prosen, Clova, Noran and Quiech. Also, he was a keen angler, and with a sufficiency of rivers, burns and lochans to fish in.

After an absence of two weeks, there was no lack of duties and affairs awaiting them, especially with Jean clearly thinking that they had been more or less on holiday, enjoying themselves.

Moreover, *she* deserved a break, having been cooped up alone there all the time. She wanted to go and see her great friend and far-out cousin Mariota, at Lintrathen, whom she had missed these weeks. She could have ridden over alone, but her father had warned her against solo journeys in unsettled times. Now, Jamie would escort her.

So, three days later, the pair of them set out eastwards, by upland tracks round the skirts of Balduff Hill, past two of the farmeries and sheep-runs, to a drop in the land-level which brought them to the glen of the Kilry Water, and this led them down into the wide basin which held the Loch of Lintrathen, this well over a mile long and half that in width, offering a fair vista with its wooded banks and background of soaring peaks, the Ogilvy highlands.

This Ogilvy connection of the Ramsays was interesting and important to them; indeed they were looked upon as all but a sept of that great clan, their barony practically surrounded by Ogilvy lands. Almost inevitably, down the centuries, they had intermarried with Ogilvys of the innumerable lairdships of that name, to find themselves linked in an almost unravelable network under the chiefs – formerly Lords Ogilvy and now Earls of Airlie – Clova, Melgam, Inverquharity, Cortachy, Isla, Inverqueich and the rest. So the Bamff family had almost as much Ogilvy blood as Ramsay.

Sir David lived at Lintrathen, although his barony was named as Clova. He had no son, so his only child, Mariota, would heir his lands, and almost certainly have to wed another Ogilvy to keep them in the name. However, there was no lack of possible suitors, and it had long been something of a diversion between her and Jean Ramsay to select the lucky swain, trying them all out by looks, build, temperament, background and so on, Jean feeling almost as much involved as was her friend. Jamie hoped to be spared in this feminine preoccupation on this occasion.

He need not have concerned himself, for there was much more on the minds of the Lintrathen folk when they arrived than possible marital alliance. Only that morning news had been sent to them from Airlie Castle. The English had invaded

Scotland, under Oliver Cromwell himself. So it was war. And against Europe's most successful and determined soldier.

The Lord Protector Cromwell was always well informed of course, his spies everywhere. He had not been long in learning of Charles's arrival in Scotland, and of his coronation. He had announced the Commonwealth's anger and opposition, declaring the said coronation as not only an affront but unlawful; that there was now only the United Kingdom of Great Britain and Ireland, and that the Scots had no right to appoint a king over their part of it, and that he was going to take and imprison this Charles as he had done his father. He had hastened north in person, to lead his Ironsides over the border, and was even now marching on Edinburgh. Sir David had been about to despatch a messenger to inform the Ramsays.

The Earl of Airlie, it seemed, was calling for an immediate assembly of his forces, as was his duty as one of the earls of Scotland. A sick man himself, and his son the Lord Ogilvy young and inexperienced, he was appointing Sir David, of Clova, his lieutenant to act as adviser for the son and in effect commander. The clan was to muster in the shortest possible time and in fullest strength, at Airlie, ready to march southwards.

Jamie was, of course, both appalled and excited. Cromwell in Scotland! The Ramsays would play their part, he had no doubt. He would hasten back to tell his father. But what would happen? What of King Charles? Where would they do battle? Were the Scots already opposing the enemy? What would the Ogilvys' role be?

Sir David could answer all this only approximately. Undoubtedly, in this extremity, the Scots would unite in some measure to defend their land and their new monarch, Kirk, nobility and common folk at one on this at least, Covenant, Catholic, Episcopalian, Highland, Lowland, all. Charles was in name commander of his realm's forces, but with no experience of war, like young Lord Ogilvy and too many another. There were the two practised generals from the Continental and Civil Wars, both Covenanters and both

Leslies, the veteran Sandy Leslie, now Earl of Leven, and his far-out kinsman David Leslie, younger and probably the more brilliant soldier, the victor of fatal Philiphaugh where Montrose had been defeated and his cause had gone down. Presumably one or both of these would command, under Charles's authority. They might already be in action. Further than that he did not know. The Ogilvy force would assemble at Airlie on the morrow, and get their instructions from their chief.

So Jamie hastened back to Bamff, leaving Jean with Mariota meantime.

It was late that night before the Ramsays could bed down for an early start in the morning, for they had had to dash round all their farflung farmeries and little communities to summon all able-bodied men who could bear arms and had horses to meet at sunrise at the castle, prepared for war. There would not be a great many, possibly forty, but fortunately, situated and employed as they were, these would all have garrons, the sturdy ponies of the hills.

Jean, they found, had come back in the evening and brought Mariota Ogilvy with her. They would keep each other company while their menfolk were away.

In the event forty-six volunteers turned up, most enthusiastic and armed with various weaponry, broadswords, dirks, hunting spears, axes, even some pistols and muskets. All were mounted. At the head of these, bags of oatmeal at saddle-bows, Sir Gilbert and his sons took leave of the anxious girls, and led the way back to Lintrathen, which was about halfway to Airlie.

They found a number of men assembled there, just arrived down from the outlying glens, but Sir David and his main company already gone. Taking these along, they proceeded down the Melgam Water to its junction with the River Isla where, high above the water-meeting, rose Airlie Castle.

This stronghold was in a strange state. Eleven years before, while the present earl's aged father was imprisoned and the son away with Montrose, Argyll, in the Covenant's name, had sacked it and demolished what he could, reputedly even using a hammer himself in his hatred. Thereafter the Ogilvy chief had had to move eastwards a dozen miles to the subsidiary castle of Cortachy. But recently the English had come and battered that house, more readily reached than Airlie; and so the earl and family had moved back here, rehabilitating the damaged fortalice as best they could. Fortunately the strong keep, as distinct from the lesser buildings, had largely defied the Argyll spleen, and was readily made habitable again.

Below the rock-top castle, so much larger than Bamff or Lintrathen, the lower ground was already full of armed men, hundreds, perhaps one-third mounted, and more coming in. The Ogilvys scarcely looked upon themselves as Highlandmen, but as a fighting clan they could rival many such. It all made a stirring scene, high spirits prevailing however grim the prospects.

Sir David was there, and climbed with the Ramsays to the castle, where they found the great hall full of lairds and landed men at table with the earl and young Lord Ogilvy, refreshment in generous supply. Their reception was enthusiastic. Obviously Sir David was popular, and as senior cadet of the line, his leadership accepted.

The Earl of Airlie was a fine-looking man, but seeming older than his middle years, and frail, sufferings in the royal cause having left their mark. Like his father, imprisoned for aiding Montrose, he had been freed by that marquis after his succession of victories; but, wounded at the defeat of Philiphaugh, he had been captured again and condemned to death, excommunicated into the bargain by the divines. Weakened as he was, he had effected a dramatic escape from St Andrews Castle dressed in the clothes of his sister who had come to say goodbye. Captured once again by Covenant General David Leslie, he was again to be executed; but Leslie, admiring his courage, had won his reprieve on condition that he would sign a pledge not to rise in arms again against the Covenant. Now, although he was in no state of health to lead them, the Ogilvys were rising indeed, but against the English, not the Covenant.

Presently the earl beat on the table for silence. "Hear me," he called, his voice at least strong enough. "Sir David of Clova, here, has served with me, with Montrose, and is skilled in warfare. He will lead you, with my son. The horse will ride at once, the foot march so soon as marshalled. More will follow. The situation, as I am informed, is that General Leslie is laying waste the Merse and east Borderland, to deny food, forage and shelter to Cromwell's advance, the folk taking to the hills. This while our Scots forces assemble. Cromwell seeks to take Edinburgh and Leslie intends to defend that city. You march for the Burgh Muir of Edinburgh for the muster, and hope to reach there before the English do!"

"Where is the king, my lord? Does he accompany his army?" Sir David asked.

"No. He is still at Falkland. Forbidden to leave, they say. All but a prisoner. The Covenant ministers, God forgive them, hem him in. Preach at him all the time. They have held a General Assembly, forced him to sign a paper saying that he was deeply humbled and afflicted because of his father's opposition to God's good work and the Covenant, by which so much blood of the Lord's people had been shed, as likewise for the Romish idolatry of his royal mother. I believe that they will never permit him to join his army, lest they side with him against the Kirk."

The reaction to that was vehement, shouting and snarls.

"We could march to Falkland and release him," someone cried. "Free him, to come with us . . ."

"We could. But I do not see it as the wise course. Not at this stage," the earl said. "We Scots must form a united front, for once, to outface Cromwell. That is vital, now. To free the king and set the Covenanters against the rest would be to divide our strength. We must support Leslie, meantime. Later, with the English banished, we can perhaps rescue Charles."

"What size of force does Cromwell have?" David Ogilvy asked.

"They say some fifteen to twenty thousand. No very large army – others to follow. But these are his famed Roundhead Ironsides, see you. The most seasoned and successful fighting troops in all Christendom. Even at this short notice we may number three times *his* number, I judge. But we will not be a united force, nor so experienced, such as his."

"And we serve under a Covenant general!" That was Inverquharity, another David Ogilvy.

"Aye. That takes some swallowing! But David Leslie is the best soldier we have in Scotland today, since Montrose died. He, and·his kinsman, Sandy Leslie, Earl of Leven. But *he* grows old . . ."

There was more talk, but not for long. Action was now called for. The sooner they were on the march the better. It was a long way to Edinburgh.

They all took their leave of the earl, and with young Lord Ogilvy, roughly Jamie's age, went down to the assembling of the men.

Sir David discussed their route with his friend. Two great estuaries, the Tay and the Forth, lay between them and the capital. For a small party, ferries could vastly shorten the journey. But with their numbers, and the horses, this was impracticable. They had to make for Perth and Stirling, to round the two firths. That would be, by the most direct routes, thirty miles and forty-five miles. Then another thirty-five miles to Edinburgh. Their Highland garrons were sturdy but stocky, short of leg, able to cover great distances and the roughest terrain but not fast. One hundred and twenty miles: it would take them three whole days, even riding until late.

They set off without delay, a mounted force of over two hundred, which made quite a lengthy column, never able to ride more than three abreast. It was after midday, so they would not make Perth that night. But then, two hundred armed men would not be particularly welcome in Covenant Perth anyway, so they would camp in the northern skirts of the Sidlaw Hills, possibly near MacBeth's Dunsinane, having ridden by Blairgowrie and Coupar Angus.

It made no comfortable journey, for the weather broke as they were leaving Airlie, the skies having been lowering since morning, and heavy rain accompanied them, with a blustering wind. Camping out in this would be less than enticing.

In the event, the rain continuing, they sought out the most sheltered place available that night, in woodland near Balbeggie which, although the rain dripped on them through the trees, at least gave them some cover from the wind; and they managed to expose sufficient dryish wood to give them fires. Jamie, eating raw oatmeal soaked in water, and wrapped in a smelly horse-blanket, revised his opinion of the excitements of campaigning.

The weather showed no improvement in the morning, and the bedraggled company rode on, to cross Tay and through Perth and southwards by Strathearn. When his sons complained, Sir Gilbert pointed out grimly that at least it was not cold.

Normally it would have made pleasant and easy riding, Strathearn being a long and attractive valley with wide vistas to the Highland mountains, and leading into Strathallan, also fair. But in the circumstances it was merely a case of covering miles, wet and boggy miles, and trying to keep up their spirits. Sir David decided that they ought to try to reach Dunblane, where he proposed to demand, in the name of the Covenant, that his men should be allowed to sleep in the former cathedral, part of which he understood was now used as the parish kirk, and the rest more or less abandoned.

It was some thirty depressing miles to Dunblane, near the foot of Strathallan, and evening before they reached it, the wind if anything strengthening, highly unusual July weather. But at least they had no difficulty in gaining shelter, the local minister being absent at the Assembly and his session-clerk making no objections to the Ogilvy contingent spending the night in the cathedral nave which, boarded off from the chancel and transepts which now served as the parish kirk, although neglected, with broken windows, the haunts of bats, still had its roof, and so providing shelter. While the men settled in, lighting fires in the kirkyard amongst the graves and using old pews and benches for fuel, their leaders sought the town's provost's aid in providing food and drink from the townsfolk. Being prepared to pay for it, and some of the lairds hinting that they would not hesitate to take what was required if it was not forthcoming voluntarily, all in the king's and Covenant's name, the provender did in due course materialise. So a somewhat better night was passed.

Next day the conditions were no better, as the grumbling, cursing array proceeded on its cheerless way. When Lord Ogilvy, who had struck up a friendship with Jamie Ramsay and rode with him most of the time, complained bitterly that the very heavens appeared to be against them and in favour of the Puritan Roundheads, Sir Gilbert, overhearing, pointed out that these conditions would be equally bad for the English invaders, worse probably in that the land was all being laid waste before them by Leslie, to distress them anyway, denying forage for man and beast; and even Oliver Cromwell would have difficulty in maintaining his troops' spirits.

That day, in the lower ground flanking the Forth estuary, passing Stirling, the site of Bannockburn which interested Jamie, and Falkirk where he bemoaned Wallace's defeat centuries earlier, they managed to reach Linlithgow, a major ride in the circumstances, with flooding to cope with. Here they found the town already full of soldiery, like themselves making for Edinburgh, parties from the Forth valley lairdships and further west, including the Graham Earl of Airth, shamefully forfeited from the ancient earldoms of Strathearn and Menteith by the weakness of Charles the First, at Argyll's instigation, yet prepared to support that monarch's son. These had already taken over the famous royal palace, the dower-house of Scotland's queens, where Mary Queen of Scots had been born. Now it stood empty, on the shore of its loch, deserted. So, within its handsome and commodious premises, its stableyards, brewhouses and outbuildings, there was shelter for all. Some trouble developed in the town and its taverns that night between the levies of rival lords, always a problem with Scottish armies mustering.

Conditions were only slightly improved in the morning. They had eighteen miles to cover to the capital, but with rivers in spate and the ground generally waterlogged, progress was slow. Sir David sent scouts ahead to try to ascertain the position at Edinburgh and to learn whether the muster at the

Burgh Muir was still in force; and since fast horses were required for this, lairdly ones were chosen. Young Lord Ogilvy volunteered to lead, and Jamie offered to go with him, Thomas less enthusiastically going along also. They were given strict instructions.

It was good to be off on their own, able to pick their way at greater speed as they would, after all the restricted riding. They went by Niddrie-Seton and Kirkliston and, with the rain ceasing at last and the clouds somewhat lifting, there they could see ahead of them the Pentland Hills to the south, a lengthy range, the wooded hogsback of Corstorphine Hill directly in front, and further east the majestic peak of Arthur's Seat which soared above the capital city. The Burgh Muir would lie just to the south of that. At this range, eight miles, it was impossible to tell what was the situation there.

They did not get nearer Edinburgh than the village of Corstorphine however. There they found a troop of horse under the banner of the Earl of Crawford, the Lindsay chief, halted and being addressed by a small party flying the flag of the Covenant. They were being instructed, on orders from General David Leslie, to take up a position on this Corstorphine Hill. The English had reached the eastern outskirts of Edinburgh but had not yet actually assailed it. Undoubtedly they were in poor shape after their dire advance from the Borderland in these conditions, lacking food and their horses weak. Leslie was holding a line from the capital's walls, or just outside them, down to Leith, the city's port, for the English had a fleet sent up to the Forth to supply the invading army, desperately needed in the present circumstances, and the Leithers had closed the port against them. The ships must not be allowed to dock – that was one of Leslie's priorities. But a detachment of English cavalry had been seen to be making its way south-about round the city, and heading in this direction, no doubt seeking to reach and take Leith from the west. They were being harried by a small Scots force, but it was feared that they could not be held up. So the strong position of Corstorphine Hill should be occupied by as many as was possible, to halt the enemy, for the English would have to come past it, either on its east or west side. Crawford accordingly was going up to man this ridge, about a mile long. Others were already there apparently. The young men from Airlie turned and hastened back to advise Sir David.

They came up with their main body, now joined by Airth's men and others, near Kirkliston, and told them the position; so all made for this Corstorphine Hill, hoping that they would be in time. Actually they saw no sign of enemy – that is, until they were mounted up on to the ridge itself, when they could make out a large column of cavalry coming in their direction from the south, against the background of the high Pentland Hills. It seemed probable that this was the English, although whether they were being assailed from the rear by Scots was not evident; no doubt a rearguard would be dealing with that.

Up on the high ground they found perhaps eight hundred men already in place along the ridge, all cavalry like themselves. Crawford, very senior amongst the earls, had taken charge, an elderly man but capable. It seemed that the enemy – if such they were – assuming that they continued on this line they were on, were going to have to pass to the westwards of the hill. Their own objective must be to turn them back, to prevent them from getting round to Leith port from this direction. So the tactics were to wait until the English were directly below this ridge and then charge down on them, by surprise, cutting their column up into gobbets; which sounded simple but which might not be so. The trees up here, fortunately, would hide them until the last moment, unless the foe sent scouts up ahead to check. But surely that was not likely in the circumstances, in a hurried dash for Leith?

Crawford, who also had served with Montrose and was used to command, divided his miscellaneous force into four sections, each of about two hundred, and a few hundred yards apart, warning all to keep themselves and their horses well hidden amongst the trees and bushes. The roadway ran close under the hill on a sort of terrace, and presumably the enemy would have to use it, for the ground below was flooded with all the rain. Therefore they would not be riding more than four abreast, and inevitably much strung out. None to move until he heard a blast blown on a hunting horn. Then down on them at speed, to cut the elongated column into pieces. And might God aid them against these Ironsides.

Jamie and Thomas undoubtedly were not the only ones there who knew butterflies in their stomachs at the prospect of this, their first experience of warfare, and against such renowned adversaries as Cromwell's dragoons. Sir Gilbert gave them urgent orders, advice and encouragement as they sat their mounts, swords drawn, in the northernmost of the four sections.

They seemed to have a long and nerve-racking wait of it, for, having to keep well back out of sight from below, amongst the trees, they could not see down to the road. Unmounted hidden watchers would give Crawford the word when to move – and whether the enemy had any scouts ahead.

A wretched horse whinnying somewhere along the line had hearts in mouths, but seemingly no alarm was raised. The English did appear to be taking their time, but of course they had to pass through Corstorphine village, and that would delay them somewhat. And they might be assailed from behind.

The waiting horsemen were becoming restive, however nervous, when at last the ululations of the horn sounded. All along the line the leaders held swords high and then slashed them down, pointing, and plunged forward. Spurs were kicked into horses' flanks, and the charge began.

Much as all wished for a headlong and orderly hurtle down on an unprepared and strung-out foe, it was not quite like that. The hillside, although steep, was very uneven and scattered with trees, so that no compact and disciplined descent was possible, even the surefooted garrons having to slither and veer to avoid trees, bushes and outcrops, the muddy wetness of the ground no help. All along the very uneven line men were shouting now. Jamie, like the others having to keep his eyes on his route down and not to collide with neighbouring riders, could now see the extended column of horsemen below intermittently. Glances showed them to be reacting to the sudden threat, as best they could probably; but in lengthy file, orders were not readily communicated, and men had to act on their own initiative, which did not lead to coherent defence. Down there it would, at first, be every man for himself.

Stationary horsemen are always at a disadvantage against charging ones, individual avoidance their best tactic and these, of course, were amongst the most highly trained cavalrymen in the world, the veterans of the English Civil War. So the impact of the much less expert attackers was not so overwhelming as the latter might have hoped, especially with the gaps between both, in timing and spacing, Jamie Ramsay for instance failing to strike any enemy with his right-and-left-swinging sword as he drove across that roadway, with the opposition troopers reining clear on either side. All he achieved was more or less accidental, as one of the Roundhead's horses, avoiding him, cannoned into another beast, all but falling, and unseating its rider.

And, charging downhill in such fashion, Jamie was not the only one to be unable to pull up his mount at the roadway, and so plunging on down the continuing slope at the far side some way before being able to rein round for a second assault, this time *uphill*. So no great havoc was wrought amongst the Englishmen.

Not bloody havoc, that is. But as a means of demolishing a disciplined and coherent column it was very successful. Broken up into small groups and individuals, and their attackers coming down on them so raggedly owing to the terrain, however well trained the Ironsides, surprised, were unable to react in any unified way, milling about on their alarmed steeds, and, of course, unable to receive any orders from front or rear.

With the attackers pulling round, however irregularly, for a repeated assault, a very elementary counter-action followed, at least at this northern end of the column. Return whence they had come and towards the bulk of their fellows quickly became the objective, not so much flight as reassembly as a body. But done in haste, and on a fairly narrow roadway, this inevitably resulted in something of a mad rush, horses jostling each other. Admittedly it did present a difficult target for the Scots would-be assailants who, in order not to be swept away themselves in the headlong dash, had more or less to draw up and watch. But it did represent chaos along the English line where, to the south, a similar situation was developing, and riders, fleeing, advancing or fighting, piled into each other, horses rearing and lashing out in screaming panic, spilling out from the road on either side.

In all this, the Scots were no more able to be ordered and controlled than were their foes, the confusion applying almost equally, save in that they were less driven by the need to be elsewhere, to escape. For that is what clearly became the dominant and deciding factor on the English side, escape back whence they had come. Whether orders to that end were in fact issued was not to be known; but the urge communicated itself to all. With Crawford's men beginning to come along after them, the celebrated Ironsides somehow managed to disentangle themselves sufficiently to spur away southwards, hardly in column, as they had come, towards Corstorphine village.

It was a victory, of a sort.

Crawford endeavoured to maintain the impetus, waving his men on, or some of them, to pursue, to keep the enemy in flight and from re-forming. Inevitably it was the southernmost sections of the Scots force which had to be the first involved in this, and on the narrow roadway those to the north were held up. By the time that Jamie and his neighbours arrived at the further end of the ridge, overlooking the village, it was to find some of Airth's men actually coming back up the hill, announcing that the Roundheads were in full flight, heading for the Pentland Hill skirts. That threat to Leith port was now over.

Deciding that they could be pleased with themselves, however unorthodox and peculiar had been their triumphing, the Scots leaders held a hurried council. It was decided that they must proceed on for Edinburgh's Burgh Muir, to discover where their prowess would next be needed.

In high spirits, the various parts of the force were marshalled, and they left the scene of victory eastwards. Casualties on either side had been negligible, and no corpses were left on the field of battle.

* * *

At the Burgh Muir, almost a mile south of the city, they found only a comparatively small assembly, although there were many tents and pavilions pitched. The elderly Alexander Leslie, Earl of Leven, appeared to be in charge here, and was glad to welcome more reinforcements, and to hear of their success at Corstorphine Hill. The Burgh Muir, although the traditional assembly place for Scots armies, on higher ground and convenient enough, did not have any all-round view of the surroundings, at least to the east, where the bulk of Arthur's Seat rose. They had not seen any return of the vanquished enemy party.

The news was good as far as it went, in that there had been no attack in force by Cromwell as yet, who had apparently grouped his forces about a mile east of the city walls, at the far side of Arthur's Seat in its parkland there, contenting himself meantime with making a number of probes to test out the defences. These last consisted of a long line of General David Leslie's army, stretching right down to Leith, two miles, inevitably thin in parts, but with strategic reserves to the rear ready to throw themselves into any dangerously threatened area. So far there was no word of any major English assault against this line, Cromwell waiting.

So it was a matter of waiting, also, for the newcomers, something of an anticlimax for these triumphant warriors. Leven told them that they might be sent for at any time by his kinsman requiring additional support in any section of the long line. The protection of the port of Leith was the first priority, the fleet kept from landing its so greatly needed provision for the tired and hungry English. He calculated that Cromwell would be unlikely to mount an offensive against the capital itself until his men and horses were fed.

While they waited, parties of reinforcements kept arriving from all over the land, some quite large, an enheartening process. Scotland was obviously going to have a major army to confront the invaders.

No demands for assistance came from General Leslie, no

messages of any sort. Jamie, for one, had never thought of warfare as largely a matter of waiting, idle.

When, in late afternoon, a courier did arrive, it was not from Leslie but from a captain of scouts based high on Arthur's Seat, on the watch. He came to announce that the English army was in fact retiring, the main force and its flanking units down towards Leith heading back south and east whence it had come.

While most there cheered, scarcely able to believe what they heard, old Leven was less impressed. Oliver Cromwell had not come all this way just to give up tamely, he declared. If he guessed aright, the English were merely moving back to the first port capable of docking and unloading those supply ships, since Leith was denied them. The East Lothian coast was unsuitable, shallow and sandy for a score of miles or more east and south. Then North Berwick harbour was tidal and small. But Dunbar, another ten miles south, was different, deep water. That would take their vessels. Dunbar, then; that was, in his judgment, the length of Cromwell's retiring.

The cheer abated.

When, later, General Leslie came up from Leith, a man of early middle years, it was agreed, Dunbar probably, although it was just possible that the enemy might go as far as Berwick-on-Tweed to regroup, as that was a larger port and reinforcements could conveniently arrive there from all over the north of England. Leslie said that he had scouts out monitoring the English withdrawal.

The question now was whether to follow up and assail Cromwell's retiral at once, to harass him before he and his could gain their needful sustenance and while English morale was low. This was recommended by many of the Scots commanders. But the two Leslies decided otherwise. Their forces were still not fully assembled, many contingents known to be on their way but not as yet arrived. And the Kirk leaders were coming from a meeting at St Andrews with a committee of the Estates of Parliament, after the General Assembly, bringing men and funds with them. The distinctly heterogeneous Scots array, numerous as it might be, required to be disciplined, marshalled and organised as effectively as possible, and this would take a little time. They would wait a couple of days and then march south, rested and in good order, junior commanders chosen and knowing their various duties and responsibilities. Meanwhile, the capital city's services were at their disposal – at least, of the lords, chiefs and leaders.

Jamie Ramsay, inexperienced as he was, did not think this the best policy; and in this instance his father rather agreed with him. But who were they to question the generals? At least they had kin in Edinburgh, and ought to be able to pass a comfortable couple of nights, for a change.

5

In the event, the next two days represented not so much an assembling and marshalling of the Scots army as a purging of it, in the name of discipline. But it was the Kirk's ideas of discipline, rather than the generals'. The divines arrived in force, their message and determination clear, and their authority was not only heavenly but lawful, for they had the backing of the Parliamentary Committee, carefully and solidly Covenant of course, behind them, under the lead of Sir Archibald Johnston of Warriston, Lord Clerk Register, the Kirk's principal legal luminary. All Malignants were to be purged from God's host: that is, those who in the past had supported the late King Charles and his bishops; the turncoat Montrose; and the Hamilton faction. These were not worthy to draw the Sword of the Spirit against the Sectaries – this was the name they gave to Cromwell and his puritanical hordes.

This unexpected decree, odd for an army whose commander-in-chief was in theory the newly crowned King of Scots, and whose need was to unite to expel the invader, alarmed and upset the Leslies, as well as many another. For it meant dispensing with the services and troops of many there now assembled, including the Earls of Crawford, Airth and Marischal and a number of lesser lords. Much offence was given, much protest made, but the clergy were adamant. These had served with Montrose and were as good as damned, and their contribution would endanger the Lord's cause. They were not wanted. Chaos reigned in the great camp of the Burgh Muir.

David Leslie and the Earl of Leven tried hard to counter this dire decree, which in name at least was the decision of parliament, to say nothing of the General Assembly of the Kirk which was in effect ruling Scotland in the name of the

Covenant. The generals were only very partially successful, managing to gain reprieve for a few accusedly Malignant forces on various grounds. These, as it happened, included the Airlie contingent for, although the Earl of Airlie was a notable and confirmed, indeed excommunicated, Malignant, he was not present, and his son Lord Ogilvy was a minor, had not been with Montrose, and could be deemed to be innocent. That Sir David Ogilvy and Sir Gilbert Ramsay *had* served with Montrose was got over on the grounds that they were mere underlings and had been only obeying orders from the deplorable Airlie. One or two other groups gained grudging acceptance by similar devices. Nevertheless, almost four thousand men, with their leaders, were dismissed as undesirable and told to go home. Seldom could a national army have had to march in defence of its country in such a state of reduction and disunity.

So it was more than any two days later before the purged host set off southwards for Dunbar – for their scouts had confirmed that it was there indeed that Cromwell had gone, and where his ships had unloaded. However, even reduced in numbers as it was, the army was still a large one, totalling over thirty thousand, and almost double Cromwell's reported numbers. They marched, in theory, under David Leslie's sole command, for Leven, displaying his disgust at this purging folly, this staffing of an army by what he called ministers' sons and clerks, refused any joint command, and only came along as some sort of voluntary adviser; but as all knew, the real command was with the divines, and the Parliamentary Committee's Covenant convener, Johnston of Warriston, a lawyer of religious tendencies.

It was thirty miles to Dunbar, going parallel with the skirts of the Lammermuir Hills, by Musselburgh, Tranent, Haddington and Hailes, and it took the motley host two days, at the pace of the slowest, to the impatience of the cavalry, halting for the first night on Gladsmuir, west of Haddington, to the chanting of psalms. Their scouts informed them that the English were encamped, not at Dunbar itself but over a mile to the south, at the level ground of Broxmouth, where the Brocks' or Badgers' Burn reached the sea, not a particularly strong position but defended by marshy ground laid down by this quite large burn, which would tend to bog down cavalry. So, since Cromwell's famous Ironsides were all cavalry, it looked as though the so-called Lord Protector was very much on the defensive on this occasion, no doubt informed that he was outnumbered two to one, and perhaps his men not all fully recovered from the deprivations of their march north. His ships were still lying off Dunbar, and there was some speculation that he might even be contemplating evacuation by sea, although he could by no means get all his thousands aboard these vessels. He might be waiting for more shipping to come for him, or awaiting reinforcements, by land, from England – this probably more likely. Either way it looked as though the sooner the Scots attacked him, the better; in this, at least, the Kirk was wholeheartedly in agreement.

Passing Hailes Castle, at the foot of Traprain Law, they were joined by Hepburns thereof, who were useful as knowing the country intimately, and not tarred with the Malignant brush. They told them that Cromwell's patrols were active all around, scouring the area for cattle and sheep to feed the English army, and at the same time watching out for any enemy assault. Hepburn of Waughton and Luffness suggested that the best place for the Scots array to establish itself in relation to this Broxmouth position was the Doon Hill, two miles inland, an outlier of the Lammermuirs, a strong site with an all-round field of view and very difficult for an enemy to assail. There the Scots could dominate the scene, take stock, and decide on tactics. And it could be reached inconspicuously by using hillfoot tracks.

The divines saw no need for such secrecy, but Leslie, in view of the enemy patrols, and aware that Cromwell might well have reinforcements coming up from England, agreed that a hidden approach to this Doon Hill viewpoint would be advisable in the circumstances. So thither the host proceeded, by the foothills and the winding valley of the Spott Burn, as dusk was falling – as again was the rain.

The Doon Valley was no majestic height, in a land of high

hills, but it was isolated, which gave it the all-round vista, a steep northern face, protective from attack, a convenient and gentler rearward slope leading back into the foothill valleys, for possible retiral, and a fairly level and commodious summit, capable of accommodating a host of men. The Hepburn had known what he was at when he recommended this.

That admitted, it made an uncomfortable night's resting place for those marooned on the top, in rain and wind, although such of the leadership as might escaped back down to the shelter in the village, church and manse of Spott, another Hepburn place. Clearly the military life was not all fervour and glory.

In the morning, even though visibility was poor, they could see the English encampment to the north-east, over a mile away. Their own presence would be as visible to the enemy, although the English scouts would almost certainly have given notice of the Scots' arrival.

It was a strange sensation to sit there on the hill-top watching, two armies facing each other, inactive. What would Cromwell, the expert strategist, do now? Both hosts were in good defensive positions, the English less so but protected by a wide moat of marshland and the Brocks' Burn, the Scots on their height. But both to wait where they were for the other to attack seemed improbable as well as ineffective. Waiting, of course, both sides might receive reinforcements. But the invaders were at a disadvantage, in enemy country, English soil still thirty miles away, short of food, and probably morale not at its highest after the Edinburgh-Leith failure, with shipping insufficient to evacuate more than one-third of them. It seemed improbable that Cromwell could afford to wait there for long. So the Leslies calculated, and decided that *they* would do the waiting, despite the clergy's urging to go down and smite the Philistines.

As the morning passed, Cromwell made no move – at least not militarily. For around noon, a small party was observed to be approaching the Doon Hill under a white flag. So it looked as though Cromwell was seeking terms. The Kirk was loud against any such weakness being shown. The spawn of Satan must not get away with anything less than utter defeat.

71

The envoys were at least allowed to climb the hill, half a dozen officers led by a burly, soberly clad individual of early middle age, with a shrewd eye. This man introduced himself civilly to the Leslies, backed by the divines, as Lieutenant-General George Monck. Most there had heard of him, a former Cavalier general, who, when Charles the First went down, had been imprisoned in the Tower, but released by Cromwell on condition of service to the triumphant Commonwealth, and sent as commander to the English forces in Ireland. Now here he was, representing the Lord Protector.

He came, he announced bluntly, to reach a pacific settlement of the situation. The Lord Protector had come to Scotland not in any fashion to try to conquer it, but to come to an understanding and forge peace between the two parts of the United Kingdom, now the Commonwealth. There was no need for battle, enmity. They both were worshippers of God Almighty. All that was required was for the Scots to send back the Prince of Wales to the Continent, so that peaceful co-operation might be established between Scotland and England . . .

He got no further before an outcry from the clergy drowned his words. He tried again, but did not obtain a hearing. Eventually he withdrew from a pocket a folded paper, which he held up and waved. For some reason this gained him a hearing, the divines presumably respecting the written word more than the spoken. It was a form of letter, written and signed by Oliver Cromwell himself.

General Monck began to read, in a flat voice. "Friends, you take upon you to judge us in the things of our God, though you know us not. I am persuaded that divers of you who lead the people of Scotland have censured us. Is it therefore infallibly agreeable to the Word of God, all that you say? I beseech you, in the bowels of Christ, think it possible that you may be mistaken. There may be a Covenant made with death and hell. I do not say yours was so – but I pray you read the twenty-eighth of Isaiah from the fifth to the fifteenth verse. And do not scorn to know that it is the Spirit that quickens and giveth life . . ."

Monck's voice was lost in uproar, there on the hill-top – and the Scots clergy had powerful lungs. On and on the furious vituperation went, hands upraised to heaven, fists shaken, threats made. After a little of this, the English general bowed briefly to the Scots ones, ignoring the ministers, and, wheeling his horse around, led his companions back down the hill.

The Leslies, when they could quieten the militant Kirk, decided to accept a Hepburn suggestion and send a party of men to go and hold the famous pass of the Pease Dean a few miles to the south, through the narrow defiles of which the road to England ran, and a few men could hold up an army, as had often been contrived in the centuries of warfare between the two realms. This would, it was hoped, prevent Cromwell escaping southwards, or reinforcements reaching him from Berwick-on-Tweed.

There was, of course, much discussion and debate as to General Monck's mission. Most of the Scots accepted it as a sign of weakness on the enemy part, although not all approved of the way it had been rejected.

All that miserable damp day, with a chill wind off the North Sea, the Scots waited, the divines angry and impatient, the troops doubtful, some leaders agreeing with the clergy, more with the generals, not to attack meantime. David Leslie, as evening fell, ruled against any move, even for leaders to go back to Spott for the night, in fear that the English might just possibly try a night attack, perhaps able to approach and climb the steep hill in darkness. The ministers, led by Cant, Blair and Dickson, with a particularly vocal one named Henry Pollock, decided to brave it out on the hill-top also.

It was another cold and unpleasant night, and with little sleep for those not used to the rigours of campaigning. By dawn, the divines had had enough. This was not only folly and misery, they declared, but shameful lack of faith. Down with them all, upon the Sectaries, the enemies not only of the Covenant and Scotland but of the Almighty. Destroy utterly the traducers of God's Holy Word!

When the Leslies protested, the Lord Clerk Register Johnston came to them, speaking with the voice of parliament.

He ordered them to do as the ministers demanded. And at once, while it was not yet full daylight, and the enemy would be unready. To disobey him would be tantamount to treason, he announced.

Although Leven still stood out, the younger Leslie, sighing, yielded. He gave the order to assemble for advance, but pointed out that this could not be achieved in a few minutes.

They would attack in three sections of roughly ten thousand men each, and not directly northwards at the enemy encampment. There was, Hepburn told them, rather firmer ground to the south. So once down this hill they would swing away south-eastwards for a mile or so, and then wheel round northwards, one section actually along the shoreline, one in the centre, and one on the slightly higher ground on their left. But as well as these, to confuse the enemy if possible, a small detached force would go and station itself to the *north* of Cromwell's encampment, where there was some woodland flanking the Brocks' Burn. These were to show themselves against the background of the trees, and this would disguise the fact that they were not a large company, only the front for many. That should force Cromwell to reserve part of his army to cope with this projected threat. Possibly because of the Malignant background of the Ogilvy contingent, this last duty was imposed upon them. They were not to remain idle there, of course, but when the moment was ripe, to advance across the burn and attack the foe, as it were from the rear.

All this arranging and marshalling in sections took some time, inevitably, to the loud impatience and denunciation of the clergy, whose cry was Smite! Smite! Smite!

At last the move was started downhill, the horses slithering and slipping on the steep, wet terrain, the ministers leading with distinctly breathless psalms, the rank and file tending rather to curse.

There was no possibility now of the English failing to observe their move, for although still dull and overcast, it was daylight. At the foot of the Doon Hill, the Ogilvy troop, plus a few others, parted company with the rest, to head straight on, to near where the Spott Burn and the Brocks' Burn joined, the three sections of the main army moving off to the right, southwards. They could hear trumpets blaring in the enemy camp, the Roundheads readying themselves for the fray, an ominous sound to Jamie Ramsay.

Sir David in command, they rode on, distinctly doubtful as to their role. Unfortunately the trees which were to be their background cover were on the wrong side of the larger stream, so that they had to cross the Spott Burn to reach them. This was not difficult, but it did mean that they would have to ford the Brocks' Burn later, if they were to advance against the English, although it did also mean, admittedly, that if the enemy assailed them, they likewise would have that disadvantage.

They reached their position without any hindrance, and there found themselves alarmingly close to the invaders' encampment, barely half a mile away. There was much stir apparent amongst the enemy, as was to be expected. Would any come in this direction? Sir David was not entirely certain as to his duty. Were they merely to pose a threat? And if no attack on them developed, were they to move to the assault? And at what stage? And if they were assailed, and by a large force, were they expected to stand and fight, against odds, or retire to rejoin the main army?

Owing to the lie of the land, that main host was soon lost to sight, to the south-east. But it was not long before they could see the English army moving off in that direction – or most of it, for a sizeable force remained behind, facing in *this* direction, as expected and desired. So it was again a matter of waiting, apparently. This was odd warfare, Jamie and his brother, and Lord Ogilvy, agreed.

For a while they just sat their mounts and stared across at their opposite numbers some five hundred yards away, the burn intervening in its channel. That was obviously marshland beyond the burn, so difficult ground for cavalry to cover. Sir David sent scouts northwards, down to the coast, to see if it was practicable to advance that way, round-about, when the time came, if advance there was to be; and, since the same problem would apply to the enemy, to leave a watch there to warn if there was a similar outflanking attempt by the English.

At last they heard the sounds of battle, thinly, at a distance, carried on an easterly wind: musketry, the clash of steel, shouting. But they could see nothing of it, a low swell of ground, north and south, not to be called a ridge, intervening. The lines of English cavalry facing them did not move.

Their scouts came back from the shoreline, to say that it was perfectly possible to get round that way, that the Brocks' Burn spread itself as it entered the sea, to form shallows which could be splashed across with ease. They had left the required watch.

Sir David was still in a quandary. How long were they to stand there idle while conflict raged elsewhere? That is, if the enemy did not come against them here, presumably around that shoreline ford. Were they in fact of any service waiting here? Admittedly, because of that woodland at their backs, the enemy line would not know how many, or how comparatively few, they were, and might refrain from assault. Merely the threat of them was obviously immobilising quite a number of Cromwell's men. But it did seem a waste just to remain inactive there while battle raged beyond the swell of that farmland. The Ogilvys were not used, nor inclined, for this sort of role.

No word came from the shore, and fidgeting, wondering, they sat their horses.

The first indication of any development, strangely, came with the unexpected break-up of the cavalry line facing them, as it began to turn away and head not northwards for the coast but due eastwards, soon to disappear beyond that swell in the land, leaving only the tented encampment with the odd dismounted figure to be see. Did this imply Cromwell's defeat, and these English going to his aid? Or was it a mere device, to reach the coast further on, and then swing round unseen to come back and cross the ford, in attack? There was discussion on this, and if it was indeed the former, whether now themselves to advance, either directly across the difficult stream, or to go on down to the ford and across there, for the main battle scene.

Then they saw something to alter their perceptions altogether. It was men streaming into sight over that swelling ground, raggedly, mounted and otherwise, in no sort of order, in small numbers and larger groups, and heading north-westwards towards the hills. Staring, the watchers wondered, and their hearts sank. The English would not be fleeing in that direction. North-east perhaps, towards Dunbar and their ships, or south for the border; but not into the trackless Lammermuir Hills. So, was this just some wing of the Scots army which had been overrun and was now in flight? Or was it . . . ?

As more and more decamping stragglers appeared, with no signs of halting to regroup or to make a stand, the watchers could not blink away a recognition of the probable situation. That was the Scots army, not in retreat but in headlong flight. Whatever had happened, a large part of it was fleeing the scene, and making for the anonymity of the hills. It could mean only defeat, major defeat, the day lost. Grimly those by the Brocks' Burn eyed each other.

What now, then? What was the Ogilvy contingent to do? What would be expected of them?

Sir David hastily conferred with his lieutenants. Was there anything that they could usefully achieve? If it was indeed complete defeat, then their fewer than three hundred men would make no difference, at this stage. Sir Gilbert said that all that they could attempt was to seek, as a disciplined troop, to cover the rear of these fleeing men from any pursuit, possibly give them opportunity to regroup, reassemble, aid in some way. This was agreed, although with doubts expressed.

So it was hastily back to the higher ground whence they had come, the flight before them showing no signs of slackening, indeed numbers increasing. When they reached the fugitives, most mounted but some afoot, men-at-arms, clansmen, some ministers, even a few lairds, and these paid no least heed to them in their haste to be elsewhere, it was evident that there was in fact little that they could do. Panic was now the master. They saw none of the actual leadership.

It was decided to ride on southwards, against that human stream, to see whether at least they might help in some orderly withdrawal. But when they reached a position where they could see much of the area before them, it was to perceive that there was no point in proceeding. A chaotic scene opened before them less than a mile off, on lower ground – chaos except in that clearly there was some order, some discipline, seeking to contain the milling confusion and medley; and in the circumstances that could only be Cromwell's Ironsides, rounding up disorganised cavalry, preventing the foot from escaping, taking prisoners by the hundred, the thousand. It was obvious that utter disaster prevailed for Scotland, and their own comparatively small company would throw itself away ineffectively in seeking to intervene now. Unhappily, they turned back, to join the sorry exodus.

Presently they were caught up by a faster-fleeing group led by none other than the Lord Tullibardine. He was slightly wounded, as were some of his Murray men, and cursing breathlessly. Those devil-damned clerks, he shouted. It was all their fault. The divines! Complete and utter shambles. Leslie should never have heeded them. They should not have left Doon Hill. Went into battle singing psalms! Got in the way of the cavalry. Purblind fools!

For a Covenant stalwart that was almost sacrilege.

Sir David asked questions. What now? What of the Leslies? Clearly they had lost this battle, but had the English suffered great loss also? If the Scots rallied, might they not still be able to defeat a weakened Cromwell?

Tullibardine could answer nothing to all that. He did not know whether the generals had escaped. Many had fled, yes, but there were vast numbers taken prisoner. He had only just got away, himself. Thousands were slain. No one was controlling the withdrawal. No word of a rally. David Leslie and old Leven might have got away, and be aiming to make a stand somewhere – he did not know. As to Cromwell's men, he did not think that they had suffered greatly. They had formed a disciplined and well-led host, the Scots a psalm-singing divided horde. He, Tullibardine, was for back to Perth, as fast as his horse could carry him!

As they rode into the skirts of the Lammermuirs and realised that they were not in fact being pursued, they slackened pace somewhat. But there was no sign of any reassembling of the fugitives, any drawing up, all heading on approximately westwards, back towards Edinburgh. They met up with the Earl of Kinnoull and a party. He was as angry and disgusted with it all as was Tullibardine. But he did think that the Leslies and other leaders had effected an escape. He had seen them heading off in the opposite direction from this, due southwards, possibly to link up with the force sent to hold the Pease Dean pass. So there might still survive a small command of ordered men, subject to discipline. But it would be at some distance, detached from all this flight. And not sufficient to tackle Cromwell again, not now, of that he was sure. They would probably make for Edinburgh, through the hills also, by what routes he could not tell. He, Kinnoull, was heading back for the capital, and advised that they all should do so now, and wait for the Leslies there. At least they ought to be spared the attentions of the Kirk!

This was agreed, and they rode on by the hillfoots, gathering quite a company as they went. It was still only mid-forenoon. The Battle of Dunbar had lasted only an hour or two.

At Edinburgh that evening they, and a great many others, waited for news of their generals, but none was forthcoming. They did not imagine that the victorious Cromwell would stage another assault on the city, not immediately at any rate; but scouts were posted on Arthur's Seat to keep a watch. Alarm and despondency reigned.

The Ramsays had kin in a house in the Canongate, and there they passed a night, comfortable in body but less so in mind and spirit.

There was still no sign of the Leslies in the morning, nor, thankfully, of any English approach to the city. All day they waited, but no word nor instructions reached them. Most of the fugitive troops who had not already done so followed Tullibardine's example and started for home. And by evening, Sir David decided that, in the circumstances, there was little else to be done. They would wait another night, and if there were no orders nor tidings in the morning, it was back to the Angus glens for them, sorry warriors. How they would face the Earl of Airlie was another matter, Jamie indeed wondering what they could say to Jean and her friend. He decided that he would have to concentrate on the little victory they had gained on Corstorphine Hill, the only time that he had actually drawn his sword even though not bloodied it.

Still without news next day, home called.

6

It was some time before tidings of any certainty percolated through to the Angus glens – and grim word it was when it came. The scale of the disaster at Dunbar was even worse than had been feared, utter and appalling defeat, horror and carnage. Over three thousand of the Scots were dead, the wounded unnumbered and ten thousand taken prisoner. The English losses were unknown, but not thought to be great. Stories of why and how it had all happened were legion, but unreliable and often contradictory. Cromwell was back at Edinburgh, inside the city now, not besieging it. David Leslie and the Earl of Leven were at Stirling, preparing to hold that narrow and strategic neck of central Scotland between Highlands and Lowlands, as so often it had been held before against English invaders. Dire news indeed, but no instructions with it, no orders as to reassembling in arms.

After an interval, the Ramsays rode over to Clova, escorting Mariota Ogilvy home, to try to discover what, if anything, now was required of them in the national interest. They found Sir David at least better informed. Cromwell's reinforcements from England had now arrived, both by sea and land, and he now held a fairly firm grip of much of southern Scotland, declaring it part of his Protectorate. David Leslie was not assembling any major army at Stirling, which perhaps wisely Cromwell was not attempting to attack meantime, well aware of its dangers for invaders, with the Forth estuary on the one side and the vast bogs of the Flanders Moss on the other. Leslie apparently was planning a very different move, a campaign, free of clerical guidance now. He had relieved King Charles from his all but imprisonment at Falkland, and taken him to Stirling Castle. With Cromwell in Scotland and inevitably preoccupied in the subduing of the land to his will, Leslie was proposing what could be a possibly brilliant gesture. Leaving Leven in command at Stirling, he would take a quite small but carefully selected and fast-riding force, and the king with him, and make with all speed, but as secretly as possible, for the west of England, by Glasgow, Dumfries and Carlisle, an area where the invaders thus far would not be strong, if indeed present at all. The royalist cause in England was known to be by no means dead, only dormant, and the Roundhead Commonwealth unpopular with the common folk, especially in the western counties and Wales, where much of the nobility and gentry also remained loyal to the formerly reigning house. Taking Charles there, crowned now as King of Scots, could be just what was needed to relight the royalist torch, and not only in the west. A rising there around the king could well spread all over the land. At the very least, it ought to bring Cromwell himself hastening south to try to quench such flame, and so rid Scotland of his feared presence.

All agreed, at Clova, that this sounded a gallant and worthwhile venture, however ambitious. And whatever else, it ought to give Leven time to rally Scotland out of its present dejection, to rise and repel any occupying English forces which Cromwell might leave behind, if and when he departed.

David Ogilvy said that he had been to Airlie to see their chief the day before, to discover his wishes in this situation. The earl had thought that, together with other leaders in these parts, Crawford, Kinnoull, Airth, Erroll, Atholl and the like, they ought to try to form a fairly united party, to be able to act as one when the opportunity presented itself, so-called Malignants as they almost all were! The Earl Marischal was said to be with Leslie at Stirling – indeed it was whispered that his was the conception of the counter-invasion of England – so he would not be included in this proposed alliance, since presumably he would be away with Charles to the south. Airlie wanted, therefore, all his lairds and chieftains to maintain their manpower in a state of readiness to re-muster for action at short notice, and this, of course, included the Ramsays. The winter would soon be upon them, and not the best time for the

82

glens-folk to rise in arms; but they would be prepared for swift response, for no one knew how the situation would develop. No one indeed knew when Leslie and the king would make their move or Leven demand the assistance of all loyal men.

It was all very uncertain, but none made objection. At least, apparently, the clergy were lying very low.

The Ramsays went back to Bamff just a little cheered. They would be ready to play their part.

It was October now, and the bad weather continued. It would make for an early winter.

It did – and a strange winter it was, and not only for the dwellers in the remote Angus glens. All Scotland, and possibly much of England also, waited and wondered. It was soon known that, almost stealthily, David Leslie and King Charles, with a hard-riding force, had left Stirling, and thereafter more or less disappeared from men's ken, Buckingham presumably with them. Nothing was heard of them as November was succeeded by December and Yuletide. They might have been swallowed up in the Cumbrian or even the Welsh mountains. Certainly no great royalist rising was reported in England. Cromwell would know something about it, no doubt, for he was always well informed; but whatever he knew, it was not enough to send him hastening southwards from Edinburgh, although he was reported to make brief and hurried visits to London to see to matters there, even though his Commonwealth lieutenants and nominees beat a well-worn trail to Edinburgh over the affairs of the two kingdoms. However, the strange silence and mystery over King Charles's and Leslie's whereabouts and intentions did have the effect of keeping Cromwell as it were on his toes, ready for a departure, and so postponed any major attempt to subdue all of Scotland to his rule meantime.

But more minor gestures in that direction were made. One of his lieutenant-generals, Lambert by name, sallied over to Hamilton, not far from Glasgow, and defeated a force of militant Covenanters there, and then turned northwards towards Stirling. Leven, defending the narrow neck of the land at Stirling, assembled such strength as he had in the great Tor Wood, to oppose, as Wallace and Bruce had done so long before. Cromwell's military genius countered this, however, by assembling shipping to take his troops across Forth at Queensferry, to get behind Leven. This manoeuvre took time, enabling Leven to send a part of his modest army hastily down to Inverkeithing, on the main shore, where the said ships would dock, to try to prevent a landing. A small battle was fought there, led by Sir Hector Maclean and his clansmen from the Highland west, wherein they at least gained much glory, even though they failed in their endeavours, Sir Hector refusing to retire in the face of overwhelming odds, wielding his broadsword in the thick of it, and as one after another of his personal banner-bearers fell at his side, crying "Another for Hector!", always being heeded so that seven banner-bearers died beside him before he himself fell. This gallantry resounded throughout the land, but it did not prevent Cromwell from marching north-westwards and reaching Perth, cutting off Leven at Stirling, and forcing him to retire into the Highland fastnesses.

Still no word came of King Charles and Leslie.

In all this, life for the Ramsays, like so many others, remained superficially normal, although with inevitable under-lying tension and readiness for sudden and drastic change, when the call came. Snowed in on their high-ground barony, Yuletide was passed in getting the cattle and sheep down to shelter, a large task. Jamie, whose responsibility this mainly was, with his team of helpers, swords laid by, by no means forgot the national crisis in his physical efforts and consequent weariness, and wondered, wondered, questioning his father, who was desperately concerned about it all, and hoped that David Ogilvy would be able to get word over to them, if and when necessary, despite the snows on the hills. The said snows should, at least, be protecting Leven's hiding forces.

It was in fact early February before they learned that Cromwell had at last left Scotland, whether for good this time none knew, but apparently he had been gone for almost two weeks, leaving that General Monck, who had come as envoy up to the Doon Hill, in command at Edinburgh, with

Lambert at Perth and Stirling. If Cromwell had gone south because of some information he had received as to Leslie's and Charles's activities, no such information reached the Scots.

It was Sir Gilbert's guess that what was happening was that Leslie had found less enthusiasm for a royalist rising in the English West Country than he had hoped for, and that he and Charles and party would be going around secretly seeking to arouse support and promises of men and arms for war once the campaigning season arrived. Cromwell might have learned of such, and their approximate area of operations and intend to nip any potential rising in the bud there and then.

As a belated spring advanced, no action appeared to be called for meantime by Leven, parliament or the Kirk. A most curious hiatus prevailed in Scotland. General Monck, like apparently everyone else, seemed to be waiting.

It was April, and the snows all but disappeared except on the high tops, before there was a call upon the Ramsays, from David Ogilvy. Monck had at last demonstrated his abilities as Lieutenant-Governor of Scotland for the Protectorate by making another ferried crossing of the Forth at Queensferry, with an army, marching through Fife while his ships sailed off eastwards and northwards around Fife Ness to the Tay estuary, and there re-embarked, to ferry his troops across to assault and take Dundee, a surprise and surprising move. Dundee was the third largest seat of population in the land, but something of a backwater nevertheless in national affairs. But it was a useful starting point for any assault on north-east Scotland, Aberdeen and beyond – and, unfortunately, uncomfortably near to the Angus glens. With Lambert at Perth and Monck at Dundee, the Earl of Airlie and neighbouring lords were becoming concerned. A council of war was to be held at Airlie Castle, and Sir Gilbert Ramsay was amongst those urged to attend.

That man felt that such a conference was overdue, and went, taking his sons with him.

Airlie Castle was almost as busy as when last they had been there, even though this was not exactly an assembly in arms. A large company of earls, lords and lairds were there, not only from Angus and Strathmore but from Fife and almost up to Aberdeen itself, and of course they had not come alone, each bringing a suitable escort of armed men to befit his rank and dignity. So the castle was full to overflowing, and the Countess of Airlie was hard put to it to provide hospitality and accommodation for all, the castleton as well as the castle itself and its outbuildings being crowded with men. Large as the establishment was, it all made for distinctly cramped conditions.

Sir Gilbert was happy to share a room with his friend David of Clova, but his sons had to be squeezed into what was really a small harness-room above the courtyard stabling. And it was there that they discovered that, if they thought their quarters less than roomy or well furnished, they were as nothing compared with the next apartment, a store for horse fodder turned into temporary sleeping accommodation for no fewer than five young women: the Ladies Marion, Margaret, Mary and Helen, daughters of Airlie by his first wife, long dead; and Christian Ogilvy, his niece, daughter of the late and gallant Sir Thomas, brother of Sir David, who now lived at Airlie Castle. Despite being dispossessed from their own chambers they were a cheerful and far from bashful lot, which was perhaps just as well, for the fodder-room could only be reached through the harness-room in which the Ramsays were to roost, so that much toing and froing was entailed, much laughter, mirth and apologies involved. And the eldest of the five, aged twenty, was quite the most beautiful creature Jamie, for one, had ever set eyes upon, dark-haired, delicately featured, slenderly built and with a wide smiling mouth – this was the niece Christian. Even Thomas was moved to remark on her looks, by no means a usual reaction with him. To be rooming next door to this highly decorative and outgoing company more than made up for any discomfort and inconvenience as to quarters.

That evening's meal, extraordinarily adequate as it was for so great a number, as regards provision, was less so as to accommodation, for all the nobility and gentry could not be seated at table in the great and lesser halls, and some of the smaller lairds and sons thereof found themselves eating in the vaulted basement kitchen. But hot as it was there, and busy with comings and goings, again there was no complaint for even with all the castleton women pressed into service for the diners, the Ogilvy family found it necessary to help out, and the Ramsay brothers did not judge it entirely wishful thinking on their part that the girl Christian and one of her cousins, Helen, seemed to pay particular attention to their neighbouring roomers.

Later, well fed, washed after a fashion and bedded down in somewhat anticipatory mood, the young men, far from seeking immediate slumber which might well be disturbed, waited for their next-door – only there was no door – occupants to arrive, these presumably having been helping with the clearing-up process after the major repast. When the five girls did appear, showing no signs of weariness either, there was much roguish glancing, chuckling and nudging in evidence, and thereafter a certain amount of passage back and forth, in various stages of undress, for unspecified reasons, presumably feminine. Even when that unfortunately ceased, still a deal of whispering and giggles emanated from the adjoining room, enough to keep Jamie from his sleep, although his brother was less affected.

It was long before silence reigned in that stableyard, one way and another.

In the morning, the great ones held their conference, lesser folk left to their own devices. It did not demand a great deal of initiative on Jamie's part to knock innocently at the non-existent door of the fodder-room while some of its denizens were engaged in a tidying-up process, and seek guidance as to what might be worth doing that forenoon, places to visit nearby for instance, not exactly seeking a guide but implying that such would be welcome. Various suggestions were offered by the three girls present, including going to look at the waterfalls on the Melgam Water, known as the Loups of Kenny, the Abbot's Cross, boulders in the shape of a crucifix high on the shoulder of Strone Hill, which marked the former boundary of Arbroath Abbey lands, which came to the Ogilvys at the Reformation; and the standing-stones at Baldovie. Since this last was proposed by Christian, who said that the Strone Hill was too far away to go and be back by midday, this Baldovie was the inevitable choice, three miles up the Cromie Burn apparently. Only, of course, Jamie Ramsay had no idea how to get there. Directions were supplied, but were sufficiently involved to permit mystified confusion, and as hospitality demanded, Christian, or Tina as she was called by her cousins, offered to conduct him. Unfortunately, the Lady Helen, the youngest of the quartette, aged sixteen, said that she would come along too; so Jamie felt it advisable to convince Thomas to accompany them – who would have been quite content to spend his time in the castle library.

So presently the four of them set off on horseback, Tina trying to calculate just how distantly they were related, for the Ramsays had more than once had Ogilvy female forebears.

The Cromie Burn was a comparatively modest tributary of the River Isla, coming down in a fairly straight course from the heights of the Forest of Kingoldrum, lacking the dramatic rocky defiles and cataracts of some of the other headwater streams. But it had the advantage of possessing only a narrow cattle-track up its length, and a curious and still narrower bridge to cross, which meant that there could be no more than two riding abreast, and often not even that. Jamie might not yet be much of a soldierly tactician but he was developing social strategies.

He and Tina chatted pleasantly enough, companionably, about this and that, Jamie ensuring that they kept well ahead of the other pair. Inevitably the disaster of Dunbar came up, and he had to confess that it had been a most inglorious as well as terrible occasion for Scottish arms, and was unable to claim any gallant contribution on his own part, nor even any real participation. But he did again make something of the Corstorphine Hill business, inconclusive as this might have proved in the long run, and was rather surprised by the quite shrewd questioning on military procedure which this aroused. It did not fail to occur to him that this young woman, a full year older than himself, was no simple lass, and unlikely to be any easy conquest, however friendly.

Three miles up the burnside, and just before the small laird's establishment of Baldovie, they swung off left-handed uphill to where, on a sudden but no very major height, rose the remains of a stone circle. There were others in the Airlie vicinity apparently, but this one had one of the remaining monoliths carved with Pictish symbols. Dismounting, the four of them examined and discussed these strange and quite elaborate decorations, trying to guess what they represented and meant. One was a crescent with what seemed to be a broken spear, or arrow in the form of a V superimposed; another an animal of sorts, with nose, eyes, ears and forepaws, but hindquarters more like a coiled serpent, and a trunk-like appendage sweeping back, not from nose but from forehead; the third and fourth were fairly obviously a mirror and comb. This was more in the studious Thomas's line of interest than Jamie's, and he hazarded a guess that the mirror and comb represented a female influence – which had Tina protesting that men could be just as concerned with their appearance – and that therefore the other symbols could well have expressly male significance, Helen gigglingly declaring that there was an old tradition that men had tails, like monkeys. Perhaps this odd creature was the Pictish notion of their remote ancestors, to which Tina added that the serpent-like tail was entirely suitable in that case. None of them could put forward a guess as to what the crescent and broken arrow could mean, Jamie's tongue-in-cheek suggestion that it might commemorate the tombstone of a man who failed to defend his woman with a bow and arrow which broke, drawing suitable condemnation from the others, this stone circle having been, as they all knew, a sacred place of sun worship for their ancestors.

Thomas said that there were normally thirteen upright stones in a circle, but here only five survived, and was told that there was an old ruined chapel in the neighbourhood with some carved stones built into the walling, which could have been brought from here. They exchanged opinions about the Picts, or more correctly the Albannach, and Tina was able to twit the young men on their mongrel background, for the Ramsays were originally of Flemish origin, coming across the Channel of England with William the Conqueror, settling in

English Huntingdonshire and only reaching Scotland in the twelfth century, with King David the First; whereas the Ogilvys were of pure Celtic or Albannach descent. Jamie recognised that he would have to keep his wits about him with this one.

He, for one, would have liked to ride on, suggesting that they might visit this ruined chapel Tina had mentioned to see the other inscribed stones, but that young woman said that they must get back, to help her aunt with the midday meal's preparation for the host of so hungry idle men. Suitably chastened, Jamie made quite a feature of helping her to remount her horse. And again he managed to get her to himself on the return journey, she telling him of her father, Sir Thomas Ogilvy, a great supporter of Charles the First, raising a regiment for that king and afterwards aiding Montrose notably, and dying at the Battle of Inverlochy aged only thirty-nine, his courage and dash renowned. Jamie rather wished that he had not made so much of that little skirmish at Corstorphine.

That afternoon, it transpired that Airlie and Crawford would address the company, or the leadership part of it, explaining the situation, what had been decided at the council and what was required of them all. So the great hall was crowded to hear. Jamie did not fail to notice Tina coming to squeeze in unobtrusively at the back, the only woman present.

Airlie, who was an eloquent man, led off. He said that the long interval and lack of action since the Dunbar Drove, as it was being called, was like that shameful defeat, the result of disunity, and not only in the realm at large but in the Covenant ranks themselves. These were divided as to whether to support King Charles in theory and oppose the English occupation, these being known as the Engagers, and those who thought it wiser now to co-operate with Cromwell and Monck against the monarchy, on the grounds that the Roundheads were at least religiously inclined, and holding Charles as a mocker of his Covenant oath, this persuasion led by Johnston of Warriston and another prominent divine, the Reverend Samuel Rutherford, rector and principal of Edinburgh University, these being called the Protesters. There was a third grouping known as the Resolutioners, who sought to unite the Scots and even to bring in the former Malignants and royalists – such as themselves here – a nation divided indeed, the fatal disease of their countrymen.

In these circumstances, and with Monck as close at hand as Dundee, it had been decided that they must set up a barrier of sorts, as it were, to any further northern advance by the occupying English forces, this to stretch if possible right across the land from south-west to north-east, more or less following the skirts of the Highland Line. The various earldoms, lordships and baronies represented here more or less covered most of this front, long as it was, territorially; so there was no need for all actually to remain mustered in arms all the time, but to be ever ready to defend their own areas, and prepared to assemble into a large striking force at short notice, if called upon. The main problem was Monck's ability to transport his troops by sea, something that they themselves were not in any position to counter, there being no Scots navy as such. So the English could re-embark, all or some of them, at Dundee, and sail up to Aberdeen or Speymouth or Inverness, and there effect a landing *behind* their own long front. This was a possibility which they had to consider; but it would admittedly present difficulties for Monck also, for it was one thing to land an army by sea and altogether another to maintain it against a hostile population. So their proposed line, in effect cutting Scotland in half, might suffice, and the English hesitate to embark on a seaborne northern campaign while south Scotland was restive behind them. They themselves could only wait and see what transpired. Meanwhile they would send messengers up to the north, especially to Huntly and his Gordons, to try to form a similar line protecting that coastline; and Huntly, being a staunch Catholic, was particularly well placed to involve the mountain Highland clans, fierce fighters and almost all Catholic also.

The Earl of Crawford then took over, and listed the various family and baronial areas, defined their respective responsibilities and named their military commanders, with all the other practical arrangements. This Airlie Castle was as good a central base as any, better than his own Finavon Castle too far to the east, or Southesk's Kinnaird, or for that matter Erroll's or Kinnoull's Gowrie castles to the west; also near enough to Dundee to be able to keep a sharp eye on Monck without being very liable to attack. So here would be their headquarters, from whence orders would come for action. Was it understood?

There was some further discussion and declarations, but no real objections to the general planning, and the gathering broke up. It was still only mid-afternoon, which was a disappointment to Jamie Ramsay at least. For they could, and would, be back at Bamff in less than two hours, whereas he had hoped that they would have to spend another night next door to their so pleasant female company, now alas ruled out.

He did however contrive a farewell to Tina Ogilvy not, sadly, alone, but sufficiently emphatic to leave little doubt as to his abiding interest and hope for further contact. Her smiling and nodding acknowledgment did not commit her to anything, but at least was no discouragement. His father eyed them sidelong as they mounted and rode off.

7

Remotely situated as it was, news of national events was slow in reaching Bamff unless specifically sent, as by Sir David Ogilvy. So much of what went on in Scotland that year of 1651 was not learned by the Ramsays until considerably later. But they did hear that Monck, who oddly seemed to have chosen Dundee as his preferred base, was by no means having it all his own way at that city. A meeting of the Estates of Parliament had been held secretly, and the Protesters – that is, those prepared to work meantime with Cromwell and Monck, including Argyll and Loudoun – had been voted down by the Engagers, led by the Marquis of Hamilton, who had got a resolution passed to co-operate with the Malignants and royalists, including the Airlie-based faction, as it was being called, against the occupying forces. To this end, Hamilton had mustered quite a substantial company of troops in his own area of Lanarkshire and the south-west, and Lambert had been sent by Monck to deal with them, and so had much depleted his Dundee numbers to send with his lieutenant-general. This circumstance encouraged the Dundee magistrates and citizens to rise in revolt, actually succeeding in driving Monck and his remaining men out of the walled city to the dock area and his ships. So when Hamilton's not very successful attempt was put down by Lambert, and that man returned to Dundee with his men, Monck exacted vengeance. He stormed the city, and after a warning that all citizens must remain in their own houses, slew all men, women and children found in the open streets, it was said to the number of almost one thousand, the greatest bloodshed of the occupation, so far, and a staining of Monck's name as an honourable man. This was to serve as an example, it appeared.

Those based on Airlie prepared for action now, and sent out warnings to be ready.

It was late July.

Another item of news reached Bamff in August. The Kirk, furious that the Protesters had been outvoted in parliament, and that Monck, on Cromwell's orders, was sanctioning lay preaching, which they saw as a blow to their cloth and sure to produce grave heresy, had held a stormy General Assembly at St Andrews, and this had resulted in a further split in the Covenant ranks. Andrew Cant had condemned the parliament as enemies of God, and clashed with the Moderator for this year, the Reverend Robert Baillie, and Johnston of Warriston the Lord Clerk Register. Loudoun had been accused of adultery as a discrediting tactic, and the extreme Protesters had actually marched out and off to Dundee to join Monck – although how that man would welcome this clerical contingent was open to doubt. But it did mean that there was a break in the ranks of the divines and their closer supporters in parliament.

This added confusion in the unhappy land had an unexpected result for the Ramsay family. For in late August the Estates of Parliament decided that still another meeting was urgently required, after this Assembly division and the Dundee massacre, to try to build some sort of united front against the occupying English, belated as it was, the Earl of Leven as theoretical commander of the king's forces in Scotland demanding it. And since the Airlie faction, Malignants although they were, had shown the way with their barrier arrangements, it was decided that the meeting should be held in that area. Since a town appeared to be required for such a session, rather than any mere house or castle, and secrecy from Monck's spies and informants advisable, the most remotely situated town of the district was selected – Alyth. So, of all places to hold a parliament, on 28th August, 1651, Alyth took its unexpected place in the annals of the land as host to the Three Estates of Scotland, three miles from Bamff House.

In the event no very large numbers attended, only some forty members, although they of course brought sundry supporters with them. Even so, the little town-house and tolbooth was too small to accommodate them, and the session was held in the parish church, whether the minister approved or not.

As a baron, Sir Gilbert Ramsay was entitled to be present, although he seldom had exercised that privilege previously; and since he had a laird's pew in the church's gallery, he took his sons to watch the proceedings. They found the gallery crowded with other onlookers, in the trains of members of the Estates.

From the first, the Convention did not look as though it would be one of enormous consequence or produce the required united front, not only because of the sparse attendance but in that it was distinguished more by who was absent than who was present. Argyll, Loudoun and Johnston were not there; Hamilton and others of the lords of the south-west whom Lambert had defeated had not been seen since; and the northern chiefs, Gordons and others, had elected not to venture down into dangerous semi-occupied territory, some, like the Marischal, being away with King Charles of course. Airlie himself was insufficiently fit to attend, but Crawford, Kinnoull, Erroll, Southesk and others of the "faction" were present, Malignants who had not found it advisable to appear at parliaments for many a year. Whether Leven and the other Covenant supporters were pleased to see these, however indicative of unity, was doubtful.

In the absence of Loudoun, who was still Chancellor of the Realm and should have presided, Leven himself took the chair, and called upon one of the more moderate ministers, there in only a watching capacity, to open the session with prayer, the Reverend James Sharpe. This the divine did, at some length.

Then Leven initiated the discussion by fairly briefly sketching in the divided and chaotic state of the realm, emphasising the urgent necessity for a unification to drive out the English occupation. Monck and his subordinates had shamefully demonstrated their wicked and ungodly tyranny by the massacre of the citizens of Dundee. The time for unity was over-past indeed, but the more urgent now in that he had just had word from England that his kinsman, General

David Leslie, with King Charles in the West Country, had at last succeeded in amassing a host there, which it was hoped would grow sufficiently to allow a march on London, to put Charles on the English throne as *they* had done over his older Scottish one.

This aroused a stir throughout the church.

So now was the time for Scotland to play its part, Leven went on. He was scarcely a rousing speaker, an elderly man now with a flat voice, however able a commander in the field. They must sink their differences as to religion, policies, and prejudice as to government, and try to form the unity for Scotland's cause and very existence. Here, along the Highland Line, it had been shown that it could be done. He called upon the Earl of Crawford to inform parliament how this had been achieved, for the guidance of all.

Crawford had not a great deal to say, praising Airlie's initiative and emphasising the loyalty of their colleagues, their recognition of the overall need for working together and the divisive folly of much of the leading clergy. He explained their arrangements for a state of readiness to be maintained along the entire Highland Line, and a continuing watch kept on Monck's movements in the Dundee area, with liaison kept with the Marquis of Huntly and other lords up in Aberdeenshire, in case of a seaborne invasion there by the English. He especially mentioned the services of the Lord Gray, the noble whose lands were closest to Dundee – Broughty Castle, House of Gray, Pittendrum and others – pointing out the risk that he had run in keeping up his links with Airlie, and informing them of what went on in the Monck camp, most notable and admirable in a staunch Catholic who had suffered much for the royal house, had been declared excommunicate, fined heavily, and was in fact owed thirty thousand pounds by the crown for yielding up the sheriffdom of Angus, hereditary in his family.

This example of Malignant loyalty, there present, rose to acknowledge. A man of late middle years, Andrew, eighth Lord Gray, was grandson of the famous Master of Gray who had for a time more or less ruled Scotland during James the Sixth's younger years, known as the Machiavelli of Scots politics and the handsomest man in Europe. Gray spoke well, refrained from any attack on the Kirk and Covenant, and urged the need for an assembly of shipping, merchanters necessarily but still capable of transporting troops, to counter the English facility for moving forces by sea. Because of the ever-present danger from English piracy in the North Sea, most Scottish merchant shipping was based on the west coast ports, on the Clyde, Dumbarton and Glasgow especially, also at Largs, Ayr and elsewhere. If some of this shipping could be brought north-about to Aberdeen, it could provide a threat to Monck which could be very useful.

This suggestion provided a deal of discussion, not all there considering it possible. But thereafter Gray produced another talking point, and one which raised the temperature of the parliament notably. He revealed that he had a very useful informant installed in Dudhope Castle in Dundee, where Monck was now lodging, and this man had been told by one of the servants that he had overheard, while waiting at table, Monck and Lambert discussing an order of Cromwell's that the Scottish regalia, crown, sceptres and sword, should be sent south to him in England, from Edinburgh Castle, as token of the ineffectiveness of Charles's coronation as King of Scots, and sign that Scotland was now securely part of his Commonwealth Protectorate.

Uproar greeted this announcement, the Scots being ever readily aroused by such symbols and tokens, possibly as part of their Albannach heritage. On every hand it was demanded that somehow the regalia must be rescued, and hidden in some secure place.

Leven had difficulty in weaning the discussion away from this subject. A small committee consisting of Gray, Crawford and the former Lord Provost of Edinburgh, Sir William Dick of Braid, was appointed to endeavour to deal with this dire problem. Dick was a notable character, once reputed to be the richest man in the kingdom, a prosperous merchant who had advanced twenty thousand pounds to Charles the First – and never seen a penny of it back, needless to say – and although a moderate supporter of the Covenant, advancing parliament a further one hundred thousand merks, had provoked the wrath of the divines and was actually fined instead of repaid, his wealth therefore dwindling. But he was highly thought of in the capital, and the best man to entrust with this project.

The session returned to the practicalities of forming the so essential united front against the occupying forces.

This inevitably was not something which could be settled expeditiously, with so many cross-currents of loyalty to be steered through, and presently Leven called for a break for refreshment, the discussion to be resumed in an hour or so. Provisions were not available in the church, and the members and supporters had to go out and get what they could in inns, ale-houses and the like, Alyth not being strong on catering for the gentry, especially in large numbers, however authoritative.

Sir Gilbert, being local, knew where to go, and took a little group to the house of a friend, a bailie of the burgh, this including Crawford, Gray, Kinnoull, Sir David Ogilvy and Sir William Dick aforesaid. Needless to say Jamie and Thomas attached themselves to this party.

They had to wait for some time before the flustered mistress of the house was able to produce viands – as others would be doing elsewhere – during which interval they discussed the problem of saving the regalia, getting it out of Edinburgh Castle and transporting it to a haven of safety. Various hiding places were suggested but none was considered sufficiently secure and in safe hands until Sir Gilbert came up with the proposal of Dunnottar Castle. None could be more loyal than the Earl Marischal, who was presently with King Charles; and he, Ramsay, had fairly recently been at Dunnottar and had been struck with the impregnability of that stronghold. He could think of nowhere more secure, on its isolated rock-stack. This idea was accepted with acclaim.

The problem of getting the precious objects there was not so readily disposed of. Lord Gray said that he had a private vessel, more than any fishing-boat, normally berthed at his Broughty Castle, but that being so uncomfortably close to Dundee in today's circumstances, it was at present kept at

Arbroath, which was conveniently near to his northern seat of Redcastle, on Lunan Bay – none so far south of Dunnottar in fact, although nothing like so strong – where his wife and daughter were now domiciled. He could have his ship taken down to near Edinburgh, not Leith port which was in English hands, but some haven nearby, this to transport the regalia northwards. But how to get it out of Edinburgh Castle? They all looked at Sir William Dick.

That man said that he had been considering the matter. The present governor of that fortress was one of Cromwell's colonels. But with Monck more or less based on Dundee, and little happening in the capital, this Roundhead colonel was dwelling in more comfortable quarters in the city, indeed in the Palace of Holyroodhouse, and only visiting the citadel intermittently. So, with many of the servants there still Scots, and necessary supplies of food, drink and fuel having to be brought in daily, it ought to be possible to smuggle in men to the castle in the guise of fuel-porters or the like, collect the regalia and smuggle it out again, in the empty carts. This device had been used in the past, with success. Then get it down to the ship, and away.

Food and drink had by this time been produced, and the diners were in animated discussion as to who should do what, and when, to bring it all about, when they were rudely interrupted. A man burst in on them, one of the Ramsays' own people, to announce disaster. The town was full of Monck's troopers, he declared, panting. Hundreds of them. They had been betrayed. They were capturing all the great ones. They were everywhere. They had the town surrounded. All was lost!

In the shock and dismay, Sir Gilbert took charge. Escape. They must escape, get out. Nothing they could do about the others, not with hundreds of troopers in it. He knew this town, its surroundings. This house, it was well placed for an escape. Its orchard backed on to the Den, or nearly so, to the lip of the ravine of the Alyth Burn. Out through the back door. Avoid the streets. Through the orchard. Forget their horses. Get down into Alyth Den. Narrow. Twisting. They would not be caught there. Troopers could only ride singly, if they were seen and followed. Easy to avoid them, even ambush them. To the Den with them. And after it, to safety up in the Forest of Alyth, and Bamff House.

There was no arguing, no alternative suggestions, in this extremity. The ten of them, leaving their meal, hurried out into the house's garden and down through the orchard. They could hear shouting and the clatter of hooves on the cobbled streets behind them. A gate in the back wall opened on to a narrow strip of grassland and then to trees which flanked the Den. No one was in sight here.

Three earls, a lord, two knights, a servitor and the two young men ran across the grass and, breathless, reached the trees' cover. Before them the ground dropped steeply into the long, twisting ravine which represented escape, safety.

They panted, looking back. It seemed somehow feeble, now, almost shameful, to hurry off, abandoning their colleagues. But what could they do against hundreds of Roundhead cavalry, ten of them, unarmed as they were? Better that *they* should escape, at least, for the cause.

The Ramsays led the way down into the wooded trough of the foaming river, and on up its winding, rocky course, northwards.

No pursuit developed, with no reason why it should. Their whereabouts, and therefore their flight, would not be known to the English, even if their actual identity was. In single file they hurried on up the defile, thankful but grievously concerned. Who was responsible for this? Who had betrayed them? What would happen to the others? Could any have escaped besides themselves? What was to be done now?

That three-mile walk over very rough terrain was taxing for the older members of the party, the Lord Gray and Sir William Dick. However, they all made it to Bamff House eventually. Sir Gilbert reckoned that they would be safe there, remotely placed as it was, but sent down a group of his people to keep watch on the Den and give warning of any approach, unlikely as this seemed.

Jean saw to their comfort and refreshment, with Jamie's and Thomas's help.

That evening, with no alarms forthcoming, they discussed their future plans. Crawford, Sir David and the other lords were for getting back to Airlie as swiftly as possible and raising a company of armed men for prompt action. It was possible that the English troopers might well remain in Alyth overnight, before carrying their prisoners back to Dundee in the morning. They had a score of miles to go, and, with their captives, would not ride at great speed – and they had had to reach Alyth in the first place. So they and their mounts would not be fresh. Also they might well be scouring the vicinity for extra prisoners. It might just be possible to intercept them, on their way back, and effect a rescue. This idea, needless to say, appealed to all. Sir Gilbert said that the Ramsays could provide horses, mere garrons necessarily now, but good on the rough country.

The urgent matter of the regalia also preoccupied them. Something must be done about this, and at once, or it might be too late. Monck might already have sent his orders. What was possible?

Gray suggested that he and Dick should accompany the others as far as Airlie, but then leave them, to proceed on to Arbroath where his vessel was berthed. They could sail in it to the Firth of Forth, possibly making for Newhaven just west of Leith port, and then try to negotiate the extraction of the precious relics from their keeping-place in Edinburgh Castle, get them down to the ship, and take them up to as near Dunnottar as was possible, Stonehaven probably. He, Gray, was well known in the capital, as Catholic, Malignant and royalist, indeed had served a term of prison in the tolbooth there, so he would be better not to be seen and recognised in Sir William's company. But the ex-Lord Provost, who had been a respected Covenant figure, would arouse no suspicions in his own city. He would have to enlist help, of course . . .

Greatly daring, Jamie Ramsay offered to go with him and act assistant.

This gesture was accepted, even if Sir Gilbert looked doubtful.

They all wondered what the outcome of this day's disaster would be, assuming that there was no rescue of the prisoners possible. Presumably Leven would have been captured with the others, therefore there would be no recognised commander of Scots forces, no experienced general. And no parliament – or at least only those members who had not attended. Argyll's and Johnston's group, the wretched Protestors, would have it all their own way. Possibly it was from them that Monck had learned of this Alyth meeting? None there would put it past Argyll, as unscrupulous as he was clever.

They sought their couches that night, minds far from easy, and intent on a notably early start in the morning.

At first light they were on their way to Airlie, by Lintrathen, nine miles. The English, assuming that they had passed the night at Alyth, would have that twenty miles to go to Dundee, by the shortest route, by Meigle and Newtyle and Auchterhouse. That would take them through the Glack of Newtyle, a long pass of the Sidlaw Hills, highly suitable for an ambush, this some ten miles from Alyth. Could they themselves possibly get to Airlie, raise a troop of horse, and hasten to Newtyle in time to intercept? It would all depend on when the Roundheads left. Would they be in any hurry in the morning? Having achieved their objective, they might well not be. And they might well still be looking for the missing earls and parliamentarians themselves. So there was just a chance. They must take it. Sir David said that he could pick up some forty or fifty men at short notice at Lintrathen, and come on after. And the Ramsays were providing a score, their watchers from down at the Den.

Despite lack of sleep they made good time to Airlie, at least, leaving David Ogilvy at Lintrathen to round up his men, the garrons doing well by them. At the castle, the Earl of Airlie was, of course, shocked by their news; but immediately gave orders for people to be assembled from the castleton and nearby, at all speed.

Gray and Dick, who could add nothing to any intervention attempt, lacking men here, were eager to be on their way for their own venture, with quite a lengthy ride to Arbroath. However, Jamie did manage a brief meeting with the young women of the establishment, not seeing Tina alone, but gripping them all with his account of the happenings at Alyth and his present sally to try to rescue Scotland's regalia. Their reactions were various, but Tina did urge him to be careful on this Edinburgh affair, squeezing his arm to emphasise her concern, which that young man found encouraging. But this was no occasion for such pleasant dalliance, and all too soon he was saying goodbye and God-speed to his father and brother, as well as to the girls, and was on his way with the two older men southwards.

They went by Eassie and Glamis and Kirkbuddo and Carmylie, across great Strathmore, some thirty miles, wondering as they rode how the rescue attempt of their parliamentary colleagues went, none of them over-hopeful in the circumstances, as well as feeling somewhat guilty in not themselves taking part, whatever their own responsibilities.

Their garrons were not built for fast riding, and it was early afternoon before they reached Arbirlot and then the seaport town of Arbroath, with its great wrecked abbey where the famous Declaration of Independence had been signed three hundred years before, demanding the freedom of Scots and Scotland for all time coming – a suitably encouraging token, Jamie asserted, for their present endeavour, his elders raising sceptical eyebrows.

They found their ship easily enough, tied up at a jetty in the outer harbour; but finding the skipper and crew was another matter, in various houses in the town. This took time, and it was soon obvious that they would not get to sea that day. It was no long voyage ahead of them, but some provisioning had to be arranged, and vessels could not just sail off without preparation. The trio settled for the night at a change-house near the harbour recommended by the skipper, and were not long in bedding down, for it had been a long and tiring day, and another early start was required. They were concerned with haste, in fear that they might not be in time to save the regalia – if save it they could.

*　　*　　*

It was, Gray reckoned, some sixty miles by sea to Leith, due south for two-thirds of the way, then west up Forth. With the prevailing south-west breeze, not strong but consistent, a certain amount of tacking was required, to use the wind, which of course added to their mileage considerably. The two-masted craft was built for comfort and utility rather than speed, and the skipper reckoned that their voyage would take them all of eight hours. So even with their early start it would be late afternoon or even dusk before they made harbour. Sir William said that this might be no bad time to arrive. They could tie up at Newhaven, a mile or so west of Leith, the main fishing village for the capital, and hire horses there to take them up to his town-house in the city, anonymously as it were, in the half-dark. Since the Cromwellian occupation, the city gates were not locked at night, with much of the English soldiery encamped outside the walls, so there should be no difficulty of ingress. He could thereafter, in the night, go to work on trying to arrange matters for the morrow's endeavour.

They made an uneventful sail of it, all of much interest to Jamie, whose first sea voyage it was; he had been out on fishing-boats in the Firth of Tay before, that was all. He found the actual sail usage fascinating, especially in the tacking process, the crew's work in handling, raising and lowering and reefing as ordered. Late August as it was, the seas were not rough, although there was a steady long swell. Fortunately he was not humiliated by being seasick. There was no difficulty as to navigation, for they were never out of sight of land all the way, indeed passing within a mile or two of Fife Ness, past St Andrews.

They made good time of it, in the circumstances, but turning to beat up the Firth of Forth, between the Ness and the Isle of May, much more of tacking was required, for now they were as good as sailing into the wind. So there was no question of arriving at Newhaven before dusk. They beat their way back and forward across the long, wide estuary, near the Bass Rock at one stage and off the Fife shore at the Earlsferry on another. Gray fretted, but Dick asserted that this did not signify overmuch.

Lights beginning to twinkle on their left were identified as Leith port, at length, where Dick said many English ships were still stationed. Soon thereafter, considerably fewer lights represented the fishing community of Newhaven, no large place.

They encountered no difficulty in docking, finding sufficient space amongst the fishing-craft. Their difficulty commenced on landing, in finding mounts to be hired, fisherfolk not being strong on horses. Eventually they acquired two, leaving Lord Gray at the ship, as agreed, to have all in readiness for a swift getaway, hopefully, in due course.

This decision was not contested, and Sir William and Jamie set off alone.

They rode up by dark lanes, avoiding the main highway between Leith and the capital, by Bonnington and Pilrig, to the skirts of the Calton Hill just north of the great Arthur's Seat, and were able to enter the city by the little-used St Andrew's Port, and so into the street called Leith Wynd. They saw remarkably few people on the way, and even in the city itself there was not much activity evident. Of course, Sir William knew all the back streets and wynds where no great passage of folk was to be expected of a late evening. Such change-houses and ale-howfs as they passed were notably quiet – a sign of the impact of the Puritan Roundhead troops in occupation, no doubt.

By these back-ways they at length came to the Dick town-house in Byres Close off the High Street, a fine mansion despite its cramped approaches, but then, all the old city on its long and narrow ridge between the castle and Holyroodhouse was cramped, had to be, space being precious, and houses and tenements rising as high as seven and eight storeys in consequence. This house of Sir William's, he explained, had been the abode of the famous or notorious Adam, Bishop of Orkney, who had married Mary Queen of Scots to the Earl of Bothwell after Darnley's death. He, Dick, required a town-house, especially when he was provost, even though his estate of Braid was only four miles away, and he had another property even closer, at Prestonfield, or Priestfield as it was called before the Reformation.

Leaving Jamie to be well looked after by a cheerful, bustling and comely housekeeper, Sir William went off to try to make his arrangements for the morrow, telling the young man not to wait up for his return, for he might well be long enough. He did not foresee any particularly early start for the next day's activities. Well fed, Jamie was glad to go to a much more comfortable – and cleaner – bed than he had occupied the night before.

It was indeed sun-up before the housekeeper knocked on his door to waken him to a prodigious breakfast. Sir William was out again, she informed, but would be back shortly – he seemed to require very little sleep of a night did Sir Will, she asserted. He had already eaten.

Presently the knight appeared, differently clad from heretofore, indeed in distinctly shabby old clothing. He was in reasonably optimistic mood, declaring that unless an unforeseen hitch developed, there was a good chance of success for their day's endeavour. He had arranged with the wood merchant who supplied the fuel for the castle fires to have them taken up there in the wood-cart, with his own man Dod, in a couple of hours' time, covered under a sort of canvas tenting, with the firewood all carefully arranged around, to hide them. The fuel-store up in the citadel was inconspicuously placed beneath a barracks block, so there ought to be little difficulty there in avoiding identification. Sir William knew where the regalia was kept, in a small chamber off the great hall. Getting it out and away would be the major hazard.

There appeared to be no hurry, despite the urgency of the problem, for they waited a while, Jamie impatient to get on with it all. Then the delay was explained, and surprisingly, by the arrival of a woman in the yard, on a fine horse but scarcely dressed to match, wearing old, all but ragged clothing but nothing ragged about her bearing, and with the housekeeper greeting her as m'lady. She was of middle years but strikingly good-looking and with a sparkling eye and ready smile.

Sir William introduced her as his wife, the Lady Anne; and it appeared that she was going to accompany them on their venture, unlikely as this seemed. She greeted Jamie genially and declared that today they were going to give a twist to the Englishmen's tails – women seeming to be preoccupied with men's alleged tails. Jamie, who had been looking on the day's attempt as in the nature of a dangerous mission indeed, wondered at this light-hearted attitude, indeed at the female presence altogether. Sir William explained that his wife's intention was possibly to create some sort of helpful diversion.

They set off, promptly now and on foot, down from this close off the High Street to the lower-level Cowgate. Clad as they were they attracted no special attention from passers-by, hangers out of windows and gossiping women. Near the west end of the Cowgate they entered a wide yard, stacked with timber, uncut on one side, sawn logs on the other, where men were working with saws, axes and wedges. At the far end were two carts, laden, each with a heavy work-horse between the shafts.

Two men came forward to greet them. One proved to be the Dicks' own servitor, Dod; the other introduced as Peerie Pate, the wood merchant. The latter, looking admiringly at the Lady Anne, declared her a bonny sight to see, and said that all was ready. He himself would drive the first cart, with Dod and yon stot Dougie. He hoped the bit tent he had made in the cart wouldna be ower uncomfortable.

They were led to one of the carts, already piled with cut wood. At least, so it looked, although on closer inspection and the removal of some boarding, it transpired that the pile was in fact hollow, the cut logs carefully built to enclose a cavity lined with sail-canvas. Into this the three gentlefolk were to climb and then be covered over.

Lady Anne, laughing heartily, hitched up her skirts and was assisted into the cavity by Peerie Pate, amidst admiring glances from all concerned. She held out a hand to Jamie, to draw him in beside her, where he found himself held to her ample bosom, to make room for her husband. Sir William, less agile, was helped in, the canvas flap was lowered and the boarding

107

replaced. The three of them were plunged into darkness, to female hilarity.

Soon the carts began to move to the clatter of horses' hooves on the cobblestones. James continued to be clutched warmly and most comfortably against pleasantly heaving femininity, while Sir William hoped aloud that the log-pile would not collapse on top of them. It was certainly an odd mode of transport for a former Lord Provost of the capital, the granddaughter of a Highland chief, even for Jamie Ramsay of Bamff.

They made a bumpy journey of it out of the Cowgate into the Grassmarket and up the West Bow to the Lawnmarket, which in turn led up, ever climbing, to the ancient tourney-ground before the castle gatehouse on its rock-top site. Dick explained that the device of hiding in the fuel-cart was not really his own idea; it had been done at least once before when, in weak James the Third's reign, his brother, the Duke of Albany, imprisoned in the fortress, had been smuggled out thus to freedom. It was unlikely, surely, that the English guards would have heard of this exploit.

Presently, with the cobbles giving place to smooth turf and earth beneath hooves and wheels, the inmates realised that they must be out of the streets and up to the tourney-ground. This was confirmed when they heard Peerie Pate shouting jocosities, presumably to the gatehouse guards, and declaring that he was a day early with the wood. Answering cries reached them, none sounding in any way suspicious; and then their wheels were rumbling over timber, the planking of the drawbridge. Thereafter it was cobbles and outcropping rock again, and they knew that they were inside the fortress. They could hear the other cart trundling along behind them.

Soon they were halted, and Pate came round to open their flap and board to let them out. A' was weel, he assured – naebody aboot. Oot wi' them. And gallantly he unloaded the lady.

They were in another yard of sorts below a towering building, evidently a barracks block, a row of arched entrances to vaulted cellars opening there. This was where the logs for the castle fires were stored. It was not a place where the garrison would be apt to visit.

Now for the test of it all, or the beginning of tests. The scheme was for the four of them, with the Lady Anne, to climb up to the higher level of the rock summit on which the great hall stood, carrying sacks of logs over their shoulders, saying if challenged that these had been ordered to be taken to the two fireplaces therein for some function planned for shortly. Once there, they would empty the wood on the hearths and take the sacks through to the adjoining small chamber where the regalia was kept, apparently in chests, put the precious items in the bags and then return to the carts thereafter. Simple in theory, but . . . !

Shouldering their burdens, Jamie, Dod and the mournful-seeming Dougie followed Sir William up round the barracks block, Lady Anne, unburdened, with them, leaving Peerie Pate and the other driver to unload very leisurely the rest of the logs from the carts and stack them in the cellars.

The fuel-carriers were soon up into the more frequented parts of the citadel. There was no large garrison in residence at present, with no need for it, but some men-at-arms, off-duty guards, servants and even a few women were there. Presumably some of officer rank also.

They came on three men hoisting buckets of water from a well in another yard and filling it into troughs. It seemed extraordinary that water should be available up there on top of the rock, but of course no castle could exist without such supply in time of siege, so a well was a prerequisite of any fortified site. Presumably this well-shaft was very deep, and the process of hoisting the water up was effected by buckets on long ropes pulled up by means of a turning drum with two handles. The men paused at their turning labour to eye the log-bearers.

The man Dod shouted at them, mockingly, that they had a real easy task there. If they wanted real work let them down to the cellars and help them bring up more wood. This sally was greeted with comments unsuitable for female ears; but Lady Anne hooted a laugh, and in broad Scots gave back as good as she got.

The carriers trudged on with their loads.

The great hall was on a still higher level, across quite a wide courtyard. Here two men were engaged in more handle-turning, but of a more ominous sort, using a stone wheel to sharpen the blades of swords, knives and axes. Dod tried his earthy humour on these also, but the resultant replies were less appreciative and in English accents. Presumably these were Roundhead troopers.

Sir William ignored them, and moved on towards the hall door. Not so his wife. She went over to the Englishmen, laughing at them almost provocatively to engage them in flirtatious converse, all challenging womanhood, again speaking in broad Scots. Jamie and the other two followed Dick with their loads.

The hall's massive door was shut but not locked, and lowering their burdens they opened it, with much creaking. Tramping within they were thankful to find the great apartment empty. There were large wide fireplaces at each end. Dumping his sack at the first of these, Sir William hurried across the hall to a doorway halfway up the far side, and tried the door-handle. Astonishingly, considering what was kept within, this was not locked either; of course, Scotland's crown, sword of state and sceptres were not items any thief would find easy to dispose of. Opening this door, Dick entered, Jamie following with Dod, Dougie keeping watch at the outer door.

This was a small chamber, ill-lit, furnished only with a table, two forms and a couple of chests, these last obviously ancient, one large, one smaller. Tried, these did prove to be locked.

They had come prepared for this. Dod produced from his belt a small axe, apt for any woodchopper, and went to work without delay, Jamie being sent back to make adequate blanketing sounds by emptying logs on the hearths with as much noise as possible, Lady Anne now with them again, to produce her own quota of banging. Dougie reported no enquiring approaches.

When Jamie and the lady, with the now empty sacks, went back to the side chamber, it was to find both chests broken open, and Sir William and Dod lifting out their contents, the same which had been carried in state at Scone the year before. The sword and one sceptre, being long, were in the larger chest, the crown, the lesser sceptre, a pair of spurs, and a jewelled ring wrapped in two silken ensigns, in the other. All but overawed as they were by what they had in their hands, no time was lost in bundling the precious symbols of sovereignty into the empty sacks, the long sword requiring two bags to enclose and hide it. Shutting the chest lids, and observing that the axe damage to the locks area was not too noticeable, the four of them emerged into the hall with their new burdens, closing the chamber door behind them.

Now for the next test.

Out in the courtyard, they found that a third man had joined the sword-sharpeners and was eyeing them interestedly, and exchanging remarks with the others. But as they came closer it was evident that it was not the men nor their burdens which was particularly concerning him but the Lady Anne. Perceiving it, she emitted a throaty chuckle, pointed at the newcomer, and strolled over towards him, hips swinging suggestively, and declaring that he was a better-looking man than the other two but a pity that he had such narrow shoulders, for she liked men with broad ones. The regalia-carriers strode on as though unconcerned; if Sir William was, at his wife's antics, he showed no sign of it.

At the lower level, the water-hoisters were resting from their labours, and at a jerked word from his master, Dod handed the wrapped sword of state to Dougie and moved over to them, declaring that they were weak, and could he give them a hand, adding that they would not do for woodmen. This brought forth insulting and very physical rejoinders, and with Lady Anne coming up, the spiced verbiage and contumely reached new heights, or depths, to ringing female laughter. The other three men marched on.

It was all as simple as that. They saw no other denizens of the fortress before reaching Peerie Pate and his fellow-driver, waiting for them with every appearance of nonchalance, both carts now empty. When Dod and his mistress came after them, deliberately not hurrying, they all of course exchanged glances of triumph but acted as though all was normal. There were windows in the barracks block above, and it was always possible that they could be watched. So Peerie Pate had backed his cart as close in to a doorway of one of the cellars as could be, this to prevent anyone above seeing down to what went on with it.

And with reason. For now the trio who had not been visible on the way up must again not be seen on the way out, past the guards at the gatehouse, and now there was no elaborate covering of logs to hide them. So Pate had them climb on to his cart once more, and to lie as flat as possible on its floor, side by side, there to be covered with the sail-canvas as, Lady Anne remarked, good, quiet corpses. It was to be hoped that they would not be obvious thus. They took the regalia under with them.

Thus Jamie was again in very close proximity to this extraordinary Highlandwoman; indeed she held his hand there in the darkness, whispering confidentially that the sword-hilt was digging into her bottom, as the cart began to clatter over the cobbles again, her husband congratulating her dryly on her abilities in bemusing mere men. Jamie also declared his admiration of her distraction tactics, and got a squeeze beyond their already close contact in acknowledgment.

When they heard Pate shouting remarks loudly, they knew that they were back at the gatehouse; and then they could hear and feel the hollow rumbling and shaking of their wheels on the drawbridge-planking as they crossed the moat beyond. They were out on to the soft grass of the tourney-ground without the cart being halted.

The thing was done.

The trio remained under cover until safely back in the Cowgate wood-yard. There they emerged to hearty plaudits and elation all round, everyone talking at once.

Sir William took charge. He considered that there was no great likelihood of the damaged chests in that hall chamber being discovered quickly, with little reason why any should look therein. But it was possible, and best that they should get the regalia down to Newhaven and the ship as quickly as

112

possible, and away. And there was the matter of the safety of Peerie Pate and his men to be thought of. The probability was that the loss of the regalia would not be discovered for some time – unless, that is, General Monck did send to have it taken to England shortly. Then suspicion might, or might not, fall upon the wood merchant. Dick was not prepared to have serious trouble descend on his helpers. He suggested therefore that they gave them that day to get safely away in the ship, and then, on the morrow, went back up to the castle and asked to see some officer in charge, there to declare that he, Pate, had been taken captive at pistol-point by a group of Malignants who had forced him to carry them, hidden, up to the citadel with his cartloads of wood. What they had done there he did not know, his attackers having left him at the wood-cellars. But he felt that he had to report it, he and his being good supporters of the Covenant. That ought to clear him of any accusation of collusion when the regalia was discovered to be missing. But if it did not, then he was to send word to him, Sir William, and he would seek to ensure that no penalties were suffered by them for this day's good work. Meantime this purse of gold pieces was a token of appreciation. And would Pate have a cartload of timber taken down forthwith to Newhaven harbour, the regalia hidden therein, while he and James Ramsay rode down in normal fashion?

The woodmen declared their satisfaction with all this, adding, optimistically perhaps, that they could look after themselves, but did not refuse the gold pieces. All parted on the best of terms, with good wishes for the remainder of the regalia epic.

Back at the Dick town-house, Sir William changed back into respectable but sober clothing, and they took their leave of the Lady Anne, Jamie receiving a smacking kiss and a hug, with the hope that she would see more of him in less extraordinary circumstances.

Then it was to horse and back down to Newhaven, seeing many Roundhead troopers in the city streets now, but none paying them any attention.

They found Pate, Dougie and the wood-cart waiting at the

harbour-arm, and Lord Gray eyeing all cautiously from the ship. There were fisherfolk about, but getting the cart as near to the vessel as possible, the transference of the sacked regalia was effected without any undue interest being aroused, to sighs of relief from some at least of the company. Farewells followed to the woodmen, and presently to Sir William also, Gray being urgent to be off, and the knight seeing no point in sailing north again with them. Jamie had got on well with Dick, and was quite sorry to part from him, sharing in such an adventure having drawn them together quite notably despite the disparity in ages.

So sails were hoisted, and they moved out into the firth. It was unlikely that there would be any hitch in their plans now.

Gray was treated to a full account of all that had transpired.

8

The voyage north proved uneventful, and quite speedy, for now the breeze was behind them and tacking but little required. They were not heading back to Arbroath now, of course, but considerably further up, for Stonehaven, or Stanehive as Lord Gray called it, a sail of perhaps thirty miles more. But with following winds, this ought not to take more than six or seven hours, which meant dusk again for their landfall, for they had left Newhaven in early afternoon, all their exciting activity actually having taken considerably less time than it might have seemed in retrospect.

Making good time, they passed Arbroath as the sun was beginning to sink; and soon thereafter Gray was able to point out his northern seat of Redcastle, at one end of the wide Lunan Bay, and towering Red Head, one of the loftiest cliff features on the east coast of Scotland, at the other. There was a little fishing community here at mid-bay, called Ethiehaven, with the famous Cardinal Beaton's house of Ethie Castle nearby, but with no berthing suitable for a vessel of their draught, otherwise they could have put in, for Redcastle, to spend the night. Montrose harbour lay some five miles to the north, but if they were going that far, they might as well proceed on to Stanehive, dock there, pass the night on the ship, and hire horses in the morning to carry them and the regalia to Dunnottar.

Actually it was fairly dark before they passed Dunnottar's mighty rock-stack, and they could only make out the loom of it against its cliff background from a mile or so off. So it was wholly dark when they reached Stonehaven. However, their skipper knew the harbour and was able to nose his way in cautiously amongst the fishing-craft and tie up without any great difficulty. Gray took Jamie and the crew ashore to have a meal in a waterside change-house. They returned to the vessel to sleep.

It had been a full and memorable day.

In the morning, they hired three garrons in the town, two to ride and one to carry the precious sackloads, as pack-horse, this because of the difficult shape and length of the sword and larger sceptre, which would have looked odd to carry personally. In this, the Earl Marischal's country, they did not need an escort, and Gray and Jamie set off southwards alone.

When last that young man had ridden this way, in the train of the king to be crowned, he had not anticipated that he would be returning thus with the very crown involved in the occasion.

They had only two miles to go before their goal came into view, soaring up from the waves, a dramatic sight always. Riding down the twisting cliff path to sea-level, and then climbing steeply, they came to the first of the series of gatehouses of that daunting crevice, ringing challenges therefrom greeting them.

"The Lord Gray to see whoever holds Dunnottar for my lord Marischal!" Gray shouted authoritatively – and Jamie added, less so, "Tell the Lady Mary Keith that Jamie Ramsay is here also."

Inevitably they had quite a wait while their message was conveyed up past the other gates and into the spread-out establishment beyond, the recipients found and the reply returned.

At last there came the desired reaction. A different voice shouted down. "I am George Ogilvie of Barras, who holds this keep for my lord Earl Marischal. I welcome the Lord Gray. Enter, my lord."

"Jamie! Jamie!" came a still more different welcome, high-pitched and excited. "Jamie Ramsay!"

That all sounded satisfactory. The gates clanked open, and they climbed to them.

Their reception was somewhat complicated in those narrow portals, where with the guards, there was not much room for three horses, their dismounted riders, the stockily

116

built youngish man and the lively girl, distinctly incoherent explanations adding to the confusion. But Mary's attitude was warmly enthusiastic at least, and for the first time Jamie realised that he might be facing another kind of complication here at Dunnottar, as Tina Ogilvy's lovely features rose before his inner eye to challenge those of Mary Keith.

However, that was for hereafter. Meantime there was a flood of talk as, leading the horses, they moved off uphill, the girl clinging to Jamie's arm.

Up in the rock-top castle amongst the wheeling seabirds, the welcome of the rest of the Keith family was kindly enquiring, the pack-horse's precious burden was unloaded and carried indoors to the main keep's vaulted kitchen with much exclamation, wonder and further disjointed explanations. Gray stripped off the sacking covers and the talking ceased abruptly, as all eyes were riveted on the contents, in awe, Jamie almost as spellbound as the others, for in fact he had not had more than hasty glances at the items hitherto. And the regalia was in itself a sufficiently exciting challenge to the eyes, irrespective of its significance to Scotland and its long and dramatic history.

The crown itself, of course, gripped the prior attention, gleaming, shining, glowing in jewelled splendour. On a base rim and diadem of gold above white ermine fur, a succession of fleur-de-lis interspersed with pearled rosettes rose to support two golden arches, these surmounted by a small orb topped finally by a cross-pattee adorned with more and large pearls, all the gold studded with diamonds and rubies which glittered, sparkled and gleamed redly. The basic parts of this crown were traditionally said to be Bruce's own, in gold from Crawford Muir and rubies from Elie in Fife, the pearls from the Tay at Perth. The arches and surmounting decoration were thought to have been added by James the Fifth, who took a great interest in the royal symbolism.

The great sword, long, two-handed, the haft also jewelled and worked in filigree, strangely with what looked like a silver oyster-shell joining handle and blade, was a gift from Pope Alexander the Sixth to James the Fourth, as indeed was the long sceptre, although his son, James the Fifth, had had this remade, for reasons unspecified; as indeed were the reasons for the gifts in the first place, they probably being more concerned with the excellent work done by Bishop Elphinstone for Holy Church in Scotland than for any particular papal regard for the king: the printing for the first time of Church Service books, or Liturgies, and the founding of Aberdeen University. This sceptre was indeed less than convenient to handle, almost as long as the sword, although highly ornate, so that the lesser one was apt to be the one used more often, and the more beautiful in fact.

Where to bestow this treasure? There was some discussion as to the safest place, until Lord Gray pointed out that all Dunnottar was equally safe, which was why it had been chosen. Would not the most suitable resting place for the regalia be that castle chapel which he had seen, with its little graveyard? This was agreed, and all trooped out of the keep to deposit Scotland's honours behind the altar in the sanctuary directly above the waves.

Thereafter there was much recounting of events and adventures, by Jamie, to the ladies of the establishment, while Gray conferred with George Ogilvie, requiring him to sign a written undertaking to guard, protect and retain the precious national symbols in this place, with his life if need be, this paper to be sent to King Charles, to reassure him of their safety. Seeing this document, indeed signing it in turn as witness, Jamie noted that these northern Ogilvies spelled their name with an ie rather than a y, for some reason.

It was then that Jamie learned that, while Gray was going to leave, to return to his vessel, and go to find someone in what authority there was left in Scotland to tell of the whereabouts and safety of the regalia, and to send off the signed paper to the king in England, Jamie himself was to be left here at Dunnottar meantime, more or less as guardian of the honours – to his considerable surprise. Gray was insistent upon this. Privately he told the younger man that he knew nothing about this Ogilvie of Barras, never heard of him before today; presumably he was trustworthy if the Marischal had appointed him to keep this castle. But he might be an extreme Covenanter, or otherwise weak in his loyalty, and the nation's very emblems of sovereignty could not be left solely in his hands; clearly the Lady Margaret Hay and the young Keith womenfolk did not count in his estimation. He, Gray, would endeavour to find out what further steps were to be taken about this situation, and inform Jamie in due course. So he must remain here, as representing himself, Dick, Crawford and the rest of the Airlie faction, who had taken this vital matter upon themselves, until instructed otherwise.

Astonished, that nineteen-year-old could only wag his head in bemusement.

When the Lady Mary Keith heard of this decision she did not hide her satisfaction. Her aunt and sisters seemed quite happy about it also; and George Ogilvie raised no objections. He was a somewhat silent and stolid man, but amiable in an undemonstrative way.

After a meal, Gray said his farewells, and with the three hired horses set off back for Stonehaven and the ship.

Mary Keith, who now seemed to look on Jamie as some sort of hero as well as a good companion, made a point of vacating her own bedchamber in the circular angle-tower so that he could occupy the same room as he and Thomas had shared before, she moving up to the attic apartment directly above – to the young man's rather doubtful appreciation. He was not at all sure how he was going to handle this situation. He liked Mary very much, and had enjoyed their association of the year before; but Christian Ogilvy had cast a more powerful spell upon him in the interim, and she was seldom out of his thoughts. Admittedly no sort of understanding had been reached between them, but he felt nevertheless some sense of commitment, however one-sided, a loyalty to her. And Tina was a young woman, indeed a year older than himself; whereas this very nice Mary was but a lassie of sixteen years, however well developed. He was going to have to watch his step, here. And yet, he could not deny that he enjoyed her company and person, and certainly would not wish to seem to reject or offend her . . .

That very evening the problem began to surface. Seeking an early retirement after his so active days and disturbed nights, Jamie apologised for leaving the family when making from the table to the lesser hall fireplace, for the late September nights were chilly up there on that windswept rock, and bidding all goodnight, headed out for his angle-tower.

In his room he found the regulation steaming pail of water for washing, brought there presumably by one of the serving-wenches. He had removed his doublet and one of his riding-boots when a tapping sounded at his door. One boot off and one on, he hobbled over thereto, and opening, found Mary holding a large jug, this also steaming. She laughed heartily at sight of his state.

"The water Katie brought will be all but cold by now," she announced. "I have more hot here, to warm it up."

"Thank you . . ." He was reaching out to take the jug when the girl brushed past him with the water, evidently concerned to add it to the other herself.

He turned back to watch her at it, declaring rather feebly that it had been quite warm enough for him as it was. The jug emptied, she put it on the floor, and turned to eye him up and down, biting her lip, her assurance suddenly gone. Then, with an exclamation, she threw herself forward into his arms.

Those arms, to be sure, could do nothing else than go round her in an embrace, clasping her rounded and eminently embraceable body to his own. Moreover, with face upturned to his, and lips open, he had no option but to kiss, whatever contrary emotions were at the back of his mind. And, of course, he was honest enough not to pretend that he did not enjoy the sensation.

So they stood, holding each other, the girl's person distinctly heaving, her lips moving against his. It was a little while before he realised that those lips were in fact doing more than caressing; they were seeking to form words. He drew back his own somewhat.

"I think . . . that I . . . should go . . . to my room!" she got out.

He supposed so also. "Yes," he said, knowing that he should feel relieved. "Yes. I think . . . it best."

She did not dash off, however.

He drew on decision, with a deep breath, and congratulated himself not only on this strength but on a flash of genius. "Yes, and you can help me take off this boot!" he declared manfully.

Mary produced a giggle at that, and released herself, to kneel and reach out for the booted leg he raised to her.

As she tugged, and he all but overbalanced, suitable hilarity replaced emotion. When the knee-length footwear eventually came off, the girl toppled back with it, and Jamie was able to hoist her up and lead her to the door, all sufficiently naturally as not to seem in the least anxious to be parted.

There Mary did present him with another and fairly lingering kiss, however, before reluctantly setting off upstairs.

He proceeded with his delayed ablutions with mixed feelings.

In the morning Mary proposed an expedition to inspect the lobster-pots which the Keith girls set along their nearby coastline, and which had to be tended every two or three days. The season would soon be over and the seas apt to be too rough for the girls' boating, but they were still getting catches. This suggestion was greeted with enthusiasm by her sisters, even though the proposer had almost certainly intended it to be only a two-person ploy. But there was no refusing the family, and presently Jamie found himself escorting all four Keith sisters down past the gatehouses, to the little fishing hamlet at the cliff-foot, and the girls' boat, their Aunt Margaret having urged care. Elizabeth was fifteen, Joan thirteen and Isabel twelve, a lively lot.

Jamie had never had opportunity to try his hand at lobster-fishing, although it could hardly be termed that, being more in the nature of dredging and extracting. The boat was loaded with two large baskets with lids, optimistically, and with these and the five occupants, was distinctly cramped as to space, for it was not large. It seemed rather low in the water to Jamie, but the girls seemed unconcerned.

He and Mary sat side by side on the centre thwart, with an oar each, and after a few false starts managed to row in fair concert, with advice from the sisters, especially as to how deep the young man plunged in his oar-blade, as compared with Mary's, so that, with his extra man-power, he did not enforce an erratic course. The two bodies, inevitably touching and working in rhythm, produced a not unpleasing mutual reaction, he discovered.

They headed northwards, up-coast, at first, the sea reasonably calm, with its normal North Sea swell, which tended to roll the craft sidelong, to squeals of joy from the Marischal's daughters, and to Jamie's problems with his oar-depth. The lobster-pots, it was explained – they were not really pots at all, but cages of a sort – were anchored on the seabed, never far out from the rocky shore, their whereabouts marked by floats made of pigs' bladders blown up on the end of ropes. They would spot these floats readily enough.

The first marker they came to occasioned some alarm in the male rower, for the three younger girls all leaning over the side to hold and steady the boat against the rope and haul it up tipped the waterline very close to the waves indeed. But his companions did not seem to foresee any danger, and he forebore from urging caution. Clearly the pot, or cage, at the rope's end took quite a deal of raising, and this was explained when at length it appeared on the surface, for it proved to consist of a board with four arched sapling boughs hooped over it to support an enclosing net, tentlike, with a funnel entry at one end, also of netting, held open at its circular mouth by wire, but left loose at the tail-end, this so that the caught lobster, coaxed in by the fish-head bait inside, easy of ingress, would be quite unable to get out. As well as the bait was a heavy flat stone, to act anchor on the sea floor. Unfortunately on this occasion that was all that was inside, no lobster. Cries of disappointment from the crew.

The cage lowered again, carefully, and the float left bobbing on the waves, they pulled on, Mary explaining that if they found half of their pots containing a catch they were in luck. She said that sometimes she did the lobstering alone, which raised her further in the man's estimation.

The second pot, nearby, did prove to contain a catch, a fair-sized, reddish-black creature with two daunting waving great claws and no fewer than eight lesser ones. Jamie was interested to see how this horror was to be got out of the dripping cage without injury to the extractor. But the girl Elizabeth seemed nowise concerned. She merely tipped the contraption so that the captive slithered about therein and when it was tail-on to her, swiftly slipped her hand down the net funnel, caught the creature by the said tail, and drew it out, claws still waving but quite unable to reach back to her hand. She dropped it into one of the baskets, closed the lid, and then without any fuss, collected a fish-head from the foot of the other basket – evidently deposited there for them by the fishermen – and inserted it into the pot, distinctly old-looking and smelly as it was, lobsters apparently not being over-particular about such details.

Had any of them ever been nipped, bitten? he asked. They laughed at the very suggestion.

They rowed on for perhaps a mile, servicing half a dozen more pots, but collecting only two more crustaceans. Mary explained that they placed their cages in chosen spots where experience, and the fisherfolk's advice, told them lobsters were apt to frequent; it was of no use just putting them down anywhere along the shoreline. It had to be in specific locations, and with rocky bottoms.

This all proved quite a slow process, however interesting, even challenging. They turned back, to tackle the south-wards shore.

There they did better, winning no fewer than seven lobsters, an unusually good haul. Mary was pleased. They would be able to leave some of their catch with the local folk at the hamlet, who were always kind to them, and moreover kept them supplied with bait.

Returning, to beach their boat and draw it up on the shingly sand, they had a few words with the women of the hamlet – their men were out at sea, fishing. They were thanked, but not at all obsequiously. It was good, Jamie felt, that these earl's daughters and their local people should be on such easily friendly terms. Some lords' offspring would be otherwise, he recognised. It was a hungry little party which thereafter climbed back up to the castle, exchanging remarks with the duty guards, Jamie with a less than comfortable burden, for he had volunteered to carry the lobsters, in a sack over his shoulders, and they still moved and squirmed about. Could they bite through the sacking and his fine doublet?

Much recounting and description descended upon Aunt Margaret.

George Ogilvie was not present, Jamie noted. It seemed that he in fact spent most of the days at his own lairdship of Barras, four miles to the south-west, looking after his affairs there. Perhaps the Lord Gray had something, in deciding that a second watcher was required over Scotland's regalia.

When Ogilvie returned that evening, however, he brought news of other matters to preoccupy them all. Word had reached him at Barras of disaster for King Charles's forces in England. They had been defeated by Cromwell at Worcester, with major losses on the royalist side, sixteen thousand against the English twenty-eight thousand, the king betrayed by an English traitor who objected to him admitting Catholics to his army. There had been a massacre at Worcester city after the defeat. Charles had managed to escape, apparently by the ingenuity of a young woman, and was said to have fled to the Continent. As to the fate of the Earl Marischal and his brother, Sir John Keith of Benholm, there was no news.

The effect of these tidings on all at Dunnottar was dire. The girls' father and their uncle, Lady Margaret's husband – what of them? They had been close to the king. Anxiety prevailed.

That night, Jamie had no problems over matters of the heart.

In the morning, wishful to help the worried family in any way that he could, he suggested that he might go down to Redcastle, Lord Gray's house on Lunan Bay, to see if he could learn anything further about the disaster and its consequences. Gray was a man apt to be well informed, had to be to have survived as he had done, a leading Catholic. If anybody reasonably near at hand would have fairly certain news of the battle in these northern parts, he would. It was only some thirty miles to Lunan Bay. He, Jamie, could ride there in a day, easily, and be back on the morrow. It was the least that he could do.

That was gratefully accepted.

So, borrowing a horse, he set off southwards, to ride by Kinneff and Inverbervie, where Bruce's son David the Second had been wrecked and rescued, down that fierce coastline, past Benholm, Johnshaven and St Cyrus, to the gentler shores around Montrose with its great and all but enclosed tidal bay. Not far beyond that, over higher ground now, he came to the Boddin Head, the northern promontory of the very different bay of Lunan, almost four miles across to where the towering Red Head of Ethie closed the view. Not far down, on a rocky mound above the sandy shore, where the incoming Lunan Water helped to make a circling defensive moat, rose the redstone Gray stronghold of Redcastle. Jamie arrived with the dusk.

He was well received by Lady Gray and her step-daughter, known now as Anne, Mistress of Gray, since her only brother had been killed in France. The part he had played in the regalia episode had been told to them by Lord Gray, and they were admiring, more so than he deserved, he felt. Gray himself was absent meantime, having gone only that morning the dozen miles or so to Kinnaird Castle, the house of the Earl of Southesk, the great Montrose's father-in-law, this when he had heard of the Worcester defeat. Southesk would be as well informed as anyone, for he had a large family, all married to folk in prominent and influential positions, six daughters and four sons with whom he kept in close touch. Gray would be back next day, however, almost certainly.

Jamie, all but royally entertained, spent a comfortable night in this so different castle above the waves, although these waves were rolling in over sandy beaches, not crashing and spouting against cliff-foot rocks.

With Anne Gray he went walking along that magnificent

beach in the morning, southwards towards Ethiehaven and the huge cliff of Red Head. She was a quiet girl of about his own age, plain-featured but well built, and quite easy to deal with once he got her talking. Quite factually she informed him that she was promised in marriage to her kinsman, William, eldest son of Sir William Gray of Pittendrum, older than herself and already with an illegitimate child, but not unkind, she thought – this to keep the Gray lordship, to which she was heir, in the family. Jamie did not know whether to condole or not. But her composed way of putting her future fate did give him some sort of an idea for his own possible use.

On their return to Redcastle they found Lord Gray already back from Kinnaird. His news as to the Worcester defeat, and the situation in England, was grim. Charles had been proclaimed King of the United Kingdom at Penrith in Cumberland, but advancing southwards from there, west of the Pennines, had been confronted by Cromwell at Worcester. Unfortunately very few of the hoped-for English royalists had joined his army, less than two thousand, and these mainly Lancashire Catholics, which had offended the Puritans. Short of cannon and ammunition, the Scots had fought bravely enough, but had been driven back and into the city, where all control of the scattered army was lost. Charles and some others, including Buckingham and the Earl of Derby, with the Scots Earl of Lauderdale and about sixty horse, had managed to escape northwards, a young woman called Jane Lane apparently somehow leading them away by devious routes, the king intending to flee to the Continent. But many of the Scots leaders had been captured, including General David Leslie himself, and amongst the others, the Earl Marischal and his brother, the Erskine Earl of Kellie, the Gordon Viscount of Kenmure and the Lord Boyd. Cromwell had despatched these southwards, prisoners, to incarceration in the Tower of London. Here were sad tidings for the Keith family.

So now the royal cause, and Scotland's with it, appeared to be lost. What would transpire remained to be seen, but Monck clearly would now be undisputed ruler of the northern kingdom, for Cromwell, and the nation left more or less leaderless. Gray saw no immediate hope of betterment, alas. The cherished freedom for which so many Scots had fought and died down the centuries was no more.

Refusing to accept this, but unhappy indeed, Jamie set out on his return journey to Dunnottar.

Anxiety and depression for the Keith family was inevitable, of course. But in that young company an atmosphere of gloom could not survive for long. There was nothing that they could do to help the captives in the Tower, except pray for them, and this they did. Life had to go on.

Jamie's position now was a strange one. He felt himself to be very much the uninvited guest, although no least hint of his presence being anything but welcome by all was manifested. But he wondered for how long he was expected to remain there? The Lord Gray had insisted that it was essential that he stayed on. The regalia must have a guardian other than just Ogilvie, of whom he seemed slightly suspicious. But in the circumstances now prevailing in the land, these national symbols might be left at Dunnottar for long enough, months, years perhaps. Surely he was not expected to remain here indefinitely? What would his father have to say about it all?

The Keith girls ensured, at any rate, that their guest's visit was not a weariness, concern for their father and uncle notwithstanding. They organised outings, did some ordinary fishing, although the weather was becoming chilly for that, whether down at the cliff-foot or out in their boat. They rode abroad, visiting places of interest, Pictish forts, circles and symbol-stones, of which there were many in this area, caves in the cliffs, ancient chapels and monastic sites, now mainly ravaged since the Reformation, and the houses and castles of kinsfolk and friends, not a few of whom were in a similar state of anxiety about menfolk amissing – Fetteresso, Urie, Muchalls, Fiddes, Benholm. Since they had been warned not to inform any of the hiding of the regalia at Dunnottar, Jamie's continued presence had to be accounted for otherwise, and almost certainly assumption would be made that some romance was in the air. And of course the lobster-pots had to be serviced every few days.

Mary's obvious affection for the young man would tend to foster notions about their relationship, to Jamie's discomfort – not helped by the other girls' smiles, occasional nudges and the like. He sought to keep the association within reasonably moderate bounds, but found it difficult at times, and not only on account of Mary's feelings, for his own male reactions were by no means inconsiderable. Tina Ogilvy seemed a long way off, and quite probably she had no great interest in him anyway. Yet she it was whom he tended to think of, last thing of a night, and not only then. And she it was who featured in his dreams. It was all very difficult.

It was the fourth night after his return from Redcastle that, after the usual and quite comprehensive kissing at his bedroom door, and Mary's reluctant leave-taking for upstairs, there was a development.

Jamie was in his bed and wondering when he was going to see Tina again, when a tapping at the door preceded its opening, and Mary, candle in hand, was asking whether she might come in. Apparently she needed some item of clothing from one of the chests in this room; it was, after all, her own normal bedchamber.

He certainly could not say no, and she came in, wearing a bed-robe. He by no means looked the other way or shut his eyes as she moved over to the table on which his own clothes lay in a heap, set down her candlestick, and went to open the lid of a wooden coffer and pick out some garment therefrom. This over her arm, she crossed to his bedside, saying that she was sorry – although she scarcely sounded it – and hoped that she had not awakened him.

It was a delicate situation, as he was very much aware. He was a young man of very normal appetites, and could not just lie there, blankets up to his chin, eyeing her. And she was well worth eyeing, for her bed-robe had opened somewhat with her stooping over the coffer, and although the light of the candle over on the table was not strong, it was sufficient to reveal that she was unclad beneath and her breasts were not wholly hidden, or indeed a glimpse of a white leg further down.

Jamie sat up and, since he slept naked, even more of himself was displayed. He assured her that he had not been asleep.

Mary fluttered a somewhat nervous laugh. "I . . . I required this shift," she said. "For the morrow."

"Yes."

"I should have remembered it, before."

"No matter."

"You are not . . . fashed? Displeased?"

"Why should I be?" He reached out to pat her arm – which was perhaps unwise.

She leaned over him, at that, and bent to stroke his hair, then changed that to a kiss on it, which brought her bosom close indeed and the more evident, challenging. He drew back, just a little, and took a deep breath, summoning up words in lieu of action.

Her words came first, however, on a titter. "You have hairs on your chest, Jamie!"

"*You* have not!" Again that was not what he had thought to say. He drew on his reserves. "Sit you down, Mary lass," he urged, and patted the blankets part-way down the bed.

She acceded immediately, and a little nearer than his patting, and reached for his hand.

"See you, Mary," he began, less than assuredly. "I have something . . . there is a matter I must tell you of. I should have done so ere this." He was recollecting what the Mistress of Gray had told him, back on the sands of Lunan Bay, and seeking to modify the like to his own needs. "I have . . . there is a young woman. A lady. At Airlie. For whom I have . . . strong feelings. We are not betrothed, but have . . . regards for each other. An understanding. We, we are close. Her name is Christian Ogilvy. She, Tina, means much to me. I should have told you . . ."

Mary had gone very still. She did not speak.

"You understand, lass? I would wed her, if I might."

The girl rose from the bed, drew her robe closer, picked up

129

her shift, and began to make for the door. Then she paused, and turned.

"Why did you not say? Before?"

"I suppose . . . because I found you . . . so kind. I enjoyed your company, your friendship, your kindness. I am sorry."

"I am sorry also," she said quietly. "Sorry." She left then, hurrying out.

He gazed after her, in the dark now. It was long before he slept that night. Was he a fool? Or worse?

In the morning, he was all but reluctant to appear at the breakfast-table, the last to arrive there. All greeted him cheerfully, and he was surprised to receive a quick smile from Mary. Even so, he was not at his most outgoing that morning.

It was Sunday, and church-going was customary. Although they had their own little chapel in the castle – indeed it had been the parish place of worship before the Reformation, less than convenient as this must have been for the majority of the parishioners – this had been changed and the local kirk was now nearer Stonehaven, on the bank of the Carron Water, once the site of an ancient St Bridget's Church. Yet this was not the Keiths' chosen place of worship, for the minister there was a rabid Covenanter, and they preferred to go six miles southwards to Kinneff, where there was a more moderate clergyman, indeed a friend of the family, who often conducted services in their own castle chapel. Kinneff was also the place of worship for Barras, so George Ogilvie frequented it. But it seemed a long way to ride, there and back, for Sunday worship, to Jamie Ramsay.

However, that Sabbath's journey had its compensations, for, strung out on the fairly narrow road, the seven of them, plus sundry retainers, had to be; and they rode two by two, and Jamie found himself partnered by Mary Keith.

She explained the church situation to him, telling him that the Reverend James Grainger was not only a fine preacher and something of a scholar, but also a most amiable man whom they all liked. He visited Dunnottar frequently with his wife, whom they all looked upon as almost another aunt. If only the Kirk had more Graingers!

This intimation, from the saddle, not only whiled away some of the miles, but made for easy converse where some strain might well have prevailed between these two. And presently the girl found it possible to speak of their more intimate and mutual concern, even though her voice did tense a little.

"Jamie, I have been thinking much. Since last night. I, I hope . . . you spoke of friendship, did you not? I hope that we may remain friends, good friends?"

"Yes. Yes, indeed – that is my wish also, Mary. Good friends. We must indeed. If, if you will be so good, so kind. After what I told you."

"Yes. While you bide at Dunnottar, it could be uncomfortable, foolish, for us to keep each other at a distance. To treat each other as though at odds. When we like each other. As we do, do we not? Foolish, no?"

"I more than like you, Mary lass, believe you me!"

"I am glad. So – we remain friends, yes? Little changed. That is not wrong, is it? I will not forget your Christian, was it? Christian Ogilvy. Nor need you. Nor *should* you! But we can still enjoy each other's company, can we not? Without hurt to any. You do not judge that . . . unsuitable?"

"I do not, Mary. I, I thank you. That is as it should be, yes. You are good, kind. And wise. Wiser than I have been. A man, and a woman, can find pleasure in other than just, just . . ." Not knowing how to finish that, he left it thus.

She glanced quickly behind her, to see how close were the next couple of riders, and reaching over, gripped his arm for a moment, but herself added no words.

The day was the brighter for that exchange. Oddly, however, they did not find much more to say to each other for the not-long remainder of the journey, although they glanced over frequently, sometimes smilingly, sometimes consideringly.

Kinneff Church, almost on the beach of a section of the coastline briefly free of cliffs and crags, was larger than many country parish kirks, but then it had a number of fishing communities along the cliff-foots to serve, Crawton,

Caterline, Whistleberry as well as Kinneff, and also quite a large inland farming area. They were greeted at the door by a smiling and rather handsome man of middle years, whose black gown did not altogether disguise a tall and muscular frame, the Reverend James Grainger. Behind him stood a plump and comely woman, who kissed the Keith girls and eyed Jamie interestedly, almost assessingly. He was told that this was another Christian, the minister's wife.

The service thereafter was one that he could take part in, however unsuitably preoccupied was his mind with other matters. It had more of praise and prayer and holy joy than some of the Kirk worship he had had to attend; and the sermon was shorter than usual, but gripping, well reasoned and less accusatory and condemnatory – in fact it had Jamie listening intently, which, in his present state of mind, spoke for itself. This James Grainger was clearly a pastor, an evangelist, a leader of his flock and not a driver, as were all too many.

On the way back to Dunnottar they actually discussed that sermon, something that Jamie could not recollect ever having done before.

That evening, at bedtime, Jamie bade them all goodnight and proceeded to his angle-tower alone. It was not long, however, until there was a tapping at his door – but it did not open thereafter. When he went to it, he found Mary standing there, candle in hand. She did not come inside.

He eyed her for a moment, being very much aware of her questioning expression. Then he took the candlestick from her and put it down on the floor. He had barely straightened up before she threw herself into his arms, in a sealing of their compact.

Hugging each other, they kissed.

It was the girl who broke free eventually, and ran off upstairs, with no rearward glances. Jamie went back to his bed with mixed emotions, but on the whole well pleased. The day before she had asked if this behaviour with each other would be wrong, and indicated that *she* did not think so. For himself, he reasoned that he should not feel guilty. There was surely much that a man and a woman could enjoy with each other, if they were fond, short of the ultimate act of love which should, must, be reserved for the chosen one. What would Tina Ogilvy think – if she was in the least concerned with him at all? Airlie seemed a long way off; and there was that warm young female readying herself for bed in the room just above. Being a distinctly masculine young man held its problems and temptations, but its rewards also, of course.

In the morning, Mary proposed an expedition to Fowlsheugh, the cliff area not far down the coast, which was particularly favoured by the seabirds for roosting, mating and nesting. It was not the best season, of course, with the nesting and breeding not coming for four months yet; but there would be much to see nevertheless. If Mary thought that she would demonstrate this to Jamie on their own, she reckoned without her sisters. They would all go, that was definite.

Just why the birds chose this stretch of cliffs, on a cliff-girt coast, was not explained. But they did, in their wheeling, diving, screaming thousands, the air alive and loud with them. A quite dizzy-making path surmounted the cliff-tops, and along this the four girls and the young man trooped, leaving their horses tethered well back, Jamie the least confident. He noted stout stakes set into the ground here and there, near the edges, with ropes coiled round them, and wondered.

He was not left wondering for long – and if dizziness had manifested itself before, now it doubled. For, halting presently beside one of these posts, Mary explained their use, and quite obviously they themselves were about to use them. Uncoiling this rope, it proved to be knotted at foot-long and regular intervals. This, firmly attached to the stake, was lowered over the edge, to act as a sort of stepladder for intrepid climbers. And, it seemed, such climbing was much practised here, for these cliffs were a source of revenue for the Earl Marischal, this mile-long stretch cut up into eight distinct sections and let out to tenants, who had the right to collect birds and eggs from all the ledges, crevices and cracks of the precipice. Not all the birds were edible, to be sure, but not a few were, their eggs likewise. There was quite a trade in them apparently.

The girls vied with each other in pointing out the various

kinds of fowl, sundry species of gull, herring, black-backed greater and lesser, common; also kittiwakes, guillemots, razorbills, shearwaters, petrels, fulmars and divers of more than one sort, the fulmars, sailing with unflapping wings exploiting the wind currents and eddies, especially fascinating. But apparently these flying fowl were not what they had come to see, at least not especially. It was the roosting ones which were the main attraction seemingly; they could not only be viewed but approached and sometimes actually touched. Because of the slight overhang of the cliff-tops, however, they could not be inspected from above to advantage; so it was necessary to descend by the ropes, using the knots as footholds and grips. This they had come to do.

Blinking, Jamie pursed his lips.

Mary demonstrated at one post, while her sisters made for others nearby. First of all, without the least trace of embarrassment, she kilted up her riding-skirts high, to tuck them between her thighs and hitch them securely into the belt she wore. Long and shapely legs thus free for action, she showed Jamie how the start of the descent had to be effected, without barking knees or knuckles on the rock of the overhang, this involving first lying on the stomach and lowering the legs over the edge, to feel with the toes for the rock face, and then, arms and legs both extended, commencing a walking-down motion. This process could be continued if desired right down the precipice; but to get close to the birds on their ledges and shelves it was more convenient, once below the lip of the cliff, just to see the knots as foot- and hand-holds, stepping down knot by knot, but being careful not to graze fists and knees on juts and protruberances of the rock. She did not need to emphasise the need for a firm grip on the rope, but pointed out how to use both inner sides of the feet for effective pressure above each knot.

Her pupil sought to pay due and necessary attention, and not be distracted by those long white legs.

Mary then showed him the technique of getting over that first edge, telling him to wait until she was well down before following her. She would shout. And if, by any chance, he got stuck or was in difficulty, he was just to stand still on one of the knots and call, and she would come up to him. He did not comment on these instructions. So, lying down, and using the V-form posture of outstretched arms and legs, she eased herself over, and disappeared from sight.

For his part, after glancing along and seeing only the youngest of the sisters still on the path, Jamie allowed himself a hasty ascertainment that the thick rope was securely fastened to its post, knelt with his back to air and sea and, taking a deep breath, waited.

Soon the call came. Mary was saying something, not just shouting, but amidst all the cries and screamings of the gulls he could not make out words. Tensing himself, and gripping the rope tightly indeed, he worked his legs over the lip, and gingerly edged himself outwards rather than downwards, with feet seeking the cliff face to press against. He took some skin off his knuckles in the process, despite all the good advice.

Actually, once over the lip, he found the exercise more simple than he had anticipated, the walking-down movement against the pull of his outstretched arms coming almost naturally, the knots on the rope large enough to be reassuring. From knot down to knot he went, rather loth to change to the alternative movement of standing on the rope itself. He was wondering just how such change was to be effected, which foot to detach from the wall to feel for the knot, when he found himself staring into the beady eye of a large fowl with a notably sharp beak not two feet away. That eye looked baleful and the beak as though it might shoot out and strike at any moment – and this had the effect of removing anxiety about feet, legs and grip quite remarkably, so that he discovered himself to be stepping down that rope, out of range, at a fair pace and not worrying over the process.

He saw other birds now, all around him, squatting on ledges, huddling into cavities, preening themselves on the dried seaweed of old nests, alighting and taking off, singly, in pairs or groups. Fowl on the wing were swishing past his head close enough for him to feel the draught of them. No expert on seafowl species, he could not name them all, although he did recognise the still-winged, floating fulmars.

Now, above the screeching, he heard Mary more distinctly; and looking over, perceived that she was only a dozen feet or so below him, face upturned. She was telling him to look right, and pointing. A puffin, she was saying, evidently pleased.

He looked as directed and there, perched on a little shelf, was an extraordinary creature indeed, a bird about one foot high, sitting upright, black and white of body but with a head which was largely beak, triangular as to shape and vividly coloured in red, blue and yellow, with bright orange feet, its eye bearing a most disillusioned expression, quite unlike that other creature's hostile look, sad rather. Jamie had never seen the like.

"We do not often see puffins here," Mary was calling up. "Is it not a wonder? So coloured. No other bird is like that. But if there is one, there will be others nearby. Jamie, you are not unhappy on the rope?"

He could scarcely have described his reaction as happy, but he nodded. "What now?" he asked.

"All the other birds to see. Do you know which is which?"

"Not most of them. The gulls and fulmars, yes."

"That just to your left is a kittiwake. There are more guillemots. And there . . ."

He was given his lesson in identifications, as they descended lower and lower on that rope. He hoped that he was not expected to remember it all. He was also wondering whether the ascent would be more difficult.

A score or so of feet above the waves, they came to a sizeable ledge, large enough to stand on, or preferably to sit. Mary did that, and patted the rock beside her.

"Is it not a place to see?" she demanded. "We are in the realm of the seabirds, their kingdom. Although sometimes there are seals." But she was not looking down to the surging tide, but left-handed along the precipice. "They will be well enough. We come here frequently." Clearly it was her sisters she was referring to. A sort of buttress of the cliff projected at this level, and hid the area where the others were. She gave a little laugh, and when he sat beside her, an arm went around Jamie's shoulder, opportunities not to be wasted.

He responded suitably, and hugging each other there amongst the concerned fowl, they kissed. Those long bare legs were very evident, and Jamie found the urge to stroke irresistible. His hand was not repulsed.

Presently cries from above interrupted, and drawing apart a little they glanced up, with sighs. Because of the topmost overhang they could not see anybody at the summit path, but obviously it was the sisters back there and growing impatient. So it had to be the rope again.

Mary said that he should mount first, clearly not from any undue modesty but so that if he was in any difficulty she was just below to guide. In fact, he found the climbing easier than the descending, with less feeling for knots with the feet, the arms pulling him up strongly. He passed that puffin again, its gloom unchanged, Mary calling that she had spotted another to the left not far away. Then she was reminding him about care to be taken in surmounting the final overhang, the V-position advisable.

Eager hands helped him up over the lip, amidst a flood of announcements, exclamations and questions. Had he seen this and that? Elizabeth had seen a puffin, Isabel swearing that she had spotted a seal, her sisters scornfully declaring that it was only a weed-hung rock moving with the tide. Joan asked, giggling, what he and Mary had been doing all that time?

They coiled up their rope round its stake, skirts were let down, and they set off back to the horses, loud in chatter.

When they got back to the castle, it was to be a surprise. They had visitors: Jamie's father and brother, with the Lord Gray. Great was the to-do.

Sir Gilbert announced that they had come to relieve Jamie of his vigil, at least temporarily. He had done nobly guarding the regalia thus long, but deserved a respite. Thomas would take over for a spell.

The Keith sisters were scarcely elated, Mary becoming unusually quiet.

The visitors had news to impart. Cromwell and his Rump

Parliament, as it was being called, had declared Scotland to be now incorporated with England in his Commonwealth, no longer a separate entity, and both without king or House of Lords. He was going to send up Commissioners to enforce this. All Scots crown property was to be confiscated. Argyll had fled to his Highland seat of Inveraray, but an English General Dean had gone to assail it, captured him and sent him to imprisonment in Edinburgh Castle. But his elder son, the Lord Lorne, a more valiant character whom his father had had appointed Colonel of the Royal Guard, young as he was, had escaped at the Battle of Worcester and was now back in the Highlands seeking to arouse the various clans, as well as the Campbells, to take up arms and be ready to move southwards – this the more urgent requirement as Cromwell had also declared all clansmen released from feudal service, in a move to separate the chiefs from their followers. Crawford and the "Airlie faction" had been in touch with Lorne, and hoped to co-ordinate their activities against Monck and Lambert in the spring. This last was the only uplifting tidings brought.

But something else the visitors had brought, other than such news. King Charles had left his private papers behind at Perth when he and Leslie marched into England, and these had been collected by Tullibardine, on word of all crown property being confiscated, and handed over to Gray for safety. He had brought them here to Dunnottar, to deposit with the regalia.

Jamie's reaction to all this was mixed. He would see Tina – that was his first thought. And, in a way, he would be glad to be back to his own life at Bamff, of course. Yet, now he came to consider it, he had been happy here at Dunnottar, in a remarkably carefree existence, despite the theoretical responsibility for the regalia. The company had been good; he did not pretend that Mary's presence and fondness was not a factor of some consequence. As for the national situation, he had to admit that he had become somewhat detached from it all up here, which was probably unworthy of him. This of Cromwell's declaration that Scotland was now part of his English Commonwealth was, of course, ridiculous, but no doubt Monck and his lieutenants would seek to enforce the edict in every way possible. He shed no tears for Argyll in Edinburgh Castle, but was glad that his son, Lorne, was proving a better Campbell chief. But it all seemed somewhat remote for him now. Perhaps he had been too long up here?

That evening there were no bedroom-door goodnights, with Thomas sharing the tower apartment again with him.

In the morning, then, it was farewells, with kisses from all the Keith girls, and from the Lady Margaret Hay also, although Mary's embrace, public as it had to be, did outdo the others. The parting with George Ogilvie was less emotional, that quiet man merely declaring that he would expect Jamie back, in due course, since it seemed that he and his brother were to take turns in their assistant guardianship of the regalia, this arranged between Lord Gray and their father.

So the trio rode off southwards, to much waving, for Redcastle first and then the Lunan Water to Forfar and into Strathmore. How soon could he find excuse to visit Airlie, Jamie wondered?

9

In the event, no excuses were required, for Sir Gilbert found it convenient to make for Bamff, by the Lunan Water valley and then the Isla, which took them close to Airlie Castle and Lintrathen. The Ogilvy earl was always well informed, and would apprise them of latest developments, and himself should be told of the depositing of the royal papers at Dunnottar.

So two days after leaving the four Keith sisters, Jamie was being greeted and warmly, by the four Ogilvy ones, and their cousin Christian, a quite arousing experience for any young man. And, to be sure, Jamie was aroused. The sight of Tina, lissome, smiling, all but brought his heart up into his throat, and he knew then, without the least doubt, if he had not known for sure before, that this was the woman he wanted for his own, however pleasant and pleasing others might be, one in particular. But, of course, that was only *his* conviction; his task would be to infect Tina with a similar desire, or if that was too much to hope for, a warm liking for him. He would waste no time in setting about this endeavour, or making a start.

The first difficulty was, to be sure, to get her alone. First he was required to give the Earl of Airlie a full account of the regalia extraction and present situation; and then to listen to his seniors discussing the latest reports of the national state of affairs – and this without exhibiting any unsuitable impatience. They were especially interested in the Lord Lorne's hopes of raising a Highland army, reckoning that he ought to be able to muster over a thousand of his own Campbells. Traditionally the various clan chiefs of the north-west were not particularly interested in what went on south of the Highland Line; but if Lorne could arouse and unite them in a great sally into the Lowlands, even Monck might have his hands full.

They themselves would join in this, of course; and Airlie had word that the Cunningham chief in the south-west, the Earl of Glencairn, was intending to raise revolt in that area. Actually, this insolent decree of Cromwell's claiming to release the Highland clansmen from feudal service – anyway, a total misunderstanding of the Highlanders' attitudes to their chiefs, which was of a patriarchal association and loyalty, not a feudal duty – was probably a gift to their cause, in that it would anger the said chiefs and might well arouse them to a united action such as seldom was their wont. And Highlandmen were amongst the world's most doughty fighters.

Interesting and encouraging as this discussion was, Jamie's preoccupations were elsewhere, indeed partly concerned with geography, local geography. He was casting about in his mind for somewhere to suggest that they should go, the young people, that is. It must not be very far away, for unfortunately they were not going to stay the night at Airlie, Bamff being only eight or nine miles off, and Sir Gilbert anxious to get back to Jean, who had again been left on her own, admittedly with Mariota Ogilvy from Lintrathen, for overlong already. He decided that the Loups of Kenny, a series of waterfalls in the ravine of the Melgam Water, would serve. Actually he had seen them before, but his hosts were not to know that. They were less than two miles away, to the north.

Young Lord Ogilvy had been listening in on all this discussion, but after the regalia account, with less than fullest attention, for undoubtedly he had heard it all ere this from his father. So presently Jamie caught his eye, and jerked his head downwards. The other young man was not averse, and shrugged. At the next pause, Jamie cleared his throat and asked the earl if he might be excused meantime. He had promised the Ogilvy girls that he would tell them of the Dunnottar episode, and he would be expected to do so before they headed back to Bamff. Airlie nodded understandingly. His son muttered something vague and rose also. They made their escape.

Now, of course, Jamie was stuck with David Ogilvy as well as his sisters. But at least he ought to be able to get into Tina's company, even though not having her to himself. They went in search of the girls.

They found Tina and Helen preparing fruit for a boiling of plum and bramble jam, in the lesser kitchen of the keep, while Martha, the chief kitchen-maid, dealt with the quite involved operation of draining run honey from combs in the required amount to provide the necessary sweetening, a sticky process. Jamie wondered whether his suggestion of even a brief excursion would be welcome in the circumstances, or whether it might be more acceptable to offer to help with the fruit? But both young women asserted that they would be happy to show their guest the Loups of Kenny, and that the jam could wait. They would tell the other sisters who were bringing more fruit from the orchard storehouse. And they would hear all about the regalia adventure as they went.

So presently all seven of them were on their way, on foot, up the riverside, for horses would be only a liability in the rocky defile with its cataracts. David Ogilvy had to listen to a second rendering of the crown, sceptre and sword saga, prompting the teller now and again over details. The latter, needless to say, made every endeavour, vocal as he had to be, to walk mainly beside Tina on the narrow, twisting pathway, and to help her, usually quite unnecessarily, over steps and stones and obstacles. More than once he found her eyeing him with a sort of assessing amusement, and wondered whether perhaps he might be overdoing it.

The waterfalls and cascades reached, were duly admired, although it was explained to the visitor that the time to see them was in the late spring, when the melting snows off the mountains sent down great quantities of water, and these ravines could be filled with a mist of spray. They all sat for a little beside the highest of the falls, hoping that perhaps they might see salmon jumping; and here, perched on a spur of rock, Jamie did manage to get an arm round Tina's shoulders and delectable person, to counter the possibility of her falling off; and lest this was altogether too obvious, clutched Helen on the other side also. The Dunnottar section of the story, duly edited, was still being told.

Enquiries were numerous, and questions even quite probing as to the resident family there, the girls having heard of the Keith sisters. The recounter had to pick his way fairly carefully there, and not with entire success, it seemed for, before they rose for their return journey, Tina remarked that he did not appear to have been much involved with this Barras laird who spelled his name oddly, but considerably more with the young women of the establishment, especially the one called Mary. This awkward deduction had to be explained away with some nicety, and this while not wishing to do any injustice to the said Mary.

On the way back to the castle, Jamie made a point of changing the subject, asking heedfully after Ogilvy family doings since last he had seen them all. But he did not lessen his attentions towards Tina.

He found his father waiting for him a little impatiently, ready to be off. So there was no further opportunity for would-be dalliance, and a matter of prompt farewells. But by bestowing fairly chaste kisses on all the girls, starting with the youngest, Helen, he was able thus to salute Tina last and, although hardly lingeringly, less conventionally. She by no means broke away, although she did eye him once more with that assessing look in her lovely eyes.

"Come and see us again, and soon," she told him. And although that was a conventional-enough invitation, Jamie cherished it, perhaps over-hopefully, as they rode off.

On the way to Bamff, his father told him that the earl and he were considering the possibility of sending young Lord Ogilvy and himself, before the winter snows made such travel too difficult in mountainous country, to make contact with Lord Lorne and the Highland chiefs, to try to work out a plan of joint action against the occupying forces.

They found all well at Bamff, Jean, although glad to see them returned, by no means so concerned at being left alone with her friend and cousin Mariota as her father seemed to assume. Jamie, thereupon, had more recounting to do.

The very next day he got back into his normal routine,

so neglected recently, connected with the cattle-stock and sheep being brought down from the higher ground for winter pasturing, and the stocking up of fuel for the fires. Much of all this had been looked after by their folk, of course, but some checking and supervision was always called for, especially with the timber extraction; a great deal of wood was required for the house and the villagers' fires. Jamie found it no misery to be thus busied, but he did miss stimulating feminine company, especially when Jean went off to Lintrathen with Mariota, for a deserved break. He often wondered how Thomas was getting on at Dunnottar, and of his relationship with the Keith daughters.

It was only a few days however before that routine was again interrupted. David, Lord Ogilvy, arrived at Bamff, to announce that his father and the Earl of Crawford had decided that the mooted visit to the west Highlands should not be delayed. Crisis had developed. Monck had learned of the abstraction of the regalia. Not only that, but of its present whereabouts. Some wretched traitor had betrayed them. Sir William Dick had been apprehended and sent prisoner to London. Others concerned had been punished also. Monck would no doubt send a force northwards, sooner or later, to retrieve the crown, sceptre and sword – for he had already taken the actual throne-chair from its place in Stirling Castle and sent it south to Cromwell – so he obviously considered these symbols to be important for Scots morale. Dunnottar was a secure hold; but could it withstand a full siege by an English army? For almost certainly that was what would happen. The Highlanders must be informed, and persuaded to move a strong force to some threatening position nearby, to inhibit, if possible, any large-scale assault by Monck from Dundee. And this must be done at the earliest. Ogilvy was to take Jamie back with him to Airlie forthwith, to receive fuller instructions, and then to depart for the Highland west.

All this, of course, much concerned the Ramsays, father and son. The thought of Dunnottar Castle being under attack was dire indeed, the Keith girls endangered. And Thomas. Jamie wondered whether he would not be better to go up there, to warn them to get out, to go to one of the other Marischal houses, Fetteresso, or Benholm, than to go away to Argyllshire seeking the Lord Lorne and the chiefs; but his father said no. Any messenger could be sent up to Dunnottar to warn them. Much more important that the Highlanders should be notified speedily, and convinced that action was necessary. No ordinary couriers would serve for that. Lord Ogilvy, Airlie's heir, and himself, two young men of baronial rank, riding hard and fast, would be the ones to achieve this. Airlie was right in that.

So Jamie found himself heading back to Airlie Castle a deal sooner than he had expected.

He had come to like and trust David Ogilvy, which was just as well if they were going to be partners in this Highland enterprise; and on the way eastwards he thought to take a risk and confide in the other on quite a different matter. After some preamble about the Keith girls, he announced that he had become much attracted to another young woman, Ogilvy's own cousin Tina. He found her very much to his taste, and would hope that she might just possibly not altogether dislike him! The trouble was that he could never see her alone. If it could possibly be contrived, even for a brief interlude, he would be much beholden. Did David think that he could arrange this – and *would* he?

Jamie was surprised at the other's reaction. Ogilvy laughed aloud, and asked if Jamie thought that his attentions towards Tina had not been perceived and discussed? His sisters had been much tickled by the situation, and bantered their cousin over it all, claiming her to be much honoured by having the regalia hero seeking to court her.

Much exercised by this, Jamie was the more concerned, anxious. Was Tina upset? This was most unfortunate. It might well put her right off him. How did she take it?

David reassured him. She seemed nowise upset, smiling rather, telling her cousins not to be foolish, yes, but not being stiff about it. What her deeper feelings might be he did not know; but she was not in any way displeased, he thought. All the girls liked him, she no exception, he was sure.

Not entirely heartened, Jamie repeated his request. Would

David try to contrive a meeting with her, away from his sisters? Ogilvy promised to do what he could.

In the event, no private congress was possible that evening, for they arrived at Airlie just as the meal was being served in the lesser hall, with Crawford and Kinnoull present, all welcoming the two young men, and Jamie receiving smiling greetings from the girls, but being seated at table between Crawford and the Lady Marion. He did manage a few exchanges and numerous glances across the board with Tina, but that was as far as it went. And after the repast, he and David were taken into Airlie's private chamber, with the other two earls, for a conference and their instructions – for they were to be off westwards at first light in the morning.

The talk there, to Jamie at least, seemed endless. The young men were treated to a prolonged exposition as to the likely attitudes of the various Highland chiefs and how to deal with them. These were nearly all Catholics, of course, and this must be remembered always. Lorne himself was not, but he *was* a Campbell, and although a better man, in their judgment, than was his father, Argyll, fell to be dealt with carefully. Cameron of Lochiel and MacDonnell of Glengarry were known to be strongest for the royal and national cause. The MacGregors were also loyal, but they hated the Campbells, and with reason, for they had deprived them of much of their lands, and getting them to co-operate with Lorne might be difficult. Then there was the question of involving the Gordons, much further to the east but nearer to Dunnottar, Catholics also, their chief, the Marquis of Huntly, loathing Argyll, and therefore possibly his son. Crawford thought, if the young men found difficulty, it might well be more practical to leave Lorne and the west Highland clans, and concentrate on the more centrally based and easterly ones, the MacNaughtons, MacGregors, Robertsons of Struan, Farquharsons of Inverey and others known to be loyal. These would not be able to raise large numbers, as would some in the west; but if they could act together they could probably produce at least a couple of thousand broadswords, which, with the Gordons, might be enough of a threat to save Dunnottar.

As well as this sort of guidance, the emissaries were told the best routes to follow, what to avoid, where the different chiefs were to be found, and the like. They were to take an escort of only two horsemen with them, these carefully selected by Airlie from his people, and them all well mounted on chosen garrons good on the rough country they would be covering. Two would be best, for the larger the company the slower it advanced, especially in the Highlands, also the more attention it attracted. Pate Ogilvy, son of the bonnet-laird of Baldovie, and Kenny his younger brother, would serve, both excellent horsemen and reliable characters. With these two they would be on the western seaboard in five days, lacking mishap, some one hundred and fifty miles, to seek out Lorne first and then, after assessing reaction, move on. Inveraray still being held by the English, Lorne was believed to be based on the original Campbell castle of Innischonnel, sited on an island in Loch Awe.

When Jamie wondered, though respectfully, why all this Highland mustering was necessary in the circumstances, and a force from *this* area of Angus and Atholl could not be used instead, he was reminded of Monck's main strength based on Dundee and Perth, both only a score of miles away, and there no doubt largely to keep an eye on themselves; also no doubt well watched and reported on by spies and informers. Any mustering of forces hereabouts would be swiftly assailed; whereas the west Highlands were far beyond easy English reach, save for that of the small enemy garrison at Inveraray.

So it was then bed for the young men with, unfortunately, the young women already retired. There would be no tapping at bedroom doors here, Jamie judged ruefully.

In that, however, he was mistaken. At least, in his sleep he did not hear anything of the sort; yet next morning early he was awakened by his shoulder being shaken. He opened his eyes, to blink. And there was Tina Ogilvy standing at his bedside, lamp in hand to amplify the dim dawn light coming from the window. She was shaking her head, but smiling.

"You sleep soundly, Jamie Ramsay," she said. "It grieves

me so to rouse you. But you are to ride at sun-up, Davie says, and it will soon be that. Breakfast awaits you, downstairs."

He sat up, seeking to gather his wits. He saw that she was clad in a bed-robe. "I . . . thank you," he got out. "Yes, we go early. I am sorry. Sorry that you have been roused. Thus early I should have . . ."

"Think naught of it. I ever awake at cock-crow, only doze thereafter. It was no trouble. I, we had to say God-speed, forby."

"Yes. We were kept late, last night. Being given our instructions and the like." He took a deep breath and reached out to touch her arm. "Tina, I wanted to tell you, *have* to tell you. Have wanted to tell you, ere this. That, that I much admire you. More than admire. That you mean much to me. I have felt this for some time. I, I want you to know it. I told David . . ."

"Indeed? Then I am flattered, Jamie. You are kind."

"Not kind, no. Never that. I am . . . much affected." That was not the way he had meant to put it. He was not very good at this, especially when he was less than fully awake, lacking practice. "Tina, can you understand? I want you to know that I find you very much to my taste." No, that was not the right note and phrasing either. "I, I . . . you delight me!"

"Do I? How strange! But I am glad, even though I do not know how this can be. For we do not know each other so very well, do we!"

"I know enough to be sure in this, Tina. And it is my hope that, that you can come to feel something for me also."

"Oh, but I do, Jamie. I do. You said, did you not, that you admired me? Why, I know not. But I admire you, and what you have done."

"What I may have done, or tried to do, is of no matter. It is *myself* that I would wish you to have some feeling for. Even only a little. You say that we do not know each other so very well. But if in time, as we come to know each other better, then, then it is my hope that you might come to favour me with some . . . affection."

"I think that I do that already, Jamie."

"Do you?" He sat forward eagerly and reached out to grasp her arm. "Do you? In truth?"

Perhaps she felt that she had gone somewhat too far and fast in encouragement, for she drew back, but only a little, just a hint of backing off. "Why, yes," she said. "We all do." And if that might seem too general, too distancing, she added, "We are friends, good friends."

He released her arm. "Friends, yes. But I would wish to be . . . especial friends, you and myself."

"Like your Lady Mary Keith, at Dunnottar?"

That gave him pause, as probably it was meant to do. "She, the Lady Mary, is a friend, yes. As are her sisters. And as are your cousins here. But . . . this is different. It is more than that that I feel for you, Tina, believe me."

"Then I am the more . . . appreciative. And I thank you." She summoned a little laugh. "I shall not forget. But, see you, you are scarce clad for lengthy discussions at this hour, Jamie – you must be getting cold." He was, of course, sitting up, naked. "Nor am I, for that matter. Besides, Davie will be thinking that I have failed to wake you. Or that you have fallen asleep again, he down at the breakfast-table. Now, I shall leave you to dress. And we will all bid you farewell presently." She leaned over, kissed the top of his head briefly, and made for the door.

"Thank you! I thank you!" he called after her, fervently.

"There is warm water for you, here at the door," she called back, and was gone.

Rising, he knew mixed feelings. Joy at that kiss, after his declarations. And dissatisfaction with himself for making such a poor performance of it, given this opportunity.

When he got down to breakfast, he found all the Ogilvy girls there, but not their elders, David impatient to be off. Also at the table, although not eating, were two young men, the brothers Pate and Kenny from Baldovie, short, stocky characters who looked solidly reliable despite their curly heads and boyish grins. They did not say much in present company, but clearly were nowise reluctant to be involved in this venture.

Jamie hastily bolted down his porridge and cream, cold meat, oatcakes and honey, and declared himself ready to be off.

Five garrons were awaiting them in the courtyard, one extra as pack-horse bearing gear, blankets and the like, also some oatmeal and cold venison in case of feeding difficulties in lonely Highland glens; moreover, this beast could be used as an alternative mount if required. Then it was goodbyes, and Jamie was favoured with another kiss from Tina, this time on the lips – but then Marion and Helen gave him that parting salute also. Was it imagination that their cousin's lasted just a little longer than the others', however?

Being instructed to take great care and to come back soon, the four of them mounted and rode off, with much waving back from Jamie Ramsay at least.

10

None of the young men underestimated the size of the task they had been allotted, in sheer mileage and difficult travelling conditions, as well as in the eventual dealings with the strange and all but unknown Highland chieftains they were being sent to persuade, even though they by no means dreaded it all. One hundred and fifty miles, Airlie had said, over a wild and upheaved land of mountains, rivers, lochs and bogs, and amongst a people most Lowlanders considered to be barbarians, all but savages. *They* did not think of the Highlandmen so, they lived too near to some of the clans for that, and knew enough of the Gaelic tongue to make themselves understood; but they recognised that they might well meet with difficulties other than just travelling conditions in the glens. For one thing, the clansmen were apt to charge mail, a sort of toll, for permission to pass through their territories; and Airlie had provided his son with a bag of silver pieces to pay out where demanded. This was one of the reasons why only the two Baldovie brothers were providing escort: the larger the company the higher the mail usually, unless they were in the nature of a powerful armed band which could ignore such pecuniary demands – but such would have to be prepared to fight its way past the consequent assemblies of the offended chieftains. Four well-armed young men was assessed as just about right.

At least they did not have to consider such questions for that first day, as they rode due westwards, by Rattray and Blairgowrie and up the West Lunan Water, past the string of lochs of Rae, Drumellie, Clunie, Butterstone and the Lowes, to the great River Tay at Dunkeld, thirty miles. This route was along only the skirts of the Highland Line, the drove-roads fair and the going on the whole good compared with what they would have to face hereafter. Nevertheless they were well pleased to reach Dunkeld's change-house by nightfall, for these garrons, broad-hooved and short-legged, although essential for the more taxing Highland travel, were not fast.

The brothers Pate and Kenny proved to be cheerful, companionable and accomplished travellers, and the four were quickly on excellent terms.

Dunkeld was as far west as Jamie, or any of them, had been hitherto, a place of renown from past ages, although its great cathedral was, since the Reformation, much damaged and abandoned, wherein lay the tomb and effigy of the notorious Wolf of Badenoch, son of Robert the Second, the prince who had hunted men, like deer, for sport, and who had burned down that other cathedral, at Elgin, because the then Bishop of Moray would not advise the Pope to give him a divorce. Now his bones lay in state behind the former high altar here. But long before that Dunkeld was a place of note, right in the centre of Scotland, where the Tay had gouged a deep defile and pass through the steep, rocky hillsides, to form the very gateway to the true Highlands. The name itself revealed its importance, the dun or fort of the Keledei, the Friends of God as the leading community of the ancient Celtic Church was called, and who, after the raiding Vikings had made a desert of their Iona, brought their establishment here, where the mountains sank to Birnam Wood: the same forest from which Malcolm Canmore used the tree branches to be carried by his army to disguise its march on King MacBeth's stronghold, near Perth, when Birnam Wood came to Dunsinane.

From now on the four would make less easy journeying. In the morning they set off, directly northwards now, up the steep banks of Tay, the main problem here the fording of the innumerable burns which cascaded down the slopes to feed the main river, scores of them, intimation, if that was needed, that the Highlands were very much a terrain dominated as much by water as by heights and depths; and where the water, where it was not falling and rushing, created lochs which had to be circumnavigated, or lay less deeply on low ground to form impassable bogs. Those first ten miles of the second day left the travellers in no doubts as to the need for the advice and cautions of their elders back at Airlie on progress through the clan country. It took them until the afternoon to get out of this throat of territory and thankfully turn westwards again at Logierait, where the river made its great right-angled bend, as the mountains drew back somewhat. And here they had to pay their first mail, or toll, to representatives of a minor branch of the house of Stewart.

If the going was somewhat faster here, it was the more costly, for the Grantully Stewarts' terrain soon gave way to that of the Clan Menzies, around Aberfeldy, still more demanding, and, with Castle Menzies nearby, in a position to enforce their claims. They got only as far as the township of Kenmore, at the foot of Loch Tay, that night. And here they had to pay Campbells, who had stolen the land from the Menzies in typical fashion.

The young men were learning that in this land distances were assessed in days and silver pieces rather than in miles. But at least they ate well enough for their money.

Next day they had to follow the shores of Loch Tay for almost twenty miles, again fording headlong burns by the score, under the mighty mountain mass of Ben Lawers and Meall Garbh, eventually to reach Killin, where another branch of the Breadalbane Campbells had to be placated. They did not halt here, although it was late afternoon, but pressed on up Glen Dochart, past its renowned cataracts, to reach high Ardchyle, where Glen Ogle joined Dochart, former MacGregor country. Everywhere around them the mountains soared, dramatic scenery even though the riders' minds tended to be otherwise preoccupied. They were going to require all their silver before this mission was accomplished, although admittedly the mail-paying was often linked with the provision of hospitality, if that word could be used. They reckoned that they had now come halfway to their initial destination on Loch Awe-side.

This Dochart was a long glen, probing westwards under the impressive mountains of Ben More and Stobinian, MacNab country now, a small clan, however proud; as small it ought to be, Jamie observed, since the name meant Sons of the Abbot, and abbots were not supposed to have sons, although in the ancient Celtic Church things might have been different.

When Glen Dochart joined Strathfillan, at Crianlarich, the travellers looked about them interestedly, for Strathfillan was famed as the place where Robert the Bruce suffered a series of blows soon after his coronation and his defeat at the Battle of Methven, near Perth. Fleeing westwards here, he parted from his wife, daughter and brother Nigel, never to see the last again; and was thereafter ambushed by Lame John MacDougall of Lorne, cousin of his Comyn enemies, and so nearly captured as to have his plaid torn from his shoulders, the jewelled brooch which held it in place with it, to become a trophy for the MacDougalls, known as the Brooch of Lorne, a story known to them all. That afternoon they passed the spot where the ambush took place, still known as Dalrigh, the Field of the King, before they reached their night's halting place at Tyndrum. Here they were again in former MacGregor land, now Campbell, as they would be for most of the rest of their journey to Innischonnel.

David Ogilvy explained the strange MacGregor situation, as his father had told him. There was now no chief of that clan, indeed in law no clan at all and no person of the name. For James the Sixth, that Wisest Fool in Christendom, on Campbell's persuasion, had proscribed the very name in 1603, the year when he went south to take over Elizabeth Tudor's throne, making it an offence punishable by death to be called MacGregor, and hanging the chief, MacGregor of Glenstrae, and many another of them. But, of course, the clansmen still existed, by the thousand, scattered over these central Highlands, and strangely, were known to be loyal to the grandson of King James, Charles the Second. Their slogan, to be sure, was "My Race is Royal", for they were descended from a brother of Kenneth mac Alpin, Gregor, who united Picts and Scots in the ninth century. Dealing with these chiefless MacGregors was likely to be part of their mission, according to Airlie and Crawford, for they were stout fighters, their defeats having been by law and treachery rather than in battle.

From Tyndrum they had to climb high over another pass and into Glen Lochy, this the very spine of Braid Alban, beyond which it was, as it were, all downhill towards the western Sea of the Hebrides. Glen Lochy itself, under lofty Ben Lui, was dull, barren and all but deserted, no mail being exacted until ten miles on they came to its junction with Glen Orchy, where not only had they to pay their way but any passage was disputed by truculent Campbells until they explained that they were on their way to visit the Lord Lorne, son of Argyll himself, at Innischonnel, which word gave them passage.

Soon thereafter the land began to open out before them splendidly to a vast basin amongst the mountains cradling Loch Awe, huge Ben Cruchan overlooking all and providing the Campbell war-cry, "Cruachan! Cruachan!". Far ahead were the dark jaws of the Pass of Brander, where Bruce had eventually defeated his enemy Lame John MacDougall. Beyond lay the sea loch of Etive, just out of sight. Loch Awe itself was one of the major freshwater lochs of Scotland, thirty miles long.

When the four reached its shores it was to see a large castle facing them on a peninsula, Kilchurn, the main seat of the chief of the secondary branch of Clan Campbell, Glenorchy. The present chief, Sir Robert's, loyalties in present circumstances were not known; but the Campbells were traditionally expert at choosing the winning side in any national dispute, and Jamie was wary.

They were accosted, of course, by armed men, but were relieved to learn that Sir Robert was not at present in residence here. After all, he had seven castles; indeed his father, who had achieved the fall of the MacGregor chief and proscription of the name – and a baronetcy to go with it, as well as MacGregor lands – had been known as Black Duncan of the Cowl, or alternatively of the Seven Castles. On stating that they were on their way to visit Lord Lorne, they were allowed to pass, almost reluctantly.

Innischonnel was up at the far south end of the long loch,

the best part of a day's travel yet. So they got only as far as Cladich, where a stream came down from Loch Shira, and they bedded down in a barn of a farmery, their fifth night out. They had covered the ground fairly well, they reckoned. They had been blessed by good weather, to be sure.

Actually the drove-road down Loch Awe-side was the easiest part of their journey since Dunkeld, there being even rough and ready timber bridges over most of the incoming burns, a great help and a sign of Campbell care for their own comfort. The slopes were more gentle here, and more populous than any seen in the Highlands hitherto, the land clearly well cared for and cultivated, the Campbells evidently having their virtues as well as their failings.

At the northern end, the loch was dotted with islands, but south-westwards there were none; that is, until the four reached journey's end where, rounding a little headland, they were suddenly confronted by the sight of towering walls of an ancient-type fortalice, basically just four lofty curtain walls some fifty feet high, presumably enclosing a courtyard, and almost wholly occupying an islet some hundreds of yards off-shore, a frowning, hostile-seeming place indeed. Undoubtedly this would be Innischonnel, where first the Campbells, the Wry Mouths as the name meant, had founded their lordship in Argyll.

The young men drew up their garrons to gaze at as unwelcoming a prospect as they had ever seen, despite the beauty of the surroundings. No sign of life showed, no access was evident. There was a wooden jetty down at the lochside, but no boats. No castleton either. If this was Lorne's refuge, it was clear why he had not been captured, like his father at Inveraray, which was none so far away as the crows flew, over the hills to the south-east.

For a while they sat their mounts and wondered. Was the place deserted? Then Pate declared that he could just make out a faint film of blue woodsmoke rising over one corner of the fortress, so at least there was a fire burning somewhere therein. They decided to shout their presence, if it was not already observed. Cupping hands to mouths, they hallooed long and loud.

There was no answering call.

They kept up the shouting until they were hoarse and beginning to despair of achieving any results of their long journey, when they perceived a small boat appearing from round the far side of the islet, rowed by two men. This came halfway to the shore and then stopped. One of the oarsmen shouted.

"Who come to Innischonnel unbidden? And why?" That was a lilting Highland voice.

Glancing at the others, David called back. "The Lord Ogilvy, and others. To speak with the Lord Lorne."

That produced, after a pause. "Who? What name?"

"Ogilvy. The Lord Ogilvy. Son to the Earl of Airlie."

Jamie added, "In the cause of King Charles."

The effect of these announcements was a silent turning round of the boat, to be rowed back whence it had come.

They waited and waited. Was Lorne not there?

At length another boat came round into sight, a much larger one, indeed a flat-bottomed scow rowed by no fewer than six men with long sweeps. This moved over towards the jetty but stopped just short of it. A man, not in tartans as the other two had been, and standing in the bows, called.

"I am MacIan, chamberlain here. How do we know that you are whom you say that you are, whatever?"

David spread his hands. "I tell you, I am the Lord Ogilvy. My father is the Earl of Airlie, High Sheriff of Angus. And here is James Ramsay of Bamff, son to Sir Gilbert. We have come far to speak with Lord Lorne. Sent by my father and the Earls of Crawford and Kinnoull."

These noble names appeared to create the desired impression, for the oarsmen dipped in their sweeps, and the scow moved in to the jetty. The travellers dismounted.

"What do we do with our horses?" Jamie called.

"Bring them," they were told. "We do not leave beasts there, at all."

They led the garrons down the steep bank, and a gangplank

was pushed out from boat to jetty for them to board, the animals not liking the narrow crossing and having to be coaxed. There proved to be sufficient space for them all, the craft obviously built to carry horses and cattle. The so-called chamberlain – only the Campbells, in the Highlands, would so style their stewards – was not in any way forthcoming. The scow was pulled round, heavily, and rowed out to the castle.

Round the north-eastern side of the islet, much was explained. From landward the tall stern walls had seemed to occupy all the space; but at this side there proved to be a grassy area of broken ground outside the walling, of no great extent but large enough to graze a couple of milk-cows and to support timber stabling for horses. In the centre of this stretch was a sort of alley or crevice in the rock, with steps cut in it to give access to an arched gateway defended by an iron portcullis; and, round the corner from this, out of sight of the land, a larger jetty, at which another scow and no fewer than six rowing-boats were moored. Innischonnel became more understandable as Lorne's refuge.

Now it could be seen, also, that there were in fact two squares of the curtain walling, joined together, that to the north somewhat lower and less massive than the main one, presumably some sort of open courtyard as adjunct to the fortress proper. It was to the guarded gateway into this outer rectangle that the steps led up.

At the jetty the visitors were ushered up the narrow, twisting pathway which led round to the crevice steps, while their garrons were landed and turned loose, further over, to graze beside the two cows and clucking poultry. This round-about and constricted approach was clearly the only access to the castle.

The portcullis was up, and there was no need for the usual drawbridge over a moat. They all climbed up to a sort of platform under the arched gateway to find themselves, as expected, in quite a large open courtyard, uneven as to flooring because of the naked rock on which it was based, and flanked on three sides by lean-to buildings. Left-handed across this they were conducted to another guarded doorway in the much more massive walling of the main fortress, steps rising to its narrow portal. And in this a man stood waiting.

Archibald Campbell, Lord Lorne, was in his late twenties, and so only slightly older than any of his visitors, a man of some bearing although not handsome, of medium build, and clad in Lowland garb. They all eyed him as keenly as he eyed them, for he had the reputation of a fighter, unlike his sire, and had behaved bravely at Dunbar, and reputedly also at Worcester, from which débâcle he had made a resourceful escape. The fact that, with his father Argyll a prisoner in Edinburgh Castle, he had elected to instal himself up here in this remote hold, to seek to raise the Highlands for King Charles, instead of joining the exiled monarch on the Continent, as had so many, spoke for itself. And he was still, in name, Colonel of the Royal Guard. The four considered him with due respect, therefore.

"Which of you is Airlie's son?" he asked. "I have met him, the earl. A good man."

"I am," David said. "And this is James Ramsay of Bamff. We greet you, my lord."

"You have come far to do that, I think! I shall be interested to learn why? But come you into this poor house."

He led them through a passage in the thick walling into another courtyard in the centre of the tall, square building, a very much enclosed space containing the castle well but no lean-to buildings. The fortalice was here seen to consist of two towers, neither much higher than the parapet walk surmounting the curtain walling, with lower wings completing the rectangle. Turning to the left, he ushered them into the larger tower, and upstairs to a distinctly barren hall where, however, a cheerful fire blazed, the source of Pate's smoke presumably. He gestured to flagons and platters on the great table.

"Refresh yourselves," he invited, pouring liquor into pewter tankards. "Here's a health to His Grace."

They all drank to that, and sat.

"So, to what am I indebted for this visit?" Lorne asked, without preamble. He was clearly a man who did not beat about the bush.

David Ogilvy glanced at Jamie, for he was apt to let the other, just a little older, take the lead. "The three earls, my father, Crawford and Kinnoull, have sent us to seek your help, in the king's cause," he began, less than confidently. "It is on the matter of the regalia . . ."

"The regalia! I understand that it has been saved and is secure in Dunnottar Castle, the Marischal's house near to Aberdeen."

"Saved, yes, but less than secure, we fear. Monck now knows that it is there, and has declared that he will have it, and send it south to Cromwell in London."

"Dunnottar is a secure place. Why it was so chosen, I presume."

"To be sure. But could any hold in the land withstand a siege, and the English artillery? Cromwell's cannon are powerful, renowned." Ogilvy coughed. "Your own Inveraray did not so withstand."

"M'mm. It is a deal less strong a place. But is the regalia so vital to the English that they will send an army, with cannon, to gain it?"

"Cromwell wants all symbols of Scotland's nationhood and independence in his hands. Like the English kings before him," Jamie put in. "He would have no more Scotland. Have us just part of his English Commonwealth. That must not be."

"James Ramsay was with the Lord Gray and Sir William Dick in getting the crown, sceptres and sword out of Edinburgh Castle and up to Dunnottar," David added.

"A worthy exploit," Lorne commended. "But, what do you want of me?"

David looked at Jamie.

"The earls believe that the regalia must be preserved here in Scotland, at all costs," the latter went on. "They believe that it is only a question of time until Monck sends up a force to Dunnottar – for they are kept well informed at Airlie. Indeed, it is a fear that such may already be being sent. Although with winter almost upon us, and not the best time to move armies and cannon in flood and snow, probably Monck will wait until the spring. We – that is those who sent us, the Angus earls

– want the English to be discouraged from so doing. They want a threat posed to any Roundhead force. Based in the hills near Dunnottar. Not for a battle, it is to be hoped, but enough to give Monck pause. In those Mearns and Deeside hills the Ironsides and their artillery could be at a distinct disadvantage."

"So . . . ?"

"If a Highland force, used to the hill country, was to base itself on the high ground inland from Dunnottar, the high ground of Fetteresso and Drumtochty, the earls believe that Monck would be concerned, inhibited, not risk an attack. And you, we understand, are seeking to raise such Highland force, my lord."

The other eyed them all. "I seek to raise the clans, yes. With support from the Lowlands. But not to sit in the Mearns hills, to protect the regalia! My aim, my friends, is to march south, in due course, in great strength, and to drive Monck and his like out of Scotland. To repair the follies of Dunbar and Worcester."

The others could only applaud that, but Jamie went on. "My lord, that is as it should be. But need the two causes be in opposition? It will take you, and the others, some time to arouse and muster all the clans that you need. And to prepare them for full war. Meantime, could you not send a lesser force to muster in the Mearns hills? As well there as anywhere, no? And to keep in touch with the Gordons none so far off. Would that not serve both our aims?"

"I do not see it so. You do not know the clans, my friend. I do! Think you that they would sit quietly there waiting? They would be raiding into the low country. Taking the cattle. And the women! Driving all back to their own lands. That would be the way of it. It would not serve. Besides, is the regalia worth it all? So vital? They represent symbols, yes, but only that. Taken south, they could be recovered one day. And if not, replaced. Scotland can survive without them, if need be. King Charles could have another crown made. And the sword and sceptres, I understand, were gifts from a Pope in Rome! No, I do not see this as *my* strong duty."

"They mean much to the folk of our land," David asserted.

"The king himself means more, the man himself, not the symbols."

That could not be denied, of course. Jamie tried again. "The king is far away. And may remain afar for some time. Years perhaps. The symbols may be all that we have to keep the nation's pride alight."

"Was it doing so locked up in Edinburgh Castle? Or now in Dunnottar? See you, my friends, I do not deem it unimportant, the regalia. But it is not, to my mind, the prime importance. That is to raise the clans in sufficient force to assail Monck. And that task is great enough for myself. And Lochiel. And Glengarry, who are with me in this. I am sorry. But I see my duty otherwise to your wishes."

His visitors eyed each other. That mention of Cameron of Lochiel and MacDonnell of Glengarry as Lorne's colleagues in his great endeavour more or less inhibited them from going on, as had been their instructions, to seek to involve these also. Yet they must try further, somehow, somewhere.

"Who could we approach then, my lord?" Jamie asked. "That would not run counter to your plans? Some lesser, more easterly, clans? You are mainly concerned with the great clans of the north-west Highlands and Islands, are you not? Camerons, MacDonalds, Macleans, MacLeods, MacDonnells and the others. And your own Campbells. What of MacGregors, MacLarens and the like? They will not be your main concern. And be nearer Dunnottar for a swift strike. MacNaughtons perhaps also. And Macfarlanes . . ."

"MacNaughton, at Dunderave, is too near the English occupying our Inveraray. But if you thought to use the scoundrelly and proscribed MacGregors, I would not object. Nor the MacLarens, Buchanans and suchlike. But the MacGregors are outside the law."

"Does such law still rule in Scotland, under Monck, my lord?"

The Campbell frowned. "It is the king's law. King James, and his successors."

"And we seek to preserve the king's crown!"

162

There was no point in creating ill-feeling. David diverted somewhat. "The MacGregors are the largest clan, are they not, whatever their name and the law? And fighters. But they have no chief, their leaders all hanged. How could we reach them? Who could we approach?"

Lorne stroked his chin. "They are scattered, yes. Largely leaderless. You would have difficulty in mustering them. But there are one or two chieftains of septs which . . . survived. Glengyle would be your best to see. If you are set on this. Donald, of Glengyle. You know Glen Gyle? It is at the head of Loch Katrine, in the Trossachs. East of the head of Loch Lomond. Glengyle himself was not involved in most of the troubles which brought down the MacGregors. He was too young then. So he and his escaped the king's righteous wrath, in the main. Thy are proscribed with the rest, to be sure. But he is, I would say, as honest as any of the name is likely to be!"

They nodded acknowledgment of what lay behind this recommendation, from a Campbell.

"Then there is Roro, in Glen Lyon. Old Roro escaped, but is now dead. His son is still chieftain in that remote place. These two might serve your purpose."

"We thank you," David said. "To reach these, how should we go? Are the English like to trouble us on the way? We do not know this country well."

"If you avoid Loch Fyne-side you should be safe. That is the long sea loch south of here, on which lies Inveraray. They hold that, unfortunately, where they can be supplied and sustained by sea. Otherwise they are not in the Highlands. You came by Glen Orchy and Glen Lochy, yes? Then go back that way, and over into Strathfillan. At Crianlarich turn south, down Glen Falloch. You will reach Glen Gyle that way, but scarcely easily. As to Roro, in Glen Lyon, ask Glengyle to direct you."

Clearly Lorne was neither wishing nor expecting them to go on north-westwards to Lochiel, Glengarry and the rest. And his final remark on the subject, on his authority in these Highland territories, left his visitors in no doubt as to where they stood, when he mentioned that King Charles had sent him a commission as lieutenant-general, the only such now not a prisoner.

While less than a genial host, Archibald Campbell provided for them well enough that night, leaving them largely to themselves. He no doubt sensed their disappointment with his attitudes and priorities. They ate plainly but adequately, and slept in more of comfort than in the Cladich barn.

In the morning they were off northwards again, down Loch Awe-side, whence they had come, hoping that their silver pieces would not run out.

It was strange how journeys always seemed shorter when retracing steps than when coming. They made good use of it to Glen Orchy, and over the Lochy pass to Tyndrum in Strathfillan – and they did rather better mail-wise, being now known to the toll-gatherers. Next day they reached Crianlarich by noon, and there, instead of proceeding up Dochart, turned due southwards down Glen Falloch, new country for them, Macfarlane territory. They wondered whether to visit Macfarlane himself, down at Tarbet on the west side of Loch Lomond; but they had gathered from Lorne that he was under Campbell sway, so decided to ask MacGregor of Glengyle about that, approaching him first.

At the head of Loch Lomond, almost as long as Loch Awe, ten miles on at Ardlui, paying Macfarlane mail, they enquired their route to this Glen Gyle. Distinctly suspiciously eyed, they were directed to go back a little way and across the valley floor, then down the east shore of Loch Lomond for two miles, to Ardleish. Then turn off into the mountains, and climb over the high pass of the Lairig Ducteach, three rough miles, to the Gyle Water, and so down to the head of Loch Katrine where Glengyle dwelt. Clearly it was a very remote and detached area, no doubt why the Glengyle MacGregors had survived. Jamie had an idea that his hero, Robert the Bruce, had found temporary refuge hereabouts three centuries earlier.

They got as far as Ardleish that night, where they were to leave the loch shore, and put up at a cowherd's shack where, after learning that they were heading for Glen Gyle next day, they were well treated, for the little family proved in fact to be MacGregors although they were having to call themselves MacEwan, the herd's father's baptismal name, since they could no longer, by law, use their own surname. When they learned, further, something of their visitors' mission, they were the more friendly, although much concerned that they had had to spend a night with the damnable Argyll's son at Innischonnel. The little family went so far as to refuse payment for the night's hospitality, although David left one of his precious silver pieces with a little girl as they took their departure in the morning.

The weather had been kind to them hitherto, for late October; but this day, the first of November, winter suddenly descended upon them and these uplands, and the travellers took their steep ascent in a chill east wind and flurries of snow, the high tops already white.

Jamie, despite the problems these conditions might impose on them, was not displeased. An early winter was to be welcomed, in that it might well delay any English assault on Dunnottar. Admittedly a force could march north from Dundee by the coastal route, without having to thread any snow-filled passes through hills. But rivers would be high, fords deep and bogs flooded, bad conditions for cavalry and even worse for oxen-drawn cannon. If Monck had not already started out . . .

Their own travel became difficult indeed as they climbed to the pass, and they were thankful that they rode the sturdy, sure-footed and untemperamental Highland garrons. Ordinary Lowland horses would have been hard put to it to pick their way up, through new snow obliterating tracks and covering rocks and soft ground on that steep and broken ascent. Blowing almost horizontally from the east in their faces, the snow coated chilled horsemen and their steeds in white.

It seemed a long climb to the grim gap between Ben Ducteach and another peak apparently called Cruach, even though MacEwan had said that it was only a couple of miles, dire miles in any weather but in snow conditions taxing to the utmost. They eventually made it, however, but the other side was almost as difficult, with them still having to pick their way over hidden hazards and the visibility only yards. Fortunately there was a break in the snow showers presently, allowing them to see a valley opening to the south-east, shallow at first but deepening into quite a major glen, and running almost straight down, possibly two or three miles of it until it reached the dark waters of a loch – no doubt Glen Gyle and Loch Katrine. Thankfully the riders made for this. Although the snow resumed again, they were down into the gut of the glen and following the stream before it did so; progress was still slow and unpleasant, but at least they could not lose their way.

The journey to the House of Glengyle from Ardleish was only some six or seven miles as an eagle might fly, but it took the horsemen most of the day.

In the lower parts of the glen they passed quite a number of shacks and cot-houses, but in these conditions few folk were in evidence and such as were did not challenge the visitors, however much they may have wondered at their arrival. No mail was charged. They had no difficulty in finding their goal, for Glengyle House, although no large castle, was a substantial semi-fortified house set just above the loch-head, backed by ancient trees There was somewhat less snow at this lower level.

Donald MacGregor of Glengyle, chieftain of the Dougal Ciar sept of Clan Alpin, proved to be a big man in his thirties, of strong features and a proud bearing. He was obviously surprised to see mounted visitors, in Lowland garb and coming down from the mountains, but welcomed them civilly to his house without immediately demanding the reasons for their so unexpected calling. Clearly casual visitors were rare at Glen Gyle. His wife, oddly, was a Campbell, sister to Campbell of Glenlyon, which might have had something to do with his survival here, and Lorne's attitude.

In the circumstances, they could not be long in broaching the subject of their visit, Jamie leading off this time. He announced that they came in the national cause, and in that of King Charles, and hoped that MacGregor of Glengyle, whose race was royal, would hear them with understanding and caring, an introduction which he had been preparing as they rode. He emphasised the name MacGregor deliberately.

The other inclined his head. "The king has no more leal supporter," he said strongly. "Would that there were more of them. And prepared to act. I served with Montrose, that great one. And daily curse the man who brought him to his death, MacCailean Mor – Argyll!"

Was this a hopeful start, having just come from Argyll's son? "Argyll is now imprisoned in Edinburgh Castle, for good or ill! But his son, the Lord Lorne, is made of better stuff, is he not? We have come here from him, at Innischonnel."

"That one sent you to me?" Glengyle sounded as though he doubted it.

"He told us where to find you. And believed that you might help."

"Help *him*? Or help King Charles?"

"Help our cause, and the king's. We seek to preserve the king's crown for him. The Honours of Scotland."

"Are they under threat, whatever?" Evidently the situation regarding the regalia had not reached these glens.

Jamie explained, with David interjecting details of his part in the saga thus far, the MacGregor clearly much interested.

When it came to the test, the seeking of active aid for their project, the callers found that they had little or no persuading to do. Glengyle saw the point at once, and more or less volunteered his assistance. What could he do to help? he demanded: so different an attitude to that of Lorne.

They detailed their ideas of a watching, waiting force to pose a threat, in the Mearns uplands, to any assault on Dunnottar by the English, and were promptly, practically but sympathetically questioned as to timing, numbers and tactics, a man of action this most obviously.

On the subject of numbers, they discussed how many might be required to make a threatening force, and this of course would in turn depend on the size of any English detachment sent. This could be guessed at only, but it seemed unlikely that for so limited an objective as taking a single castle, however strongly placed, a large body of troops would be deemed necessary. It was not, they thought, the numbers of men which would be the important factor, but the cannon needed to batter the stronghold into submission. One Roundhead regiment, then?

Glengyle said that he could raise five hundred men from here, Balquhidder, Inversnaid, and Strathyre. Some MacLarens might join them.

Impressed, Jamie mentioned the MacGregors of Roro. Would they be likely to assist? Lorne had spoken of them.

Yes, Glengyle agreed. Young Roro was a sound man. And he acted chieftain to a large number of leaderless Gregorach up in Rannoch, and in Glen Strae itself, their former chief's territory. Roro could probably raise another five hundred. He himself would go and see Roro and seek to arrange it. Would one thousand men be sufficient?

All but left speechless by such reaction, his visitors sought to declare their gratification. They had thought of themselves as having to go to see Roro; but if Glengyle would do so, it would be much more effective, as well as sparing them the further difficult travel. One thousand Highland broadswords would be magnificent, if such could indeed be mustered. They had not hoped for so many. Was it possible?

Glengyle dismissed that with a wave of the hand. The Gregorach did not do things by halves, at all. But when? That was the great matter. When, and for how long, would they be needed?

The others admitted the difficulties in this aspect of it all. The timing. When would Monck act? They had no absolute certainty that he would send a force at all. But the information the earls had received from their spies in Dundee indicated that he, Monck, was determined to have the regalia. And the only way to get it was to send troops to reduce Dunnottar Castle. He might already have done so, to be sure, but they hoped and prayed not. It seemed most likely that he would wait for the spring, with conditions more favourable for the heavy English cavalry, and especially the cannon, oxen-drawn. The chances were, therefore, that it would be April before an attempt was made. This, presumably, would better suit the MacGregors also?

Glengyle, shrugging, said that the Gregorach were not to be prevented from operating by winter conditions. And they had no cannon to drag through bogs, flooded fords and snow-filled roads. But, yes, he could move a force of his people into the Mearns hills by April. But for how long would they have to wait there? He admitted that the Gregorach would not be good at idle waiting – which was what Lorne had indicated also.

Jamie and David conceded the difficulty here, this of timing. It might well be too late, if they heard at Airlie of an English force setting off northwards for Dunnottar, to send word here to Glen Gyle, the MacGregors to assemble and hurry eastwards. Admittedly oxen travelled very slowly anyway, the more so when having to pull massive cannon and cannonballs. The English cavalry could probably make the journey to Dunnottar, say, seventy miles, in three days. But the oxen would do well to cover it in ten, with a score of rivers to ford. Monck could send cannon by sea, of course; but was that likely? They would not be anticipating attack on the way. Also there was nowhere close to Dunnottar where they could unship large artillery; and since it was all hostile country for the English, they would need to send troops up first to secure the harbour. Stonehaven was not large enough. It would have to be Aberdeen. That would entail a full-scale assault on that city. No, the cannon necessary would almost certainly go by road, and slowly. Would, say, eight days give time for the MacGregors to get mustered and into position?

Glengyle nodded. If they were prepared, ready, yes. How far from Glen Gyle and Roro to the Mearns? One hundred miles? More? Running gillies could cover thirty miles a day, and better, if need be. In Montrose's army they had done so often. And over roughest country. Given notice, they could have men in position in under eight days, yes.

His guests were much heartened, admiring, and said so.

Glengyle asked about Lorne's plans, and they told him of the intention to raise the north-western great clans, and the hopes of assistance by the Earl of Glencairn and his Ayrshire levies; also the lieutenant-generalship conferred. The other reserved comment.

Thereafter they passed a pleasant evening, Lady Glengyle proving to be a friendly and competent hostess. The visitors were intrigued by this MacGregor-Campbell union, but could not say so. It was the more strange in that Glen Lyon had originally been MacGregor territory, like so much else; yet Glengyle had married the sister of its present laird. The fact that there was still an enclave of MacGregors in long Glen Lyon, at Roro, added to the mystery. They were not enlightened on this.

In the morning, although it was still very cold, the snow had stopped, and the travellers were for off. Glengyle advised them as to route, as far as Perth. They would wish to avoid that city, of course, with its English garrison. If they went down this Loch Katrine-side and through the Trossachs by Lochs Achray and Vennacher to the Falls of Leny, at the foot of Strathyre, then up that strath to Loch Earn, passing Balquhidder – all this in former MacGregor country – they could then turn eastwards by the River Earn to Comrie and Crieff. From there, up the Sma' Glen to Strathbraan, which would lead them to Dunkeld, which they knew. Say sixty miles in all. In these conditions, two days, on good garrons. Another day thereafter and they would be back in their Angus glens. If they were asked for mail as they went, to say that they were under the protection of MacGregor of Glengyle, on his business, and they would be spared.

Astonished at this last, from the so-called proscribed and landless Children of the Mist, they left that hospitable house with many expressions of acclaim and gratitude, hoping that Glengyle had a good reception from Roro, and assuring him that they would send word just as soon as they learned of Monck's expected move for the regalia. If he had already moved, they would inform, probably sending these brothers, Pate and Kenny Ogilvy.

It was homewards for them, then, well pleased with their mission.

11

Jamie could have left his companions near Alyth, to turn north for Bamff, but declared that he ought to accompany them right to Airlie, to help David give account of it all – but in fact, of course, in order that he might see Tina again. They had been away exactly two weeks, and covered well over three hundred very difficult miles. They were quite sorry to part from Pate and Kenny, with whom they had become very good friends.

Their reception at Airlie Castle was rewarding. Kinnoull had departed but Crawford was still with David's father. The two earls were much impressed with the young men's efforts and their hoped-for results, although disappointed in Lorne's attitude. They much applauded Glengyle, and declared that he must be rewarded in due course, in some suitable fashion. There was no word of any move by Monck in the Dunnottar direction, although reports said that he spoke of the regalia often. The English were presently preoccupied with sporadic uprisings in the west country of Lanarkshire, Renfrewshire and Ayrshire, headed by Glencairn and Eglinton and Cathcart, these threatening their garrisons at Glasgow and Paisley. Monck was said to be urging Cromwell to send up more troops from England.

So the situation was finely balanced meantime.

There was news about Dunnottar itself. Thomas Ramsay was to be relieved in his spell of duty up there shortly. Lord Gray was arranging that his own nephew and heir to the title, William of Bandirran, should go and take over as assistant guardian of the regalia for a while, to succeed Thomas; and Airlie had nominated young David Ogilvy of Inverquharity to take a turn at it thereafter, with Jamie possibly doing another spell there later. This succession of watchers was necessary, for Barras had his own lairdship to see to, and could not be at the castle all the time.

This interview over, Jamie went in search of Tina Ogilvy.

He discovered that the girls, except Helen who was not well, had all gone off on a day's visit to Lintrathen to see their cousin Mariota; but since they would be back with the darkening, that would not be long. Jamie decided however not to wait, but to go and meet them. David had had enough of riding, and left him to it.

In fact he met the four young women only a couple of miles up the Melgam Water, and great was the stir his appearance created, with cries, exclamations and much manoeuvring of horses to get close enough to embrace the returned traveller from the saddle. He enjoyed being so evidently popular, but did not fail to note that Tina was the least effusive, although she greeted him with a warm smile. She was the oldest of course, and possibly felt that she had to give an example in ladylike behaviour.

Answering clamant demands for details as to the Highland venture, Jamie found that unfortunately they were most of the way back to Airlie before he could contrive to be riding beside Tina at the rear. There he found that his eloquent account of the mission had inexplicably dried up; and the young woman appeared to be quite content to remain silent also, in contrast to the chatter ahead.

"I . . . I have missed you," he managed to declare, at length.

"Have you, Jamie? I would have thought that you would have been far too much engaged in your important affairs for anything of the sort, women's small concerns far from your mind. Unless, of course, you met some attractive Highlandwoman on your travels?"

Was that encouraging, or the reverse? "No. No – the only woman we saw was the Lady Glengyle. That is, apart from cottage folk. She was kind, but . . . older."

"Ah. So no Mary Keiths! So you missed us, you who seem to attract the women!"

"It was you I missed, not, not . . ." He gestured forward,

less than kindly perhaps, and plucked up his courage. "Do I attract you, Tina? At all? A little?"

"Oh, yes. To be sure, You are quite good-looking. And something of a hero into the bargain!"

"That is not what I meant," he asserted. "I meant *me*. Myself. James Ramsay. The one who thinks so highly, and so often, of you."

"Do you? I wonder why?"

"You are beautiful. And kind. And, and altogether admirable. All that I judge a woman should be. The woman I want!" That came out in a rush. "I told you, back in that bedchamber, that morning."

"You were half asleep then, if I recollect aright. And a man can say odd things when he is in that state."

"I meant it then. And I mean it now. Why do you doubt me, Tina?"

"Say that I have had other young men saying similar things to me, now and again!"

"Have you? Yes, you will have done." Even to himself that sounded distinctly flat. "Did you . . . have any of these . . . were you taken with any of them?"

She gave a small laugh then, and reached over to pat his arm. "Not particularly," she said.

"I should not have asked that," he admitted.

"I forgive you, Jamie. To tell the truth, I think that I like you rather better than any of them!"

It was his turn to reach over and squeeze. "I . . . am . . . glad." That was heartfelt.

"Any, so *far*!" she added, but with a smile.

"M'mm. Then I needs must make haste, no? Before another comes to you."

"There is no real race, see you," she observed, judiciously. "I am not like Mariota, at Lintrathen, heiress to all Clova and half of Glen Isla. Suitors line up to seek her favours. She finds it amusing. We have just been discussing the situation with her."

"I am not concerned with such," he assured. "Lands and the likes. She is my sister's friend also, and good company.

174

But that is not for me. I, I want *you*! Not what I might win with you."

"That is a comfort, perhaps!"

He shook his head. She did not seem to take him seriously. "I shall keep trying, Tina. And hoping," he told her. They were by now turning into the castle stableyard. "I am only the second son of no great laird. But, I love you!"

She reined up and turned to look at him directly. "That is the first time that you have said it," she declared. "I wonder why?" And she dismounted.

Jamie was left wondering also.

That evening, after the meal, it was pleasant in the great hall, round the fire, with clarsach and lute, playing, singing, and the young men encouraged to elaborate on their recent experiences in territory none of the others, even the earls, had ever penetrated or had cause to. Much interest was shown in Clan Alpin, the MacGregors, whose plight was now investing them with a sort of aura of romance. Helen, evidently feeling better, had joined them.

When, with no more logs being put on the fire, retiral was indicated, Jamie found himself escorted to his bedchamber by all five of the Ogilvy girls, with even competition to carry in the steaming pail of washing water, their brother left to find his own way to his room. When, thereafter, Tina hustled them all out, rather like a henwife shooing out poultry, Jamie made a point of kissing them all goodnight in robust fashion, so that he might do likewise, or approximately so, with the older girl, in rather more lingering fashion. She gave him her lips, but then, so did the others; only hers did open just a little.

He decided before he slept that he was probably entitled to feel encouraged.

In the morning, having no excuse to delay his return home, Jamie was delighted when Tina said that she would escort him on his way. Sadly, that produced acclaim from her cousins, all deciding to do the same, even David. So seven strong they left Airlie, the guest deciding that he was altogether too popular – but gratified also, of course, in some measure.

When they parted, at Lintrathen again, there was more

kissing and hugging, inevitably less intimate. But Tina did contrive to murmur a few words near his ear.

"Come back soon," she said. "I shall not forget your belated confession."

And what did she mean by that, he wondered, as, with much backward waving, he rode off.

Welcomed home by father and sister, both clearly happy and relieved to see him and eager for his tidings, Jamie was quickly back into the daily routine of the estate. With both sons away, much work had been delayed, especially the quite major preparations which had to be made for winter conditions up in these Highland Line foothills, so that he did not have too much time for cogitation and deep dwelling on affairs of the heart, although Tina was never very far from his mind.

He did, however, after some debate with himself, find time to consult his sister on the matter, hesitantly as he approached her. Jean was an eminently sensible and down-to-earth young woman, but not lacking in fondness for her brothers nor in some understanding of their needs and problems. Perhaps she could help.

"Jean, I would esteem your advice," he began, one evening when their father was down in Alyth town. "I could do with some guidance. On a privy matter."

"Guidsakes!" she exclaimed, wide-eyed. "This is not like you. What's to do? Are you unwell? Sickening?"

"No, no. Nothing of that sort. It is . . . otherwise. I have come to have . . . I have developed some, some affection for Tina, for Christian Ogilvy."

"Mercy upon us, that is no news! Everybody knows it. Mariota tells me that the Ogilvy girls, the cousins, talk of little else these days, when they visit her."

"Eh? You say so? Save us, how can that be?"

"Jamie, use such wits as you have! Think you that we women are as witless? Blind? You men show your feelings clearly enough."

"You mean . . . they all know? And Tina? She has known also. And for some time?"

"To be sure she has. But are you really serious in this concern, Jamie? It is no mere passing fancy? Like the Keith girl."

"Of course not. Tina is . . . especial. But if she has known all along, then, then it is the worse. For me. She does not appear to take my regard seriously. She does not mislike me, I think. But she puts off any, any advances. Smiles at them. Even though she urged me to go back there, soon."

"She would not smile, and urge you back, if she had no interest in you."

"I want more than her interest. I want her caring, her feeling for me as I feel for her. My love returned. How do I gain that? In what am I failing?"

"Have you said it? In so many words. Or *one* word, indeed – love! Have you told her that you love her?"

"I think so, yes. I did, yes. One time. All that she said was that she wondered why. I seek more than that, Jean."

"You told her once! A woman needs more avowal than that, lad. Any woman of spirit. You have to press your suit. She must perceive that you are in earnest. Men can make a play for women all too readily. Desiring only their favours. With no concern for true love. You would not want your Tina to prove so easy to get? If easy for you, then easy for other men also."

"M'mm. Perhaps. But she must know how I feel. How deeply. I have made it clear enough, I swear! Without, without showing it all to others. Many times. Shown that I prefer her company to that of the others. Once, even in my bedchamber . . ."

"Sakes, you got that far, the pair of you?"

"No, no. I was abed when she came to waken me. Early. We were to ride for the Highlands, David her cousin, and myself. I had slept late. There was nothing more. But . . ."

"The fact that she did come into your room, and alone, not send a servant, says much, I think! Was it then that you told her that you loved her?"

"No. Not then. At least, I did say that I admired her. More

than others. I think I said that she was very much to my taste. Something of that sort."

"When did you tell her? This of love."

"I think – yes, it was as we were entering the castle yard. Preparing to dismount . . ."

"Oh, Jamie Ramsay, what a fool you are! Where women are concerned, at any rate. That is not how to woo. You must tell her much, how beautiful she is – and Christian *is* good-looking – how every inch of you needs her. How she outshines all her sex, for you. How you would challenge all men for her. How you would be lost without her. And tell her time and time again that you love her – that is the most important part of it. You cannot say it often enough."

"You think so? All words, words!"

"More than just words, to be sure. Actions have their place, but have to be more carefully, discreetly used. Your words need not, should not, be discreet. With your actions, her reactions have to be considered heedfully. Not to offend. But words of love can be a deal more telling and insistent. Did you not learn anything of all this from Mary Keith?"

"I was not in love with Mary. Only . . . friendly. Enjoying her kindness . . ."

"Aye! You men! From what you have told me, I . . . well, never heed. But heed the rest of what I have told you. You may be good at saving regalia and acting the hero. But you are not much of a lover, I fear, my dear brother – or at least, in declaring your love."

He shook his head. "Why do women need such handling? Or, no, not handling. I mean all this of what you call wooing? When a man is making it very clear that he cares."

"Say that we have got to be very sure. Both of ourselves and of the men who seek us. When a woman gives herself, it is no light giving – not for honest women. There are the other sort, of course, but not the kind to fall in love with. Men, clearly, can be less – heedful."

"So! Then the sooner that I go back to Airlie, as Tina said, the better. And start to woo her, as you tell me. The trouble

178

is, it is so difficult to get her alone. Always the others girls are there."

"Except when you need awakening in the morning!"

"That was . . . David, her cousin, sent her up. He was at his breakfast. I must go back. Soon."

"No-oo. I think not, Jamie. Be not in too great haste. Leave her to wait a little. If she indeed said to come back soon, and does have something of a care for you, then the waiting may well aid you, make her the more wishful to see you. And be the more kind and forthcoming when she does! I think that you should bide your time, lad, a little."

He frowned. "That would be . . . not to my liking. Difficult. Feeling as I do. Waiting. Doing nothing. When she is so important to me. Hard to thole. And perhaps cause her to think that I do not care so much, in thus staying away. Unless . . . unless you could help, Jean? Could you not invite Tina to come here? For a visit. Mariota comes often. Why not Tina with her? Then we could contrive to see each other along . . ."

"That would not serve, Jamie. Not at this stage. To invite Tina here, without her cousins, or some of them, would look too obvious. Singling her out. Too much of a declaration. She would be embarrassed, and probably have to refuse. Later, perhaps. But until you have her admitting caring interest in you, *you* must do the calling."

Glumly he considered his sister, and wondered whether he had been wise in confiding in her.

In the days, even weeks, which followed, Jamie wondered the more, all but found himself scowling at Jean on occasion, when the cost of taking her advice taxed his patience greatly. To be in love, and to have the loved one living a mere ten miles away, and not to be able to go and see her and proclaim his ardour was trying in the extreme for a young man of Jamie's active nature. And no word came to him, in the interim, from Airlie Castle.

Not that he in any way hung around and moped. It was a particularly hard as well as early winter, and this occasioned much work with the cattle and sheep stock, the fuel situation and even the water supply, with ice a continuing problem.

Despite the hard conditions, Thomas arrived safely back from Dunnottar at Yuletide, having been relieved there by the Master of Gray. For that quiet character he was almost voluble on his experiences up in the Mearns, apparently having much enjoyed his spell of duty there. Clearly the feminine company had been to his liking; and although he did not go into much detail, even when cross-questioned by his sister, as clearly Mary Keith in especial had had quite an effect upon him, an expert in bringing out the man in any male. The other girls had commended themselves also, to be sure, and he had been taken fishing, lobstering, cliff-climbing, visiting and church-going. The brothers were able to exchange anecdotes and reminiscences, and to assist each other in dodging some of Jean's more shrewd probings.

So a pleasant enough Christmastide was passed at Bamff, despite Jamie's preoccupations – and despite the prevailing distresses in the land at large.

For distress there was in Scotland that winter, apart altogether from the hard weather. The English occupation was biting as hard as the frost, its effects becoming ever more rigorous and tending to trouble all, high and low, townsfolk and countrymen. Trade was at a standstill, deliberately put down, and in consequence poverty was widespread in all classes. Taxes were imposed by the occupying regime on a scale never before experienced, and the proceeds sent to England. The numbers of the Roundhead military were costly to feed and maintain, and their rule harsh. Imprisonments, fines and banishments were imposed on the gentry and nobility, many Kirk ministers being dispossessed of their livings. The folk of the Highlands, and of the skirts thereof, which included these remoter Angus glens, were the fortunate ones, however grim the weather conditions.

In mid-January word came of a new English measure. Cromwell sent up a command that deputies from all the shires and burghs of Scotland were to assemble at Dalkeith, in Lothian, to meet commissioners his parliament was sending north, to give official assent to the incorporation of the northern realm in the English Commonwealth, this under pain of dire punishment if there were any refusals. Once his incorporation was signed and effected, a convention was to be held in Edinburgh – no longer a parliament, it was to be noted – to select and appoint twenty-one of its members to go and attend the parliament in London, this being now the government of Scotland. And the point was made that the erring Scots should be grateful indeed that the English parliamentarians were so generous towards their defeated enemy as to allow them representation in the governing body.

The reaction to all this in Scotland need not be catalogued; but what was there to be done about it, with a powerful and efficient English army controlling the Lowlands, most of the nation's leaders either dead, imprisoned or overseas, and, so far, no Highland host coming to the rescue – as indeed how could one, in these winter conditions.

Sir Gilbert was, of course, much exercised over all this, for he was a member of the Scottish Estates of Parliament, even though he did not attend all its sittings, and had not been at its last sparsely attended meeting in August when it had sat under Monck's dictatorial supervision. So he, Ramsay, was presumably one of those expected to present themselves at this meeting with the English commissioners at Dalkeith. Whether to do so or not concerned him not a little.

In the circumstances, he decided to go and consult Airlie, and Crawford if he was still available. Jamie would have wished to accompany him, needless to say, but his father saw no need for this, and detailed much that would keep his sons busy at Bamff, with the frozen water situation particularly grievous, with its effect on the mill-wheels, water-driven, requiring a difficult and much less efficient horse-driven system of grinding having to be contrived to produce the essential meal for men and beasts. There were three mills on the barony properties, and Jamie had been put in charge of this situation and was finding great problems in keeping them all working. He did ask his father to convey his greetings to David Ogilvy and his sisters, and especially to cousin Christian, which had his sire eyeing him thoughtfully. Jamie sometimes was concerned that Sir Gilbert had ideas of finding suitable and landed brides for him and Thomas, like so many another of their kind, and indeed already had made remarks about the suitability of the heiress of some Fife laird called Lumsdaine for Thomas. Jamie certainly did not want to push him into any abortive marriage plans or wife-seeking on *his* behalf by premature indications of interest in the landless Tina.

Returning after two nights away, and declaring the difficulties of travel conditions, Sir Gilbert had much else to declare. The English commissioners had already arrived at Dalkeith, and Monck was angry that the Scots deputies were not there to greet them. Johnston of Warriston was hastily collecting amenable Remonstrants to attend, indeed the meeting probably had been held by this time, so there was no question of him, Ramsay, going there. Not that Airlie would have advised it anyway. The earl himself, being all but house-bound, certainly could not have gone even if he had desired to; and Crawford, who was back at his own castle of Finavon, was likewise refusing to attend, Kinnoull also. It would be a very small and unrepresentative gathering, which would further displease Monck. So far as they could gauge, about the only earl at Dalkeith would be the Campbell, Loudoun, the Chancellor, although whether there could now be a chancellor for Scotland, with no parliament to chair, was questionable. The convention which was to be called in Edinburgh to confirm the Union and the Protectorate would no doubt be equally unrepresentative.

There was no news from the Highlands, and Lorne, not surprisingly.

There were tidings from London, sad tidings. Sir William Dick was dead, had died in the Tower. Whether it had been by execution or maltreatment was not revealed, but he had been in good enough health at the time of the extraction of the regalia. Jamie grieved for him. He had liked and admired Sir William. He felt for the spirited and unconventional Lady Dick.

On the regalia situation Sir Gilbert had to report that the Master of Gray, having served his six weeks at Dunnottar, was now being relieved by David, son of Sir John Ogilvy of Inverquharity, distant kin of Airlie, as arranged. Which meant that Jamie himself was due to go next, in another six weeks, to replace young Inverquharity.

That word resolved all Jamie's indecisions. It meant that he would be going north for a further six weeks, in early March. He was certainly not going to put off seeing Tina before then, whatever his father thought or his sister advised.

He concocted excellent excuse for going over to Airlie in person now. If and when Monck did send up a force to collect the regalia from Dunnottar, it could well be once the snows had melted and the worst of the flooding was past, that is, probably early April. Which meant that he, Jamie, would almost certainly be there when it might happen. He required the earl's guidance as to what should be done, how he should react and urge the others to react. It would be a sufficiently challenging situation.

Sir Gilbert could not deny that, and raised no objection to his son's visit to Airlie now. Nor could Jean.

Snow, ice or none, he was off the following week, on the first day of February.

12

On his father's advice, Jamie did not take the direct and shortest route to Airlie, over the high ground to Lintrathen and down the Melgam Water, but went south by Alyth and Shanzie, working eastwards, still through foothill country but less high and with the frozen snow less deep. At least there was no difficulty in crossing burns and rivers, all being solid ice and able to bear his garron's weight.

His reception at Airlie was heartening – heartening even though it was in fact critical. That is, from the girls, including Tina. They had expected him back long before this. The travel conditions had not prevented his father from coming. Why not himself? They were disappointed in him. Tina admittedly was the least vocal in this, but she did indicate some reproach.

He had his excuses ready, of course. Conditions at Bamff, the frozen water, the mills having to be converted to horse-power, and the difficulties of transporting meal and fodder, cut timber for fuel buried under snow and having to be dried out, the people as well as the stock having to be looked after. To be sure, much of this applied to Airlie also, although it was set on significantly lower ground. Acceptance was only moderate.

The Earl of Airlie himself did not criticise, but said that he was glad that Jamie had come. He had in fact been going to send and ask him to do so, for this matter of the regalia-guarding was highly important and possibly reaching a vital stage. He had thought much on the situation, and had travel conditions not been so bad would have asked the Lord Gray to come and confer on the subject, since he was so much involved in the project. The big question was whether to leave the regalia at Dunnottar, now that the English knew that it was there, or to remove it secretly elsewhere. Yes, Dunnottar was as secure a

184

place as could be found in all Scotland to hold it; but now that the secret was out, even that castle could be battered into submission by English cannon, he imagined. Cromwell had perfected artillery warfare as no one else had done, and even Borthwick Castle in Lothian, considered impregnable, he had managed to reduce. So it might be wisest to remove the regalia, and hide it somewhere else. There was no stronger hold which would be any better, so it would be a matter of taking it secretly to another place, an unsuspected spot, not necessarily a castle at all. This might be wisest, in the circumstances. Yet it held its dangers also. Someone might give the secret away to the enemy, deliberately, or in gossip, idle talk, or even have the secret wrung out of them by torture. These English could be ruthless, as they had shown all too clearly. And if the regalia was not strongly defended in its new hiding place, it could be captured easily enough.

Jamie admitted that these thoughts had also occurred to him and to his father and brother. They had not come to any firm conclusion, but could think of nowhere that would be proof against possible betrayal, deliberate or through talk. It might be possible to smuggle the items out of the castle unseen, possibly at night; that was not the problem, nor in finding some unlikely hiding place. It was the danger of it becoming spoken of thereafter. The word could well get out and somebody talk. And it was certain that Monck and his lieutenants would not rest, nor be gentle, in their efforts to locate it. Jamie thought of the Keith girls, and how they might be subjected to cruel questioning, but did not elaborate on that. And there was the garrison of forty men and a few women.

Airlie said that, on the way north, Jamie should call in at the Redcastle of Lunan, and seek Gray's views on this vital matter. Meantime, they would be wise to consider the situation assuming that the regalia remained at Dunnottar and an English force did arrive to besiege the castle. The MacGregors' efforts might be successful in some degree; but if he knew Monck, and a force was deterred from making the assault, then he would just send a larger and stronger one, for he was a very determined man.

Jamie had to admit that also. Even Glengyle could not be expected to keep the Gregorach permanently assembled in arms in the Mearns.

So, then, a siege of Dunnottar sooner or later. Cannon battering it into submission. What then? If it came to that, Airlie suggested, there was only the one course to follow. Bundle the regalia up into canvas, or even fish-nets, and lower it by night down the castle cliffs into the sea. It would be safe there.

All but appalled, Jamie stared at the earl. Sink it in the sea! The Honours of Scotland. Was that not unthinkable? The regalia cast into the waves. Better that than in the Tower of London, he was told grimly. The symbols of the nation's sovereignty would at least still be in Scotland.

But the crown! The jewelled crown. And sceptres. And sword of state. On the bottom of the sea. Even if they were not swept away in storm, lost, what would the salt water do to them? Ruin. The end of them.

Not necessarily, Airlie thought. Metals did not always suffer in sea water. Think of iron anchors and chains. The jewels might be at some risk, or their setting, although the pearls came from salt water at Perth. But if some were lost, they could be replaced. And if the sacking or netting cover was heavily weighted, it ought not to be swept away from the bottom in storms.

Jamie still did not like the idea; but the earl declared that even if the regalia was lost thus, it would be better than having it mocked at in English hands.

Agreeing to consult the Lord Gray on this in due course, Jamie took his leave, and went in search of Tina, wondering how to get her alone.

In the event, he did not have to try very hard for, finding the Ogilvy sisters scattered at various tasks around the castle, he learned that Tina had in fact elected to go down to Airlie Mill, apparently to discover whether the miller and his sons had considered harnessing horse-power to turn the great wheel, whether indeed they knew of the procedure which Jamie had described for doing so. This, of course, sent the said expert off hot-foot down to the mill also, nowise suggesting that any of the other girls should accompany him. He was gratified that Tina had heeded and sought to make use of his report so promptly and practically.

There were more mills than one at Airlie, but the castle's own one was situated just below where the Melgam Water joined the River Isla, half a mile to the south. Hastening thither, he found Tina in converse with the elderly miller and two of his sons, considering the mighty but immobilised water-wheel, its blades firmly anchored in ice, she seeking to explain the process Jamie had described in less than detailed fashion.

"Ah, there you are, Jamie," she exclaimed. "I thought it just possible that you might make an appearance. This is Jock Carnegie and his sons Dougie and Tam. I have been telling them about how you are getting over this ice problem up at Bamff. But I am not sure of exactly how you convert to milling by horses. Our friends here would be glad to know, for they have been unable to use this mill for some time, and are having to drive wagons down to another mill two miles and more away, where your Alyth Burn joins the Isla and produces a greater flow, which has not wholly frozen over. This every two days or so, to take the corn there and bring back the meal we all need. That mill still can grind, with much breaking up of ice needed to keep a flow of water."

Jamie greeted the men, who declared that they knew of horse-mills, to be sure, and how they worked, but not how this water-mill could be adapted, as the lady said that it could.

Glad to explain, Jamie said that it was not really difficult so long as they could contrive sufficient space for the horses to work. The process of using the power created by the driven vertical wheel to turn the grinding-stones was effected by a series of large spindles and cogs, at right-angles, as they knew. By detaching two of these, and changing the direction of the angles, to the lesser follower wheel from the first pit-wheel, the drive could be obtained from inside the mill itself – that is, if there was sufficient space for the horse, or horses, to work. If not, and the animals had to work outside, then a great deal more mechanism was required, as they had found in one of their own mills at Bamff, requiring outside gearing. The men understood these directions, even if Tina did not, rather lost in talk of overshot, vertical, pit and follower wheels, heights of fall, great cogs and lesser, and the like. They all went round looking at the various parts and assessing. But, as Jamie had said, the vital factor was space for the horses to work. But Carnegie decided that, with much clearing of piles and sacks of unground oats and various impedimenta, they ought to be able to clear enough room for one horse to work, turning a windlass in continuing circles, linked to the existing gearing. They could effect that. But there just was insufficient room for two beasts to work. Jamie agreed, but said that even one would be enough to produce a fair amount of power; better than having to go miles over snow and ice to get the meal elsewhere. Training the garrons to do the necessary circling movement, hour after hour, was another problem, but with patience it could be achieved. The alternative, horses outside, transmitting the power by rotating long poles and cogs at different angles, would be much more difficult, although easier on the horses.

Leaving the millers suitably impressed and sending off to consult carpenters needed to fashion the gear, the pair from the castle left them to it.

Jamie was now concerned that they did not return to the said castle forthwith. These were not ideal conditions for walking, but he suggested at least a short stroll, nevertheless, and in the opposite direction. The young woman, well wrapped up against the cold, voiced no objection; and when, quite quickly, she slithered on a glassy stretch of ice, he protectively took her arm and hung on to it thereafter, for safety's sake.

They walked thus for a while, in silence, Jamie wondering how best to begin what he had come to say.

"It was good that you thought to come and tell these millers," he declared at length. "Good that you, that we, could help here, perhaps. But good also that this way we could see each other. Alone, I mean. That has always been my difficulty, Tina – to see you alone."

"Is that so? And you have wanted to do so? Why, Jamie?"

"Because – to tell you. Tell you that I love you. Love you."

"But you have told me that already."

"Yes. But only once, I think. And, and you made but little . . . comment!" He gripped her arm the tighter. "I wanted you to know. Know that this is important to me, very important. *All* important."

"Is it? Yet it has not brought you to Airlie for long, Jamie!"

"No-o-o." How to explain sisterly advice? "I have had much to see to." He knew that sounded feeble indeed. "And, and I was not sure that you wanted me to come. Sufficiently."

"Yet the last words I spoke to you were to come back. And soon."

"Yes. But that could have been but . . . civility." He paused. Was that perhaps an uncivil thing to say? "You are always kind, and that could have been just a small kindness. I could not be sure. I have debated it long, too long perhaps."

"Debated just what, Jamie?"

"Debated whether you were just being kindly, civil. Whether my coming back soon meant more than that to you. Whether *I* mean much to you, Tina?"

"To be sure you do, Jamie. Would I be walking here with you if you did not?"

"But . . . yes, that is good. But, sufficiently? For me to hope? Hope that you might come to return my love?"

She achieved a small laugh there. "Surely you do not really wish it returned to you? This love of yours, Jamie? I would have thought that you would wish me to keep it!"

"Will you? Will you keep it, then? My love." He was not counting the number of times he had said the word, as Jean had advised. "And my hope that you may come to find some such love for me also?"

"I think that you may hope, yes."

He halted then, there beside the frozen river, and since he was holding her, she had to halt also. He pulled her round to face him, urgently.

189

"Tina, I want more than hope. I have been hoping for long. Too long. Could you love me? As I love you?"

"Jamie, there is love and love. There is liking, fondness, affection, caring. And there is the other that men call passion. Which do you seek from me? And what do you have for me, yourself?"

"All!" he said. "All!" And suddenly he was tired of words, all this exchange of words, whatever Jean had counselled as to wooing. That was not what he wanted. He threw both arms around her, pulled her strongly to him, and bent to kiss her, masterfully, almost fiercely. And kissing, although her upturned face was cold, her lips were warm, and not tightly closed.

They stood there, in the snow, and some part of the man's mind recognised that her arms were around him now also. The fierceness of his kissing, although that continued, changed and mellowed and deepened – and was undoubtedly returned.

Time stood still, as they held each other, wordless now at last.

How long they stood there, beside a cataract of ice's strange beauty, they were not concerned to know. But presently the more languorous lips drew apart and, gazing deep into each other's eyes, they turned by mutual consent and started to walk back whence they had come, holding hands but still unspeaking. Every few paces the man half turned to look at his companion, and smiled, and she nodded her lovely head in return.

They said few words indeed on that walk back to the castle, words seeming now to have become almost superfluous. Jamie, for one, felt nothing of the bitter cold, the joyous warmth within him all that he was aware of, his heart singing however inactive his lips now. Tina squeezed his hand frequently.

In the courtyard, at the keep door with its iron yett and shot-holes, they paused, to face each other.

"The world has changed," he said simply.

She nodded.

"Yet you have not said that you love me!"

190

"I love you," she said then, equally simply.

And hand in hand they entered the building together.

They made no announcement to the Ogilvy family, but unless the girls at least were very heedless and unobservant, they could not have been unaware of some new closeness and understanding between these two. That evening, by the lesser hall fire, passed normally enough, with music and some storytelling, the chatter easy except when, after the earl's retiral to bed, it inevitably came round to the regalia situation and Jamie's role at Dunnottar, when Tina's features became less relaxed, the possibility of siege and warfare not to be avoided, and concern evident. Oddly enough, this was somewhat dispelled by the girls' wonderings about the Marischal's daughters, and whether they would remain in their home in these circumstances, and Marion's roguish remark that Mary Keith might be less adventurously inclined – this with a significant glance at Tina. That young woman smiled, and said that the Keith girls, if still at Dunnottar, being, she understood, women of spirit, might well be stimulated to further exploits. Jamie waved a dismissive hand.

When yawns told their own story and a move was made bedwards, some indication of family perception was evidenced in that none of the sisters, although they all kissed Jamie goodnight, actually escorted him to his bedroom door, only Tina doing that. There, beside the steaming pail of water, she paused.

"This has been a notable day, Jamie," she said. "For us. A day to remember, no?"

The man could not prevent himself from wishing it to be a night to remember also, but could and did restrain himself from saying so. "To my joy," he declared. "My great joy. And, and gratitude. You have made me a happy man, Tina."

"I deserve no thanks. But perhaps you are as grateful to whoever controls our destinies. Were we destined for each other, Jamie?"

"I do not know. All I know is that I love you beyond all words that I can speak. Words can say so little sometimes."

"Your words have been . . . very acceptable! In the end."
She produced her little laugh. "If . . . belated!"

"Yes. We do not need words now, do we!" And he drew her
to him.

"Oh yes, we do. Women need words of love. As well as
other . . . tokens! I like . . ." She got no further, with her
lips sealed by his.

They stood, he hungrily, she yieldingly, for a while, his
hands beginning to stray. She did not stop this, but presently
she used her own hands to push him gently from her.

"I know . . . what you would wish . . . . here and now!" she
got out, a little breathlessly. "I do not say that . . . I have not
some . . . sympathy! But your water will be getting cold, here!
As will mine, above. Perhaps as well, to cool ardour a little!
Dear Jamie, have patience. And you, *we*, can dream tonight,
at least! Sweet dreaming, my dear."

Reluctantly he let her go, with a last lingering kiss, and
watched as she disappeared up the lamp-lit winding turnpike
stair. She was right, of course, right. But . . . !

Jamie Ramsay lay long awake thereafter, thinking, imagin-
ing, savouring. But when he awoke in the morning, he did not
remember dreaming at all.

After breakfast, since it would not take him all day to ride back
to Bamff, even in these conditions, Jamie decided to go down
Airlie Den to the mill again, and see whether any progress
had been made on the suggested alterations. Needless to say,
he anticipated that Tina would go with him. Unfortunately
David also expressed an interest in this subject and decided
to accompany them; and when his sisters heard, they all
came. They had all been restricted as to exercise these icy
weeks. So it was quite a party which descended upon the
Carnegies and two carpenters from the village whom they
had enrolled, and who were busy with saws, adzes, axes
and other tools – and who became distinctly embarrassed
to find themselves watched at their labours by the bevvy of
ladies from the castle. However, Jamie's expertise was of help
to them, indeed to the extent of them having to reject some part

of what they had constructed, in that certain cog-spokes were too widely spaced for horse – as distinct from water-power, and replacement required; although whether this made the visitors the more popular was questionable, however interested the workmen were in the theory of it all.

Back at the castle thereafter there was time only for a hasty send-off meal if Jamie was to get home before darkening. There was no sense in any of the Ogilvys escorting him into the deeper snowdrifts and ice-sheets of the higher ground, but David and Tina did declare that they would see him some little way on his difficult road, and he did not protest too hard that this was unnecessary.

It was David's mount, a well-bred riding horse rather than any garron, which demonstrated its unsuitability for these conditions quite soon by slithering and floundering and thus bringing the escorting to an early finish. Jamie would have wished that David would have turned back alone, then, and Tina, more sensibly mounted, continue at least a little further, and out of sight, but could hardly say so.

It was farewell then, but the visitor did take the opportunity to make a suggestion which had been on his mind for a while. It was David to whom he put it.

"Do you think that, if the weather improves sufficiently and the snows lift, you and Tina, with perhaps one or two of your sisters, could be prevailed upon to come to Bamff for a short visit, David?" he asked carefully. "I will have most of a month before I have to leave for Dunnottar, and it would be good to return a little of the hospitality I have received at Airlie?" Although he addressed David, he looked at Tina.

They both agreed that that would be a pleasure, if it proved to be possible as to weather. But, David asked, with an eyebrow lifted at his friend, whether they needed to bring the other girls? So he was not wholly lacking in percipience.

At least that allowed Jamie to rein his garron close to Tina's and to kiss her again, however briefly.

"Come if you can," he urged her. "Else it will be months before I see you again."

"I . . . we will, if we are able," she reassured. "But, Jamie, if we cannot, then take good care of yourself, up there at Dunnottar. I wish, I wish that you did not have to go. If the English do assail that castle, you could be in great danger. Cannon-fire. Fighting. Possible hurt, possible capture. Why must it be *you* who goes, again?"

"I have been concerned with the Honours all along," he pointed out. "It is my duty. But they may not come while I am there. They may well delay, with all this hard weather. The roads, for cavalry and oxen, will be slow in clearing, with much flooding once the snows melt."

She gripped his arm. "Come back to us safely – if I do not see you before then. You are precious now, see you! Precious!"

"That sends me away joyous!" he said thickly. And reining his beast round quickly, he was off, before emotions took over too evidently. It was some time before he steeled himself to look back and wave.

13

That winter was the hardest and longest in living memory. By March the snow still held the land in its grip; and when Jamie set out northwards for the Mearns conditions were little if any improved – and there had been no visit from Tina and David. He imagined that the girl would have essayed it, if he knew her and her spirit; but David might have been less eager; or it might have been his father, Tina's uncle and guardian, forbidding the hazardous journey. As responsible for the welfare of his brother's daughter, it was quite possible that he would not see Jamie Ramsay, a landless second son, however ancient and distinguished his ancestry, as a suitable suitor and match for Tina, and consider it his duty to find her a better-endowed and more worthy husband. This dire notion was apt to come between that young man and his sleep on occasion, for marriage of course was now his urgent aim. He would be of twenty years in July. Airlie had four daughters of his own to find husbands for, to be sure . . .

With more instructions regarding care to be taken and behaviour recommended from the family, he left Bamff early in March, snowflakes still falling. He would have chosen to go via Airlie, although that was scarcely on his way, but his father insisted that his best route, in the circumstances, was south by Alyth and into Strathmore at Meigle, then east by Glamis to Forfar, and so, avoiding Brechin, to the coast at Montrose – this to avoid the surely difficult crossings of the many rivers flowing down from the Angus glens, especially the large ones of Isla, Clova, Prosen, Wastwater and Esk. He would have to cross Isla at Crathies, just before Meigle, but there was a good bridge there. The rivers would be in a bad state, all but unfordable. The difficulties of the journey would be major, without unnecessary complications.

That first day certainly proved Sir Gilbert's point, for Jamie got only as far as the township of Meigle, a bare mile beyond the bridge over the Isla, and a mere eight miles from Bamff. The ground had sunk here to the almost level floor of great Strathmore, little more than one hundred feet above sea-level, however distant the sea, from nearer one thousand at Bamff, and the effect was a blanketing of snow, all but level for mile upon mile, so deep as to hide all roads and tracks, walls, hedges and obstacles completely and, what was worse, small watercourses and their dipping channels. So riding was a matter of very slowly seeking to pick a way in the right direction at a walking pace, and slow walking at that. The ice itself was not so thick at this level, but that was almost more dangerous, for it meant that beneath the snow-cover the garron's weight might break frozen flooding below and cause a collapse. Jamie could have got somewhat further, for the days were lengthening now; but these were no conditions to spend nights in sheds and barns, much less in the open air, and there was a change-house at Meigle, and no other such eastwards before Eassie, six miles. At least there were no problems as to accommodation, for there were just no travellers to compete with at the inn, and his arrival greeted almost with astonishment.

Next day it was a similar round-about and probing progress, mere guesswork as to where the road lay much of the way, and cold riding indeed. Jamie had more or less to let his sturdy and wise-seeming garron find its own best routes, and a great fellow-feeling developed between man and horse. Passing Eassie's ale-house, both obtained much-needed sustenance at midday; and by dusk reached Glamis, ten miles, a sizeable village where there was a choice of hostelries. He did not risk calling at the great castle of the Lyon family, now Earls of Kinghorne, nearby, being unsure of the allegiances of the present lord, since he was, Jamie understood, married to a sister of one of the Covenant generals.

On down Strathmore the following day six miles brought

him to Forfar, the county town of Angus. And here the conditions changed somewhat, for Jamie had been advised by his father to move out of the great strath proper at this point and head eastwards, by the ancient priory of Restenneth and the lochs of Fithie, Rescobie and Balgavies, to Guthrie, in a subsidiary vale, making for the sea by following the Lunan Water. Sir Gilbert had believed that the conditions would be considerably less difficult the nearer the coast he got, where snow and ice were usually less severe. He in fact got as far as Guthrie that night, a fourteen-mile day, on which he congratulated himself and his mount.

Still eastwards thereafter he went on, by Frioch, to follow the frozen Lunan to Inverkeilor. And as he neared Lunan Bay at last, he was able to see, as foretold, that snow and ice here had less of a grip, indeed the Lunan had actually flowing water at its centre, the first he had seen for long, however little of it there was in the circumstances. After the prevailing whiteness everywhere, it was a change indeed to see the level plain of the sea, in movement, however grey and sullen it looked.

At Redcastle, the Lord Gray welcomed him, expressing surprise to see him in such conditions. He had heard that travel was all but impossible inland, and all his news had come by boat, the fishing-craft from the havens of this coastline able to operate normally. However, this state of affairs would at least delay Monck's projected three-pronged assaults northwards.

Jamie, assuming that the other was referring to the Dunnottar situation, expressed wonder and question as to it possibly being three-pronged, only to discover that Gray was speaking of a quite different operation. It seemed that he had learned something which Airlie had not been told, at least when Jamie had last seen him, namely that Monck was sending three different forces northwards to counter any Highland rising against his occupation regime. Gray even had the names of the commanders – how he got this information he did not disclose – with a General Dean to lead the main force north from Perth, making for Inverness; a Colonel Lilburn heading for Lochaber; and a Colonel Overton actually sailing from Ayr, allegedly to Kintyre and the west Highland coast, and – here was the key to it all – taking the Marquis of Argyll with him in order to persuade his son and his Campbells to abandon the projected rising of the clans. Presumably that crooked carle, MacCailean Mor, had agreed to co-operate in return for his release from Edinburgh Castle.

Astonished and concerned, Jamie could not but know a grudging admiration for Monck's initiative and strategies. But at least these weather conditions would make any Highland advances by land impossible, although the sea foray, presumably with smaller numbers, could well be feasible. How would Lorne react to that, with his own father and chief of the great clan against him?

Gray did not know, but judged that it all would put back the project of any Highland rising very considerably. These English knew what they were at; and were always able to exploit the Scots' weaknesses and divisions.

Jamie wondered whether it could all affect his MacGregor project? He thought not, probably. He told Gray of this, and that David, Lord Ogilvy, had agreed to hasten over to Glengyle to inform that chieftain just as soon as word was received of any move being made towards Dunnottar. The other sounded doubtful as to any Gregorach success in halting seasoned Roundhead cavalry and their cannon. But he agreed that the state of the roads and travel difficulties were bound to put off Monck's various expeditions for some considerable time.

Incidentally, he informed that his nephew, and heir to the title, had quite enjoyed his spell at Dunnottar and had found much to praise in the Keith daughters, especially the eldest. Jamie reserved comment.

In the morning he set off northwards on the last lap of his journey, about twenty-five miles. He hoped to cover this in one day, in this improved travelling.

Arrival at Dunnottar itself, all but clear of snow, was sufficiently rewarding, Jamie being greeted like some long-lost brother, although as far as the Lady Mary was concerned, his reception was scarcely brotherly. They all had been awaiting his coming for days, they said. It was so good to see him. Why he seemed to be so popular that young man did not know, but he could not deny a certain satisfaction. The man he was replacing, the other David Ogilvy of Inverquharity, might possibly have been entitled to feel a little nettled at all this display of esteem for his successor, even though he himself appeared to be on good terms with the castle's occupants.

There proved to be a new denizen of the rock-top fortalice, or at least new to Jamie. This was Sir John Keith of Inverurie and Kintore, youngest brother of the Earl Marischal and the girls' uncle, who was temporarily acting replacement for Ogilvie of Barras, the castle's keeper, who seemed to have a variety of duties and responsibilities elsewhere. Jamie had met Sir *James* Keith of Benholm, the other brother. He preferred this one, a cheerful and quite lively character, much younger than the earl, who was clearly on excellent terms with his nieces and with his brother James's wife, the Lady Margaret Hay.

Jamie had arrived just in time for the evening meal, which proved to be hearty in more than the provender, high spirits prevailing. For a stronghold under threat of enemy action, the atmosphere seemed notably carefree. Not that the new arrival would have expected or wished for gloom and apprehension; but he wondered whether they were all taking the situation sufficiently seriously. Long-delayed English action might be leading to a possibly dangerous assumption that there was nothing to fear?

Another aspect of that first meal also raised some little concern in Jamie. He found Mary sitting beside him, and more than once he felt her hand reach out to press his thigh. So, whatever alternative interest she might have found in his various substitutes, she had evidently not forgotten their earlier amities, which could now present him with problems.

He, of course, explained to them all the situation prevailing, as far as he knew it, with the English occupation, Monck's efficiency and ruthlessness, the Highland hoped-for rising and threats thereto, and his own efforts to involve the MacGregors in countering any assault on Dunnottar. He had general attention, but got the impression that these

Keiths were less convinced than he was of the dangers of attack, both on account of doubts as to whether the English were sufficiently interested to mount an expedition, and their belief in the impregnability of their castle. He did not want to seem alarmist, but thought this attitude unwise. But perhaps he himself was over-fearful? Lord Gray had not thought so, at any rate, and he was much more aware of the true state of affairs than were these good folk skied in their eagle's nest of a fortress.

More personal concerns reasserted themselves when, after an almost boisterous evening of singing and Highland dancing in the great hall, with some competition among these sisters to have Jamie as partner, Mary made it clear that she alone was going to take the newcomer to the bedchamber reserved for him in that seaward-facing tower on the cliff edge. Goodnight kisses all round had him involuntarily comparing these four sisters with the four Ogilvy ones, with their similarities and their differences; and then he was led off, Mary's arm linked in his.

Deliberately, as they crossed to the tower, he asked how she had got on with the succession of other regalia guardians, brother Thomas, the Master of Gray, and this David Ogilvy, as indication that he looked on her affectionate gestures as not likely to be unique to himself.

She trilled a laugh. "Oh, they have all been good company," she asserted. "But none so good as yourself, Jamie. Your brother Thomas was kind, but he is very serious, is he not? So fond of books and papers. Will Gray was jaunty but a shade raw, if you understand me! And David Ogilvy plods somewhat, and prefers Elizabeth, I judge. You please me best!" And she squeezed his arm again against her rounded person.

"M'mm. I thank you. But you show me too much favour. I mean, you are too kind, too generous . . ."

They were climbing the tower stair by now, and came to the landing which led to Jamie's room. The girl opened the door.

"We must see that all is in order," she declared, entering.

He cleared his throat as he followed her in. "I have to

say something, to tell you, Mary, that Tina Ogilvy and myself, Christian Ogilvy, are now promised to each other. Not betrothed yet, but promised. I told you of her before, you will mind. So . . ."

She turned, in the lamplight. "I have not forgotten," she said. "But we are still friends, are we not?"

"Friends, yes. To be sure. Only . . ."

"Only you, or we, must not go too far in our friendship? Is that it?"

"Well, yes. That would be . . . unsuitable. Wrong, Mary."

"Your Tina is a fortunate woman! But . . . she would not begrudge me a little fondness?"

"No. No, I think not. Only – so long as you understand."

"Understand that I must be very modest? I fear that I am not a very modest creature, Jamie! Do you wish that I was?"

"It is difficult," he admitted. "I enjoy our friendship. But must keep it within bounds. You see, I love Tina Ogilvy."

"Love! Oh, yes, love. And you do not love me?"

"I am fond of you, yes. But my heart is with Tina, you see."

"There are shades of love, I think. But I will not forget. And must be content with your modest tokens, yes?" She gave a little laugh and came to fling her arms around him and give him a not particularly modest kiss. "Goodnight, then, Tina's lover! I will only console you, for her absence, in great moderation!" And with that she was gone to her chamber directly above.

Jamie rubbed his chin. Had he got away with that remarkably successfully? Or not? He would undoubtedly discover in due course. And he was here for weeks.

He discovered also that the castle's denizens, not wishing to remain cooped up like fowl on their rock-summit, day in, day out, were in the circumstances doing a lot of sea-fishing from boats. The weather, however cold, had not been stormy on the whole, and the sea in consequence fairly calm, making the fishing practicable and not unpleasurable, so long as the fishers were well wrapped up. And it was not entirely a matter of the sport, a pastime. With the Mearns hills frozen and all roads and tracks inland blocked, fresh beef and mutton, and meal also, were in short supply, so that fish was a very necessary supplement to the diet. Fortunately these waters abounded in a variety of fish, flounders and rock-cod inshore, haddock, whiting and herring further out. The Keiths and their guests held competitions, apparently, as to which boat could make the best catch, much rivalry engendered.

That very next day Jamie became involved. The three men were each allotted a boat, down at the fishing haven – young Inverquharity was putting off his departure until the morrow – each with two female companions. Jamie found himself, needless to say, with Mary; also her aunt, the Lady Margaret, a pleasant, quietly competent person who seemed to find much gentle amusement in the antics of her nieces. Mary decided that they should go for flounders this day, or flukies as the locals called them, declaring that she knew an excellent place to find them in large numbers, much better than the spot below the castle cliff itself where she had taught Jamie the art of catching them. This was a sort of inlet with a sandy floor, called Thornyhive Bay, over a mile to the south, which also had the advantage of the semicircle of cliffs sheltering them from the cold south-west winds, even though these were not strong, her aunt commending that decision, for sitting still in an open boat could be a chilly business.

The fisherfolk, men and women, helping them to push out the boats, with much challenge and raillery, the three trios rowed off in their different directions. Mary and Jamie sat side by side on the central thwart with an oar each, as they had done on the lobster-fishing, which ensured maximum physical contact and a pleasing mutual motion, the Lady Margaret in the stern eyeing them amusedly. They steered southwards around the castle rock and on along the cliff-foots beyond. Jamie asked whether they were heading for the Fowlsheugh area but was told they were not going so far. There was another good patch for flounders further on in that vicinity; but the sooner that they got started with the fishing, the larger their catch would be apt to be, said feminine logic. The other two boats would have to row considerably further out to sea if they were after haddock and herring, and this would give themselves the advantage.

It fell to be explained that flatfish preferred a sandy bottom and not too deep water; and this coastline being preponderantly rock-bound and cliff-girt, large sandy patches and comparative shallows were at a minimum. This Thornyhive that they were making for was the largest of these and the most hopeful.

The Lady Margaret, less competitive than Mary, suggested that if they got tired of fishing, or too chilled, they might take their visitor to see the Ladies' Gallery, a most notable feature of this coast, a little further south, the source of many a legend, this being a passage through the cliffs, negotiable by boat, and in which the echoes were extraordinary. But her niece was concerned to win the day with their catch; another day perhaps.

When the horseshoe-shaped little bay probing into the cliffs informed them that they were approximately over the required sandy area, a weighted stone on a rope was lowered to anchor them, and the messy business of baiting hooks with lug-worms commenced, these gathered for them by the fisherfolk. Jamie was again surprised that delicate and ladylike fingers were prepared to accept the staining of the sandy brown fluid coming out of the punctured bait.

For this boat-fishing, they used little spars, each with three hooks on a foot of gut, to be let down by each fisher, weighted with a nugget of lead, and when this touched bottom, the line to be raised that foot so that the worms were just touching the sand, Jamie was reminded. So, already cold fingers stained brown, he lowered his spar over the side hopefully, unwinding his line from its wooden frame and wondering how he would know when it touched bottom, in the sway of boat and water. Actually he felt the dunt quite clearly. But as he was raising it, almost immediately there was a further slight bumping over his forefinger, and he assumed that he had not raised it high enough, but the tugging continued. Mary told him to draw up at once. Wet line landing in a tangle, he pulled – and was surprised and delighted to see a fair-sized curling and flapping flatfish, brown on one side, white on the other, hanging from one of the hooks, its weight suddenly evident as it came out of the water. He had never expected such instant success. Mary declared that he had been very lucky, for her own and her aunt's lines remained untouched. She also indicated that one of his other hooks was now without its bait; so his line must have landed almost on top of a pair of flukies, and one had managed to suck off the lug-worm at once, without being hooked.

Much pleased with himself, Jamie rebaited the two hooks, and was left with a flapping creature on the floorboards at his feet. Not quite sure of the procedure now, he looked at Mary, who picked up the fish by its tail and banged its head sharply on her oar-shaft and handed it back to its catcher. Thus taught, the young man lowered his gear over the side again, disentangling his line. Mary, fishing from the other side of the boat, told him to move a little nearer to the bows with the said line, or the sea's movement might cause his tackle to catch on hers.

Lady Margaret was next to get a bite, and drew up a fish, smaller than Jamie's. However, his condescending congratulations were scarcely in order, for quite quickly she got another catch, of a size equal to his own; and then Mary emphasised the situation by collecting a larger one than either.

Thereafter, with nothing seeming to happen to his line for some considerable time, and the women both landing fish, Jamie became somewhat deflated. Mary suggested that he drew up again, and doing so it was to find the bait gone from all three hooks. He was informed that probably he had not threaded the worms on sufficiently securely, enabling the flounders to suck them off easily. A further demonstration of twisting the worms round the hooks, like knitting as was explained, left him educated without being edified.

He did rather better after that, but still not so well as his two companions, which made him wonder whether his fingers were less sensitive to the slight tugging which indicated nibbling fish. And on another occasion, drawing up a flounder, two hooks were unbaited again. This was a sport for experts it seemed.

After a couple of hours of this, and catches becoming infrequent, Mary decided to move on to another area, again where cliffs receded somewhat. Jamie was quite glad of the exercise of rowing to warm him up, surprised that he seemed to be feeling the chill more than the women did. They wondered how the other boats were faring. They could see one of them, far out.

Their second pitch was not so profitable as the first, but they did win a few more fish before, the cold becoming just too much, they decided to call it a day. They were running out of lug-worms, anyway. Lady Mary said that they should have thought to bring along a flask of whisky, to help warm them; she was sure that her brother-in-law would not have omitted such precaution, he having a taste that way anyhow.

Counting their catch, they found that they had twenty-three flounders, and one crab which had somehow got itself hooked, a reasonable haul they all agreed.

Back at the haven, they found that they were the first boat home. Elizabeth, Joan and Ogilvy's craft came in as they were handing over half of their flounder catch to the fisherfolk, apparently a normal procedure. This trio declared that they had had good luck – that is, until they heard the flounder total, which was almost double their own, although they claimed theirs would weigh as much, herring, whiting and haddock. They said that they had passed Sir James's boat on their way in, and its occupants had been grumbling about poor sport. It looked as though Mary's team had won the day.

Later, after a meal consisting largely of fish, the more satisfying in that it was self-provided, the evening was spent more sleepily than the previous one, round a well-doing fire, the warmth and their full stomachs, after the cold fishing, seeming to make them mildly soporific. But there was nothing soporific about Mary Keith's goodnight at Jamie's bedroom door eventually, as she clung to him and all but shook him into some retaliatory gestures, a frank young woman indeed. She called back, as she mounted the further stairway, that it was a pity that she was not permitted to teach him more than flounder-catching.

Some time that night Jamie was awakened by the noise of a gale and driving rain battering the glass and wooden shuttering of his window, something no one in Scotland had heard for long.

In the morning, it was still blowing wind and pouring rain, but the air warmer than they had felt it for months. The thaw had come at last, in late March.

For the next four days the wet, warm and blowy weather did not let up, and life in Dunnottar Castle was restricted to indoor activities, apt to be galling for young people, Lady Margaret being the least concerned. Ogilvy, of course, had to postpone his departure, for these conditions would make travel all but impossible, with snow and ice melting and flooding everywhere. He did not appear to be greatly upset by this, finding Elizabeth's company ample compensation. For his part, Jamie recognised that had he been fancy free, he and Mary could have reached quite advanced stages in their relationship. That they did not she could not hide her regret, even though she most evidently did hold herself back; and even the man knew some physical frustration, however much he knew that he ought not to, with so much proximity and time on their hands.

The weather remaining mild and windy even when the rain ceased, another preoccupation was seldom far from Jamie's mind: the English reaction to changed conditions. Given some time for the floods to drain away, the rivers to sink and fords become passable, the occupying forces would be on the march, up to the Highlands and possibly here to the Mearns. What had been all along at the back of his mind now came to the front. Preparations. They ought to be making preparations for that eventuality. But what?

He held frequent discussions with Sir James and Ogilvy on the subject, finding them less concerned than he was, convinced that Dunnottar's strength and position would be adequate against any attack. Large numbers of men would make no difference. And cannon, Jamie put to them? What of cannon-fire, Roundhead artillery? Where would they base these, he was asked? There was no high ground near enough to the rock-top fortalice to allow effective cannon-fire; and based down at shore-level as near as they could get, the artillery would have to shoot up at such a steep angle as to be quite ineffective at battering down the thick walling.

Jamie was not convinced. Cromwell had perfected cannonry to a great degree, the secret of many of his victories, range much increased. And there was another thought which had occurred to him, when they were out fishing: boats. Even though Monck could probably not find sufficient ships to come and assail Dunnottar by sea, especially with this Ayr–Kintyre army to transport to the Highlands, could the English perhaps take boats from the many fishing havens along this coast, not small craft like their own rowing-boats but sea-fishing vessels, and base their artillery thereon? That way they could overcome the steepness of the angle of fire, and with long-range pieces could possibly demolish the castle's defences.

The others had to admit this danger, but pointed out that no firing from the sea could reach and damage the series of fortifications and gatehouses in the ravine, land-facing, which led up to the fortress, the only access. Men, therefore, however many, still would not be able to get up.

That was true. But siege – what of that? If Dunnottar was besieged, cannon or none, for how long could it hold out?

There could be no clear answer to that. It would depend on the provisioning, would it not? And the numbers of mouths to feed. They had unending water supply from the well. It would be a matter of laying in stocks of food, large stocks.

This was agreed. They had an ice-house in the castle, dug out like a small cave, and it would keep preserved a certain amount of meat and fish. But not enough to sustain them for very long. The problem would be, in this milder weather, to prevent the food from going bad. So there was no point in starting to stock up at this stage, except for salted provision, which would keep more or less indefinitely. Would they get any warning of an enemy approach? To give them a chance to bring in supplies?

Jamie said that Lord Gray had told him that if he could gain any word of an English advance to the Mearns he would send a message, probably by boat. They must hope that this came about, and that they were given sufficient time to collect ample sustenance.

George Ogilvie of Barras arrived at the castle on the same day that young Inverquharity took his departure, the coastal roads now being passable for a determined horseman. The others lost no time in consulting him, and found him concerned and practical as to the defensive situation, agreeing with most of Jamie's points and contentions. Although he had been much absent from the castle, he had not abandoned his responsibilities to the Earl Marischal as keeper thereof, apparently. He had sent urgent messages to parliamentary and Kirk leaders suggesting that, now that the English knew the whereabouts of the regalia, it should be removed to some new and secret hiding place; and if not, that the defences of Dunnottar should be strengthened, best by a protective force being sent up to guard the castle area; but he had had no response. He had thought about the problems of provisioning if they were to be besieged, and had come to the conclusion that if this happened it would be sensible to reduce the garrison of the fortress itself; with the fewer mouths to feed the longer they could hold out and the more chance of the attackers giving up the attempt. So long as they had sufficient men to man the various gatehouses, no large company actually within the castle would be necessary, since the enemy could not get into it save through these all but impassable portals. A force camped around Dunnottar would be advantageous, but not inside. The cannon situation did worry him, but he did not see what could be done about it. He wished that he knew more about artillery and the ranges of the most modern weapons; so much would depend on that. If the guns could be placed on the top of the hill opposite the castle, and their shot still reach the defensive walls and gatehouses in the approach ravine, then they were in trouble indeed. How far was it across the yawning gap? More than quarter of a mile – nearer a half? Surely that was beyond the range of even Cromwell's famed cannon?

So the priorities, meantime, were to lay in all supplies possible of salted meats and fish, also meal, honey and other foods which would keep, and to make plans for other and more perishable provisions to be available at short notice nearby, if required. Also to strengthen defences as much as was possible, ensure that the fishing community were warned that their lives might well be troubled by the English; indeed that they ought to be ready to move away to neighbouring havens, with their boats, if necessary, upset as this would be, but better than enemy occupation and possible mishandling. Finally, to reduce the garrison of the castle as much as was feasible. Most of the men came from Stonehaven, so they would not be too greatly inconvenienced.

Oddly enough, in this last respect, Barras was going to add to their numbers by one, for it seemed that his wife Janet was determined not to be parted from him for what might prove to be quite a lengthy period – this attitude possibly being one of the reasons for his frequent absences from his duties at the castle. She had decided to join them, siege or none. She would be arriving in a day or two.

The days which followed were uneventful in major happenings but busy enough. The weather redeemed itself, producing mild spring-like conditions as April progressed, which of course had its disadvantages also, in that it would make travel for armed forces more possible. But it did allow fishing.

During this period Jamie's relationship with Mary Keith settled into an acceptable mould – acceptable to the man at least. They enjoyed each other's company and interests, physical contact being frequent but kept within bounds. Sometimes the goodnights on the stairway landing were somewhat prolonged, but Mary now accepted that Jamie had to be loyal to Tina, and did not tempt him too far, although clearly she found this restraint taxing. They were as good friends as a warm-blooded young man and young woman could be without allowing nature's impulses to have their fuller expression.

When Janet Ogilvie arrived from Barras, she proved to be a handsome and obviously strong-minded creature, indeed more positive and much more voluble than was her husband, but friendly and good company. She was already a friend of the Lady Margaret's, and soon was on good terms with Sir John and Jamie. And accompanying her, although not to stay, came Christian Grainger, the minister's wife from Kinneff, evidently a close associate of Janet's, plus a tirewoman to help with the female baggage from Barras. It seemed a strange development for a fortress under threat of attack. But it was to be noted that there was no suggestion that any of the womenfolk should leave Dunnottar in the circumstances, even though Lady Margaret could easily have taken her nieces to the safety of Benholm Castle, her own home, not far away.

Before Christian Grainger departed for Kinneff again, she and Janet had to see the cause of all the upheaval, the Honours of Scotland, in the little chapel of the castle, which, when unwrapped from their protective covering, held the group all but in awe, both over the beauty of what they saw in the glowing jewels and in the significance of it all, the drama and history behind it, and what it meant to their nation.

Janet Ogilvie settled in quickly, becoming a popular member of the household. She went fishing with them and took part in all activities; also proved to be a notable singer and entertainer for their evenings at the fireside. It was one day with her in the boat with Mary and himself that Jamie saw another craft sailing up from southwards, and not just a fishing-boat, larger. There was something about it which was familiar, and he realised that it was almost certainly Lord Gray's personal vessel, in which they had transported the regalia. Was this the promised warning? Telling his companions, he waved, standing up. But the ship was fully a quarter-mile seaward, and passed on. Watching it, they saw it presently turn in towards Dunnottar haven. That was enough for the fishers. They drew in their lines and got out the oars.

They found Gray's vessel moored at the boat-strand, and, with their catch, hastened up past all the gatehouses and fortifications to the castle. There they discovered the skipper of the craft with Barras and Sir John. He brought the dreaded news from Gray. How that lord got his tidings was not disclosed, but of course he owned Broughty Castle near Dundee as well as other properties thereabouts, and would have no lack of resident informants. An English force had set out from that city for the Mearns two days before, seven hundred men and four large cannon. He even knew the names of the commanders, General Lambert and a Major-General Morgan. They were coming for the regalia.

His hearers eyed each other. How long had they got? Two days when Gray got the news, three days now. And say seventy-five miles to cover. Roads still difficult, flooding receding but leaving much soft ground, rivers still running high for fording. The heavy cavalry could be here in another day or so. But the artillery? Would Lambert and his troopers leave the ox-drawn cannon to come on ahead? Or would they stay with the guns, slow as they would be? All four men thought that they would stay. Cannon were precious, and the English would not be likely to take the risk of them falling into enemy hands. How many miles a day would the oxen cover, in these conditions? Slow-moving creatures anyway, and with the heavy loads to drag, cannonballs as well as cannon. Eight miles? No more than ten, at any rate. Seven days, say, at best. So, they had perhaps three days to prepare, to get in the stocks of fresh meat and other provisions, three very busy days. And then . . .

Jamie wondered whether Airlie had got the information as speedily, from his own sources in Dundee, and Lord Ogilvy sped to the Trossachs and Glen Gyle? Would the Gregorach be on their way?

While the men were occupied in ensuring the maximum meat collection and delivery, Janet Ogilvie suggested that James and Christian Grainger, down at Kinneff, should be informed, so that, when the English got near there, they could send a fishing-boat up to Dunnottar quickly to give last-minute warning. Mary and her sisters agreed to see to this.

Dunnottar prepared for assault. The last time it had done so it was against the great Montrose's force, when the Marischal had yielded to persuasion rather than to siege. What persuasion would be effective now?

14

It was only two days later that a boat from Kinneff arrived, with the Reverend Grainger himself as passenger. He came to tell them that the Roundhead army had travelled rather more quickly than anticipated. They were at Inverbervie, a mere four miles south of Kinneff. To avoid the vast flood-plain around the Montrose basin, they had apparently left the coast road at Arbroath and ridden due northwards, by Frioch and Brechin and Laurencekirk, to come back to the coast down the Bervie Water, by Arbuthnott. They had camped last night at Inverbervie township. So they were only a dozen or so miles from Dunnottar.

Although so long prepared for this eventuality, now that it was a reality the situation had a great effect upon them all. This very day the enemy could be upon them. The knowledge concentrated and preoccupied their thoughts notably. Despite all the preparations, there was still much to see to.

Jamie of course was especially concerned about cannon. Had they reached Inverbervie so soon? If so, they had made better time of it than he would have expected. Grainger said that his informants, fishermen, had not mentioned cannon, merely that a great host of horsed soldiers had descended upon their little town and more or less taken it over.

When, after a blessing upon them all and their establishment, the minister took his departure, Jamie and Mary accompanied him down to the haven and his boat, and saying farewell, agreed that it might be some time before they saw each other again. They found that his boatmen had already told the local fisherfolk of the position, and these were promptly preparing to pack up their belongings, or some of them, and leave their houses for temporary alternative shelter and fishing bases elsewhere nearby, at Kinneff itself, or Catterline or Crowton and the like, this being a notable coast for fishing havens. None of them wanted to endure an English army's occupation.

Back at the castle, the surplus men of the garrison, mainly the older ones, were sent off to Stonehaven, many thankful to be going. Then the great gates were closed and barred and the portcullis lowered. How long would it be before they were opened again?

The womenfolk were checking over the food stores and trying to calculate for how long they would last. The only addition possible now would be such fish as they might be able to catch from that cliff-foot ledge of theirs – no major supply. Some form of rationing would almost certainly be necessary. Needless to say, this was a new and extraordinary experience for all of them. There was no panic, but less chatter than was apt to prevail.

It was in the late afternoon that the first horsemen appeared, not many, a mere troop, obviously a scouting party. They drew up on the high ground opposite the castle, to gaze across, sunlight gleaming on helmets and breastplates. Presently they dismounted, and about a dozen troopers set off down the steep slope. At its foot, they climbed only a little way up towards the mouth of the all-important ravine-like alleyway, and considered the defensive situation. The watchers could imagine their reactions to what they saw. Then they moved round to the shore and the fishers' cottages, now abandoned, boats gone. They were there for some time, before climbing back up the hill in their awkward long riding-boots, to the horses. Soon thereafter a trio of riders set off southwards.

"I wonder what their report to Lambert will be?" Sir John said. "Not very encouraging, I think."

"They will have been assessing cannon-range," Jamie asserted. Cannon were very much on his mind. "So much depends on that."

"I say that we are safe from their cannon," Barras declared. "No ball could reach us here."

Jamie reserved judgment.

The sun was sinking to the Mearns hills when the main mass of the English force came into view over the Uras and Bourtreebush moorland folds, a seemingly vast host riding in an endless column. There might be only seven hundred of them, but at a distance it looked like more. Seven hundred horsemen can make a daunting sight. They came on, in no hurry, to the high ground opposite, Jamie noting that they flew no banners nor pennons. These were determined, professional and efficient soldiers, not concerned with flourish or display.

It was not long after their arrival that there was a development. A dismounted group came on down the winding path to the shore-level, and this company was different from the previous one in that three of its members wore wide-brimmed felt hats instead of helmets. It was quite possible to ride down this steep track, with care taken by man and beast – the castle inmates and their horses did – but perhaps for heavy cavalry mounts it was not advisable. Anyway, these callers came on foot, although themselves scarcely shod for the terrain.

At sight of this oncoming party carefully picking its way down, Barras, Sir John and Jamie made their own way down past the intervening defences to the lowermost gatehouse and barrier. Clearly this was to be in the nature of a parley, but Barras took a flintlock musket with him, possibly to reinforce his message.

The newcomers came up much closer to the frowning gateway arch, walling and portcullis than had done the scouting group, before halting. There a trooper raised a bugle-horn to his lips and blew a resounding blast, which echoed from the cliffs around, for attention, most commanding and authoritative. Then one of the hatted individuals stepped forward and raised an arm.

"Hear me!" he called strongly. "I am General Lambert, of the Lord Protector's army. I come at Commanding-General Monck's order to receive from you the Scotch crown and other items belonging to the former monarchy which we are informed reliably have been brought here. The Lord Protector requires that these be sent to him, at London, for his care and keeping. Deliver them up to me forthwith, and you in this hold will not be molested. Fail to do so, and you will suffer, and grievously. You hear me? I, Lieutenant-General Lambert, command it. Tell whoever holds this place."

Barras, who was not a notable vocalist, nevertheless raised his voice, as strongly, from one of the narrow gatehouse window slits. "I hear you, Englishman, I, Ogilvie of Barras, keeper of this castle for my lord Earl Marischal of Scotland. I do not accept that you have any authority, nor your Monck, nor yet the man Cromwell, to lay hands on Scotland's Honours. They remain in my keeping until such time as King Charles orders otherwise. Hear you *me*!"

"Fool! Whatever your name," came back to them. "Are you blind, as well as witless? Do you not see that I have the means to take what I demand?" The general turned to gesture up the hill towards his masses of armed men.

"How will you take it, Englishman?"

"You and yours will learn soon enough if you do not heed me, I promise you! We have not come all this long road for nothing."

Sir John raised his voice. "I am the Earl Marischal's brother, Sir John Keith of Kintore. Barras here is under orders, equally with yourself, General. The regalia has been entrusted to his keeping. He will yield it up to none. You cannot take it, I say. Your journey has been fruitless."

"We shall see about that! You shall hear further from me, fools!"

"And hear you *this*!" Barras shouted, and raising the primed flintlock, fired a shot from it well above the heads of the group below. And as the echoes died away, added, "If you think to delay your departure and have further word with us, come not so close next time, or the shots will not be aimed so high!"

Jamie was quite impressed. He had not thought Barras had it in him to act thus.

The English party turned about and went to climb back whence they had come.

The trio at the gatehouse eyed each other. Barras turned to give his orders to the grinning guards there, and then led their own climbing way up to the rock-top citadel.

Declaring it all to the women thereafter sounded sufficiently defiant and spirited. Jamie was the least vocal this time. He was still wondering about artillery-fire. He had heard from his father about English culverins cannon-royal – an odd name for Cromwellian pieces – demi-culverins and serpentines, the second throwing balls of up to fifty pounds, which could smash and topple masonry with ease. It was the range that he was not sure about. And those called mortars, these it was said could fire at a high angle where ordinary cannon could not. If they had mortars brought against them . . . ?

Dusk descending soon thereafter, with camp-fires beginning to glow redly up on the high ground landwards, it was agreed that early bedding was advisable, for the enemy might well be active from first light. But not all would bed down in their rooms. The three men would take it in turns to command the night-watch, in case of English attempts in darkness. Not that this was likely at this stage, before the enemy had had opportunity to prospect and to sum up the possibilities of assault. Barras would take the first night's watch.

That evening, on the stair landing, Mary was especially emotional and requiring comforting and assurance, the feeling of being surrounded by foes and besieged affecting her considerably, however prepared they had all been for it. The man well understood, and held her close. Her sisters would be less fortunate.

Up betimes, sunrise did indeed see groups of the English exploring, surveying all around, high and low – or as nearly so as they could, for of course only a semicircle of inspection was available to them, the seaward aspect being out of sight save from boats, and the boats had gone. This was the only visible enemy activity all day, save for a group of Roundheads making the gesture of firing muskets from as near as they dared come to the lower gatehouse, a mere intimation, sufficiently harmless as not to be worth the garrison firing in reply and wasting precious ammunition, its only effect being to send up clouds of screaming seafowl from the surrounding cliffs. That is, until early evening when two boats came southwards, filled with men, obviously requisitioned from Stonehaven, to assess the situation from seawards. These were not allowed to come too close, with musket-shots warning them off. Not that they were likely to gain much encouragement from what they could see from that side, only sheer, frowning cliffs.

There was still no sign of cannon arriving on the high ground.

That night it was Sir John's turn to take the watch-duty. He was not called upon to do more than inspect the guard to ensure wakefulness and readiness.

In the morning they all awaited events. By now Lambert and his officers must have learned the problems facing them, and could not be too happy as to their prospects. At any rate no major moves developed, although they did send down quite a large company to the boat-strand and fishers' cottages, presumably more as a threat than anything else, for there was nothing that these could usefully do from there. Assault hung fire. The assumption was that Lambert was waiting for artillery. None had appeared by nightfall.

It was Jamie's turn on watch, and he said his goodnights more publicly than heretofore. He decided, instead of going up and down on visits from the keep, that he would take up his stance in the little gatehouse chamber with the three men on duty there, where he could take spells of keeping the lookout. He found that the guards were keeping a lamp lit all night, partly for their own benefit but also to let the enemy see that watch was indeed being kept throughout, for the light would be visible through the slit windows. But after inspecting the beacon containing pitch-pine doused with lamp oil which was kept ready to light on the gatehouse battlements, in case of need, and coming back into the lamp-lit chamber thereafter, he decided that the lamp should be extinguished, for he had seen out much more clearly without it to affect his night vision. It was the second day of May, and actually it was never really pitch dark of a night, although sight was limited and outlines less than clear. Better watching without the lamp.

They took it in turns to doze, two on, two off, Jamie taking the first spell. Watching, at one of the slit windows, his mind wandered over a variety of subjects. Tina, of course, first and foremost; always he was thinking of her, hungry for her, wondering what she was doing, hoping that no other men were thinking to have her, for her attractiveness and sheer beauty were undeniable, even though she was no great heiress. He wondered about Glengyle and his MacGregors, whether they had managed to achieve anything, whether indeed they had ever reached these Mearns hills. He wondered about possible attack, trying to put himself in the place of the enemy commanders and guessing how they would seek to solve *their* problems. And always his mind came back to cannon, especially mortars.

Three hours on, and he and his companions handed over to the other pair. They had seen nothing, no hint of movement in the darkness, heard nothing save the calling of night birds. He lay down on a blanket on the floor to sleep.

It seemed to him that he had barely closed his eyes when he was wakened by a shaking of his shoulder and an urgent voice.

"Maister, I'm no' sure, but I think they're oot there! I canna just right see onything, but there's sort o' movement, y'ken. And I thocht I heard a big noise like steel on stane . . ."

Jamie was up and over at the slit window before the man had got that far, waving him quiet, peering out. The darkest hour is just before the dawn, they say, and it did seem darker than before to him. But – yes, there was movement out there, movement rather than forms to be seen, and not far off.

"Quickly, light that beacon!" he called to the others, up the stairs. "They are there." Even as he spoke, he heard the clink of metal. He was on his way up to the open parapet walk of the gatehouse.

The beacon flared into light, smoky but strong, even as he arrived. At first its glare only dazzled his sight, so that he could make out nothing there beyond the walling. But then, eyes adjusting, he saw them, the ranks of men coming up the slope, flame actually glinting on their armour, men by the score, the hundred. Need for any silence gone, he heard shouts, commands.

He gave a brief command himself. "Muskets! Fire into them!" he cried.

He hardly required to order it, for his companions, anticipating this, were ready. Shots rang out, two shots only, for there was no rapid fire with flintlock muskets; but yells from the dark mass probably indicated hits; indeed bullets could hardly miss some target. Jamie hurried down for his own musket which he had forgotten to bring up with him in his haste, to add to the enemy discouragement.

The Roundheads fired back, of course, in vastly greater volume, but their shots rattled harmlessly on the masonry, with the defenders crouching down behind the crenellations. The likelihood of any hurt being suffered was remote.

Quickly the remainder of the garrison arrived down to assist with their fire, and there were more cries and screams, more enemy shooting also, of course, much more, salvoes. But apart from the danger of flying splinters of masonry, there was little menace in it.

Presently Barras and Sir John arrived, wakened by the noise, but by that time the attackers, their surprise failed, recognised that there was no advantage for them in this, no means whereby even if they could reach the walling and great iron-protected gates, they could open these or climb up. They had begun to move backwards out of range, presumably taking their casualties with them. A few parting shots were fired, to hasten them on their way, and the engagement was over.

First blood to the defenders.

Back up at the castle, the women were much excited and demanding of details, praising their menfolk and, being still not dressed, save in bed-robes, were the more appreciated themselves. It was nearly dawn, and not worth while retiring again, so a celebratory repast, better than a mere breakfast, was prepared and enjoyed. Elated as all were, however, they did not fail to wonder what Lambert's next move would be.

They had to wait until early afternoon before they had an answer to that. A small fleet of fishing-boats appeared from the north, more than the total of the Stonehaven craft, so the English must have raided the smaller havens of Cowie,

Muchalls and Stranathro further up the coast. They were all crammed with men. After marshalling some distance out, the squadron moved in, in good order, towards the cliff-foot.

The defenders had not failed to anticipate something of the sort. The garrison, with crowbars and pick-axes, had, during the weeks of waiting, dug out major supplies of large stones and boulders from the rock-top, and these were poised ready to hurl down. They waited until the first line of boats was almost at the cliff. What the attackers were aiming to do then was questionable, for although it might be possible for one or two individuals in the boats, spry ones, to clamber up to that little ledge where Mary and Jamie had fished, no numbers could do so, no room for such, and there was no other place where it was possible to ascend.

Then Barras ordered the rocks to be rolled over, and these went bounding and crashing down. Not all landed on boats, of course, some hitting projections and being flung outwards and sideways, others splashing harmlessly into the water. But some did smash into the craft and men, to dire effect, breaking bodies and timbers, to bellows and shrieks and bloody confusion. Shots came up at the rock-hurlers, but ineffectually because of the steepness of the angle of fire again, and the cornices of the cliff-top which largely hid the defenders. Some boats came to the rescue of their fellows, while others rowed further out to lessen the steepness of the shooting, although this to be sure increased the range. Barras ordered no waste of ammunition.

After drawing back to a safe distance, and leaving three boats sunken, the fleet waited for a little, as though undecided, and then turned and rowed off whence they had come, to the cheers and jeers of the garrison, feminine voices amongst them.

This little victory did warn the defenders, however, that another similar attempt might be made by night, when some attackers might be able to get up to that ledge, and from there up the steep, winding ascent to the castle. Precautions they would have to take to bar the ascent temporarily with judiciously placed and held rocks, also to contrive more beacons on this seaward face of the stronghold, the cliff face itself being inevitably in the shadow still but the light probably having a restraining effect. And watch would have to be kept here, also.

Mary it was who promptly volunteered to help provide this from her, and Jamie's, tower-room windows – possibly with motives not altogether defensive. If so, her planning was rather invalidated by her sisters and the two older women declaring that they would take part in this vigil, taking turns as the men did on the landward-facing side. All this meant, of course, that much temporary bedding was necessary in the tower for five extra females, in Mary's room and in the still higher garret chamber normally used only as a store. So there would be a distinct lack of privacy in that sea tower of a night. Mary's ingenuity would be taxed, especially with light from blazing beacons illuminating things unnecessarily.

The denizens of Dunnottar Castle were becoming just slightly cock-a-hoop, with still no cannon appearing.

Two days later, with no further attack developing, the watchers saw quite a major part of the force on the high ground, almost half, they calculated, ride away southwards. What did this mean? Could it be connected with the MacGregors? Or was it merely that the English commanders felt that so large a force as seven hundred men was unnecessary there, in the circumstances? That half this would be equally effective if it was to be just a matter of siege? Cannon? If it was some move to obtain the essential cannon, surely over three hundred men would not be required to see to this?

No further seawards attempt took place, by night or day, almost to the Keith girls' disappointment.

It looked like siege then. Was that something of a relief? Or the reverse? There was some debate on this.

15

The day after the departure of half the Roundhead force, there was a new initiative from the residue. A party came down the hill, on foot, around noon, and under a white flag, no muskets in sight. This came to within hailing distance of the lower gatehouse, halted, and a bugle-horn was blown. Although Barras and the others had hastened down at the sight, they deliberately kept the callers waiting for quite some time. The bugle sounded again.

At length Barras called, confidently, sarcastically, "To what are we indebted for this visit, Englishry? We were dining."

"Then we regret disturbing you, sirs," came back. That was not Lambert's harsh and dictatorial voice, much more civil, almost affable, and with a Welsh lilt to it. "I am Major-General Morgan, now in command here. We feel that this confrontation is unfortunate and unnecessary. We can continue to hold you penned in your hold for as long as need be, until you have to yield through lack of victual – as in time you must. But that is to inflict much distress and hardship upon you, and we understand that there are ladies with you. Better, wiser, more suitable for all, that you should yield now, with honour. You have proved yourself worthy defenders, men of spirit. Why prolong your ordeal to its inevitable end?"

"What end do you speak of, Welshman? When you ride off, empty of hand, as your Lambert appears to have done?"

"Not so. General Lambert has urgent concerns elsewhere. Against rebels. We remain, and will do so. Till when you can no longer sustain yourselves with food and drink. That must come, since we can prevent all supplies reaching you. You may be dining this day, but sooner or later you will dine no more! Much better to surrender what has been unlawfully deposited

223

here, now, according to the Lord Protector's command, and save further distress. This is all that we ask: give us the crown and sceptres and we will leave you. You will go free, be not harmed. You may retain this castle, if you so wish. No proceedings will be taken against you. The crown and sceptres, these baubles of past and discredited kingship, that is all that we require."

"You have a nimble tongue, General Morgan," Sir John answered him. "But you waste your eloquence on us. We do not yield. Ourselves, or what is entrusted to our keeping. Scotland's Honours are not for upjumped English squires. Nor Welsh ones, either! Tell your Monck and Cromwell that. We are well supplied here. Probably we eat a deal better than you do, in your camp. We suggest that you be gone!"

"You are unwise, sir. You cannot hold out indefinitely. We shall have your crown and sceptres eventually. We can wait, *you* cannot. Think on it, think well. We will come back for your answer, tomorrow. Meanwhile, I regret having spoiled your dinner. May you have the good sense to be able to enjoy many more! A good-day to you." And gesturing something like a salute, the major-general turned his party round and led them off.

"A different man from Lambert," Sir John commented. "But no less determined, I judge."

"Think you that Lambert can have gone to deal with the MacGregors?" Jamie wondered, as they climbed back to the castle. "That may be what this Morgan meant by rebels."

The others, who had never taken his MacGregors really seriously, offered no opinions.

The defenders, despite what had been said, relaxed no whit in their precautions and watching, by day or night. But that afternoon, Mary led a little group of anglers down to their ledge, to fish for flukes. Unfortunately they now had no lug-worms, and had to bait their hooks with scraps of bacon rind, beef gristle and the like. They caught only a few fish, but at least suffered no attentions from the enemy, for of course they could not be seen from landwards.

Next day was Sunday, and when the promised and smaller

group of Roundheads came down to enquire the results of second thoughts over surrender, it was still another voice which hailed the gatehouse.

"I am Colonel Styles," the defenders were informed. "Major-General Morgan has gone to church, but sends his compliments. And hopes that you have come to the wise decision."

"We have indeed," Barras gave back. "We have decided that we do very well here, and shall continue to do so. We hope that you and your general will perceive that you can serve your cause, however wrongous, better elsewhere, and go back whence you came. Preferably back to your own England!"

"Then you are witless fools!" they were told, and without further parley the party turned and strode off. The colonel with the Yorkshire voice was a man of fewer words than his Welsh superior, who seemed also to be a man of religion. They wondered which church he had gone to, the nearest at Stonehaven, or Dunnottar's own parish kirk at Kinneff? The Roundheads were said to be strong on religion, to be sure, although of the stern and puritanical sort. They also wondered what Morgan would think of the Reverend Grainger's service – although, as a Welshman, he might be no Puritan.

That night, as though to emphasise that, Sabbath or none, the castle occupants were to be taught their folly, there were two assaults, just before dawn, simultaneously, on landward and seaward sides of the rock, this causing at first considerable confusion and alarm, and the hasty transferring of members of the garrison, and somewhat random musket-fire. But with blazing torches tossed down the sea cliff to add to the beacon light, it became evident that the situation on this side was in the nature of a diversion, only four boats being visible and the shots therefrom merely a demonstration. Most of the men returned to the gatehouse and kept the enemy at bay as before. Soon these withdrew also, so that probably the entire procedure was likewise a demonstration that the defenders need look for no respite.

The day following passed without incident.

For that night, Jamie had a suggestion. Let them show

these Englishmen that they were not the only ones who could mount surprise sallies. Those four boats of the night before were now, they could see from the northernmost angle-tower, beached down at the strand by the fishers' cottages. There did not appear to be any of the enemy in evidence down there permanently. A party could slip out of the castle in the dark, with axes and hammers, and smash the timbers of those boats so that they could not be used again against them. What of that?

The notion was well received. It was Janet Ogilvie who made the point that if up at the camp they heard banging and smashing going on, would they not send troops down to investigate and perhaps attack or capture the axemen? Jamie declared that he thought the cliffs would blanket the sound or at least confuse the guards as to where it came from. But even if not, it would not be obvious that it was not coming from the castle itself, possibly some new defences being erected?

That was accepted. And when Jamie said that he would lead the smashing party, Sir John, whose turn it was on duty, declared that he would go with them. It was to be hoped, however, that no enemy assault would develop at the same time, and so cut off the party. To provide against any such risk, it was decided to send a couple of men a little way up the track towards the camp, with a horn, to give warning if they heard any of the enemy coming down, before hurrying back to the gatehouse.

That gatehouse caused Barras to add another detail. The iron portcullis, when raised and lowered, was apt to make a loud clanking and scraping noise, which might alert the enemy. They would have to raise it very slowly, almost inch by inch, and anoint the hinges and chains with goose grease, to try to ensure quiet.

So, late that night, a group of ten, armed with axes and picks, lifted the portcullis only sufficiently for them, stooping, to get under its iron bars, raising it as possibly no portcullis had ever been before to try to prevent creaking. It did make a little noise, even so, but not sufficient, they thought, to be heard at any distance. They gauged that if they kept close under the walling, at first, they would not be seen from the camp, with the beacon's light leaving a shadow there. Once out of that glow, they could head directly and normally down to the shore.

First of all, there, they had to ensure that there were no troopers sleeping in the cottages. This confirmed, they proceeded to the boats. These were sturdily built craft – they had to be for fishing in those waters – and they were not of the smallest sort. So smashing them sufficiently to ensure that they would not be readily repaired was going to entail a deal of hard work, and noisy work inevitably. There was just no way of lessening the last, so instead of trying to, they all went ahead with their axes just as quickly and vehemently as they could, and hoped that, even if they were heard up there, they could do the necessary damage and then get back to the castle before they could be intercepted.

Turning the boats over, they smashed and banged and hammered at the bottoms like madmen, the din sounding to them deafening. Jamie found it extraordinary for the sort of satisfaction their destruction gave him, the breaking and splitting and splintering, appealing to some deep and reprehensible instinct, for these were, after all, the property of friendly fishermen.

No warning came down from the pair of watchers halfway up the hill.

It was all very basic and simple work, and did not take them very long in fact. Leaving four craft which would not sail again for some considerable time – for repairing them here, with no boatyard, would be scarcely possible – the wreckers returned to the gatehouse, sending up a man to bring back the watchers. Once all were within, the portcullis was lowered again, with a clang now. The guards inside said that they had heard the banging clearly enough; but those up the hill declared that very little of it all had reached them.

Without feeling that they had done anything to be particularly proud of, the party decided that they had struck a small blow against their foes, even though these could, of course, go and purloin new boats, if they deemed it worthwhile. It was, too, a boost to morale for the castle-folk, however modest, for this feeling of being penned in and besieged did tend to affect them all.

For their part, as the days passed, the women kept an eye on the food stocks, and began to express just a little anxiety. The fishing from the ledge went on daily, but with diminishing results, for there was not an inexhaustible supply of flounders on that modest patch of sand below. There was plenty of fish further out, no doubt, and lobsters caught in their pots, but no way of getting at them. Rationing was instituted, not drastically, but enough to raise some grumbles amongst the garrison. At least the castellans were thankful that they had got rid of the horses, leaving them at various nearby farms, for providing forage for these would have much added to their problems.

They began to lose track of the days, with differing estimates as to how long since the English had arrived. Two weeks? Or more?

At least no cannon had been seen to be delivered, and assuredly they would have known of it quickly enough if they had!

The atmosphere of confinement increased, and affected them all variously, and some more than others. Jamie in fact was one of the worst affected. He was very much of an active, not to say urgent, nature, far from placid; his brother Thomas would have reacted quite differently. To have to do practically nothing all day, save for fishing from a ledge, was anathema to him. They all did organise sporting exercises, challenges and games, archery, quoits, fencing, wrestling for the men, ball-games for the women. The women were, in fact, much the best at bearing with the inaction, seeming to be able to concern themselves with tasks and interests about the house and in the small garden-ground beside the chapel where, as May progressed, plants were sprouting. Unfortunately it had never occurred to the Keiths to grow vegetables there, with no need to do so on such shallow rock-top soil. They could have done with vegetables now.

Jamie had to restrain himself, day after day, over Mary's

availability, reduced rations appearing to have no effect on her outgoing and affectionate nature. Fortunately for his resolutions, the other females continuing to occupy the sea tower did limit opportunities for dalliance.

Another aspect of their incarceration was the isolation, the feeling of being cut off from their fellows, from any information as to what went on outside their own walls, what was happening in the land at large, and to their own families and friends. They wondered about so much, about the Highland situation and whether the three English sallies thereto were proceeding, and whether this would put an end to Lord Lorne's efforts. What of the south-west stirrings against the occupation? What else might Monck be up to? Jamie was concerned about the MacGregors, needless to say. And so on. But it was the general sense of exclusion, enforced detachment from the rest of the world, which grew on them all, and the men in especial.

They had another white-flag call from Major-General Morgan an unspecified number of days later, all count of days by now being lost. He was, as before, reasonable, mannerly, seeking to be persuasive, declaring that they must now surely perceive that their situation was hopeless, with no possibility of relief or any outcome more favourable to themselves than his renewed offer of pardon and freedom from reprisals if they but delivered up the crown, sceptres and sword. These would have to be handed over in the end, since the castle could not hold out indefinitely, whereas they, the besiegers, could remain in position so long as needful. Morgan declared himself especially concerned for the hardships being imposed on the ladies, saying that this was a most unsuitable and unnecessary ordeal for them. He went so far as to announce that Mistress Grainger, the parish minister's wife, was much troubled over their situation, and had asked him to do whatever he could to lessen their distressful state. Accordingly, he had come to offer again an amnesty and pardon, despite the defenders' continued obduracy. Surely as gentlemen and men of some judgment, they must see reason in this?

When Barras gave him his brief and forceful answer, still Morgan was not yet wholly rebuffed, saying that he considered them foolish and mistaken. But he would be prepared to allow the ladies to leave the castle, free and unharmed, until their men came to their senses. Women should not have to suffer for men's stubborn folly.

Barras rejecting that also, was told at least to put it to the ladies, as was their simple due. And if they decided to accept his offer, to send up a messenger to the camp, and he would arrange it swiftly and favourably. He might even get Mistress Grainger to come and escort her friends out, to reassure them by her presence.

Which said, Morgan turned and left them.

His hearers pondered it all. Did he think that by detaching the female presence in the castle he would hasten male capitulation? They judged that it would not all be gentlemanly concern for the other sex, for these Roundheads were not notable for such behaviour.

Needless to say, no messenger was despatched up to the camp, the ladies being at one in rejecting the offer without the least hesitation, indeed scornfully. They did wonder about General Morgan, however, interested in the man himself, rather than his present efforts.

Siege continued, with a necessary tightening of the rationing becoming evident to all.

16

In the circumstances, two days later, the defenders were surprised to see that white flag being brought down the hill again, and with it not only the major-general on foot, but two women mounted on garrons picking their way knowledgeably. None would do that who did not know the twists and turns of that awkward track; and as they drew nearer it could be seen that one was indeed Christian Grainger. This set tongues awagging, needless to say, and wonderings, especially when Barras recognised her companion to be Anne Lindsay of Cuichbarnes, his own sister-in-law. They appeared to be carrying packages. What could this imply? Surely these two would not lend themselves to any attempt to persuade surrender?

Nearing the gatehouse, the little party halted, and Morgan raised his voice. "The keeper of this castle," he called. "I would have word with him, inform him."

"I am here," Barras shouted back. "And wondering that you keep better company than your usual, sirrah!"

That was ignored. "I have here with me Mistress Grainger and her friend," Morgan said. "They come to offer some caring and comfort to your unfortunate ladies. They may remain at the castle here for an hour or two. When they are ready to leave, make a signal up to my camp and I personally will come down and escort them back." And turning to Christian Grainger, he gallantly aided her down from the saddle. Anne Lindsay dismounted without aid.

As, astonished, the watchers stared, the general swept off his broad-brimmed hat in a bow, and waving his escort round; this unusual Roundhead left the ladies, to lead the way back uphill.

Suspicious of his motives, Barras waited to give orders for the portcullis to be raised to allow the visitors to enter the gateway until the soldiers were some distance off. They all did call down welcome to the unexpected guests, however.

The ladies came, carrying their bulky burdens, and leaving their horses to be looked after by the castle guards. Greetings with the three men were somewhat incoherent at first, exclamations and questions started and not finished, emotion uppermost. Anne Lindsay, a big, plain-faced but hearty woman, asked after her sister Janet. But out of it all, presently, Christian Grainger came out with it.

"We have come for the regalia, the Honours!" she announced.

The men stared, wordless.

"We have planned it all, my husband and I both," she told them. "That is why Anne and I have brought all this." And she gestured to the bundles they carried. "Clothing, much clothing. And a distaff and flax. We think that it will serve. And these riding cloaks which we wear. James believes that we can do it."

Still mystified, her hearers eyed her unbelievingly.

On their way up to the rock-top, Christian explained. She had told General Morgan, who came to worship at their church, that the ladies cooped up in the castle required succour, comfort, interests, and probably some change of clothing and gear. He had allowed them to bring all this, but expected them to try and convince the said ladies to leave the stronghold. The distaff and flax were ostensibly to spin thread for their embroidery work. Something long like this was necessary to disguise the sceptres. The sword of state, they feared, would be too long to hide and would have to be left, hidden somewhere. The crown would go out wrapped in the clothing. She and Anne would take these away for her husband to bury under the pulpit of Kinneff kirk, so that, when the castle had eventually to surrender, the Honours at least would be safe and no inkling available to the English as to where they could be. That is, if this was agreed and permitted by them, its keepers?

Astonished and much impressed, the men were at one in

their praise and admiration for this brilliant scheme, and its authors. To be sure they agreed it all. The like had never occurred to any of them. It was, they judged, as ingenious as it was seemingly practical. So long as the Honours got safely past the general on the way out. It would be tragedy indeed if there was any suspicion then, and search made, all their efforts and long guardianship thrown away.

Christian said that she believed that Morgan, who was obviously a ladies' man, would not actually search them; and they would wrap up the items most carefully. She had mentioned the distaff's awkward length to him, deliberately, on the way down from the camp. And it was approximately the same length as the longer sceptre. But she and her husband had thought of the possibility of discovery at the gate, and believed that in such dire eventuality the regalia could still be saved. The general was not likely to bring down with him, to collect them again, more than the four men he had as escort just now; why should he? So, if the garrison's men were to be watching and ready, if the secret *was* uncovered, they should be prepared to rush out and overpower the Englishmen – for there would be many more of them – recover the Honours and take them back inside. It would mean leaving the portcullis up a little way, but that ought not to be a problem. Her husband had suggested, at first, that in the event of such discovery, they might in fact capture the general, and take him to hold as hostage, but on consideration, they decided that this would hold little advantage and would much complicate her own and Anne's situation, for they would then have to remain in the castle also, which would help no one. Better to leave Morgan free to take them back up to the camp, angry as he would be. He might seek to punish them in some way, but what could he do, save berate them? However, it was to be hoped that nothing of the sort would be necessary, and the regalia be carried off undiscovered.

By this time they were all up at the castle, and its female denizens had to have all this explained to them, to loud exclamations of acclaim. Nothing would do but that they must go there and then to the chapel, to uncover the Honours and see how they could be wrapped up safely and disguised. The sword, all agreed, was too large, long and heavy to be smuggled out, and must be hidden otherwise; fortunately it was the least important of the regalia and the most readily replaced. Mary suggested that they might do as she had once suggested for all the items, hide it on the sea-bottom attached to a rope and float, like one of their lobster-pots.

Uncovering the crown and sceptres, and again awed by their beauty and renown, it seeming sacrilege indeed to wrap them up in clothing and the distaff's canvas. All agreed that the results of doing so appeared very similar to the bundles which the visitors had brought in, although the crown, hidden in cloth, did look somewhat bulkier, as well as being much heavier. But Christian said that the larger bundle would seem to any man to be merely more discarded women's garb, taken for washing or repair. It all ought to go as they planned. Her husband James would be praying for them forby, she added.

So it was back to the keep for the only very modest and token refreshment available for the visitors, and while this was being offered, they all heard such news as their callers could give them. To Jamie's satisfaction he learned that Glengyle and his MacGregors had not failed them. It was them that the castellans had to thank for no cannon having reached Dunnottar, for the local story was that the ox-drawn column, left well behind by Lambert's horsed force, had been ambushed and set upon by the Gregorach in the Inglismaldie area, the escort routed and the cannon sunk in the bogs of the flooded North Esk River. Possibly it was word of this which had sent Lambert off with half of his troops, although if so, he had not returned. The visitors had had no tidings of any battle between the Roundheads and the MacGregors thereafter, but perhaps the latter had returned to their own mountains with Lambert pursuing, duty done. Or more likely, the general had gone off to assist one or other of the English thrusts into the Highlands which were said to be proceeding.

Other news which might interest their hearers was scanty. Thirty Scots representatives had been ordered to go south to London to serve as delegates in the English parliament, this to general resentment, in that it was declared that it was for the embodying of Scotland with England. The Reverend Robert Blair, one of the foremost divines, had declared that the nation's embodiment was when as a poor bird is embodied with the hawk which has eaten it up. Angered by the Scots' reaction, Cromwell was said to have commented that they were so senseless, this generation, of their own good, that scarce a man of them showed any sign of rejoicing. Otherwise, news was only of continuing oppression, divisions amongst the Kirk factions, and the like.

When it was felt that probably it was time for the visitors to depart with their precious burdens, Barras went down to the gatehouse first, to muster all the garrison and inform them of the procedure should there be any search of the women, and the regalia discovered, the situation with the portcullis, and the leaving of the English general unharmed if possible. Then all the company in the castle escorted the visitors down, while Barras hung out his own version of a white flag from the gatehouse battlements as signal to the enemy camp that the two ladies were ready to take their leave.

Amidst distinctly tense farewells and good wishes on all sides, the portcullis was raised just sufficiently for the two garrons to get out, by which time they all could see the English party coming down the hill again. Christian and Anne were assisted up into their saddles, the latter carrying the sceptres across her saddle-bow rather awkwardly, as she had done with the distaff, and the former with the now heavier bundle of clothing containing the crown, this before her and partly covered by her cloak. Thus they waited, only the three men beside them, the castle ladies remaining under the gateway arch, with guards ready to rush out to the rescue if need be.

Morgan was seen to have his four men only with him again, to the watchers' relief. As he drew near, Barras, Sir John and Jamie drew back to the portcullis, saluting the horsewomen. These decided not to ride to meet the general, just in case a search developed and men could come to their aid, in which case the shorter distance out the better.

Coming up, Morgan doffed his hat once more. "So, you have

235

not convinced the other ladies to come with you, mistresses," he said. "I judge that as regrettable. They will only suffer the more, and unnecessarily."

"They are determined to remain, General," Christian told him. "They are none so ill-placed. But the better for our visit. They thank you for your courtesy."

"I do not make war on women," he declared. "But their own men, here, should have persuaded them to leave, I say." He raised his voice. "You are foolish," he called to the three men. "Your stubbornness will profit you nothing."

When he got no reply to that, the general turned and gestured towards the hill, landwards. The two mounted ladies waved to those at the gateway and urged their garrons forward, Morgan and his men walking alongside.

The sighs of relief from all left behind might almost have been heard by the departing group. Oddly, Jamie for one felt almost guilty over this taking advantage of Morgan's civility.

There was not likely to be any hitch in the procedure now.

They all found it a strange sensation to be climbing back up to the castle, siege resumed, with the object of the siege no longer valid. For how long should they continue to hold out now, then? – that was the question. An odd situation.

17

That matter of when to yield did continue to preoccupy all in Dunnottar Castle in the days which followed, for of course there was no question but that yield eventually they must. The English, not knowing that their objective was gone, would undoubtedly continue the siege; and food was running low. The men did not wish to impose more hardship on the women than was necessary, nor on the garrison indeed; but they were agreed that the longer they could resist, within reason, the better for the safety of the regalia. For, of course, once they did yield, the besiegers would expect to find their trophies in the castle; and when they did not, there would be searchings, enquiries and demands – that was certain. The longer that was after the two women's visit, the less likelihood there was of any link being suspected with that incident, and therefore with Kinneff kirk. At all costs the secret must be preserved, however determined the interrogators. What they were all to say in such inevitable questioning also became a matter of concern to all.

Meanwhile, there was another decision to make: what to do with the sword of state? It was accepted that Mary's suggestion of hiding it in the sea was probably a good one. But that was not so simple, to have it recoverable and yet its hiding place not obvious. Just to throw it into the water, below their cliff face, with rope and float attached, would not do. It would be far too readily found there by diligent searchers. Amongst the Keith girls' other lobster-pots, with their so similar floats, would be safest – but how to get it there without a boat? And there was no way that they could think of to acquire a boat.

Mary again it was who came up with the answer: they should build a raft. That ought not to be too difficult. There was much timber stored in the castle, for the many fires necessary, and the beacons. They might even dismantle some of the beaming in storehouses, to produce longer material. A quite large and substantial raft . . .

There was some questioning as to the practicality of this, but Jamie for one agreed that it ought to be feasible. They would have to sail the raft by night if they were not to be observed. And another thought occurred to him. When, after surrender, they were questioned as to where the regalia had been taken, here was an answer that they could give, and with some truth. They had cast it into the sea, rather than let it fall into English hands. That might well be believed. They could even keep the raft, to show how it had been done, to help their story to be believed.

This was accepted, for they would have to say something to their no doubt angry questioners.

The building of the raft was commenced without delay, after considerable discussion as to construction and size. It would not require to be very large, for two people would be all that was necessary to paddle it and take the sword. But it would have to be reasonably high out of the water to be safe to sail in the open sea, yet not too heavy to get down the cliff intact. Could they make it more buoyant with floats of some sort?

They used bladders, those of cattle, sheep and pigs, for their lobster-pot floats, and kept a store of such available. But these would not do for a raft designed to carry folk, not large enough. Casks, Barras suggested. They had the small casks in which they kept their honey wine, ale and the like, these now almost all empty. Four, or better, six casks tied to the ends and centre of the raft would help to keep it up and manageable, he thought.

So there was much sawing, hammering and tool-work, joists from the store-roofing the main timbers, firewood serving as cross-bars and bulk, with the casks secured at ends and middle, rope and cordage being used to bind all together firmly. Paddles had to be fashioned also, three of these in case one got lost overboard. The thing would make unwieldy navigating undoubtedly, but given reasonably calm seas, ought not to be too difficult for the paddlers. Almost without discussion it was accepted that Mary and Jamie would man the raft.

They had good assistance in building the contraption, men of the garrison glad to assist, two of whom proving to have had some experience in boat-construction. All there took much interest in the proceedings, glad of something to preoccupy them.

Meantime, the besiegers contented themselves with waiting, patiently or otherwise, although no doubt they constituted a nuisance if not a menace to the surrounding area's inhabitants.

In two days the raft was finished and pronounced reasonably seaworthy by the proclaimed experts. The problem now was to get it down to the water, heavy as it proved to be. Fortunately the castle was fairly well provided with rope, for this was required for various purposes, in particular the raising and lowering of the barriers, less than portcullises, at the intervening defensive posts behind the main gatehouse. So the plan was to lower the raft down the cliff on ropes, a difficult if scarcely delicate task, requiring much care and prospecting in the process. Even so, they discovered that the rope available was not sufficient, in the needful two lengths, to let the thing down all the way, almost two hundred feet, in the one stage; so that a projecting spur had to be found whereon the craft could rest, part-way, and where the rope-handlers could descend in order to continue with the lowering process – this proving quite the most difficult problem of all, that cliff being notable for being all but unclimbable except for the difficult enough single route down to the fishing-ledge; and there was no convenient halfway resting place for the raft on that descent. So much prospecting on ropes had to be done, and it was the Keith girls who did it, skirts hitched high, experts from their long practice at the Fowlsheugh precipices. Eventually a possible part-descent was mapped out, not so far down as they would have liked but enough to get the raft almost halfway down. It might not quite reach the water on the second lowering, and probably would have to be dropped the remaining few feet, with a cord attached to one of the thick ropes, and held secure, so that they did not have the thing floating away thereafter.

One small problem remained: how to mark the float to be tied to the sword so that it could be identified in due course when the time came to retrieve it, amongst all the other lobster-pot floats? Yet not to be too obvious. As usual, the imaginative Mary Keith came up with a solution. A short length of harness leather securely wrapped round the head of the float would not look strange and could seem part of the plugging of the blown-up bladder; but none of the other floats was so tied. Leather would be best – braiding or coloured cord could be washed off in rough seas. Not that it was to be expected that there would be any close inspection of lobster-pot floats by the enemy; but this for safety. And, of course, to guide themselves back to find the sword, eventually.

All was prepared then, and they remarked amongst themselves that there was so much more ado about getting rid of the less-important sword than there had been over the vital crown and sceptres. The weather was good and the sea remained calm. It was decided that they should make the attempt that same night.

They had to wait until late, of course, for it was almost June and darkness was brief. Indeed it was never wholly dark, and the raft-handlers and cliff-climbers, their eyes adjusting themselves to the gloom, found their tasks less difficult than they had anticipated. Again it was the girls who performed the most testing part of the venture, in lowering themselves down to the projecting spur of rock where the raft was to rest, part-way. Jamie and two of the garrison joined the four young women on this, less nimbly, and found it in the half-light a hair-raising experience. They all had to huddle together tightly, amidst much feminine giggling, on the very limited and uneven perch.

When at length shouts from above heralded the raft's bumping and scraping descent, it was difficult indeed to receive it and hold it steady there, in that cramped position, bulky as it was, while the two ropes came slithering down to them, one with a lengthy thin cord attached to it which must be held, to ensure retention of the raft later on. The seven of them were just too many for their awkward stance; yet all their muscle-power was needed to hold the heavy construction on the next stage of its lowering, its three paddles tied to the rope binding.

Somehow they got it down, although, as they had guessed, when the ropes were fully extended the weight remained the same, so that obviously it was still not in the water. Owing to the underhang of the cliff, they could not see down to sea-level. But they calculated that it could not be far above the water, and they could risk letting go of all save the cord. They did not hear the resultant splash because of the noise of the sea, but the retained cord did not run more than six feet or so before it went slack.

Now they all had to clamber up again, Mary left holding the cord. Then Jamie collected the awkward sword of state, with its float, and, to the good wishes of the others, commenced their next difficult descent, the sword no help. Fortunately, by this time he knew almost every inch of the way, so that, going slowly, he got down to the ledge safely. There he found Mary, speedier, had already retrieved the raft, dragging it along bumping against the rock, to immediately under them.

Getting down on to it was the next hazard, six or seven feet below. Jamie was able to help the young woman over the edge and down, she slipping the last foot or so. There, she panted up that the raft was very unsteady to stand on, so he told her to sit, while he knelt on the ledge and handed the heavy sword down to her. Then it was his turn to lower himself, which he did rather less successfully, only just avoiding missing the raft altogether, teetering on the raised side or gunwale and then managing to collapse inboard and partly on top of Mary and the sword, with the rocking of the contraption beneath him.

Regaining breath and sitting together on the already wet flooring, uncomfortable indeed as to posture, but thankful to have got thus far, they unhitched two of the paddles. The raft seemed to be floating well enough, and higher than they had expected, those casks responsible, no doubt. But when it came to propelling and steering, they were less pleased. As a craft it was unwieldy in the extreme, and being somewhat lopsided, difficult to guide with their paddles. At first they largely went round in circles, possibly caused not only by the construction of the thing but by the strengths and depths of their paddling. However, after some trial and error, they managed to get going approximately forward, still zigzagging but on a reasonably sustained course, and this southwards, heading for a lobster area which would be impossible to see, even in daylight, from the enemy camp.

They had, according to Mary, fully half a mile to go on this less than easy voyage. They were thankful indeed that the sea was calm, although the swell did tilt them oddly, no doubt owing to the fact that this raft was flat-bottomed, unlike a keeled boat. Their paddling together improved, however much they managed to splash themselves and each other, a wet procedure altogether.

It seemed a long half-mile, but at last Mary declared that they must be nearly there, and began to look out for lobster-floats. These proved hard to find in the shadowy half-dark, being so low-set.

Peering about them, at length they discerned one, and soon another nearby, for they tended to be planted clustered fairly close together over likely rock and sand beds. Choosing a spot not far from these two, and very much aware of what they were doing with that symbol of the nation's sovereignty, carried before the monarchs at so many coronations and important ceremonies and parliamentary openings, they picked up the sword of state and lowered it over the side. It went down a lot faster than any lobster-pot and, clutching the rope, they felt its dunt on the bottom. Then, eyeing each other, they turned to peer up at the dark looms of cliffs overlooking this vital spot, but could distinguish no obvious landmark to help identify the site, before casting the rest of the rope and its float overboard.

Silent, now, for a little, they turned the raft around and paddled back whence they had come.

When they reached the landing place beneath the ledge there were two more problems: first, to get themselves up, and then the raft itself, which was to be left thereon as intimation to the enemy that they had cast the regalia into the sea from it. The climbing up proved to be more difficult from that low-set raft than from a boat, but with the projections of the rock face aiding them as hand- and toe-holds, they managed it. But hauling the raft up was a different matter and beyond the two of them. So Mary went off up the cliff, to bring down volunteers to help. Waiting for them there, Jamie rather wished that he had gone with her, for although it was not a cold night, wet as he was, it made a chilly interlude.

However he soon warmed up again when a party, including two of Mary's sisters, came creeping down, and they commenced the task of hoisting. The raft seemed much heavier than when lowering it. They lost one of the paddles in the raising process but that was not important. Tying the thing securely into position on the ledge, the ascent was commenced, amidst much congratulation for the rafters.

They held something of a minor celebration thereafter, modest as to refreshment as it had to be – although now all felt that there was not the same need to preserve stocks, for the siege need not go on for much longer, surely.

It was hardly worth going to bed as dawn was breaking, but on the other hand there was no need to be up at any early hour. On the stair landing, on their way thither, Mary clearly considered that she deserved a rather special goodnight send-off, and was not denied it.

18

For how long, then, to continue with their resistance to the Roundheads? The men of the garrison were already tending to grumble that there was no longer any need for them to be half-starved when there was nothing to guard here, not exactly mutinous but restive. Would a few days more make any difference? Explanations about avoiding any possible links with the two ladies from Kinneff were seen as not worth the hardship entailed.

It was decided to surrender two days later.

This decision concentrated the minds, of the leaders at least, on the likely results, for them, of the yielding. Morgan and his officers, however courteous he might be personally, would be exceedingly angry when they found out that they had been deprived of their prize, the entire object of their presence in the Mearns. Their reaction would be unpleasant undoubtedly, could be harsh indeed. They were unlikely just to express their disappointment, ask questions, and then depart. There would almost certainly be reprisals, against the men at least. Barras, Sir John Keith and Jamie agreed that their main duty now was to protect the ladies, as far as possible, also the garrison, from probable English fury and, of course, to mislead the questioners as to the whereabouts of the Honours, and when they were disposed of.

None, in fact, now really looked forward to the end of the siege therefore. But it had to come.

Around noon, then, on the third day of June 1652, Barras hung his canvas sheeting, as white flag, from the gatehouse battlements, and had a horn blown to attract attention to it, and all waited. It was not long before there was evident reaction. Quite a large party presently came down from the camp, no four or five this time, Morgan, with his felt hat, to the fore.

As they neared, Barras ordered the portcullis to be raised, and thereafter walked out alone to meet the Englishmen, as keeper of the castle.

"So, you have come to your senses at last!" Morgan greeted him, no smiles nor civilities on this occasion. "You have kept us waiting overlong, fellow. And will pay for it, I promise you! You surrender?"

"I do, General. Our supplies can no longer sustain us."

"As I told you. You deliver the castle into our hands, we representing the Lord Protector?"

"I have no option, sir. But remind you, a man under orders yourself from your Cromwell, that we here too have been under orders, to hold this strength against all comers."

"Such orders have no validity in the Protectorate! You are rebels, contumaceous rebels! And shall suffer for it."

Barras shrugged, silent.

"Your people are disarmed, sirrah?"

"I have ordered all to lay down their arms, yes."

"Then no treacherous behaviour or resistance, see you." And Morgan turned and pointed to the hill where a still larger party of armed men was coming down from the camp. "Or you will pay for it with your lives." And he waved his officers forward to the gatehouse arch. Within it, Sir John and Jamie waited. The garrison remained out of sight.

"You are Keith, your Earl Marischal's brother, he having taken arms against the Lord Protector," Morgan accused. "And who is this young man?"

"He is a friend, Ramsay by name, who happened to be in the castle visiting when you came against us. He could not escape." Barras was doing his best for Jamie.

The other made no comment but gestured to his officers and soldiers behind. "See to this place, that it is secure, all guards rounded up and held fast. Suffer no least resistance – use your swords. Then follow us up to the castle." He pointed peremptorily upwards, backed by some of his senior officers, a grim-faced crew.

The three castellans led the way upwards, silent.

As they passed the series of defensive gateways and battlements in that ravine, the newcomers were obviously impressed, commenting. At the rock-top they gazed around them keenly, noting all.

Reaching the keep, only the Lady Margaret and Janet Ogilvie awaited them, the Keith girls lying low meantime. There was no hat sweeping-off today, Morgan only inclining his head.

"The Lady Margaret Hay, sister to the Earl of Kinnoull, wife to Sir John's brother," Barras introduced. "And my own wife, Janet."

"These ladies did not accept my offer for them to leave this rebellious hold when they should have done," Morgan said, a little less stiffly. "And after I permitted comforts to be brought to them."

"This is our home," the Lady Margaret said simply. "And I have nieces here to watch over. They would not leave. I could not." She spread her hands. "Do you come within, sir? I fear that we have no refreshment left to offer you."

"This is no occasion for such, lady. I am taking over this castle, in the Lord Protector's name. You will remain in your chambers until such time as I decide what to do with you. You will not be molested, however obstinate you have been." He turned back to Barras. "Now, lead us to where you keep the crown and the rest."

The other took a deep breath. "That I cannot do, General. Since we no longer have the regalia."

Morgan glared. "Fool! Do not seek to cozen me! We have come for these baubles and will have them. You have them here. Take us to them."

"It is not possible, I tell you. For they are gone."

For a moment or two it looked as though the Welshman would strike Barras in his anger.

Sir John intervened. "You cannot have them, Morgan," he announced. "The Honours of Scotland are not for you, or for any save King Charles. We have . . . disposed of them."

"You . . . you . . . ! Disposed! What are saying? Disposed!"

"We were determined that they should not fall into English hands, these symbols so precious to our nation. You, I think, are a Welshman, Morgan. Would you allow invaders to have some Welsh sacred symbol? A relic of your St David or the like? I think not."

"Do not seek to chaffer with me, sir. I will have that crown, sceptres and sword. And all else connected with them. We know that they are here. If you do not bring us to them, we will overturn every stone of this hold till we find them."

"That will serve you nothing," Barras insisted. "I told you, they are gone."

"Silence! Do you take us for witless dolts, to be fobbed off with such a tale! Uncover them for us, or you will pay the price."

"We cannot do that, for they are no longer here."

Morgan jerked his head to his lieutenants, indicating Barras. Two of these stepped forward to grab him by the arms, and to shake him menacingly.

"We will make you speak, man – never doubt it!" the general said. "We are not here to be played games with. Perhaps the ladies should retire while we . . . question you!" The threat in that was undisguised.

"No!" Janet Ogilvie exclaimed. "Do not, sir. They cannot tell you. It is impossible."

"We shall see!"

Again Sir John spoke up. "The Honours are in the sea," he declared flatly.

"What?"

"We told you, General. We disposed of them when it was clear that we would have to yield the castle up. Better that they should be gone, at least in Scottish waters, than surrendered into English hands. We took that decision, in the end. And cast our problem into the sea."

"Liar! Dizzard! Think you that we will believe that? Your so precious baubles! Such you would never do. Do not think that we are so easily deceived. We have come for these chattels of the former monarchy, and we will have them. So you can spare us your stories. Where are they?"

"In . . . the . . . sea." That came out jerkily, for Barras was being shaken fiercely again.

"It is true. They are no longer here," Sir John reiterated. "We were determined that you should not have them. Better under the waves. Leave him, Morgan. Barras cannot say otherwise. They are gone. The sea now has our treasure."

The Englishmen eyed each other, wondering; but Barras was not released.

"You are saying that you threw it all over the cliffs?" Morgan challenged him. "I do not believe it."

"Not over the cliff," Barras said. "You might, perhaps, have recovered it from there. Below the cliff. In boats." He paused, as they all looked up. The four Keith sisters had come quietly into the rear of the vaulted basement entrance chamber, and were standing, watching, listening.

"These are the Marischal's daughters?" the general demanded.

"Yes. The Ladies Mary, Elizabeth, Joan and Isabel."

Jamie, who had not spoken thus far, moved over to stand beside the young women.

"I still do not credit it," Morgan declared. "This of the sea – it is but a tale! How could you put your regalia into the sea, if not over your cliff? You have no boat. Nor could reach one, nor summon one."

"We made a raft." That was Mary, clear-voiced. "A raft. Of timbers. We built it, and then lowered it over the cliff into the water. Then paddled it to the deeps. And sank our, our burden there."

"A likely tale! You all have conspired to deceive us with it."

"It is true. *I* helped to do it. I can show you the raft. It is still there."

It was strange that the young woman's assertions were received with more credence than were the two men's. It may have been the mention of the raft which did it. The Roundheads all eyed her keenly.

"If this is truth, where did you sink your treasures? From this raft."

"Out to sea, sir. In deep water. Where none will find it."

248

There was a pause, as the questioners considered the situation. Then Morgan announced, "I still think that you seek to cozen us – to your danger, I assure you! But show us your raft."

"It is on a ledge at the cliff-foot," Mary said. "You will have to descend the cliff, sirs. Can you do that?"

"We are not cripples, girl!"

"In your long riding-boots it will be difficult . . ."

"Can we not see it from the top? Or is this but more deceit?"

"We have said that it is truth. We are not liars. If you will come, I will show you."

"Very well. But seeing a raft will be no proof that these wretched baubles are in the sea."

"You can search the castle for them, General," Barras said. "You will not find them. We kept them in the chapel here until we decided to dispose of them."

"We will search, I assure you! Now, let us see this raft."

Mary leading now, they all trooped out across the rock-top courtyard to the seaward cliff-edge. There the young woman pointed out the beginning of the daunting track down, indicating how, from there, the ledge was not visible owing to the curvature of the cliff face.

The Roundhead officers looked distinctly offput by what they could see of that descent. None were youngsters, and clad as they were, they were hardly to be blamed for evident reluctance to venture down. Mary and her sisters, with Jamie, began to show them how to proceed, demonstrating that it was entirely possible.

Morgan looked at his lieutenants. "No need for us *all* to go down there, just to see this raft," he asserted, very sensibly.

One brave officer took the hint, the most junior probably. "I will go, sir," he volunteered, and gingerly he began to follow the young people. Jamie turned to give him a hand, which was not refused, those boots no gear for such exercise. But the girls ahead of them constituted a challenge.

Actually they did not have to go more than halfway down

before they could see the raft on the ledge. Satisfied, the officer was prompt in turning back, to report.

Now Morgan had to repeat that the evidence of the raft did not prove that the regalia was not still hidden in the castle. Barras said that they could not prevent the invaders from searching for it, fruitless as would be their efforts. The Roundheads were taken to the chapel, to be shown where the Honours had lain.

Morgan then ordered his officers to muster their men to search the entire premises, high and low, omitting no possible hiding-place, including the women's bedchambers, although he did observe that these last were to be examined with decency, however thoroughly. Let them see to it.

So thereafter there was upheaval indeed, as soldiers swarmed over all, peering, upending, opening, overturning, and in no gentle fashion. Lady Margaret in especial was much put-about and distressed by it all, houseproud as she was. The other members of the establishment went after the searchers, replacing and tidying up as best they could.

When, in the end, nothing to the point was uncovered, however many items and keepsakes the troopers might have purloined in the process, Morgan had to admit that his prize was no longer at Dunnottar, and the dumping in the sea could be no fable. Summoning the inmates to the great hall, he announced his decisions and commands.

"Whatever you have done with your regalia, you have here committed a grave offence against the Lord Protector," he declared, at his sternest. "You have held this fortress against the Lord Protector's forces, in dire rebellion. You have resisted all lawful authority. You have caused death and injury by musket-fire. You have created great trouble for all concerned with rule and order. You will pay for it, as promised. You, Ogilvie, and you, Keith, are under arrest. You will be taken south, for General Monck to decide your fate. Your properties, wherever they may be, will be forfeited. Your men will be taken to the town, Stonehaven, and locked up in such gaol as they have there, to await the Lord Protector's pleasure. And this young man, whatever his name is, will go with them. He may be but a visitor but he has aided you in all this." And he pointed at Jamie. "I do not make war against women, but you ladies have been foolish and obstinate. You may remain here meantime, but some suitable punishment may be meted out to you. That is, unless you accept my final offer of kindness, and disclose to us just where the regalia is hidden. If in the sea, then you may well have made some close note of the spot. Have you? If you reveal this, even at this late stage, I could consider lessening punishments. What say you?"

Nobody said anything.

"So be it. Justice will take its course." He turned to his officers. "See to it. The prisoners to be bound. These two to our camp. The young fellow and the other rebellious rogues under strong guard to the town, to be locked up and kept, under pain of heavy penalties. Make sure that is understood. The women may remain."

The said women, with cries and exclamations, rushed forward to embrace their menfolk, much moved and distressed, Mary coming to fling her arms round Jamie, with her sisters seeking to do the same, the officers, after a moment or two, pushing them away. It was a confused and emotional scene, as Morgan turned and strode out.

No time was given, no allowance made, for any gathering of belongings nor leave-taking, although the women did accompany the prisoners as they were marched down to the gatehouse and out, their hands tied behind their backs. Last-minute clutchings were fended off, final calls and good wishes exchanged; and then it was escort to the enemy camp for Barras, Sir John and Jamie, the women being ordered back, where they could only wave farewells. It made a sorry end to a resounding episode.

Up at the camp, Jamie found himself separated from the others, to await the arrival of the captured garrison-members. When these appeared, all bound likewise, no time was lost in marching them off northwards, Jamie with the rest, along the high ground, under a cavalry escort which harried and hurried the captives at all but a running pace, a trial for men who had been cooped up within a fortress for weeks. Fortunately they had less than two miles to go, and soon they were trotting downhill to the town.

The tolbooth of Stonehaven, overlooking the harbour, was no large establishment, by no means intended to house large numbers of miscreants; and even though it was now empty, as frequently, the place was clearly going to be overcrowded. They were herded to it, now escorted by quite a crowd of the townsfolk, which had quickly gathered, these calling out to their kin and friends, for nearly all the garrison were from the burgh. Therein they were penned in the two cells by the officer in charge of the troopers, and the doors slammed on them, and locked, all without delay or any leave-taking.

Jamie was thrust in with about a dozen others, with barely room for them all to sit, much less to lie. Remarking on this, he was rather surprised at the reaction from his companions. Seeming quite cheerful, they declared that they did not expect to have to do any lying down – they would all be out of there almost as soon as the Roundheads had gone; for almost certainly the English would not leave any troops in the town just to guard unimportant folk like themselves. And their Stanehive friends and relations would have them released before those horsemen were halfway back to Dunnottar. Was not the tolbooth's keeper brother to one of them, and the provost himself cousin to another? Threats might have been made, but these would be ignored, for sure.

And so, indeed, it transpired. They had not been in those cells for an hour before the doors were flung open and grinning townsfolk, women as well as men, were ushering them out amidst much joyous reunion after the long siege, and contumely for the besiegers and scorn that these should think that Stanehive would allow its menfolk to remain locked up, whatever they said.

As the crowd broke up, in the street, and went off with their rescued friends, Jamie found himself in the extraordinary situation of being a free man but left alone there by the harbour. At something of a loss, and with evening setting in, he decided that the only thing to be done was to seek shelter for the night in an ale-house, there being two or three of these on this waterfront. The problem now was, he had no money, not having been permitted to gather any of his possessions at the castle.

However, at the first tavern he tried, on explaining who he was, he was taken in with acclaim and assured of a bed and hospitality, no payment necessary. The ale-wife had a nephew, one of the garrison; indeed it seemed that most of the families in the small burgh had had connections in the beleaguered castle, and all these were now looked upon almost as heroes. So Jamie was taken in and treated likewise.

Later he drank ale with some of the fishermen, all eager to hear his account of events.

On his couch that night, he sought to gather his wits, and plan what to do now. Thinking about it, he came to the conclusion that probably the English would not trouble further with Stonehaven or the prisoners brought here. Why would they wish to burden themselves with the like? They would be off fairly quickly, he imagined, for the south, with Barras and Sir John having to pay the price for their disappointment over the regalia. Sympathy and commiseration for these two friends did not prevent Jamie from seeking his own best way out of the present situation. He would have liked to call back at Dunnottar to inform his friends there, especially Mary, that he was free; but recognised that the English might well leave a party there to keep an eye on the castle and possibly to continue with enquiries as to the whereabouts of the Honours. So it would be unwise to risk a visit there. He would head for home. He wondered whether to try to persuade some of the local fishermen to take him, perhaps to Gray's Redcastle, in their boat? Then he decided that, since his own garron was still presumably at the farmery of Glaslaw, a mile or so west of the castle, he might as well make his way there, as secretly as possible, collect his horse and ride off southwards himself, by unfrequented ways, avoiding at all costs the route the English would be likely to take. An early start, then, before the town woke up to the new day. He went down to inform his kindly hostess of his plans and to thank her for her goodness. She said that a parcel of eatables would be awaiting him at his room door, to take with him in the morning.

Thus prepared, and wondering how the castle women were feeling this first night on their own, he consigned himself to sleep.

19

Soon after dawn, Jamie left the ale-house quietly, with the food generously provided, and made his way through the still-sleeping town. Stonehaven was built on something of a hillside around the bay where the Carron Water entered the sea, so he proceeded from the harbour directly inland, uphill, seeing only one old man leading a milk-cow but barked at by a couple of dogs. Due westward, thus, he went for about a mile, advisedly avoiding Fetteresso Castle, a lesser Marischal house which might possibly be occupied by the enemy, before turning southwards for the farm of Glaslaw. He had ridden all this neighbourhood with Barras and Sir John when arranging for beef and mutton to be sent to the castle larders, so he knew where to walk. He had to get across the Carron Water, which proved to be something of a problem; but fortunately the river was no longer running high, and after some prospecting he was able to find a stretch shallow enough to wade over, wet as he got.

A mile south and he came to the farm; and by this time folk were up and about. He informed the farmer and his family of the situation, and was given breakfast, which enabled him to keep the ale-wife's provision for his journey, was reunited with his garron, and told of his best route southwards, avoiding the coast road which the Roundheads would probably be taking. He was advised to keep well inland, making for the Fiddes area, over high ground, keeping west of Bruxie Hill, and then on to Glen Bervie, to cross the Bervie Water at the Mondynes ford. Thereafter to make for Laurencekirk and eventually Brechin. That way he ought to avoid the English.

Thankful to be mounted again, he set off. It was strange to think that quite probably the enemy force, with his two friends, might well be riding approximately in the same direction only two or three miles to the east.

Be that as it might, Jamie made a quite speedy and uneventful ride of it, the fording of many streams coming down off the Mearns hills presenting few problems with the garron to carry him over. With food to eat as he rode, he covered a good thirty-five miles over a fairly rough countryside of hillsides, moors and bog-filled valleys, finding some satisfaction in merely riding free after all the long period of being confined within walls, to reach the vicinity of Fettercairn, where, between that village and Edzell, he bedded down in an isolated hay-barn, still having no money to pay for accommodation. At least the garron got something to eat.

He had decided to avoid Brechin, for possibly the English might choose to go that way, depending on whether they were heading for Perth or Dundee – that is, if they were yet on the move at all. The most direct route to the Angus glens was by the hillfoots to Fern, Ogil, and Tannadyce, to Kirriemuir, and thence by Lintrathen homewards, some forty miles. Somehow he must make it in a day.

Hungry indeed next morning he was the more determined to reach Bamff that night. Not having the wherewithal to buy food was a dire experience. He recognised only too well that when he got to Lintrathen it would be quicker to go down to Airlie – where was his beloved – than to proceed on to Bamff; but tempted as he was, he knew that it was his duty to go home to his father and family first, even though he would thereafter have to make his report to the Earl of Airlie.

Sheer hunger in time drove him to the manse of the parish minister of Tannadyce, where he sought for and received a poke of oatmeal, eyed distinctly askance by the minister's wife, her husband being absent, as obviously one of the gentry, but in travel-stained and tattered clothing, begging for sustenance. He knew from experience that, swallowed uncooked, the meal would swell up in his stomach and quell the pangs for a little while. He had subsisted thus many a time as a youth on the hill, rounding up cattle.

He saw no English, as he concluded that he would not if

they were making for Dundee. The weather turned wet in the late afternoon, which did not improve matters; but he was now in country which he knew, and passing Lintrathen with something of a pang, made Bamff House by dusk. Home did beckon, even though Airlie, and Tina, had beckoned even more strongly.

It was indeed a joyous homecoming, and of course totally unexpected, the Ramsays having heard of the Dunnottar siege but not knowing of the surrender. They all had been greatly worried, and heartfelt was the thankfulness to see Jamie home, safe and well. They were delighted when they heard about the smuggling out of the regalia to Kinneff and hoped-for security. There was sorrow for the capturing and eventual trial of Barras and Sir John Keith; but approval of the attitude of the Stonehaven folk, and glee at the ease of the release from the tolbooth there. Although Jamie was not to be proclaimed hero by his own family, clearly his part in it all was much admired. He underwent a deal of questioning, needless to say.

For his part, he sought information as to what had gone on in Scotland at large while he had not been at large. He learned that, sadly, Monck's three-pronged assault on the Highlanders had been all too successful, Lorne and the various clan forces prevented from linking up, and not so much defeated as dispersed. There was, apparently, criticism of Lorne's leadership, although part of the trouble undoubtedly would be that he was a Campbell, and the other clans reluctant to be commanded by such. The three English forces were still in the north, and it was reported that strong forts and barracks were being built, at Inverness, which had been taken by the Ironsides, and at Inverlochy, in the west. Elsewhere in the land there was little to tell, certainly no good news. Glencairn, in the south-west, seemed to be lying low, with another of the forts being set up at Ayr, with a large garrison. Monck's rule was tightening everywhere, and more of his forts going up at Leith and Perth. However, Cromwell seemed to be having his own troubles at Westminster, for he had dismissed with contumely what was being called the Rump Parliament, which the wretched twenty-one Scots so-called representatives had attended, and was ruling his Protectorate through his generals with a rod of iron, as Monck was seeking to emulate in Scotland. It seemed astonishing that all this turmoil, distress and bloodshed had come about as an eventual result of James the Sixth and First's personal conception of the divine right of kings, which in his own reign had been a mere theory with little practical application, but which his son, the well-meaning and too religiously minded Charles the First, had taken seriously and sought to enforce.

There was nothing to report from Airlie, of any moment. That earl's 'faction', Crawford, Kinnoull, Gray and the rest, were, like Glencairn, lying fairly low, biding their time, being too close to Dundee, Monck's headquarters, to provoke major retaliation in present circumstances. Sir Gilbert went over there frequently, to keep in touch; and David, Lord Ogilvy, had called in at Bamff two weeks before. Without actually naming names, Jamie asked if all was well with the family there, to be assured that nothing to the contrary had been reported. He could hardly ask whether any eligible and hopeful young men had been frequenting that castle.

Two days he forbore, before he declared that he must himself go to Airlie to report to the earl on the Dunnottar interlude, an announcement which was accepted as suitable – with sister Jean smilingly commanding him to give her love to Tina, if he happened to see her. His acceptance of this duty was more enthusiastic than it was of his father's announced decision to accompany his son, to hear Airlie's reaction to the Dunnottar situation, since this might well set limits to his own visit; but there could be no indication of reluctance, even though it did mean another day's delay.

They rode next morning.

Arrival at Airlie castle with his sire meant of course that they had to go straight to the earl, without any possibility of seeking out Tina and her cousins. Airlie was surprised and delighted to see Jamie, and quite enthralled when they got down to a report on the regalia and Dunnottar situation, loud in his praise of the efforts of all concerned, and the initiative shown. Jamie perhaps did not go into all the details quite as thoroughly as he might have done, having his own ideas as to what to be doing with his time here. Just as soon as he decently could, he asked after the Ogilvy family, carefully mentioning David first, then the sisters and finally Tina, wondering where they were and could he see them? To his disappointment, the earl announced that today these were all out hawking, and with that other David, Inverquharity, who was a very keen falconer. Jamie's almost urgent demand to know where the sport was taking place was perhaps unsuitable in the circumstances, but even though his father looked slightly critical, Airlie showed no displeasure and said that they had intended to go up to the Loch of Lintrathen, to hawk for waterfowl.

To think that he had passed that loch on their way here! But it was only just over two miles away. He could be there on his garron in twenty minutes. He was on his feet and asking to be excused almost before the earl had finished speaking. Both older men eyed him shrewdly, and Airlie observed, apparently casually, that Tina was very good with hawks.

Jamie, with his own quick glance, bowed and headed for the door. So the earl knew more than he had reckoned on. Was that favourable, or the reverse?

The garron was quickly pounding its sure-footed way northwards again.

Lintrathen Loch was a sizeable sheet of water, a mile and a half in length and half that across, the house at the south-western end, where such road as there was skirted. Jamie supposed that, being civil, he ought really to call in at the house and announce his presence to Mariota, but forbore, telling himself that it was quite likely that she herself might be out with the hawkers over her ground, in the circumstances.

Oddly enough, he saw the quarry before he saw the hunters, or some of them. Flying quite high, there were five ducks, mallard he judged, heading westwards. Then he noticed, higher still, a hawk gliding well above them, wings seemingly still but keeping pace with the waterfowl. At that height they must have been in the air for some little time, which meant that the hawkers must be some way off, at the other side of the loch. He hoped that they had a good and active tranter with them, the term for the man whose duty it was to retrieve both game and errant hawks, for in this sport it was all too easy to lose both, at a distance, even though the hawks were trained to circle back to their fliers after making a kill.

He could not see any party across the loch, but there was scattered woodland over there, and they could well be hiding amongst that in order not to disturb the fowl. He rode on round south-abouts.

Jamie glimpsed another hawk flying, much lower this time and after a large flapping heron; and seeing from approximately where this came, was able to assess where he would probably find the hunters, to the north-east area of the loch. Then he glimpsed a hound, being used to put up the fowl from the reed-beds, and was soon round behind it. And there, the riders were clustered, carefully placed behind a screen of low bushes but where they had an all-round view upwards, clear of trees.

There were eight of them, he counted, with three others sitting horses a little way apart, no doubt the falconers or tranters. Only two of the main group were men, young Lord Ogilvy and Inverquharity. Jamie picked out Tina right away, to be sure, and his heart lifted. How many weeks since they had seen each other? He hoped that young Inverquharity was not becoming interested in her, for he was nearest to her.

Jamie could not complain, at least, about that young woman's reception of his appearance on the scene. She must have recognised him at once, as soon as he emerged from the trees into the more open ground south of the bushes, for she immediately reined her horse round and came over at the canter to meet him, hand raised in salute and greeting.

"Jamie! Jamie!" she called excitedly – and she was not one to display much excitement normally. "You are back! Jamie . . . !"

He reined up to her beast, and caring not who watched, all but fell out of his saddle in his efforts to throw his arms around her. He was too full of emotion for any words.

"My dear!" she cried. "So you have come. At last! It has been long, long . . ." She clutched his shoulder, all but shook it, which did not help his unsteady seat. "You have won back to us!"

"To *you*!" he got out – he was not so speechless as all that.

They stared into each other's eyes, and in that moment the man knew that his doubts and fears had been needless; at least, some of them.

Then others of the party came up, full of exclamations and greetings, and that precious moment was gone. For a little there were only incoherent questionings and half-answers, hawking forgotten quite.

However, with the falcons on gloved wrists or circling about and demanding attention, this was no time for lengthy talk and discussion. Jamie saw that Mariota Ogilvy was there with them. There was a move back to the chosen position, David on one side of him, Tina on the other. Ogilvy was not long in asking after the Keith affairs, and was given answers in which Mary had to figure most prominently, the sword-sinking episode inevitably taking pride of place.

So, by fits and starts, details of the Dunnottar siege and actions came out, not the most satisfactory way of imparting the information, with the hawks, falconers, tranters, kills, hound and restive horses all to be coped with. Jamie quite enjoyed hawking, but today he was not the enthusiast. After a while of this, he had little difficulty in catching Tina's eye, and making a different sort of announcement.

"My father is at Airlie, and he will be waiting for me," he declared. "I must return. I but wanted to see you all. But keep you on with your sport." And again the glance at Tina.

That young woman did not fail to take the hint. "I will accompany you back, Jamie," she said. "David, see you to my hawk." And she reined round there and then.

Whether any of the others who heard may have thought to return with them, they were not given the chance, for the pair rode off right away, without any leave-taking. If it was all rather obvious, Jamie for one was not concerned as he led the way, and fast.

He did not follow the line of the loch shore as he had come, but struck off north by east up towards the higher ground leading to the little pass between Strone and Brankam Hills, although this was certainly not the quickest way back to Airlie. Behind him, Tina followed on, calling no questions.

Halfway to the pass, where the trees thinned out to only scattered and stunted hawthorns, he reined his beast up, almost a mile from the others, and turned in his saddle to eye the girl, silent, however eloquent his looks.

"Where are we going, Jamie?" she asked now, but sounding nowise concerned.

"Going? Going, my dear one? I care not where we are going, so long as we go together!"

She smiled. "It seems that we do, does it not?" A pause. "But . . . need we go much further? Meantime?"

That had him wondering. "You mean . . . ?"

"This is a sufficiently pleasant spot, is it not? And . . . sequestered."

Her use of that word had him down off his horse and striding over to aid her down from hers, in moments. And that helping brought her into his arms, needless to say, and with no real struggle to free herself. Holding each other, their lips met.

Patiently the garrons waited.

Her person, stirring against his own, so affected him that he had to swallow gulpingly, which was no aid to kissing. "My love," he used those lips to whisper, "my . . . dearest . . . love."

Her lips open, she sensibly did not attempt speech. Perhaps they were eloquent enough, nevertheless.

So they stood for long moments, in each other's arms. Then Tina gently freed one of hers, to point. "There . . . I . . . think," she got out, somewhat breathlessly, inevitably. She was a practical young woman, as well as all else.

He looked, and saw that she had indicated two hawthorn trees, one dead and fallen, the other twisted by the winds but with a spread of leafy cover, about a score of yards apart. He nodded, more than agreeably.

They led the garrons over to the first, and tethered them to the fallen trunk, then, hand in hand, moved to the other.

Tina disengaged herself and sat down beneath the branches, to pat the grass at her side.

"Is not the prospect from here superb?" she asked.

"I have no other prospect for my eyes but you!" he declared, sitting down, and close.

"To be sure, there are more prospects than one. Or even two."

"You mean . . . ?" That was becoming quite a litany with Jamie.

"I mean that the present one is fair. But there is the future also. No?"

"Tina, you see it? See the future? With *me*?"

"Is that over-ambitious, Jamie?"

He all but groaned. "Dear God, that is it all! All my desire. And hope. And prayer. The future ours. Yours and mine, together, lass. You, you could love me, then? You do? As I love you. Say it, Tina, say it. I have longed and waited and ached for this. Say it!"

"Would I be sitting here if I did not, foolish one? I love you, yes. Love you dearly. I . . ."

She got no further, of course, swept into his arms again and all but smothered in his appreciation and exultation. She had to protest, in the end, begging for breath and easement of person.

"Do not . . . devour me quite!" she beseeched, but not unkindly. "I am but a frail female!"

"Frail – you! I know of none stronger, in all that matters. That has been part of my worry. That you could ever yield yourself to such as me."

"So asks the hero of the regalia?" That was the first time that word hero had actually been enunciated, even though there was that hint of affectionate raillery behind it.

"No hero," he disclaimed. "I did nothing heroic. Others quite as much, and more . . ."

"None others, I think, for so long, for all the story, from Edinburgh Castle. All dangerous for you. But we can debate your heroism another time, can we not? Now, we have our . . . prospects to consider?"

He nodded hearty agreement, and he emphasised his present preferred prospects by pulling her to him again, and this time the hand of one of his encircling arms cupped one of her breasts. She did not reject it. "Most gladly," he agreed.

Again there was a little delay before less immediate prospects could be considered. "What, then, of the future?" she got out at last. "Am I foolish to be concerned with the future, now, when the present is so . . . pleasing? One of my frailties, perhaps?"

"No, no. It is but that I am so happy, so overcome with my joy . . ."

"*Our* joy! And to be continued, yes? For long? So – the future!"

"For always, here and hereafter. Would you marry me, Tina?"

She wagged her lovely head, wagged not shook. "Think you that I would say no, having come thus far? Are you going to ask me to? That is your first using of the word, Jamie."

"Well . . . yes. You see, lass, I have so little to offer. My family, although ancient, is not rich. I am only a second son. I will inherit no great lands, a farmery perhaps. Or none at all. Your uncle and guardian, the Earl of Airlie, may well have other plans for you. Would wed you one day to some heir of title and property, never to such as myself. This has all along been my fear."

"I know of no such design by my uncle. *I* am no heiress, either. My father was a second son also, you see, and slain when young. So I am no great catch either! Would your father not seek better for you?"

"I would hope and pray not! Besides, in a few months' time I will be of twenty years, and can make my own choice."

"So, we wait for some months?"

"If we must. I fear that I will but ill thole the waiting, my dear, if wait we have to. Now that I know that you will have me. I seem to have been waiting for this for too long already."

"But you have had some consolations, have you not?" Her smile was quizzical. "This Mary Keith! She seems to be a very spirited lady. And . . . friendly! You appear to have done much together."

"I . . . she is a friend, yes. A good friend. But only that, Tina. We had to see much of each other, held as we were in that castle. But I told her of you, of my fondness for you, my hopes, from the beginning. So there was no, no difficulty."

"Poor Jamie! Torn between two females! Or more, perhaps? Who knows how many of us admire the diffident hero!" She patted his arm around her. "However, this of the Lady Mary may well not displease our David of Inverquharity, I think. For he appears to think highly of her, also!"

"She spoke of him kindly, yes. And . . . of others. It may be that she is but kindly disposed . . ."

"Ah, yes. And as such, to be appreciated by men with time on their hands? Perhaps I should be grateful to her for keeping my love entertained? In all the weary waiting?"

"No! It was not like that. I, we were but friends, I assure you, Tina."

She laughed. "I know, I know. I but tease. Let Mary Keith be. We have more to speak of than that, I judge." And she turned in his arms to give a little salutary bite on the lobe of his ear.

That, needless to say, ensured that there was in fact no major speaking on any other subject for some considerable time, for Jamie took it as an invitation for action rather than more words. And under his pressure she found it easier to lie back on the grass rather than seek to remain sitting up and being all but wrestled with; so that there, under the old hawthorn tree, they found sundry ways of demonstrating their now mutually admitted fondness for each other, as men and women have been discovering since men and women were. Time obligingly stood still for them.

How long it was before a whinny from one of their garrons had Tina sitting up, neither knew. But it was time, perhaps, for she felt bound to point out that Jamie had told the hawking-party that his father had been waiting for him at the castle and he must return – that the said unspecified time ago. It might be embarrassing if the others in fact were to get back before them! Jamie could not deny that, much as he would have wished this interlude to continue. So, with a final embrace, they rose and went to the horses.

On their way back to Airlie, at a spanking pace now, Tina proved that it was not only possible to communicate in such circumstances but that constructive thought might be achieved. At a stretch where the horses could trot side by side, she voiced the results.

"I have been considering, Jamie. My uncle is likely to be seeing you, at this time, as do the rest of us, as something of a hero, however much you may deny it. In that case, he could wish to please you, even reward you, no? Certainly not to disappoint or offend. So this might well be no bad time to speak to him. Of ourselves. To ask for his niece's hand! While the farrier's iron still is hot! How think you?"

"M'mm. It might be, yes. He said kind things when I was telling him of Dunnottar. But naught that I did was sufficient to cause him to see me as a suitable husband for you, Tina, I fear . . ."

"For so brave a gallant and so urgent a lover, you fear too much, Jamie Ramsay! Try him, and see."

"Now? When we get there? To the castle?"

"Why not? I told you, while the iron is hot."

Strangely, the young man, who had not been afraid to face all the dangers of the regalia episode, extraction from Edinburgh Castle, and the Dunnottar siege and his captivity, was more than apprehensive over the prospect of approaching the Earl of Airlie on the subject of a marriage, as they neared Airlie Castle.

At least they were relieved to find the hawking-party not yet back, and Sir Gilbert not apparently fretting at his son's delayed return. The two older men were still engaged in converse and discussion.

Tina, well aware of Jamie's lack of confidence in the present situation, did her best for him. She realised that he would not wish to speak to the earl and his father at the same time, and so, after they had made known their arrival to their elders, and she said that she would obtain some refreshment for

266

Jamie, went back alone to her uncle to mention that she would like a word with him when he could spare a moment. What Airlie made of that was anybody's guess, but he might well have been not totally unprepared when, emerging from his withdrawing-room off the great hall, alone, he found not his niece but the young man awaiting him there.

"Where is Tina?" he wondered. "She wants me, she said."

"She . . . she was being kind, my lord," Jamie got out. "It is me, myself, who seeks your ear. I, I crave your indulgence. To speak with you alone."

"Ah! Now I see it! And what have you got to say, young man?"

"I would marry Tina!" That came out in a rush, not at all as he had planned to say it.

"You would? Now here is a surprise!" That was solemnly said.

"Yes. I crave your lordship's pardon. For, for speaking thus. I know that it is a great thing to ask, that I am too bold, too forward. Thus to approach you. And to seek her hand. But it is . . . it means all to me, all! I have little to offer, my lord. But I love her, love her dearly. I would *die* for her!"

"Dear me, that would be excessive, I think! So, you would have Tina to wife? And she would have you? I need scarcely ask that, or she would not have come to me contriving this interview!"

"Yes, my lord. She, of her kindness, would have me. Even though I can give her so little. I recognise well that I am no worthy match, a second son, of no inheritance. But . . ."

"But you would have her, nevertheless. And she you. So there it is. We are faced with a dilemma, it seems."

"I know it, well I know it. You may have other plans for Tina. More worthy suitors . . ."

"More worthy than the saver of the Honours of Scotland? Scarcely, I think. That is not the dilemma, lad, it is where you are going to put her. To take her, as wife, and instal her. Here is the problem."

Jamie blinked, mind spinning, as he eyed the other.

267

"Your father and I have been discussing this aspect of the matter. He can give you a farm, yes. But surely Tina deserves better than a farmhouse on some hillside, I judge, my brother's daughter. Her father heired a small property, Balfour, near to Kirriemuir. You may know it. But he never lived on it, being off soldiering. His wife dwelt here, at Airlie, when I lived at Cortachy. And she died when Tina was born. So I gave a tack of Balfour to another, a distant kinsman, meantime. Meaning Tina to have it in due course. But I can scarcely put the tacksman, an elderly man, out at short notice, until I have found him another place. Here is the dilemma. So where do you take my niece?"

Jamie was scarcely taking all this in, so overwhelmed was he by the unspoken implications of it. It was being *accepted*! He to wed Tina. Not said so, but as though taken for granted. His father and the earl having discussed it! Wits reeling, he ran a hand over his head.

"I, I do not know," he jerked. "We have not thought. I did not think that you would be aware of, of . . ."

Airlie actually pointed a finger at him. "Think you that we are all blind, boy! Everyone has known that you and Tina were making for each other. And been glad of it. So we were all anxious while you were away at that Dunnottar. But Tina will be of full age in one year's time, when she is entitled to have Balfour. I have never spoken to her of this, for here has always been her home. She would never have wished to go to live there, alone. I would have but given her the tacksman's rent – he is another Ogilvy. But, now, I will have to find him some other suitable property."

"No, my lord, no need, surely? If I may wed her, we can find *somewhere* to live together. In Bamff House there is room, until I can find another . . ."

"You have an elder brother, who will heir that. And a sister, unwed. There is no dower-house, your father says. But we will discover something, to be sure, before you come to actual marriage."

All this was beyond taking in, for Jamie, at the moment. All that he could think of was that he was being given Tina, allowed to wed her, his dream to come true. He all but flung himself forward to grasp Airlie, in his gratitude.

The other saw it, and smiled. "You wish to speak with your father? Or . . . that can wait? Off with you, lad, to your Tina!"

No second such suggestion was required. The younger man did not actually run, but was out of that hall and down the winding stairs at speed.

He found her out in the courtyard, talking to a maid-servant. With scant courtesy he grasped her arm to drag her away, the other girl eyeing them astonished.

"So-o-o!" Tina said. "You have not been long. Yet, haste is it?"

"It is . . . a wonder! He said yes. I can wed you, lass, I can wed you! Here is joy. Joy! The happiest day of my life! We will wed, my love." And there, before the staring maid, he took his bride-to-be and waltzed her round and round.

Part protesting, part rejoicing with him, she part questioned also. "Your father? He also agrees?"

"I have not seen him. But the earl said that they had discussed it all. Our marrying. So, if your uncle agrees, my father will not refuse. Anyway, I will be of age soon, and then he could not. So, my love, we will be man and wife. Can you believe it? I scarcely can."

"I will get used to the notion, I think! Given time . . ."

They went within, Jamie eager to find some private corner where he could express his delight more adequately than in mere words, and add to the delight at the same time. Tina, wagging her head over him, allowed herself to be led into a vaulted basement cellar, on the way to the kitchen, used for storing meats, bacon, eggs, salt-fish and the like. Clearing a bench of its cheeses, he sat her down, and against this domestic background proceeded to demonstrate that romance could triumph over mere conditions.

They were so engaged when voices outside proclaimed the arrival of the hawkers and, rather alarmed that these might think to deposit their game, ducks, herons and suchlike in this store-chamber, Tina pleaded for immediate disengagement, the man reluctant. However, the thought of announcement of their wonderful news to the others compensated, and they got out of that larder in time to avoid possible discovery.

Thereafter the joy of imparting the glad tidings was only very slightly tempered for Jamie by the fact that none of the young folk seemed in the least surprised, David indeed going so far as to wonder that it had all taken so long to get this far, all but dilatory lack of urgency implied, to his friend's astonishment. But there was no lack of congratulation, demands as to when the wedding was to be, and the like.

A celebratory feast would have been in order, but unfortunately Sir Gilbert, clearly lacking in the romantic faculty, had lingered for long enough at Airlie for one day, and declared that they must be off; it would be late anyway before they got back to Bamff. Like the others, he did not seem in any way surprised by developments, nor put out that he had not been consulted directly.

Farewells, then, were almost chaotic, with no opportunity for privacy, amidst much good-natured raillery and banter, Jamie assuring that he would be back very soon, and getting a whisper, with his kiss from Tina, to make it even sooner than that.

On the way home, needless to say, he brought up the subject of accommodation for newly-weds. His father did not appear to see any great problem. There was surely room for them at Bamff. The western wing of the tower-house, actually the oldest part of the building, was but little used; they could have that if they wanted to keep separate from the rest of the family. He would, in due course, hand over one of the farms – always that had been intended; only, of course, these all had tenants in them, and such had to be considered. But Jamie would not wish to take his gently born bride to live in what was little better than a cot-house anyway, would he? He could choose which farm he wanted, within reason – best to select one where the present tenant was elderly and likely to be giving up soon anyway. And Airlie was going to hand over this Balfour to the girl, sooner or later, quite a fair property, as he remembered it. Jamie was fortunate in the prospect of this unexpected acquisition. There was a small castle thereon, a mill, and two or three farmeries.

With that the younger man had to be content. Not that he was in any way ambitious for land or possessions; all he wanted was a reasonable house to take Tina to, and sharing his old home with the family scarcely was his notion of that. But he was far too happy this day greatly to concern himself with the matter. He had gained what he wanted and had so greatly longed for – Tina. The rest was not significant, there and then. As for this Balfour, he had no great wish to go sit as laird in some minor castle, in the right of his wife. Or was that but prideful selfishness?

20

Needless to say, it was not many days before Jamie was back at Airlie – three to be exact. And there, despite his surely legitimate and understandable requirements for private dealings with Tina, in the establishment of their betrothal no less, he found himself distracted by word of events on a rather wider scene. The Lord Gray had arrived at the castle the night before, for consultation with the earl.

Gray had been informed as to the outcome of the Dunnottar siege, and the saving of the regalia, by Airlie, but was eager to hear details from Jamie himself. Indeed, he had been going to come on to Bamff hereafter to see the Ramsay brothers, for there could be further tasks for them. But meantime, he had news connected with Dunnottar to impart. Sir John Keith had escaped from his captors. Just how this had been effected he did not know, and Ogilvie of Barras apparently had not; but Keith was free again, and thought to have gone north, to the much upset of Monck and the others. Jamie, of course, was delighted to hear it.

There was more than that, however. Considering the comparative remoteness of Gray's northern refuge of the Redcastle of Lunan, he always appeared to be notably well informed as to all that went on in the land at large. To be sure, his main properties were in and around Dundee, at Broughty, Castle Huntly, House of Gray, Bandirran and the rest; and with Monck more or less ruling Scotland from there, kinsfolk and servants were in a good position to learn quickly of events. And his Broughty Castle having its own haven within its outer walling, it was only a couple or so of hours sail up the coast to Lunan Bay for his messengers. But as well as that, he maintained links with other Catholic lords by means of the successors of the former itinerant friars who used to wander the country fulfilling various useful functions including news dissemination, and which the Reformation of eighty or so years before had merely driven, as it were, under cover, the services of which not only Catholics were glad to avail themselves.

At any rate, wherever Gray had gained it, he had much information to retail. The principal news related to the Highland situation. Apparently the earlier reports that Monck's three-pronged assaults had more or less demolished the loyalist clans' threat to the occupation regime were vastly exaggerated, Airlie saying that he had guessed as much, or why would the English now be building these forts up there if the danger was over? It seemed that it was in the main a matter of poor leadership on the Scots side, for which Lord Lorne was being blamed, with the result that the various Highland forces had been separated and dispersed rather than defeated; and these were now planning a new and better-led offensive on a major scale. This time the Earl of Glencairn was to be in command; and it would not be only Highland troops, a large contingent from the south-west, Glencairn's own country, being promised. Gray was commissioned to see that the Airlie faction's earls and their strength were enrolled. Hence this visit. There was to be a preliminary gathering of the leaders, or their representatives, at Loch Earn in a month's time, and it was hoped that Lord Ogilvy, Jamie Ramsay and others from these Angus glens would be present. It would be too late in the campaigning season to stage an assault thereafter, so it would have to be next spring or early summer for the action, but that would give time for the maximum mustering of forces. Much was hoped for, from this joint venture, the first really major attack and challenge to the invaders since the fatal Battle of Dunbar.

Other tidings Gray brought were that a secret meeting of the General Assembly of the Kirk had been betrayed to the English, dispersed by troops, and some of the clergy arrested. All ministers were now ordered to remain in their parishes, under pain of imprisonment, no assembling of more than three of them permitted. Gray grimly wondered whether this would improve the religious instruction of Scotland's parishioners with more preaching of the Gospel and less on resolutions, remonstrances and Leagues? English judges were being appointed to replace justiciars, sheriffs and local magistrates. And an especial campaign was being initiated by the invaders against alleged witchcraft, with torture for confessions, and burnings – this probably being used as an excuse for getting rid of folk who stood out against the occupiers' domination. And amidst all this, the Protesters and the Resolutioners continued with their own embittered bickering. God help Scotland!

Jamie agreed to go, with David Lord Ogilvy, to this meeting at Loch Earn in a month's time, and took his leave to go in search of Tina.

She was waiting for him, having heard of his arrival, although she had not managed to avoid the company of two of her cousins. However, she had a proposal. They could ride together to inspect this Balfour Castle, which one day was to be theirs apparently, some five or six miles away, which would ensure them being alone together for some considerable time – always a problem in this friendly household. Jamie agreed heartily. Meantime, she announced, her kind cousins would arrange a little feast to celebrate the pair's betrothal which, in turn, meant that it would be too late for Jamie to return to Bamff thereafter, so that he would have to spend the night at Airlie. Would this inconvenience him?

Reaction to that was predictable.

So presently they were riding north-eastwards, as often side by side as was practicable, well content. They went by a route they had followed more than once, up the Cramie Burn past Baldovie, and along the hillfoots to Kingoldrum. Tina said that she had been to Balfour only once before – although presumably she had been conceived there – and that visit was some time ago. Would they ever live there, she wondered? Jamie might not wish actually to dwell in an Ogilvy house, a proud Ramsay, claiming more ancient lineage? He assured her that he was not so proud as all that, although he would have liked to instal her in some more suitable Ramsay establishment. Unfortunately it appeared that there was none fit for her – but then, no royal palace even was that! They would see what Balfour was like when they got there.

Smiling, she informed him that the great, or infamous if he preferred it, Davie Beaton, the cardinal, who had all but ruled Scotland a century ago, as Primate of Holy Church and Chancellor of the Kingdom, had not been too proud to live in Balfour Castle, at least part of the time. Before he took holy orders, he had married Marion Ogilvy and got Balfour with her, as dowry, and had later in fact improved and added to the place for one of his children by the said Marion; although by then, he having become an abbot, he had to reduce her in stature to that of "chief lewd" as the phrase went, continuing to live with her as man and wife nevertheless. Jamie, who had never heard this story, assured that there was no likelihood of him following the Beaton example.

On the western outskirts of the little village of the Kirkton of Kingoldrum they found the castle a strange mixture of ancient and modern, of one-time grandeur and present-day modest homeliness. Situated in quite a strong position, clearly it had once been something of a major fortalice, consonant with the name of a notable family, predecessors of the Ogilvys who also probably gained it by marriage. It appeared to have been, like so many another, a structure of irregular outline, this dictated by the outcropping shaping of its site, consisting of external curtain walling, angle-towers and presumably a central keep. One massive angle-tower, with arrow-slit windows, shot-holes and an odd sloping roof, remained intact, but most of the curtain walling was gone, although some of the subsidiary lean-to buildings survived as stabling and storehouses and the basement of a lesser angle-tower remained to the north-east. But the keep had been replaced by an ordinary gabled house of three storeys, with no ambitious features save dormer windows, odd to see in such a setting. It was in fact a large farmhouse planted down in the midst of a ruined stronghold.

The visitors eyed all this interestedly, before calling at the farmhouse door, reached across a filled-in moat. It was opened to them immediately, indicating that their arrival had been observed, by an elderly woman of matronly appearance, who announced herself as "hoosehalder tae Maister David Ogilvy who was awa at Kirrie Fair the day;" most male Ogilvys seemed to be named David. When informed who the visitors were, she invited them within civilly enough, going so far as to offer them oatcakes with beakers of milk, this much appreciated.

They could scarcely go around inspecting the house – and of course said nothing about the possibility of themselves coming here to live at some future date – but they did see enough to realise that the premises were reasonably commodious and, rearranged and refurbished, could make quite a comfortable, unpretentious home. Sufficiently satisfied, they did not linger long and took their departure, leaving regards for Maister David.

This all having taken considerably less time than they had anticipated, Tina proposed that they might make their return journey by a round-about route, neither being in any great hurry to get back to Airlie. By riding due northwards from Kingoldrum for about three miles, using a drove-road she knew of through the hills, by Ascreavie, they would reach the spectacular upper valley of the Carity Burn, from which Inverquharity took its name, a tributary of the River South Esk, this forming quite a major pass through steep, craggy braesides, westwards, which after some four more miles would bring them to Balintore, another Ogilvy lairdship, from which there was a good road down to Lintrathen. Nothing loth, Jamie, who did not know this territory well, told her to lead the way. He indicated that however steep and dramatic this route, it would not be so inhospitable as to prevent them from halting somewhere along the way, for a little break from all the riding. She reassured him that this might just be possible.

Tina was right. As they went northwards, the scenery grew ever more challenging, the hills heightening and steepening, the valleys deep and twisting, the streams rushing and cascading. In present company it made most enjoyable riding, and with excellent prospects to come. They were in fact heading directly into the vast Highland fastnesses, the mountains beckoning.

In the circumstances, with all the valleys, ravines and burns running southwards from those heights, it seemed strange to come, after the first three miles, to a very definite glen running crosswise east and west, caused presumably by some curious earth movement when the land was forming, the Carity Burn, quite a sizeable stream, threading it. Turning westwards, along the foot of this, they became quickly enclosed, the hillsides rising even more sheerly above them as the valley narrowed and lifted. From farflung vistas of peaks and ridges and clefts, they were now funnelling through a straight, lengthy and deep defile. In this the early afternoon July sunlight did reach them, but soon it would no longer do so. It would be a dark and gloomy place in winter.

So straight was this mountain trench that almost all the way they could see far ahead, and higher, the jaws of the pass Tina had spoken of. Jamie declared that a better place to ambush an enemy would be hard to imagine. The girl told him that was not the way to see it all, in fighting and bloodshed, but as a passage and doorway to further delight, for she promised him that the view from the pass summit would enthral.

And she was right in this also. When at length they had climbed up between those frowning, all but threatening, walls of rock and scree, suddenly all was transformed. Abruptly their enclosure was no more, with the land opening widespread before them, a steep drop yes, but the views beyond seeming to stretch to infinity, the sun now supreme over all, hill and dale, moor and plain, forest and lochs, further than eye could see. The riders drew rein, to gaze.

"We live in a lovely land," Jamie redeemed himself by observing, with all thought of tactics and strategy banished, or almost, for there were more kinds of strategy than the military.

Part-way down that steep descent there was a clump of whins on a sort of shelf of the hillside, facing south by west into the sun, and not far from the track. That would serve them very well.

Moving on, when opposite this feature, the man leaned over to touch Tina's arm and point. Raising eyebrows at him, she shook her head over him also, but turned her mount's head in that direction without more effective protest.

At the whins they dismounted, and found prickly branches stout enough to tether their beasts to, Tina remarking that these were becoming long-suffering animals.

"The views from here are sufficient for you?" he asked thoughtfully, throwing himself down on the grass and holding up open arms to her.

"If I am given opportunity to look," she said, standing over him for a moment or two before giving a mock sigh and sinking to her knees and entering those arms.

Reluctance thereafter was nowise in evidence, even though there were just hints towards moderation, probably wise.

They remained there for more than any few minutes, and did in fact manage one or two unspoken appreciations of the vista in between closer enjoyments, seekings and discoveries. The garrons were patient indeed, had to be, since they could scarcely graze on whins.

At length it was time to go, for Tina reckoned that they had still four miles to ride down to Lintrathen Loch and then another two to Airlie, and the betrothal feast must not be unduly held up.

So there was no more patience needed from the horses, pace the requirement.

Back at the castle, they found all ready for them, the Ogilvy sisters having been very busy. The great hall was decorated for the occasion with flowers and greenery, and the girls were dressed in their best. A splendid repast had been prepared, soup and salmon, roast duck and venison, sweetmeats and fruit and wine. Tina disappeared for a little while, and returned, handsomely clad and looking quite beautiful. Mariota from Lintrathen was present as guest, and Lord Gray was still there. They all sat down at the long table, lit with candles although it was still daylight, Jamie having to be still in his riding-clothes.

The earl opened the proceedings with a little speech,

declaring how auspicious was the occasion, how joyful they all were at this espousal and how fortunate were both of the happy pair, Jamie to have won so attractive, good-looking and talented a partner, and Tina so spirited and gallant a young man, to whom all good Scots were indebted for helping to preserve the Honours and supporting the King's Grace in this grievous time. They all wished them very well, and in due course a long and happy marriage. As symbol of esteem it gave him pleasure to hand over to Tina's chosen partner a small token which had been in the Ogilvy family for exactly one hundred and seventy years, the ring which Sir James Ogilvy of Lintrathen had given to Margaret Ramsay of Bamff when he had married her in 1482 – his to use now!

Greatly moved, Jamie accepted the jewelled golden circlet, stammering thanks. He recognised that some sort of acknowledgment of the gift and the occasion was now expected of him, but did not see himself as any sort of orator.

"I, I am overwhelmed," he got out, "by this especial symbol of, of a continuing bond between our families. Of kindness by you all towards myself. And you, my lord, in particular, for entrusting your, your . . ." He paused, at a loss for what to call Tina in respect of the earl's guardianship, "in respect of your charge to me. Your niece." Recognising that as feeble, he went on hurriedly. "I am the happiest man in this land, in that Tina will have me. She deserves a deal better!" And he sat down as hurriedly, and thankfully.

But he was not finished with yet, for beside him Tina rose to speak.

"I look on myself as greatly to be envied, by being asked to share Jamie's life with him. I might have done much worse, I think!" She glanced down at him, sidelong. "It is customary, I understand, for betrothal pledges to be exchanged at such a time. And so I offer him this." And she raised her arms to unhook a slender gold chain from around her neck, drawing out from her gown the little circular Celtic cross which hung therefrom, and handing it to the man, with an incipient curtsy.

All but appalled he took it, still warm from its nesting place.

He knew that crucifix, for he had tended to find it in the way of his lips ere this, between her breasts. A wonder to have as it was, he was embarrassed, for he had not considered the matter of a betrothal pledge, and had brought nothing to exchange. Unless . . . ? Of course! He stood, and kissed her before them all, then took her hand and placed on a finger the ring her uncle had just given him, praising heaven in his heart that he had it to give.

Tina smiled into his eyes, knowingly, understandingly, lovingly; and all round the table applauded; and at David Ogilvy's suggestion, rose to drink the health and happiness of the couple.

Thereafter, with Jamie putting the chain and cross round his own neck, and touching it now and again, the meal proceeded in normal if lively fashion.

Music and dancing followed.

When it was bedtime at length, all the young Ogilvys escorted Jamie to his chamber door on the third-floor landing of the keep, with much hearty goodnighting and some kissing. But they had the discernment to leave Tina alone with him at length, when they continued their ascent to the range of attic bedrooms above.

Drawing his love to him, Jamie was now very much aware, momentarily, of similar, but so different, stair-landing good-nights in the sea tower of Dunnottar Castle, although quickly he put the thought from him.

"My beloved, we are betrothed now!" he declared, lips moving against hers. "All but . . . wed!"

"All *but* . . . !" she agreed, emphasising that but.

"That crucifix, how wonderful it is to have it. Knowing where it came from." And his forefinger probed down into the division in her bosom.

"It was all but yours anyway," she told him. "You have kissed it, if by mistake, often enough, no? And the ring, I will cherish that."

"I had nothing else to give you, I had not thought of pledges, lass."

"I know it. I was going to ask you for a kiss, as pledge, then. A sufficient gesture. But you thought quickly. And I got the kiss, too!"

"I, I would give you more than any kiss. Tonight," he said then.

"I know that also. And a part of me would welcome it. But no, Jamie, I think. Not tonight. Not yet. Let us be patient. Soon, yes. But we will be glad one day, for, for restraint. On our wedding night. So long as it is not too long to wait. Just a little more patience, my dear. Do you not agree?"

Whether or not he agreed, he nodded, but with a sigh. "At least, come inside. For a moment or two. Not to stand here . . ." And he pushed open the chamber door.

"So long as we avoid the bed!" she conceded, but gently.

Inside, their embracing was fairly comprehensive, both fulfilling and frustrating necessarily, until Tina, well aware of the latter, called a halt, and declared a goodnight. At the door again, she turned to stroke his cheek.

"I . . . promise you . . . one day . . . all we both long for, my heart," and fled upstairs.

In the morning, after another consultation with Airlie and Gray, David escorted Mariota and Jamie as far as Lintrathen, where all parted, Ogilvy saying that he would come to his friend at Bamff when his father got word of the exact timing for the meeting at Loch Earn although, in the circumstances, they might well see each other before that, Jamie admitting that this was likely.

21

In the event, Jamie had two more meetings with his betrothed before the Highland jaunt was begun, once again at Airlie and then when, at his pressing suggestion, David brought her to Bamff for a two-night stay, with the objective of making a tour round some of the Ramsay farms to see whether there were any of them in which she would be prepared to set up house with him, in preference to occupying a wing of Bamff House itself, in the event of Balfour Castle not becoming available for them for some time. So they spent an early August day, with the bell-heather in full bloom on the hillsides, riding the bounds of the Forest of Alyth, and the young woman surprised at the great extent of it all, Jamie explaining that, although large in acreage it was poor land as far as value went, however picturesque, no rich lairdship, nothing like the Airlie, Cortachy, Lintrathen or even Balfour properties. They visited the farms of Ardormie, Sheilwalls, Incheoch, Balwhyme, Kinkeadly and Gouldswell, even the far-off Derryhill, paying particular attention to Incheoch and Kinkeadly where there were elderly tenants who would not be too upset to be transferred to alternative houses in the Bamff castleton or the hamlet of Milncraig, indeed might well find the move to their taste, less isolated in winter snows, and in congenial company. They did not mention the possibility of this to any of the incumbents, of course; but for his part, Jamie had very considerable doubts as to whether he could in fact contemplate bringing Tina to live in any of these houses, even with improvements made and refurbishings, so basic and lacking in amenities did they seem to him. Much better sharing quarters at Bamff itself. Tina did not say as much, but inevitably she must have thought similarly.

She and Jean Ramsay got on well together; and this would certainly make the institution of two households less difficult. Tina was able to express the opinion that she would be entirely happy at Bamff House.

At least all the inspections offered ample opportunity for affectionate concourse, and with a parting period looming ahead of them, Jamie made the most of it, or, if not quite the most, much of it, Tina's co-operation ungrudging even though limiting as to final stages.

Three days after she returned to Airlie, David was back at Bamff. They were due at Loch Earn three days hence.

Brother Thomas set off with them next day, not exactly enthusiastic about it all but determined to play his part in the nation's cause. Jamie was anxious to go by Glen Gyle to see the MacGregor, even though this was scarcely the most direct route to Loch Earn. They went with well-wishing from Sir Gilbert, with the promise of at least forty Ramsay men to add to the eventual muster.

By Rattray they went south, to cross Tay at Perth, then on down Strathearn by Auchterarder and the Allan Water to Braco, and so across the higher ground to Doune of Menteith and their first night halt. Then on into the Highlands proper at Callander, from which they reached Loch Venachar, under soaring Ben Ledi, and so to fair Loch Katrine of the islands and forests, at the head of which opened Glen Gyle, some thirty-five more rough miles. There they found that they need not have made this detour, for Glengyle himself was preparing to go to Loch Earn the next day.

Well received by the MacGregor, they were loud in his praise over his successful intervention in the Mearns, and the effects of no cannon reaching the besiegers of Dunnottar; but lacking details, they demanded information. Glengyle made light of it, merely declaring that the Gregorach cut off the artillery train from its guards, in the Inglismaldie area, and had driven the oxen and their cannon into the bogland of the North Esk River, where the heavy pieces had sunk satisfactorily, a simple matter. They themselves had suffered no casualties. He was glad if it had helped the besieged, and wanted to hear what had happened to the regalia.

Jamie's account of it all much interested the chieftain, particularly the problems of disposing of the sword of state. It all provided an animated discussion around the table of the modest house, overlooking the loch-head. Glengyle's wife made an excellent hostess. It was from her, not from her husband, that the visitors learned that Glengyle had been a lieutenant-colonel in the service of the late King James the Seventh and Second.

In the morning, with a dozen running-gillies to support them, the four horsemen set off from the loch, not eastwards as they had come but due northwards over the mountains, wild country indeed, to reach the head of the long glen of Balquhidder, MacGregor country still in fact, although not in their name, since not even Argyll and Glenorchy, Campbells, had been able to oust them therefrom. Down this valley they rode and ran, nine miles, and then up the northern reaches of Strathyre, which eventually brought them down to Earn, a major loch.

The size of this sheet of water, fully seven miles long, presented its problems. Where was the meeting of leaders to be held? The word reaching Airlie had merely said Loch Earn; and Glengyle was no wiser. Presumably the message had come from the Earl of Glencairn himself, who, being a Lowlander, might well not know the area, and assume that this was sufficient direction. The gathering would almost certainly be held at some laird's house. But which? On the south or the north side of the mile-wide water? Glengyle of course knew the chieftains and lairds here based, but which would be the host? Edinample, at this south-western end, was a Campbell place, so Lorne might have chosen it; but it was a seat of the Glenorchy branch, not on the best of terms with the main line of Argyll. Stewart of Ardvoirlich would surely be apt to support the Stewart monarch. But there were also the properties of Dalimeanach, Coulmore, Finglen and Ardrostan on this southern side, smaller lairdships. On the north, where the hills came down closer to the water, there were, apparently, only two major houses, Dalveich and Dalkenneth.

Glengyle thought Ardvoirlich, quite a renowned place, the most likely – although he wondered how a MacGregor might be welcomed there? They were starting to head along the shore eastwards thereto when another little party came up, from the north apparently, under Robertson of Struan, equally unsure as to their destination. They trotted along in convoy.

Glengyle explained to the younger man why he was doubtful as to his reception at Ardvoirlich. It seemed that sixty-four years before, a band of MacGregors from Balquhidder had perpetrated an outrage here. Admittedly they had been provoked. A party of the Gregorach had been stalking deer in the forest of Glenartney, a royal forest unfortunately, when they had been caught by the royal keeper of the forest, Drummond of Drummond Earnoch. He had not imprisoned nor slain them, but had cut off all their ears and sent them home, as an example. The Gregorach probably would have preferred their clansmen to have been slain. This insult to the proud royal race of Clan Alpin was not to be borne. So after keeping watch on him for a while, the MacGregors managed to catch Drummond alone one day, prospecting for a deer-drive above Loch Earnside, and there had killed him. But not content with this, they cut off his head, wrapped it in a plaid, and carried it down to the low ground. It so happened that Drummond's sister was married to Stewart of Ardvoirlich. So the avengers took the head there, and asked the lady for the usual Highland hospitality, her husband being from home. While she was gone to get them modest provision, they had taken out their trophy, set it on a platter on the table, and stuffed bread and cheese into the dead mouth. The woman, returning, at sight of it fled screaming out of the house and up into the hills, where she roamed mad. The MacGregors had departed, taking the head with them. All this, needless to say, got the Gregorach into trouble with King James, and, with the Campbells making the most of it, was the beginning of the lengthy royal persecution of the MacGregor clan as a whole, with its vehement reactions, which ended in the proscription of the very name, and the execution of the chief, Glenstrae, in 1603. Even today Glengyle, like others of his name, could not sign any document or charter as MacGregor but had to use a pseudonym.

Jamie, for one, recognised that the Clan Alpin would be better as friend than enemy.

However, there was no trouble at Ardvoirlich this day, for long before they reached the house, set well back from the loch, on the hillfoot, they saw the large number of tethered horses and waiting men-at-arms and clansmen, indicating that this was indeed the scene of the meeting, and there would be a sufficiency of great ones here to ensure that the MacGregors would scarcely stand out.

Whether James Stewart of Ardvoirlich appreciated all this invasion of his establishment, whatever their surnames, was doubtful, for it involved him and his catering for the needs of not only the many notables but of their escorting hangers-on also, no light matter.

The newcomers found the leaders assembled round improvised tables in the orchard, where they introduced themselves to William Cunninghame, ninth Earl of Glencairn, a heavy-featured and solidly built man in his forties, who rather stood out as to garb, hairstyle and much else amongst all the Highlanders. They saw Lord Lorne and the Earl of Atholl, and the great chiefs Cameron of Lochiel and MacDonnell of Glengarry, amongst the others, with more arriving as they waited and ate and drank, whisky at least being in ample supply.

They learned the reason why this gathering had been called by Glencairn and not Lorne. He had been sent a commission as commander of all the royal forces in Scotland by King Charles, from France, so that Lorne was reduced to lieutenant-general, which made him look less than happy today.

Rank being very much in consideration here, Lord Ogilvy as an earl's heir was made more of than either Jamie, Thomas or Glengyle – that is, until a pause enabled David to declare the Dunnottar and regalia situation, and the parts Jamie and Glengyle had played in it, unknown to all here. After which these two were much sought after, questioned and acclaimed. Many were the queries as to where the Honours were now, and Jamie was thankful to be able to say, in all honesty, that he did not know, save that the sword of state was hidden under the sea waves. The fewer people who knew where the other precious items were the safer they would be, since folk talked, even though with no least intention of betrayal. The cannon saga also drew much praise, some wondering whether these pieces of artillery might be rescued from the bog for use against the enemy. Glengyle thought that would be difficult, having been at pains to sink them deep.

In mid-afternoon, when it was decided that no more representatives were likely to appear, Glencairn, very much in command now, ordered a roll-call not only of those present and the numbers of men, horsed and foot, which they could promise, but also of other chiefs and lairds known to be prepared to take part in a major onslaught on the enemy in due course, but not able to be here this day, with their probable contributions.

It proved to be quite a stirring occasion, as name after name was called out, and their owners seeming to vie with each other in manpower offered. Lorne, not exactly sulking today as superseded commander but a little stiff, led off with fifteen hundred foot and fifty horse, with Atholl, determined to beat this, with twelve hundred but one hundred cavalry. Glengarry called three hundred MacDonnells, and Lochiel, not to be outdone, topped it with four hundred Camerons. Struan Robertson promised two hundred and fifty, as did Farquharson of Inverey, with MacNaughton two hundred and Glengyle the same. Lesser men from the Lowlands such as Graham of Duchray, Blackadder of Tulliallan and Sir Arthur Forbes came up with their eighties and fifties, and Ardvoirlich himself rose to seventy. Thereafter, Thomas, as the elder brother, promised forty Ramsays, and Ogilvy declared that the Earls of Airlie, Crawford and Kinnoull, with the Lord Gray, the Carnegies, the Lyalls, the Fotheringhams and others, would contribute unspecified numbers, but strongly, probably as many as five thousand, and a large part cavalry. Other messages of support were made likewise.

In the end, it was reckoned that Glencairn could rely on between eighteen thousand and twenty thousand men, fully two thousand horsed, which all declared satisfactory.

Tactics could only be tentatively considered here and now, but it was agreed in general that their best strategy, assembling at various points in the early summer or late spring, would be to make a number of individual sallies against the occupation forces, to confuse them as much as possible, and also to disperse them, and then to mass for a major united assault in mid-summer, somewhere in the Highland West, forcing if possible Monck's army of Roundhead cavalry to come up and fight them in country quite unsuited to it, using the land to fight for them as Montrose had shown how, with ambushes, traps in bogs, disputed river-crossings, pass-holdings and the like.

With Ardvoirlich quite unable to put up all this company, with its attendants, for the night, a move was made as quickly as possible thereafter, with dispersal in all directions. Jamie, David and Thomas said farewell to Glengyle, who was heading back southwards as they had come, while they would ride due eastwards, along the loch and then following the River Earn by St Fillans, Comrie, Crieff and Perth, the direct route. They were all much heartened by the meeting and its prospects, and looked forward to forgathering again in the late spring, although Jamie found looking forward tended not to get beyond the next few months, if that, the prospects marital rather than military.

The trio got as far as a change-house in Comrie township that night, and were back in their own Angus glens before the next day's darkening.

22

It was not long before Jamie made an excuse to visit Airlie, and there found, amongst other things, that Lord Gray had left a message for him. Would young Ramsay go up to Dunnottar, recover the sword of state, and deposit it safely with the rest of the regalia at Kinneff, Gray of course being particularly concerned over the Honours.

This mission, reinforced by Airlie's urging, did not displease Jamie; but with his mind preoccupied by other matters, he could have done without it at the present time. However, he thought differently presently when, alone with Tina, he learned that she not only knew about the proposal but welcomed it; for she proposed to accompany him thereon. She had long wished to see Dunnottar and its inmates, of which she had heard so much. And, since it would scarcely do for a young man and woman to set off alone on such a venture, unwed, clearly they should get married promptly and be able to go in respectable fashion.

The bridegroom-to-be was delighted, needless to say. Would the earl agree?

Yes, her uncle was making no objection; so obviously Tina had done more than merely think about all this. She desired no large or elaborate wedding, and she did not suppose that he did. They could be wed in the parish church at the Kirkton of Airlie, with few but family present, just as soon as the arrangements could be made, if that would suit Jamie? And then, off to the north, together.

Overjoyed at this unexpected development, Jamie went back that evening to Bamff in a state of elation, with his news. Give her ten days, Tina had requested; as far as he was concerned, two would have been sufficient.

The Ramsays were nowise upset by word of all this, but perceived the need for haste in preparing the wing of the house for the newly-weds. Jean took charge of this, of course, and great was the busy-ness in cleaning up, painting and finding furnishings and plenishings for the hitherto all but neglected quarters, which consisted of a vaulted basement chamber, used as a laundry, which could be turned into a kitchen, and single rooms on the three floors above, ample accommodation.

The entire Ramsay family paid another visit to Airlie five days later, to discover what was required of them for the wedding. They found all equally astir there, as far as the women were concerned, the men tending to distance themselves from this activity. Mariota of Lintrathen appeared to be involved too. Tina on this occasion had little time for Jamie, although interested to hear of the furnishings at Bamff House. Wedding apparel seemed to be the primary concern of the Ogilvy girls for some reason, and the food and drink position and provision thereafter. Were nuptials always like this?

Airlie shut himself up in his withdrawing-room and Sir Gilbert with him, and David and Thomas disappeared. The central figure, the bridegroom surely, found himself almost in the way, and was sent to go and see the parish minister.

At the Kirkton, on the rising ground of what were called the Braes of Airlie, that elderly man proved to be another Ogilvy, claiming links with Inverquharity. He was more interested in the regalia situation than in discussing holy matrimony. But he took Jamie into the church, quite large for a country place of worship, briefly explained the procedure, commended the bride as a fine and bonny lass, and reverted to the subject of the Honours and the man James Grainger. Was he strong for the Covenant? Or otherwise? He had heard that these ministers up Aberdeen way were over-inclined to favour bishops and suchlike?

Jamie went back to Bamff that night wondering about weddings. They were necessary, presumably, but were the priorities right? If this was to be a quiet one, what would an ambitious and elaborate one be like?

* * *

On the eve of the great day, the Ramsays, taking their best clothes along with them, made not for Airlie Castle but for Lintrathen only. Apparently it was considered unsuitable for the groom to spend the night before the wedding under the same roof as his bride, another oddity. Here Mariota provided for the visitors most adequately, she and Jean giving Jamie much allegedly good advice. That young man took some time getting to sleep that night, preoccupied with thoughts anent the next one.

The ceremony was to be held before noon, in order to give ample time for the subsequent feasting, with the Ramsay party, plus bride, wishing to get back to Bamff before too late. So, after a somewhat chaotic breakfast, the young women concerned about having to ride nearly six miles in their fine dresses, all set out for the church, Jamie feeling almost guilty at being the cause of so much upheaval.

Reaching the Braes of Airlie they passed, and were hailed by, many folk, evidently on their way to attend the service, to the Ramsays' surprise. Seemingly the wedding was arousing much local interest, a token of the Ogilvy family's popularity and esteem. They found the church already almost full, so others would have to stand at the back. Jamie and Thomas joined the minister in the vestry, where presently they were pleased to see David Ogilvy coming to contribute moral support, not only the bridegroom wishing that it was all over. Thomas raised some alarm by wondering whether he had mislaid the ring, but discovered it in an inner pocket of his doublet. The Reverend Ogilvy kept popping out to check whether the bridal retinue had arrived.

Cheers from outside informed that it had, and the three young men were shepherded into the church proper, to stand, backs to the noisy congregation and facing the communion-table and site of the former altar, the minister hurrying off to ascertain that all was ready outside.

Then the strains of bagpipes were heard and, to cries of acclaim and delight, the earl's piper led in the bride, on her uncle's arm, all four female cousins behind, a smiling throng. Tina was looking at her loveliest, gowned simply but

291

effectively in white and silver, a circlet of Tay pearls keeping her abundant hair within bounds, and nowise appearing as though she had ridden the intervening miles to be there thus, the four bridesmaids all clad alike, and fair indeed even though none to compete with the bride in sheer beauty and the natural grace and poise with which she carried herself.

Up the central aisle they moved slowly, to the waiting three young men, Tina inclining her head left and right, faintly smiling, to the plaudits and calls of the company. Jamie all but choked at the sight of her, scarcely able to believe that all this was actually happening, and for himself. Her look to him did not help, so full of love, caring and understanding was it, leaving him all but breathless to complicate his choking, as she took her place at his side.

In fact, the man was hardly aware of what went on thereafter, although he went through the motions without too much indication from bride, brother and minister, all but dropping the ring but managing to retrieve it, and getting his fingers gripped as he slipped it on one of Tina's. Fortunately the ceremony was a brief one requiring a minimum of activity by the groom. Even when declared man and wife and the bride turned to be kissed, he was less expert at it than usual. No doubt she realised that he would make up for it in due course.

The required ministerial homily on the duties and responsibilities of a married couple thereafter was blessedly short, and moderate in content and tone, the benediction following with commendable promptitude. As all looked at each other, at the back the piper tuned up and burst into triumphant flourish.

Husband found himself leading wife down towards piper and door, and becoming aware that the pressure on his arm was intended to slow him down somewhat. Thereafter, as in a dream, he received his flood of congratulations and admonitions, the Ogilvy sisters' excitement in marked contrast to Tina's seeming almost amused composure. It appeared to Jamie a long time before they could don cloaks, mount horses, and set off back to Airlie.

The feasting which was provided there was sumptuous, and represented much forethought; but fortunately, apart from the toast proposed by the earl to the happy couple, replied to more by smiles than verbal eloquence, there was no speech-making. Even so Jamie longed for it all to be over, his one real concern to be alone with Tina. He was no misanthropist, he liked people, most people; but there were times and occasions when he felt that he was seeing overmuch of them, or all but one of them, of whom he could not see enough. As he ate and drank, and smiled and nodded, his inner voice was urgent, if repetitive, saying she is mine, mine, my wife, mine! He was almost having to convince himself.

Tina more or less had to act the appreciative recipient of felicitation and tribute for both of them.

There was a further intended treat when at last the banqueting was over, in the singing of a series of ballads, to musical accompaniment, by the Ogilvy cousins and Mariota, on the theme of romantic marriage and love, not all of which actually were entirely appropriate, however colourful and dramatic, and the sisters' enjoyment of it all most manifest.

It was with a sigh of relief that at long last the bridegroom heard Airlie announce that Sir Gilbert judged it time for the bride to go and change into travelling garb for the journey back to Bamff. Accompanied by the other girls as laughing assistants in this process, Tina left her husband's side. *He* would have preferred to have done the assisting.

Their send-off, after what seemed a considerable delay, was noisy as it was admonitory and protracted. Popularity undoubtedly had its drawbacks.

The five of them escorted Mariota to Lintrathen and then turned westwards, Jamie's ordeal nearly over. Did all men look on their weddings as ordeals? A women's institution, in fact? Tina had betrayed no signs of impatience nor preoccupation throughout.

It was dusk as they reached Bamff House, and the pair were led by Jean and Thomas to their own wing-tower. Although the temperature did not require it, cheerful fires blazed in the living-room – it could not be termed a hall – and in the bedchamber above. Pails and basins of water steamed beside

293

the latter, and honey wine and oatcakes were on a settle by the former.

Jamie accepted a special goodnight kiss from Jean when he accompanied brother and sister downstairs, together with a look from her which even in this dim light spoke volumes. Thankfully he shut the door on them, and turned to race up the turnpike stair. Alone, at last!

She was standing beside the living-room fire, sipping honey wine, and wisely, seeing his urgency, she got her beaker set down before he reached her almost at a run.

"At last! At last!" he cried, throwing his arms around her. "Oh, my dear, my heart's darling, it has seemed so long, eternity! At last we are alone! None to heed . . . but ourselves."

"Impatient one! I, I . . ." She got no further, her lips denied the formation of words by his hungry kissing. Yet, after a moment or two of gasping for breath, the said lips produced their own contributing eloquence.

At length, without releasing her, he held her a little way from him, to search her eyes. "Tina, lass, it is true? I am not dreaming this? We are wed? You are mine? And I am yours! Together. For all time. I do not but dream? Tell me that it is true. Man and wife. Now and hereafter, for ever! Say it, lass, say it!"

"I said it. In the church. Before all. I took you to be my wedded husband. Have you forgotten already, foolish one? Or did you just not hear me? Your wits elsewhere! And yet, you took me likewise as your wife. See, I have the ring to prove it. Is it not sufficient for you? Or must I say it again?"

"Yes, say it, say it. That you are mine. For ever. And none can take you from me."

"I am yours, yes, Jamie. Not to be taken from you. But are you not selfish? What of me? You are mine also, are you not? Marriage is two-sided. None to take you from me!"

"Think you that is likely? Is possible?"

"We weak women never know . . ."

"Weak! You! You, Tina, are the strongest person that it has been my lot to know. Which makes it the more

294

wonderful, scarcely believable, that you should give yourself to me."

"You make me sound like a harridan, a horror!"

Suddenly he had had enough of talk. He embraced and kissed her again, and then gestured aloft. "My dear, do you wish . . . to go up? Go first? To, to prepare for . . ." He left the rest unsaid.

"Why first? Why alone?" she asked. "I thought that you had had a sufficiency of being alone. You wish to be together, now and always." And she held out her hand to him.

So they mounted the stairs side by side, silent now.

In the firelit room above, with the great canopied bed which Jean had so thoughtfully had brought there, they stood for moments. It was the girl who pointed, this time, to the still faintly steaming pails.

"The longer we delay," she mentioned, "the colder will be the water."

Swallowing, he nodded.

"I claim a woman's privilege," she declared, lightly. "I wash first." And, with a touch to his arm, "And with a little assistance."

That had him more silent than ever.

She left him, to move over to the bed. "I have sometimes wondered what it would be like to be bathed by a man," she mentioned, over her shoulder. "Was that unseemly of me? Immodest?"

"No." He sounded a little hoarse.

She began to take off her clothes, her back to him, as he stood watching as though transfixed.

With only a short white shift left on, she turned to face him, and paused, the division of her bosom and her long white legs promising delight. Then, with a toss of her head, she pulled the shift up over her hair, which she then shook free, and so stood in all her naked loveliness, prospects more than fulfilled.

The man stared, breath held, wordless.

Tina remained thus for moments, not flaunting herself, indeed almost as though now undecided. Then, with another toss of the head, she came over to him beside the fire and the water pails.

"Yours," she said simply. "All yours. Is it . . . sufficient?"

Jamie was at his least eloquent, although his eyes, expression, posture even, with arms outstretched, said it all. "You . . . are . . . beyond all . . . perfect! Oh, woman! Woman!" And he went to take her to him.

She allowed his lips and hands free play for a while, with murmurs, never of protest nor even caution, but of pleas for patience with promise, which were, it is to be feared, largely unheeded. And, at length, she did push him away, with a laugh.

"Unfair!" she chided. "You cheat me. Myself, all-giving. You giving nothing! And . . . armoured in clothing! Besides, I am thus to wash, am I not? At least, you ought to pour the water!"

Saying something quite incoherent, he desisted in his handling and caressing, and turned to empty the two pails of now lukewarm water into the tub alongside. Then he aided her to step in. She did not sit, just large enough as it was.

Recovering his wits, if only just, Jamie stripped off his doublet and rolled up his shirt-sleeves, while Tina nodded approvingly. A soap-ball, a cloth, a towel and a panikin were there provided, and he used the last to scoop up water and pour it over her, with not a little splash and splatter betraying his excitement. Then he took the cloth and stood back a little to consider where he would start.

Tina raised arms to twist and coil up her abundant hair so that it did not get wet, which perhaps gave him the lead he required. So he started at her long and graceful neck, handling the wet soaped cloth carefully, almost soothingly, although soothing was scarcely the effect upon himself. He missed no inch, down to her shoulders, she raising arms again to aid him. Then her full and shapely breasts had him all but gasping his pleasure and appreciation, he lingering over them, back and forth as though these needed more thorough washing than the rest, the cloth somehow less effective than his fingers. In

296

fact so concerned was he at this stage that he found that the cloth needed rinsing out, and when he rose from so doing, it was to lean over and kiss the firm and pointed nipples, encouraging them.

With what from that young woman was almost a giggle, Tina also bent her head to kiss the man's hair.

Then he moved round, not exactly reluctantly, to wash the smooth back, not taking long to reach her cool, rounded bottom, and being particularly meticulous that the cleavage between buttocks should be adequately dealt with. Following the slender waist round to the front again, now he got down on his knees to do justice to the gentle swell of the belly and the dark and intriguing triangle below, which of course required a rather different treatment. Then on down those sculptured thighs and calves, with unfailing attention. He would, however, have ignored her feet, but Tina was not having that, and raised one out of the water to poke it at him.

"These surely need your service most," she declared, wiggling toes at him. "Do not shirk your duty, Jamie Ramsay, when you have been so . . . considerate further up!"

He kissed that foot, and then the other, as penance.

Straightening up, when he was beginning to go over it all again, just in case he had missed some part, she ordered the towel peremptorily, and stepped out.

Drying her had its moments also, of course, but she speeded this up by reproaching him that he had emptied both pails into the tub and so left no clean water for his own washing. Was he going to demean himself by bathing in her dirty water?

That had him tugging off shirt and breeches to demonstrate it as a privilege, and found himself being assisted in his disrobing by a naked and still somewhat damp female, which was not altogether a help, however acceptable. Getting those breeches right off required both agility and care, especially for a man aroused as Jamie was, and his helper, however willing, less than experienced in the matter.

Then, despite other urges, it was his turn to step into the tub and be poured water over and sponged down. Tina did not make quite such a process of it as he had done, but she was neither sparing nor slapdash, and did not omit any essential features, being very careful with her hands. The feel of those hands on him, and the sight of her bending down so close to him in all her rounded beauty, was almost more than the man could stand without leaping out and dragging her off to the inviting bed.

Perhaps something of the same sort of urgency affected her also, for suddenly she handed him the damp towel to dry himself, and almost ran over to the said bed, to throw herself on it, and there lie watching him, an invitation if ever there was one. Tina did not do things by halves.

It is to be feared that Jamie's towelling efforts were superficial, to say the least. Jumping out of the tub, he cast the towel away and went to her. The woman's arms came out to receive him.

Nevertheless, despite all the urgency and need, the man now sought to school himself to be gentle, realising something of her needs and feelings, emotional and physical, in a situation so new to her. With all her delectable, inviting and challenging person beneath him, he gave her time and aid, while yet so well aware of his own fiercely demanding masculinity.

That could last only so long, of course; but with Tina heaving and tossing under him, and then her biting at his shoulder, he did let himself go, in flooding fulfilment.

The woman's biting and twisting, and her gasping cry thereafter, did allow him to savour his foretaste of heaven without any self-condemnation, possessing and possessed.

Presently they lay in each other's arms, not in such drowsy bliss that they could not eye and fondle and stroke in achieved and continuing delight, their joy and wonder expressed more in touch than in words.

Unaware of the passage of time now, or of anything else save their oneness and the completion of identity, later they did not so much repeat their triumph as diversify it, less exigently but still with fervour and greater savouring, especially for Tina, who proved herself to be as positive in love-making as she was in all else.

Eventually they slept in each other's arms, all embraced.

23

Jamie and Tina set off on his errand to the north three days
later, and well pleased to be doing so as something which they
could do alone together and yet with its own importance on the
wider scene, the young woman also interested to see Dunnottar
and the Keith sisters, especially Mary of whom she had heard
so much. Jamie was just a little concerned over the prospect of
these two meeting each other, but did not say so.

They rode by Airlie where, there being no great need for
haste, they spent a few hours and had to deliver suitably
expurgated accounts as to their marital state to a highly interested audience. Then on by Kirriemuir to Forfar, the county
town, where there was a selection of inns and change-houses
for them to choose from, for the night, ensuring the privacy
and conditions which they could find reasonably enjoyable.

The following day they followed the picturesque Lunan
Water all the way down to Inverkeilor and Lunan Bay, where
at its Redcastle, they reported to Lord Gray and spent the
night in excellent comfort. Gray, as always, source, or at
least repository, for news, informed them that he had word
that Sir John Keith had got away by ship from Dysart in
Fife, for France; and that Monck and his colleagues were
said to believe that he had managed somehow to take the
missing regalia away with him. This was, of course, highly
satisfactory, however erroneous, for more than Keith, for it
presumably would mean that there would be no more English
search for the honours, and they could remain hidden at
Kinneff. That did not make it any less necessary that the
sword of state should be recovered from the seabed as quickly
as possible and deposited beside the other items. Ogilvie of
Barras was still imprisoned in Edinburgh Castle; but as far

as Gray knew there had been no untoward developments at Dunnottar Castle.

In the morning the pair were off again, taking the coastal route, by Montrose, St Cyrus and Inverbervie, new territory for Tina. It was September now and the days were beginning to shorten, so that, although they had to pass Kinneff, they did not call in at the manse, since Jamie imagined that Dunnottar might well be difficult to get into once darkness had fallen, in present circumstances. They pressed on.

Tina's first sight of the fortress, on its rock thrusting into the sea, had her exclaiming in admiration, declaring that it explained so much which had tended to mystify her hitherto. Small wonder that the English had been able to capture it only through the starvation of the garrison.

Down in the dip, they had some difficulty in gaining access, just before dusk as it was, the gates being shut and barred, and whoever kept the gatehouse suspicious and out of sight. Jamie had to do a deal of shouting, and then waiting, while presumably enquiries were being made, before at length the portcullis clanked and creaked up and the massive doors opened. And out therefrom came a single figure, running, a very female figure – the Lady Mary Keith.

"Jamie! Jamie!" she called, as she came.

That man, although he jumped down from his horse to greet her, could have done with a less enthusiastic greeting.

Tina looked on interestedly.

Mary flung herself into Jamie's arms, with exclamations and questions. But in all her huggings and babblings, her eyes were on the other woman, now also dismounting.

The man, declaring himself delighted to see Mary and hoping that all was well at Dunnottar, lost no time in turning towards Tina.

"Here is Christian Ogilvy, or Tina, my wife," he announced hurriedly. "We are wed. Not long since. Tina, here is the Lady Mary."

"I guessed that it could be none other," Tina said, smiling. "I have heard much of the Lady Mary. Have been most eager to meet her. I see that she is all that I have been told, and more!"

It was not often that Mary Keith was at a loss for words. Still clutching Jamie's arm, she stared at the other, lips parted but unspeaking now.

"I have brought Tina to see you all. And to recover the sword. At the Lord Gray's bidding. The sword of state." Jamie brought that out in something of a rush.

"I hope that you do not find my coming . . . inconvenient?" Tina asked innocently. "I promise to be no problem. How wonderful a place is your Dunnottar, that I see. And how wonderful what you, and the others, have done here. All must admire and salute you. Heroines, indeed!"

Mary found her voice. "I did not know. That Jamie was married. I, I . . . wish you well. I have heard of you, yes. But not, you . . ." She released the man's arm, shaking her head.

"We have been married only for one week," Tina told her helpfully. "It will come as a surprise to you, no doubt. I will endeavour not to disappoint too sorely!"

"No. I understand, now. You are . . . very beautiful!"

"You are kind! I can take no credit for my looks. But you – you have proved yourself in better ways, in courage and enterprise. And, with your own good looks, besides!"

They eyed each other searchingly, while the man looked on almost warily.

Then Mary produced a little laugh. "Welcome to Dunnottar!" she said. "Come," and turned to lead the way in.

Jamie decided that he should feel relieved probably.

As they led their horses up the steep incline between the succession of defensive barriers and outworks, Tina remarked wonderingly on it all, and Mary amplified and detailed. She informed that they had really no garrison in residence now, not wishing to bring down further possible English wrath upon themselves, only a few men now being needed to maintain the place. So far they had suffered no further attention from the occupation forces.

At the summit she asked Jamie about this of the sword. Why the haste to retrieve it? Was it not safer where it was?

He told her that the Lord Gray thought that it was scarcely wise to leave it there, feared that a storm could detach the float and so the position would be lost. Also that the sea water could damage it. He believed that it should be with the rest of the Honours at Kinneff, considering them to be secure there, since it seemed that Monck thought that Sir John Keith had escaped with them all to France. This news that her uncle was safe away was received with joy by the girl, although she was sorry to hear that Barras had not managed to get away with him. The Graingers would be relieved to learn that there was no suspicion that the regalia was in their church. They had been worried, naturally, that word of its whereabouts would get out somehow.

However, Mary had sad news for them. Janet Ogilvie, Barras's wife, had left the castle soon after the surrender and gone home to Barras. From there, a woman of spirit, she had set off southwards, with a servant, to try somehow to effect the release of her husband. At Dunnottar they had no details as to what she had actually attempted; all they knew was that she had been caught at it, and arrested in turn, so that she was now a captive also, just where none knew.

Saddened by these tidings, they were ushered into the keep.

The rest of the Keith family made the visitors very welcome, their interest in Tina undisguised. Jamie gathered that they had been having a dull, not to say humdrum life, more or less marooned up here on the rock-top, after all the excitements of the past, the lack of menfolk particularly felt by the lively girls. So the newcomers' unexpected arrival went down well.

They spent a pleasant evening, Tina creating an excellent impression and being notably friendly towards Mary, who began to respond. Nevertheless, when bedtime came, Jamie found himself and his wife being conducted not to his old chamber in the sea tower, of vivid memories, but to an upper chamber of the main keep itself, a gesture of some significance perhaps. Ushering them within, Mary did give him a goodnight kiss, although not of the lingering variety, but then, the others of the household had already done the like.

Alone, Tina turned to him. "So-o-o! Now much is explained, Jamie Ramsay!" she said, smiling. "I have to be the proud wife indeed, to have won so esteemed and popular a spouse! Am I not the fortunate one?"

He did not attempt an answer to that, but closed her lips otherwise.

Although not in his preferred room, he had no complaints to make as to the night which followed.

In the morning they all discussed the retrieval of the sword. Mary saw no reason why they should seek to do this secretly, or by night. There were no English up here nowadays; and anyway, the cliff-tops were seldom frequented. Tending their lobster-pots was a favourite Keith activity, so even if they were seen, no significance would be attached. The fisherfolk were back in their cottages, and boats available again. So they might as well make their endeavour right away.

Tina was not going to be left out of this notable venture; but the other young women also wanted to be involved. So it was decided that two boats would go lobstering, Mary, Jamie and Tina in one, the three sisters in the other. They would visit various pots first, then come together at the especial float – which had been constantly checked on to see that it was still in place – so that, even if they were being observed from the cliffs, nothing would look suspicious.

The six of them went down to the boat-strand, then, Jamie glad to greet the fisherfolk again. They collected the usual bait, and were aided in pushing off the two boats. Mary had brought along some sailcloth to wrap the sword in.

Tina was much interested in the lobster-fishing, preliminary as it was to greater things. She had never done this before; indeed she was not used to fishing at sea, her only occasional boating being on Lintrathen Loch. The fact that the caught lobsters, drawn up, were still alive, their great claws waving and threatening, fascinated her. She could also appreciate the way Mary and Jamie sat together on the central thwart, with the inevitable heaving bodily contact as they rowed, she catching the man's eye more than once, and winking.

They came to the vital float, with its leather circlet, in due course, and Jamie for one was much relieved to recognise the bladder still presumably in place. The other boat had got there first but, however reluctantly, the sisters had waited for their seniors, meanwhile scanning the cliffs, to report nobody in sight.

Manoeuvring their boat close, Jamie reached over to haul the float inboard, and then to tug at the rope. It came up some way, very much at a slant, and then held fast, this pulling the craft over. Quickly glancing at Mary, he heaved again, with no result save to heel the boat over somewhat.

"What? It is . . . it does not move!" he jerked, in alarm.

Mary came to pull also. "It is caught on something. The sword. Some rock, I expect. Wedged."

"Lord! Here's a pickle!! What can we do?"

"Pull it the other way. In the other direction. Row back. Try to drag it clear."

Jamie sat again, to take both oars to back-water, while Tina moved to help the other girl at the rope. But again they were brought up with a jerk, held fast.

The sisters shouted to ask what was wrong. Could they help?

Mary thought yes. Two boats tugging, and from different directions. Use their anchor-rope to hitch on to this rope.

That took a little doing, but the Keith girls were a practical lot and knew all about knots and wet cordage. Presently it was effected, the two ropes forming a Y-shaped yoke. Then, a synchronised pulling together.

At first, both craft were brought up sharply; but at the second attempt there was movement. All could feel a succession of catches away below them. Then, suddenly, there was just weight to pull up.

Eagerly pulled wet rope splattering them, they hoisted, and up to the surface appeared the sword of state, hilt first, with its curious double hook-shaped guard. Cries of triumph arose.

As they drew it inboard Tina, who of course had not seen it before, exclaimed at its size and beauty, longer than a normal sword, the elaborate hilt wrought in silver filigree, its junction with the blade covered by finely worked leaves, the long blade itself etched in Italianate design; it had, of course, been a gift to King James the Fourth from Pope Alexander the Sixth. It was all dulled and slightly corroded, but otherwise undamaged, and handsome indeed. Tina calculated that it had been carried before six monarchs since its arrival from Italy.

Then, the precious relic wrapped in the sailcloth and laid down amongst the clawing lobsters, the ropes were untied, and the two boats pulled back to the haven. Mary declared that she would treasure that special float as a memento.

Jamie took over their trophy on landing, to carry it up to the castle, observing that it was no wonder that Christian Grainger and her friend had been unable to disguise this heavy and lengthy object as any distaff for smuggling out.

That evening they held a celebratory feast of lobster meat. Tomorrow they would take the sword to Kinneff.

It was down the coast for the three of them next morning, the sword now carefully swathed in a large bundle of fish-nets, which ought to attract no attention along that shoreline.

At the manse, they found James Grainger collecting wind-blown apples in his garden. He was greatly cheered to learn that the sword had been recovered, his wife equally so. They took it into the house to unwrap it; Christian there and then set about cleaning and polishing it, declaring that it appeared to have suffered no lasting damage by its immersion.

Where to put it now? The minister said that he had buried the rest of the Honours under a slab below the pulpit in the kirk; but there was no room there for such a long object. Some other hiding place.

They all trooped into the church, and were not long in deciding that the best place to put that sword was beneath the pews, preferably at the west end of the building. They picked out an area where the stone slabs of the flooring could best be lifted and no sign of the move to remain.

The Graingers were much relieved to hear that occupying forces' leaders were assuming that Sir John Keith had escaped to the Continent with the regalia, which ought to ensure no suspicions and searchings would develop up here. The minister had been much worried about this possibility, worried about the entire situation. He had wanted to write to the patron of his living, the Earl Marischal, informing him of the position and seeking instructions – his simple duty, surely. But he had no means of communicating with the earl, in France, and instead had written to Lady Anne Douglas, asking her, if she had the opportunity, to send the word to the Marischal. This lady, it seemed, was now betrothed to the earl, whose wife, the Keith girls' mother, had long been dead. Anne Douglas was the sister of the Earl of Morton, at Aberdour Castle in Fife and was known to be intending to join her husband-to-be in France whenever opportunity offered. Jamie had hitherto only once or twice heard mention of this lady, which seemed to indicate no great affection for her at Dunnottar. But Grainger was most anxious that the earl should know the position, so as to inform King Charles that his crown was safe. If he had realised that Sir John Keith had escaped, he would not have troubled the lady. Now, presumably, he would have to write again to inform her that the sword was also recovered and hidden.

Mary Keith did not see why this was necessary, but was prepared to recognise that the parish minister's duties towards his principal heritor and stipend-payer were important to him.

Jamie helped Grainger move a couple of rows of the wooden pews and then prise up three of the stone slabs beneath, remove a little of the underlying earth, insert the wrapped sword in the cavity and then replace the slabs, sweeping all traces of activity away and restoring the pews to their places. Meanwhile Tina made friends with the pleasant and courageous woman who bore the same name as herself, declaring how greatly she admired what the other had done and the risks taken.

The visitors were given a simple but acceptable meal, and departed, duty done.

Mary took them back by Barras, inland a couple of miles; but there was no one there who could give them any news as to the laird and his lady.

Jamie and his wife spent a further couple of days at Dunnottar, enjoying the company and being shown the countryside around, Tina being especially impressed with the Fowlsheugh cliffs and birdlife; and interested on a visit to Stonehaven to see the town's tolbooth where her husband had been incarcerated so briefly. He was not a little surprised to note how friendly Tina and Mary had become, clearly appreciating each other's attitudes and characters, and frequently combining to tease and gently mock the man they both had found to their tastes. Women never ceased to astonish that man.

When they bade farewell to the Keiths, it was with promises to return to Dunnottar when possible, Jamie not forgetting that military activities looming ahead might delay that for some time.

They spent the night thereafter at the Redcastle of Lunan again, to inform the Lord Gray of the sword situation; and by fast riding, were back at Bamff by the following dusk.

24

That winter and early spring was a happy time for Jamie
Ramsay, who found married life highly satisfactory, with
Tina constant joy. A challenge also, for she was no meek
and mild wife and demanded the best in a man. She very
much shared in his activities and responsibilities in the
barony, ranging the Forest of Alyth and the surrounding
area with him, and getting to know its people, the tenants,
farmers, cowherds, shepherds, millers and woodsmen, with
their families, for however scattered, it was all very much of
a community. She had a great capacity for making friends and
receiving confidences; indeed Jamie sometimes complained
that everyone seemed to bring their troubles and problems
to her, whether she was able to solve them or not. Even
the undemonstrative and sometimes remote-seeming Thomas
opened up with her in a way he never did with others. And
Jean asserted that there must be more to her younger brother
than she had reckoned to have won such a wife.

The only shadow on the couple's happiness, as the months
passed, was the separation which lay ahead, and which might
possibly be fairly prolonged, for it was a campaign which
was envisaged, no mere assault or two against the enemy,
Glencairn ambitious to free Scotland of the occupying English
altogether, however major an undertaking. Jamie in one way
looked forward to playing his part in the attempt; but having
to leave Tina to do so was a dire thought. She was not very
happy about it either, however spirited a young woman.

In the event, the pair had longer together than anticipated,
and for a significant reason. The Lord Protector Cromwell
was having trouble on two fronts: in England, with the Rump
Parliament dismissed and the Barebones one which followed

declaiming against him, for Cromwell was a soldier rather than a parliamentarian; he was now proposing to rule without any parliament, to rumblings of discontent. His other trouble was in Ireland, where there was armed revolt. He required to deal with the former himself and so could not lead in putting down the Irish. So he ordered Monck to do this, to assemble an English fleet and take an army over the Irish Sea. Word of this came, as usual, from Lord Gray, whose sources of information at Dundee were valuable indeed. Gray had sent word to Glencairn, who recognised the advantage of waiting until Monck and his troops were out of Scotland before making his attacks, in the hope of less effective English leadership by the generals left in charge. It took some time, of course, for Monck to gather shipping in sufficient numbers, and men, at Dumbarton on the Clyde, so the Scots venture was delayed, and considerably. No complaints emanated from Bamff House.

In fact it was early August before word came from Glencairn, via Airlie, to muster. The deplored parting had to take place. Tina accompanied Jamie and Thomas, with forty-five of their people, mounted on garrons – awkward time as it was for most of them with harvest almost upon them – as far as Airlie Castle, where the faction's contingent was to assemble, and there to say farewell, a grievous matter for not only the Ramsays, although Tina sought to maintain a cheerful front and make encouraging noises towards the departing warriors.

Nominally in command, David Lord Ogilvy led a sizeable party of some two hundred and thirty mounted men westwards, for Loch Earn, to put the Scots challenge to the test.

They followed a different route from previously, to give English-held Perth a wide berth, by Rattray and Dunkeld to Strath Braan and so down the Sma' Glen to Crieff and Comrie, heading again for Ardvoirlich on the southern shore of Loch Earn, passing the intervening night at Amulree. At Ardvoirlich, Stewart thereof gave them unexpected instructions. Glencairn's tactics were to confuse the enemy, and to this end he was dividing his hoped-for force into a number of groupings, to raid into various English-held areas, thus dispersing the opposition. Lorne, Lochiel, Glengarry and other Highland chiefs were to assemble up in Rannoch, to threaten to cut off Aberdeenshire and the north-east from the Roundhead headquarters at Dundee. A force was to remain here at Loch Earn, with a view to assailing Perth. And Glencairn himself was down at Duchray, near Loch Ard in the Trossachs, from where he could descend on Glasgow and Stirling, although that mighty fortress-castle was scarcely to be tackled.

Ardvoirlich thought that the Airlie contingent should stay there, and form the nucleus of this Loch Earn force, with his Stewarts – they were the first to arrive; but Jamie felt that he ought to report to Glencairn himself, in case he had any especial tasks for them. Moreover, Loch Ard and Duchray were only some twenty-five miles away, easily reached; so it was decided that he should take the Ramsay party down there, leaving David and the main body at Ardvoirlich meantime, until they learned how the campaign was planned.

So next morning Jamie and Thomas led their people off along the loch shore westwards to Edinample, where they turned due southwards to climb up the quite steep Glen Ample and over a small pass under Ben Each, down to Loch Lubnaig in Strathyre. Still southwards they came, under soaring Ben Ledi, to Loch Venachar, turned westwards along it and then south again over the Mounth of Teith to Aberfoyle. Loch Ard was only a further couple of miles, and Duchray Castle just to the south of it. They reached it through another narrow but much lower little pass, with mighty Ben Lomond looming ahead. They were none so far from the MacGregor's Glen Gyle here.

In fact Glengyle himself was the first of the leaders they saw when they reached Duchray, a mutually pleasant meeting. He took the Ramsay brothers into the modest Duchray Castle. There seemed to be no very large assembly here.

They found the earl, with Lord Kenmure, Duchray himself and a number of other Graham and Cunningham lairds, debating strategy. They were well received, Glencairn concerned that as yet numbers were less than looked for, the expected parties of Buchanans, Colquhouns, and Macfarlanes not yet having put in an appearance. He had only just over three hundred men here, inadequate for their proposed assaults. He was still adhering to his dispersal tactics as best overall, however. He was glad to hear that the Ramsays could have another two hundred Airlie men down from Ardvoirlich in a day, if need be, under Lord Ogilvy.

It seemed that the earl's intention was to make a first gesture towards Stirling, not at the fortress-citadel of course but aimed at the strategic Fords of Frew, about eight miles west of the town, where a small English outpost was based to guard the important crossing of the River Forth amongst all the impassable bogland of the Flanders Moss; this in the hope of coaxing the Roundhead Colonel Kidd, holding Stirling Castle, out to counter-attack, and thereupon luring him westwards into this mountainous country, where he and his heavy cavalry would be at major disadvantage. It seemed a sound enough plan, as a start to their campaign; and if Kidd did not rise to their bait, no great harm would be done to their further activities. Jamie gathered that it was in fact Glengyle's idea in the first place.

Glencairn, a strange man with a long bony face and prominent nose, said that they would wait for another two or three days for reinforcements to arrive, and then strike.

Glengyle thereafter suggested that if they were going to wait these two days, why would not the Ramsay brothers come back with him to his house a mere ten miles away, for comfort, instead of biding at this overcrowded Duchray. They were glad to avail themselves of this invitation. Glencairn had no objection, so long as they were back in time; and Graham himself no doubt welcomed it.

On their way north-westwards through the Trossachs heights, the MacGregor told them that he knew why the Buchanans, Colquhouns and Macfarlanes, of this Lomond and Lennox area, were in no hurry to appear. It was because Glencairn was a Lowlander and they were reluctant to be led by such. Even Lorne, a Campbell, was preferable; the clans had their own priorities. This struck a distinctly ominous note for his hearers. So, on their way over the Mounth, Jamie sent a couple of their men northwards again to Loch Earn, to urge David Ogilvy to bring his Airlie company down to Duchray, whatever Ardvoirlich said, to add to the force there.

The brothers spent a pleasant couple of days in Glen Gyle, their host taking them deer-stalking on one of them and fishing in Loch Katrine on the other, unusual campaigning activities, while his wife proved, as before, a kind and effective hostess. Then back to Duchray.

They found that the Airlie party had duly arrived an hour or two before themselves, and had been welcomed, for otherwise only a small group under Colonel Blackadder of Tulliallan, another Lowlander, had come in, although these, thirty well-horsed troopers, were a useful accretion at this stage. Glencairn had decided not to wait any longer. They would move on the morrow.

Apart from the MacGregor's running gillies it was entirely a mounted force which set off next morning early, eastwards, for if they did successfully draw this Colonel Kidd out of Stirling Castle, it would be cavalry which they would have to deal with. They rode along the side of the infant Forth, by Aberfoyle, to emerge from the constriction of the hills to the wide flood-plain of the quickly widening river, that unique feature of Scotland which had affected its history since history was, the great and vital barrier between Highlands and Lowlands, twenty-five miles long by five wide, the Flanders Moss. This, closing the central belt between the estuaries of Clyde and Forth, formed an all but impassable obstacle for armies as for ordinary travellers, save at one or two narrow and far from obvious places, the Fords of Frew one of these. Elsewhere it was all bog and swamp, lochans and pools, a drowned land of islets, scrub forest, thickets, rushes, reeds and peat-bogs, the haunt of the wildest of the wild creatures; that is, save for the larger Loch of Menteith towards this western end, the notable sheet of water two miles by one, to one of the islands of which the child Mary, Queen of Scots had been sent for safety, at the age of five, to escape the clutches of England's

Henry the Eighth's Rough Wooing tactics, before her removal to France.

Along the north flanks of the Moss and this loch Glencairn's force trotted, the running gillies by no means holding back the horsemen. This was all Graham country, and Duchray very much led the way, indeed the lairds of two of the properties they had to pass, Rednock and Ruskie, were with the company. The MacGregors knew it all very well also, but for different reasons; secret and diverse ways across the watery wilderness were highly useful for some of them in their not infrequent raids on southern cattle-lands, as means of getting the resultant booty back into the safety of their mountains without being followed up by angry owners.

Beyond the Loch of Menteith they went for some five miles, overlooking the widest part of the Moss, to the hamlet of Thornhill of Boquhapple, where they abruptly turned off southwards into the Moss itself, but by a narrow and winding though passable track. After a mile of this, strung out as now necessarily they were, they did have to cross a shallow ford, this not the Fords of Frew but to cross the minor Goodie Water. It was a further couple of miles to the River Forth itself, now wide indeed, and they went at the ready, for the English outpost at Frew Wester was known to be about fifty strong, and they would not be likely to fail to observe the approach of a large mounted company, and take appropriate action. It was known also that they had parties based on both sides of the ford, and almost certainly when they saw the size of the advancing force, those on the north bank would retire quickly to the south side and there seek to hold the wide river-crossing from a fairly strong position.

It was now that Glengyle proved his worth, the MacGregor knowing a thing or two, as had been indicated, about picking a way across this flood-land barrier. Not for nothing was it called the Fords of Frew, in the plural, for the river here wound through an astonishing series of meanders, sometimes coiling back and round almost to meet an earlier loop; and after some five hundred yards upstream from the main ford, there was another shallowing, out of sight because of scrub woodland intervening. It was not a direct crossing, zigzag and difficult, but passable for determined men, the second ford. So, before coming into view of the outposts, Glengyle dismounted and led his eighty clansmen off right-handed, to make for this, while the mounted force waited for a while, to give the Gregorach time to make their especial contribution. They had come about seventeen miles from Duchray.

They remained stationary for some twenty minutes or so before moving on; and after another half-mile came into full view of the hutments of the enemy position. And not only were these visible but much activity thereabouts also. For they could now see the MacGregors running along the southern side of the river towards the main ford, no doubt yelling, although they were too far off to be heard; and English troopers mounting, to prepare to deal with them, those on the north side crossing the river to aid their fellows.

Glencairn saw the signal, and the Scots mounted force spurred forward to the attack.

Actually little attacking developed, for the Roundheads were no fools, and most evidently quickly saw the situation as untenable, an assault by many times their number from front and rear. So instead of seeking to hold the ford, they were not long in turning and riding off in the general direction of Stirling, before the MacGregors could reach them. There was no real disappointment about this for the Scots, for it was all as planned.

The further plan now was to pursue the fleeing English, not with any hope of catching up with them but to emphasise the threat to Stirling town eight miles away, the towering castle rock even from here dominating the landscape. So, after splashing across the ford, the mounted men rejoined the MacGregors, and all set off on the heels of the departing enemy, but in no great haste, for such was not called for now.

Both groups had no option but to proceed due southwards for a mile or so, by the only firm track through the bogland, till they reached the rising ground where the Gargunnock foothills began to rise, and where they could turn eastwards.

They did keep the fleeing enemy in sight, which was all that was intended.

About two miles from the outskirts of Stirling town, in the Touch area where they would be plainly visible to watchers up in the castle, they halted. It was just past noon. What would be the English reaction, and when? The Scots leaders had sought to time it all, as best they could; but Colonel Kidd's counteractions could only be guessed at.

Glencairn sent scouts up to the high ground of Craigniven to keep watch, and dismounted his force to rest and eat their rations. So far, so good. But if Kidd delayed any move until the next day, it could be awkward. They were unsure as to what size of a force he had in Stirling town and fortress; but it was thought that it might number at least five hundred men, seasoned cavalry. Suppose that he chose to wait for darkness, and made a night attack? The general feeling was that he would not do this; but that, assessing that the Scots involved, whoever they were, would have only about half that number, he would sally out at this impudent threat just as soon as he could muster his array. After all, there were still, in mid-August, some seven hours of daylight.

Glencairn went over with his leaders the procedure if and when the English did respond.

In the event, they did not have any long period of waiting before their scouts hastened down to report that a large cavalry force from around the rock-foot of Stirling Castle had appeared, and was heading in this direction. How many they could not judge at that range, but it looked to be at least four troops of horse.

That was good enough for Glencairn. He gave orders for retiral. His main horsed company, not riding too quickly at this stage, would return as they had come, but not seek to defend the Fords of Frew; but the MacGregors to run back along the *south* side of the Flanders Moss, in a possible diversionary move. They could cross the Moss in due course, west of the Loch of Menteith, using their local knowledge, and possibly make a useful contribution in any subsequent affray.

Jamie, Thomas and David were not alone in finding the

journey back to Aberfoyle one of the strangest experiences of their lives. They had to regulate their pace carefully, while seeming to be in full retreat; and with seventeen miles to cover that was no simple matter. The problem of keeping the pursuit well in sight but at a safe distance was no light one for a force of their size, strung out as they so largely had to be, Glencairn in fact riding at the rear of his troops, continually to glance back gauging distances. So far as they could see, once over the Fords of Frew, all the enemy appeared to be following them and none the MacGregors, which was satisfactory. The aim was to keep them at about a mile's distance as far as possible, which meant constantly adjusting their own speed, no easy task with all the different types of horses and riders, and over undulating country with many dips, burns to cross and soft ground to avoid, their track only a drove-road. The same conditions, of course, applied to the foe, only they would be seeking to catch up, not to maintain the gap. Being bait for a trap represented a new role for the Scots.

They were fairly successful at it, however, as mile succeeded mile westwards along the flanks of the Moss. Admittedly sometimes the enemy were a little too close and sometimes the reverse; but on the whole the strategy worked, Glencairn's messengers riding up and down the long column seeking to control the pace required. Matters were a little complicated by Colonel Kidd – if he was indeed in command of the pursuit – having a scouting patrol in front, sometimes well ahead, which had to be allowed for; fortunately this small group would have no desire to get really close, and risk being turned upon and annihilated.

When they got as far as the Loch of Menteith, there was the further problem of its wooded shores, which meant that the two forces were frequently hidden from each other, and distance-keeping the more difficult.

In open ground again a mile or so past the loch, tactics changed. A small rearguard of Blackadder's troopers was left behind to carry on at approximately the same pace, to remain well within sight of the foe now; and the bulk of Glencairn's company dug in spurs to hasten forward at maximum speed.

In the twists and bends of the drove-road, it was hoped that this would not be too obvious.

The force now pounded on and through the township of Aberfoyle, heading for the pass beyond, where the stripling Forth wound its way through the suddenly steep and enclosing hillsides after emerging from its two head-streams and Loch Ard. Here was the scene of operations, at last.

No time was to be lost now. Up into the scattered woodlands which clothed the foot of Craigmore, a modest but abrupt mountain, the horsemen turned their mounts to climb. It had all been prospected beforehand, and each group knew where to go, the main requirement being that they should be hidden from the riverside track below. They had to be very quick about it all. And up in their cover they found their foot colleagues from Duchray encampment already in position and waiting – no doubt had been for hours. Now it was all very much a hurried manoeuvre.

Jamie and his friends were barely in their allotted position, amongst a group of MacNaughton clansmen, with the Viscount Kenmure nearby, when they heard the clatter of hooves on the track below, out of sight because of the trees and the fall of the ground: that would be Blackadder's thirty hurrying through. Then silence, save for the unfortunate occasional whinny of a restive horse.

They seemed to have quite a wait now, and Jamie for one hoped that the English had not taken fright at the sight of this pass. But no, presently there was the sound of more hooves, which would represent the advance party of the enemy proceeding onwards. This they were allowed to do, unchecked.

Another wait, briefer this time, and then more hoof-beats and the clink of armour rising above the murmur of the cascading river. This also was allowed to go on for some time, however impatient the waiting, hidden men; for of course the track below was narrow and the foe inevitably much strung out, at two or three abreast at most.

Then, at length, Glencairn's horn sounded ululating and echoing from the hillside, and it was action. Downhill men rushed, mounted and on foot, swords and dirks drawn, all along the little pass.

What followed could nowise be described as a battle. The Roundhead troopers had no least chance to present any effective opposition or defence against the hurtling attackers, in elongated column as they were, the foremost possibly a quarter of a mile ahead of the rearmost. Cut up into groups of four or six, they had barely time to unsheath their swords and seek to control frightened, rearing horses, when the attack was upon them. Many were cut down, more unseated and trampled, some swept right over into the river. It was massacre rather than fighting.

Jamie was amongst the many who did not even get his sword bloodied. After his charging garron cannoned into an English trooper's mount, throwing the rider, he had difficulty in drawing up his beast before it too would have plunged down into the water. By the time that he had recovered control, and reined round, someone else had dealt with the unseated Roundhead. However, he himself was almost jostled out of his saddle by escapers fleeing back whence they had come. Chaos reigned in that pass, but bloody and contrived chaos, no overall order of victors or vanquished being possible. There was no question, of course, as to the outcome, only how many of the enemy would win free. Some of the English were seeking to climb up into the steep woodland from which their assailants had descended, others taking their chances in the river rather than trying to fight their way back along the track. Some men died fighting bravely, but most had other priorities.

Kenmure, nominally in the charge of the horsed men, tried to rally pursuit eastwards, with only partial success. Jamie and David joined him, with some of Blackadder's party now returning back, too late to be involved in any active part of the actual encounter. Their alarmed horses shying and rearing away from the dead and dying who littered the track, they rode, shouting their acclaim.

There was further cause for congratulation presently when they found that a large proportion of the would-be escapers had been trapped at the mouth of the pass by Glengyle and his Gregorach. Some had got past, their heavy horses cleaving a way through, but a great many more bodies lay in heaps, over eighty, some enthusiast declared.

There was no point in further pursuit, for any who had won free thus far would be unlikely to be caught in the open country, dispersed and in desperate flight. So it was back up the pass triumphant; yet many of them, including Jamie Ramsay, in unsoldierly reaction to all the savagery and bloodshed and the gruesome indications of their victory. Warfare was not all glory and martial ardour; there was revulsion also.

Nevertheless, jubilation and exultation had to reign. They had very completely won the day, the first real victory, however modest in scale, against the hated invaders, and their own casualties negligible. There was only the one disappointment: they did not appear to have killed or captured this Colonel Kidd.

The victors, with the wounded, prisoners and captured horses, trooped back to Duchray in triumph.

25

To celebrate and make use of the victory, Glencairn ordered a series of ride-outs and marches from Duchray, mere demonstrations as these were, parties of horse and foot sent here and there, openly, indeed challengingly, throughout this central area of the land, to let the people know that the dreaded occupation troops were no longer in control hereabouts. Jamie and his colleagues took part in these sallies, ranging as far east as Doune, Dunblane and the Ochil foothills townships, south to the villages of Buchlyvie, Balfron, Kippen and even to Falkirk, while others rode almost to the outskirts of Glasgow. Stirling itself they carefully avoided, for its great citadel was quite beyond any assault, and the numbers of its garrison were not known, and they could be dangerous. One result of all this was the belated adherence of the Lomondside clans, the Macfarlanes, Colquhouns and Buchanans, which much increased the numbers mustered in the Aberfoyle area, to the extent that the Graham country groaned under the need to support them all.

This situation, and word from the north that the other Highland groups had been doing their own raiding, from Loch Earn and Rannoch, decided Glencairn that a change in strategy was now due. He was not foolish enough to believe that the Cromwellian generals left in command in Scotland during Monck's absence would sit idle at Dundee, Edinburgh, Inverness and elsewhere while all this was going on; so he decided that it was time to assemble as one large army, and act as such in the royal cause.

So orders were sent out for all to gather at a suitable, convenient and safe area: Rannoch, seventy or so miles to the north, in central Perthshire, from whence they could make their major attempt at freeing at least the northern half of Scotland.

It was a cheerful and sizeable force, then, which set off northwards, almost one thousand strong, to collect the Loch Earn contingent at Ardvoirlich and then to proceed on up Glen Ogle to Loch Tay-side to reach the Strath of Appin by Fortingall and so on to the assembly area of the main Highland clans at Foss, between the great lochs of Rannoch and Tummel.

The cavalry covered that quite difficult and round-about journey through the thronging mountains in just over two days, but the foot took considerably longer. The lengthy valley of the River Tummel, stretching westwards from near Pitlochry almost to the desolation of the vast Moor of Rannoch, some thirty miles, was sufficiently wide to rank as a strath, a major depression between the mountain ranges of Breadalbane and Atholl, dotted with lochs, an ideal place for an all-Highland muster, cut off from and with no easy access to the low country, yet populated enough to support, at least temporarily, a large gathering of men. And large indeed was the assemblage which the newcomers joined, with a great variety of clansfolk and their chiefs and leaders. This was Menzies territory, and the House of Foss was serving as headquarters, that clan of course well represented, however outnumbered by the larger ones. The Earl of Atholl, whose lands neighboured to north and east, had twelve hundred foot and over a hundred horse; Cameron of Lochiel four hundred; MacDonnell of Glengarry three hundred; Farquharson of Inverey nearly as many; Robertson of Struan, Macpherson of Cluny, Mackintosh and his Clan Chattan supporters, Macgillivrays, Shaws, Macphails, Macbeans, Cattanachs, Macqueens and the rest, with up to two hundred each; and many lesser chieftains with their hundreds and fifties. Quite a representation of Aberdeenshire, Mearns and Moray lairds were there, Forbes, Gordon, Fraser, Grant, Burnet and the like, these all with mounted men. Others were still arriving, and with Glencairn's host, the total was already some seven thousand, a goodly command.

There were congratulations over the Aberfoyle exploit and

its effects, and reports of complementary gestures towards Perth, Aberdeen, Elgin, even Inverness, with details of enemy forces and garrisons. All were eager for action now.

Glencairn was nothing loth. But he observed that Lorne and his Campbells had not yet shown up – and having at least another thousand to add to their numbers. Moreover, he was the acting lieutenant-general of this array. The earl felt that he must wait for Lorne. As a Lowlander he presumably did not realise just how this decision would be deplored, just how unpopular were the Campbells amongst the other clans.

They waited two more days, three, and then sent urgent messengers to Innischonnel in Argyll, demanding attendance, while resentment seethed in the royalist camp.

With still no word of the Campbells coming, five days later the army marched.

The strategy now was to try to effect the cutting-off of all occupation forces in the north from the line of Dundee and Perth, this including of course the city of Aberdeen, a major objective. Farquharson of Inverey, knowledgeable about how best this could be effected, suggested that they proceeded to his own barony and territory of Inverey, in Cromar, at the head of the River Dee, from where they could exert control over the huge area of inland Aberdeenshire, Buchan and Moray, and be able to descend on the city itself by either Dee or Don valleys. This was accepted by the others as the first step.

To march a large army, horse and foot, from Rannoch to upper Deeside, was no light undertaking. It would involve at least another seventy miles of high mountainous country to cover, with all the problems of rounding ranges and lochs, climbing passes and fording rivers innumerable. Going by Tummel and Pitlochry, Straloch and Kirkmichael, surmounting more passes, to Glen Shee, then up over the great pass of the Cairnweill, and so down to the Dee at Braemar – that was the challenge. The foot, although nearly all Highlanders and used to hill travel, would take at least four days to do it, even the cavalry requiring more than two. Fortunately they ought not to have to encounter any English on the way, so there should be no need for especial groupings nor defensive measures.

It was now late August and the mountain land was at its loveliest, the heather out on all the moors and hillsides, the birches just beginning to turn towards golden, the bog-cotton and marsh marigolds and meadowsweet rioting on all the levels, the little white roses and the bluebells everywhere. For Jamie and his friends the ride through a spectacular country unknown to them was so far removed from anything military as to engender almost a holiday mood.

Well towards the head of a long procession of riders, topping one of the highest passes in the land at well over two thousand feet, the Cairnweill, between Glen Shee and Glen Clunie, Jamie asked Farquharson of Inverey what Cromar meant – for that is where they had been told they were making. It was explained that the huge and ancient earldom of Mar, once indeed one of the original mormaordoms or sub-kingdoms of Pictish Alba, consisted of three divisions, Midmar to the south, Braemar to the north here, and Cromar, the smallest but still large, the north-western portion, the name meaning the enclosed or remote position. And remote and enclosed it was, these mountains on their left part of it. Threaded by the upper reaches of the great River Dee, it reached westwards into the highest land-mass of all Scotland, the Monadh Ruadh, or Red Mountains. His seat of Inverey sat on the south bank of Dee just below the waterfalls of the Linn o' Dee. They would be there in an hour or so.

Presently, coming down out of the narrows of steep Glen Clunie into the wider strath of Dee was like entering a different land, fair, open, tree-clad, after the barren constrictions of the heights and their stony passes. Here, at the river, already a major rushing stream, they turned westwards, up its south bank, the six more miles to the glen of the Ey Water, near the mouth of which reared the castle of Inverey, Farquharson's seat, on a rocky knoll above level meadows, unusual for these uplands; which was as well, if their thousands of men were going to be based here. Presumably Farquharson knew what he was taking on.

The army all arrived in due course, and settled in, making as orderly an encampment of it as conditions allowed, here basing themselves for a campaign, the progress of which would be determined by events. They must wait for Lorne and his Campbells, and other reinforcements, but they would be active while they waited.

They had not been settled in at Inverey for more than a few days, making ride-outs and excursions from there more or less to show the royalist flag, Jamie and his friends busy, when they discovered how efficient were the Roundheads at gaining information, presumably employing a network of spies up and down the land. News reached Glencairn that a large English force had arrived at Aberdeen, and under none other than Major-General Morgan; so General Lambert, who had been left in command in Scotland while Monck was in Ireland, had learned of the Highland move here, and was wasting no time. It looked, therefore, as though action would not be long delayed.

A council of war at Inverey was divided in opinion as to strategy now. One view was the obvious one: to march down Dee and Don for Aberdeen without delay, and challenge Morgan to battle. He would not have as many troops as themselves, even though they were professional soldiers. Another view was to wait, let Morgan do the attacking, and hope that Lorne would arrive from the west to reinforce them. Glencairn rather favoured this plan. Down in the lower country, nearer the city, the advantage would be apt to be with the heavy armed cavalry of the Cromwellian force; whereas what had happened at the Aberfoyle pass engagement showed the weakness of the enemy in narrow mountainous territory. Let Morgan come to them, then, if he dared, and they would try to decoy him into a suitable killing-ground and teach him his lesson. If he did not venture out, however, remained in Aberdeen, they would have to adopt different tactics; but in that case Lorne's additional strength would be the more valuable.

If this seemed a feeble attitude to some of the more fiery

chiefs, the majority agreed that it was probably wise in the circumstances.

In the event, the decision was taken for them anyway. For only the very next day urgent word reached Inverey that in fact Morgan with a large English force was on the march up Deeside, heading for them.

So now it was decision of a different sort: how to deal with this imminent threat, and no time to waste. Glencairn, Aberfoyle very much in his mind, turned to Farquharson. Where was the nearest pass-like area into which they could hope to lure Morgan and deal with him as they had done with Colonel Kidd? And Farquharson was in no doubts as to that. Up-river three miles was the Linn o' Dee, where the valley suddenly narrowed into what was in effect a defile, and which continued for another couple of miles westwards to where it widened again, where the Liath Water's glen came in from the south, parallel to this Glen Ey. If they could trap the Roundheads in that . . . !

There was no time for prolonged debate, with an army to move before the English came up with them. Orders were given for a swift departure for all, westwards, while local scouts were sent in the other direction, to keep watch for Morgan's approach.

As Glencairn's thousands threaded those narrows past the spectacular cataracts and waterfalls of the Linn o' Dee, it was amply clear that Farquharson had been right. This lengthy and winding passage and track could be a death-trap for any strung-out force attacked from the wooded hillsides, the Aberfoyle situation on a much larger scale. Their own host threading it was itself strung out for over a mile, Glencairn and his lieutenants examining the ambush possibilities as they went. There were opportunities all the way, steep woodlands on one side, rushing river on the other, twists and bends by the dozen. If they could coax Morgan in here, they would have him.

When they reached the Liath Water, coming down from the major mountain of Carn Liath, there was a widening, with much open ground flanking the junction of the two rivers, which would be flooded in winter but was dry enough at present. The Highland host settled down here, in temporary encampment, five miles west of their previous site.

Leaving the mass of his men there, Glencairn and most of his leaders, Jamie, David and Thomas included, retraced their steps, on foot now, to decide on the details of their hoped-for ambushes, and who would go where. There was a superfluity of possibilities, ample hiding places for the attackers and few spots where the passageway below widened.

They were perhaps halfway through when scouts met them to report that the English were in fact none so far off, having made good time up the comparatively easily accessible Deeside, good going all the way for cavalry. They had got as far as Invercauld when these scouts had left, and were still coming on.

So it was back to Glen Liath encampment, the leaders of companies and groups to assemble their men at once and take up a succession of chosen positions along the lengthy anticipated killing-ground. There was much eagerness and excitement now at the prospect of seeing action at last.

The Airlie contingent, including Jamie and Thomas's Bamff party, were allotted a fairly central position above a sharp bend of the river. At this point on the tree-clad hillside they discovered much outcropping rock and loose boulders, which they recognised would be excellent ammunition to send rolling down on to the horsed column below, useful as a daunting preliminary to their own headlong assault. Positioning their men to best advantage, they settled down to wait.

And wait they did, hour after hour, as the afternoon wore on, Glencairn himself riding up and down the length of the pass to keep all at the ready and informed. And it was the earl who disappointingly eventually brought them the news. Morgan and his force, reckoned as numbering perhaps fifteen hundred horse, were not presently risking the narrows, according to their scouts. He had halted his troopers at their own former camp at Inverey, and appeared to be settling in. He had, sadly, presumably learned the lesson of Aberfoyle.

It was anticlimax.

However, it was just possible that the enemy might be waiting to attempt an advance by night, when it could conceivably be less dangerous, although this seemed rather unlikely. Or Morgan might be waiting till the morrow, when his men and horses were rested after their long riding. So the ambush position must continue to be held meantime, and scouts posted.

So there was settling in for a watchful night, there on the hillside.

No alarm was sounded.

In the morning, however sleep-starved, all were on the alert again, waiting. Scouts brought no word of enemy movement.

All day that was the situation. It began to dawn on Glencairn's host that Morgan was not going to risk an entry into the narrows.

Was there any way by which the enemy could reach them, avoiding this pass? Farquharson thought not. Clansmen on foot could conceivably enflank them north-abouts, by going up Glen Quoich into the heights of Ben a' Bourd, a tremendous land-mass, crossing the summits and descending Glen Darry and then Glen Lui to the upper Dee; but this was quite out of the question for mounted troops. Southwards up Glen Clunie, as they had come, there was no way across the mountains westwards. Morgan, if he was not to enter this pass, had no option but to stay where he was, or to retire.

This conclusion appeared to have been reached by the English also, for the quite ridiculous situation developed of two armies sitting there five miles apart facing each other and neither prepared to make a move – for Glencairn realised that it would be folly for him to attempt an attack on Morgan entrenched at Inverey; fifteen hundred armoured Roundheads in defensive position would present an all but impregnable front against their own lightly armed men, however superior they might be in numbers.

So they waited. Who would tire of it first? Who would get hungry first, for supplies for many mouths were a major problem? Suppose Lorne came at last, over the Cairnweill, at Morgan's back? That might offer a chance for them to move in.

The scouts kept vigil.

Jamie wondered about Donside. That river some fifteen miles to the north traced a roughly parallel course to Dee. Could the English get up to the Don and work round to descend on them from behind? Or for that matter, could they use it to descend on Aberdeen while Morgan was held up here? He was told that neither was a practical proposition.

Such questions became pointless anyway when, after a wait of four days, Morgan and his force saw the situation as profitless and packed up, to return down Dee whence they had come, presumably heading for food and forage at Aberdeen. The confrontation was over, meantime.

Now the Scots had to wait for their lieutenant-general, Lorne.

In fact, little as it was anticipated, they waited for all of five weeks, back at Inverey, waited for the Campbells. Other parties of recruits did arrive, from north and west, but Lorne did not, to the fury of the other Highland chiefs and the worry of Glencairn. It was not only the useful addition of the thousand and more men which concerned him; it was the fact that Lorne held the king's signed commission of lieutenant-general, and as such was second-in-command of all the royalist forces in Scotland, and was entitled to be consulted and involved in this and any other campaign. It was all a most offputting situation, and in more ways than one.

At least the delay and exasperation did not greatly affect Jamie Ramsay, for he and his friends and supporters were kept sufficiently busy. The tasks of themselves and other horsed companies like them was to range far and wide over the land, as it were showing the royal banner, proclaiming the fact that the occupying English were to be challenged and driven out, in the first place in this northern half of the country, and later from Scotland altogether. The high mountainous areas were, of course, not available to either side, but, once down Dee some thirty miles, a vast area of lower Aberdeensire countryside was more or less open to them for their riding and patrolling. No actual fighting developed from all this parading and demonstrating, for no Roundhead troops were actually based in the country area. Morgan may have sent out his own patrols from Aberdeen city, but if so none was actually encountered by the Scots parties.

It seemed a strange way to campaign, as autumn passed into winter, and snows appeared on the mountains and rivers began to run high, the point of it all becoming less and less obvious as travel became the more difficult. But Glencairn, who had had experience of warfare in the Highlands when heading Covenant forces against Montrose, declared that winter campaigning in the Highlands was possible for determined and experienced foot, and even men mounted on garrons; and of course, to the advantage of such as themselves, the clan chiefs agreeing with him, even though, in all this long waiting, some of their clansfolk did tend to drift quietly off home. For his part, Jamie was not long in wishing that he could do his waiting back at Bamff, with Tina.

With November upon them, the leadership made their decision, or two of them. One was to send Viscount Kenmure himself, rated as a colonel, to Lorne at Innischonnel, or wherever he was basing himself, to command attendance forthwith; the other to despatch a part of their force to Badenoch and the upper Spey valley, where they heard that a Roundhead force had been installed in Ruthven Castle, near Kingussie, as a sort of halfway station between Perth and their garrison at Inverness. If Ruthven could be recaptured and its holders disposed of, it would isolate Inverness and greatly help the overall situation.

Ruthven was in fact no more than thirty miles away from Inverey, to the west, as the eagles flew. But the mighty barrier of the Monadh Ruadh lay between. However, Farquharson assured that there were ways through this, the highest mountain-mass in the land, for resolute men, even mounted men on sturdy, sure-hooved garrons. And since this would be the most direct route for Kenmure to take to reach Lorne at Loch Awe-side, a company would escort him so far, and in

Badenoch seek to raise sufficient men of the confederacy of Clan Chattan to make the attempt on Ruthven Castle, hoping also that Lorne and his force would be brought to assist in the business. The Airlie contingent were amongst those who volunteered for this duty; and Macpherson of Cluny, one of the Clan Chattan chiefs, would accompany them, in order to persuade the Badenoch clansmen to take part.

With one of Farquharson's mountain men as guide, the company of some two hundred, mounted and foot, set off due westwards on a grey day of mid-November, not all entirely confident as to the practicality of what they were to attempt, although Jamie for one looked on it as something of an adventure to provide a welcome change from their now somewhat humdrum parading around Aberdeenshire. Kenmure himself, a Lowlander from Dumfriesshire, was distinctly doubtful about seeking to make their way through those mighty snow-clad masses ahead, whatever Farquharson said.

They went up Dee some three miles above Linn o' Dee, the river now all but a series of cascades and rapids as the land mounted. But where the Geldie tributary came in from the south, they turned up this rushing stream, their drove-road giving way to mere deer-tracks. The Farquharson called this Glen Geldie, but it seemed to Jamie a misnomer; he judged it more of a V-shaped staircase which lifted and twisted this way and that ever more steeply, mile after mounting mile, probing into the savage, rocky heights. Soon of course they were into snow, and progress had to be slow indeed, the foot picking the way for the horsemen, who in fact were more often dismounted than in the saddle, a trial for man and beast.

Geldie was a curious feature in more than steepness, for although it headed southwards at first, it gradually curved round the thrusting mountainsides to the west and presently even slightly northwards. And up here the burn threaded its way through a high plateau of moorland rather than any glen, and this made still more difficult travelling, in deep snow. Yet traverse it they must, for here was no place to linger even as the short day declined. Their guide assured them that there was only a mile or two of this. They were in fact on a watershed here, and soon they would come to the beginning of the descent on the other side, the headwaters of the River Feshie, which would lead them down into Badenoch. Actually, he said, there was only some fifty feet of rise between the two streams, although one ran east and the other west. At the Feshie, after a few more miles, they would reach woodland which would offer them the shelter they required for the night. Disbelief scarcely disguised, they ploutered on.

Where the Geldie rose they never discovered, for it disintegrated into small headstreams, and they were left to struggle over peat-hags and broken ground, more or less level, for a grim mile or so. Probably it would have been worse going without the deep snow, for this, packed hard by the wind of the high tops, at least gave them some sort of base to tread on. None was attempting to ride now, the garrons well content to be led. But their guide seemed to know where he was leading them which, with the early darkness beginning to fall, was as well. The fall of the ground was scarcely noticeable at first, but presently they came across a burn which was definitely flowing in the other direction, westwards. This was an early stage of the Feshie, they were told. Follow it.

Gradually the snow thinned and the burn grew larger and the slopes steeper. In the dusk, the sight of the first small, twisted pine tree was greeted with a cheer. Soon they were descending rapidly. And there ahead of them loomed up the dark mass of a cluster of ancient trees, a displaced portion of the primeval forest of pine, the trunks, however gnarled, set close enough together to have kept the thinner snow here from lying, all sheltered by a rocky bluff. Here they would pass the night, and thankfully. The Farquharson assessed that they had come probably a score of miles, harsh miles indeed. Another twenty-five or so to go, but down a long, recognisable and traversable valley, Glen Feshie.

They spent a much better night than might have been anticipated, the resinous pine branches making splendid fires which, with themselves wrapped in their horse-blankets, kept them warm, despite the cold venison and raw oatmeal which was their ration. After the day's miseries, there were no complaints.

Riding down Glen Feshie on the morrow could not have been more different from the day before's travail. Picturesque but comparatively straight, its slopes well back and dotted with the great old pines, there were almost twenty-five miles of it, but presenting no hazards, its river flowing fast but without many twists and bends, all so strangely unlike the other side of the mountain-mass. Progress down this had the MacGregor running-gillies keeping up with the horsemen, and the ordinary foot trailing well behind.

Kenmure, Cluny Macpherson, Glengyle and the other leaders reached the eventual junction with the great River Spey by noon, in its wide strath near the shores of the large Loch Insh. They had passed sundry clachans of cot-houses on the way, for this was fairly populous Clan Chattan country, Macpherson now taking over from the Farquharson guide, since this was part of his own territory; but he had delayed enquiries until reaching this loch, really only a widening of the Spey, at the north end of which was the township of Invereshie. Here they halted to consult its Macpherson laird as to present local conditions.

Invereshie told them that there was in fact quite a large English garrison at Ruthven Castle, seven miles to the south, he thought over three hundred. And it was a strong place, once the stronghold of the notorious and savage prince, Alexander Stewart, Earl of Buchan, nicknamed the Wolf of Badenoch. He assessed that it would require a large and determined force to reduce it, and with cannon.

This, of course, set them back more than somewhat. They were not a large force and they had no cannon, nor knew where they could obtain any. It looked as though their difficult journey had been next to pointless, although they might be able to block communications with the Roundhead garrison at Inverness.

They made camp in the levels of Invereshie, meantime.

Jamie found himself to be the only one there who had actually experienced siegery, and was able to advise that

333

without cannon, the enemy's ability to hold out was dependent on how much food they had within the walls, an obvious point but sometimes overlooked. When the English learned that a force had arrived in the area, they would assume that it would probably intend to take the castle, and so would make haste to lay in stocks of provisions and, important, forage for their horses. If they, themselves, could stop that, by surrounding the fortalice, then it would fall the sooner. But did they have sufficient numbers to do this? With more enemy than expected?

This presented his colleagues with a problem indeed. It sounded as though the Roundheads well outnumbered themselves. They required reinforcements, and on quite a large scale. If they attempted to surround Ruthven with their present force, the Roundheads would quickly perceive that *they* had the greater strength, and would sally out and seek to disperse them.

Cluny said therefore that they should lie low here meantime, at Invereshie, well north of Ruthven. Quite probably the garrison would not learn of their presence for some time, set well back from the main route to Inverness. They would send and inform Glencairn of the situation, and at the same time despatch messengers out to all the area for the Clan Chattan men, Macphersons, Mackintoshes, Cattanachs, Shaws and the others, to assemble at some hidden place, probably the Forest of Rothiemurchus to the north, ready to join them in the eventual assault on the castle.

This was agreed. And Kenmure said that, who could tell, he might be able to persuade the wretched Lorne to move up here with his Campbells, to transform the besieging host, and the situation generally. None there was inclined to put much reliance on that.

So the viscount, with a small escort of MacGregors, who knew the territory between here and Loch Awe in Argyll, departed south-westwards, by at first the high ground to avoid the Ruthven vicinity, for Glen Banchor and then Strathmashie and Glen Spean, on their long road to the west coast; while the Farquharson guide turned to make his way back whence he had brought them, to inform Glencairn.

Once again, then, it was a matter of more or less idle waiting, there on the banks of Spey beside Loch Insh. Did much of warfare consist of this waiting? Jamie wondered. Fortunately this was no unpleasant countryside to wait in, even in winter, with deer to stalk, salmon and trout to fish for, duck to shoot and forest-exploring to engage in; but this was not what they had come for. There was little useful that most of the company could do, the visiting and persuading of the local clansfolk best left to Cluny and his people.

In fact, they had less of a delay than they all feared, for three events hastened matters. Glencairn arrived after a few days, with about half of his numbers from Inverey. They had not, of course, attempted the hazardous journey over by Geldie and Feshie, but had come round the long way, north-abouts, by upper Don, Midmar and the Ladder Hills, to reach the lower Spey, then southwards. And the very day after their arrival there was the extraordinary development of a further accession of strength, the appearance of a mounted party of five score English royalists under a Colonel Wogan, who had somehow found their way northwards to Inverey from Carlisle of all places, and been sent after Glencairn by Farquharson. This enterprising Wogan had apparently been sent by King Charles in France, to land at Dover, and had made for his own calf-country of Cumbria, raised these men and come to join the Scots, the only folk rebelling against Cromwell. The morale effect at least was rewarding to all concerned.

Then the third item was the unexpectedly swift arrival of Kenmure, Lorne and the Campbell host. Apparently the viscount had not had to go even halfway to Loch Awe when he had met Lorne on his way north-east at last, although scarcely hurrying about it. So here was the lieutenant-general and the reinforcements so long awaited. Apparently they had come openly past Ruthven Castle, and had provoked no sort of challenge or evident reaction from the garrison, not surprising perhaps in view of their numbers. But they had observed how strong a hold it was and how difficult it would be to take without cannon.

Lorne's arrival, despite its awaiting and the accession of strength, presented its all too evident problems. For the Campbell was in sour mood, as inimical towards Glencairn and the other chiefs as they were towards himself. Clearly he believed that *he* ought to be the general in command, and none other. From the first there were disagreements, with the Campbell force in fact distancing themselves and going to encamp some way off in the haughs of Feshie at Dalnavert – which was probably as well, for the other clansmen looked like coming to blows with them.

Glencairn was faced with a difficult situation, in more than one respect.

At least all agreed on one matter. Ruthven Castle was unlikely to be reduced without cannon. And where were these to be found? The Highlands were the last place to look for artillery. Perhaps the Roundheads would have some at Inverness? Was there any point, then, in remaining in Badenoch with this now large army? Merely besieging Ruthven would be a waste of their numbers, when there was so much of Scotland waiting to be freed from the English yoke. Glencairn was coming to the conclusion that, after all this trouble, they would be much better to go back and endeavour to take the city of Aberdeen, and possibly then assail Inverness.

Most there agreed with this but oddly, not Lorne, now in name at least second-in-command. He declared that there were greater priorities in the king's cause than this concentration on the north-east. What about Glasgow and the south-west? Leave Aberdeen and Inverness, and head for more worthwhile objectives. Apparently this had been his contention all along.

Glencairn was prepared to accept that this must come, eventually. But with this army assembled here it would be absurd to leave the north without seeking to take Aberdeen and Inverness; anyway, the northern chiefs would not consider it. So the north-abouts move would stand, leaving Ruthven. They would march in two days.

The very next day, however, locals came to Invereshie to

inform that Lorne and his Campbells had left their camp at Dalnavert overnight and set off southwards.

Astonished, infuriated, Glencairn and his lieutenants could scarcely believe it. This was desertion as well as insurrection and shame, and coming from their lieutenant-general. Lorne could not be allowed to get away with it, or there could be no discipline enforced in the royal army. What Colonel Wogan thought of it was anybody's guess. All were of one mind – Lorne and the Campbells must be brought back.

They were mainly foot, so could not have got so very far yet. Glengarry and Lochiel, major chiefs of the MacDonnells and Camerons, were despatched with a force of three hundred horse to bring back the deserters. Jamie and his colleagues went with them, riding fast.

It was the first day of January 1654.

Passing the township of Kingussie, six miles south, they saw Ruthven Castle topping a conical hillock rising out of the flood-plain of the Spey less than a mile to the east, large and obviously a most difficult place to besiege, if scarcely so much so as Dunnottar. What its garrison thought of all this military activity going on nearby who could tell? A few miles further, beyond Newtonmore, where the Spey took its great bend south-westwards, they saw the elongated column of the Campbell host stretching ahead of them.

Quickly making up on the tail-end of this lengthy, trudging force, the chiefs shouted at them to halt, halt. Right along the mile-long line they rode, with similar commands. These Campbells were all afoot. But well in front, they presently could see the fifty or so of Lorne's mounted men.

See, and of course be seen. For ride on as they did, it soon became evident that they were not catching up with these horsemen in front. Clearly Lorne was not allowing them to do so. He and his riders were in fact bolting, evidently guessing that they were to be taken back, and deciding otherwise. The extraordinary situation developed of the lieutenant-general of the king's forces in Scotland fleeing from the envoys of his own commander-in-chief, and deserting his own thousand foot in the process.

Was ever a cause so bedevilled by dissension and division? Jamie wondered.

Glengarry and Lochiel, recognising that with Lorne's headstart they were unlikely to catch up with him, decided that their priority was to take this Campbell force to Invereshie. They gave up the chase and concentrated on persuading and ordering the bewildered Argyll troops to turn back.

This took a deal of doing, with the numbers involved, and there was much shouting, debate and threatening. Some of the Campbells flatly refused, and ran off up into the hillsides; but most, feeling abandoned by their lord, eventually did turn back, and were slowly escorted northwards again by the cavalry. Passing Ruthven once more, the Roundheads there must have been almost as nonplussed as were the Campbell rank and file.

Back at Invereshie, the astonished Glencairn ordered the returned and disgraced Argyll men to go to their former camp at Dalnavert, but to be ready to move in a couple of days, with the rest of the army. They would go northwards, round the lofty Monadh Ruadh range, to make for Aberdeenshire once more.

But the very next day they discovered that the Campbell foot had quietly disappeared. No doubt they had gone off in groups by night, into the surrounding hills; they were, after all, themselves hillmen. Presumably they all would find their way back to Argyll in due course.

So much for King Charles's service.

The following morning, however, different tidings reached Glencairn. The English garrison at Ruthven had as quietly packed up and left the castle, for the south. No doubt they had felt that, with all this coming and going of Scots troops in the vicinity, they would be better elsewhere, presumably not prepared for a siege. As surprised by this easy victory as by all else, Glencairn sent a body of Macphersons to demolish, or at the least make the castle undefendable for the future. Then the march northwards commenced, out of Badenoch.

Had it been worth it, after all?

* * *

They went slowly now, no great haste called for, horse adapting to the pace of foot. Down Spey they went, encountering no problems other than wintry conditions and the feeding of their large numbers. There was no point in seeking to conquer the high and difficult passes with this host, so they held to the low ground, covering a mere fifteen or so miles a day. This was now mainly Grant country, and they picked up more reinforcements as they went. Past the Hills of Cromdale, they left Spey at last at Craigellachie, to make for Keith, and then headed almost for the coast at Mortlach, to halt at Balveny Castle, the seat of Sir Robert Innes, a staunch royalist who had been created a baronet by Charles the First. Here it was felt decision had to be made as to their immediate objectives. Some of the leaders were in favour of assailing nearby Elgin, capital of this Moray, said to be in English hands. But Glencairn still was anxious to adhere to his original intention of taking the city of Aberdeen, third largest in the land, and thus striking a major blow at the occupying forces. In the end he had his way, and the march was resumed, due southwards now.

They went by Aberchirder and Huntly, through Strathbogie, and so to the upper Don. They were all getting used to the discomforts of winter travel by now, although scarcely enjoying it. Conditions might have been much worse, for it was proving to be a very frosty season with little new snow, at least on the lower ground, and this made for firm conditions underfoot, frozen ground, however chilly for an army overnight outdoors. All were becoming seasoned campaigners, if scarcely seasoned fighters.

Through this Gordon country they progressed, gaining more recruits, so that now they reckoned to have some fifteen thousand men, fully two thousand horsed, a mighty host with which to assault Aberdeen's English garrison. And there was still the residue at Inverey, up Deeside under Farquharson, to send for.

At length, in Midmar, they were brought up to an unexpected halt. Local Forbes informants told them that Kildrummy Castle ahead, principal seat of the earldom of Mar, had been taken over and garrisoned by the English, from Aberdeen.

Morgan had been reinforced by sea, in the city, and so was able to send a quite substantial force here to take and hold the castle. And it was another very strong place. Moreover, the enemy had brought light artillery to take it, and presumably still retained these cannon.

The army had reached a hamlet called Whitelums when they received this distinctly upsetting information. Another enemy-garrisoned castle ahead, and supplied with cannon. This changed the picture entirely, for it meant that if they proceeded on against Aberdeen they could have an English force behind them, and one supplied with artillery, of which they had none. So they could be caught between two arrays, both of cavalry and both better armed than they were. They should have made for Elgin, many of the chiefs averred.

Glencairn, as so often, was in a quandary. What to do? It looked as though Aberdeen was not for them meantime, if Morgan was being supplied and reinforced by sea, possibly from England rather than from Lambert at Dundee. Lambert could himself march north against them.

Decision withheld meantime, they sent out scouting parties to gain information and to assess possibilities, Jamie and his friends amongst these, probing down Don and Urie and Ythan to none so far from Aberdeen itself. And they learned that Morgan was indeed very active, and that English patrols were constantly ranging over the entire area, largely to purloin cattle and sheep to feed their army but also to keep an eye on all and to intimidate.

By the time that Farquharson and the force left at Inverey came up to rejoin them, Glencairn had made up his mind. It was north again for his now large host. No point in attempting to besiege Kildrummy, where Morgan would undoubtedly come to assail them, with his cannon, artillery in front and rear then. Elgin for them, and cut off Inverness. There was no dissent now.

So it was a retracing of steps in the freezing January weather, back by Huntly and Keith to the Spey again at Fochabers, then on, westwards now by Llanbryde for the Moray capital. Making enquiries as they approached, they learned that there was only a comparatively small English garrison in Elgin and, as far as was known, it had not been reinforced. Elgin was an important town but was not particularly strong defensively. With their own numbers so great now, they ought to take it without much difficulty.

In fact they marched in, after a careful prospecting, by the Pans Gate – where the lepers had been given their bread in the distant past, not allowed to enter the town – this on being told that the Roundheads had just prudently ridden off northwards, presumably for Inverness, to the joy of the citizenry. Whether that joy would persist, with the thousands of royalists arriving to occupy their town instead, was another matter. But at least Elgin was now freed, in King Charles's name. Glencairn, with another bloodless victory to his credit, took up his residence, and made headquarters at the former Bishop's Palace, now renamed Dunfermline House, and his troops moved into comfortable quarters for the first time for months.

Spirits rose, indeed became rather over-spirited for many of the townsfolk.

Morale was further enhanced, presently, by the arrival of more loyalist notables and their adherents, including the Lord Forrester and the Marquis of Montrose, second son and heir of the great one. Glencairn's intention now was to leave a force to occupy Elgin and then march on west with the main army to take Inverness, and thus to free all north of Aberdeen of the English.

And march they did, or some of them did, but by no means the majority. For a courier from the north, from much further north than Inverness in fact, from Dornoch in Sutherland, came to create consternation in the royalist army. He brought a letter from one General Middleton to announce that *he* now held a new commission from King Charles appointing him as overall commander in Scotland, superseding Glencairn, Lorne and all others, and requiring Glencairn and his army to repair to him at Dornoch, where he had arrived from France, without delay.

The effect of this extraordinary missive was as dire as it

was dramatic. It changed all, and not only for Glencairn. The army's leadership all but exploded. Was the king run mad? To change commanders now! And this Middleton! A man of no account to most of them, and with a history of side-changing. What had got into Charles Stewart and his advisers?

John Middleton of that Ilk was a small Mearns laird, of old family yes, but small acres, who had become a soldier by profession in the most humble fashion, starting as a mere pikeman in the Hepburn Regiment in France, and working his way up, fighting for whoever would pay him best. Deciding to join the Covenant army, he was given a colonelcy, fought against the great Montrose, being indeed second-in-command to David Leslie at Montrose's great defeat at Philiphaugh when his behaviour towards the defeated prisoners was notorious for its savagery. However, he had remained attached to Leslie and when the latter adhered to King Charles in 1650 had done the same. He had fought well at Worcester, and was wounded and captured, and thereafter imprisoned in the Tower of London. Presumably he had escaped from there and got to the Continent. And now here he was, come to command them all, earls, lords, clan chiefs and leaders of their own large levies of men. Not if they knew it!

Glencairn was not only grievously upset and offended but perturbed. What did this portend? How had it come about? Was he to obey this summons? Would, could Middleton lead a royalist army, a united army, to possible victory? Would the magnates obey him? One, he knew, who would never accept this command, and his own demotion, was the Lord Lorne!

That evening there was a great debate in the hall of the former Bishop's Palace, a council of war indeed, even though not to plan military action. And from the first noisy contributions and assertions, it was obvious that the great majority there taking part were not prepared to serve under this upjumped and unreliable Middleton. The great clan chiefs were especially vehement, Lochiel, Glengarry, the Mackintosh, Cluny Macpherson, Grant and the rest. They were *not* going to take their forces to place under the man at Dornoch, king's commission or none. The same applied with most of the lords, young Montrose leading the opposition against the man who had so harmed his own renowned father. And how did they know that it was not all a trick, a shameful device? The man was a time-server, all knew. He had proved that more than once. Might he not be, in fact, in *Cromwell's* pay? How had he got out of the Tower of London, when so many another languished and died therein? It could all have been arranged, so that he could go to France, work upon the young and inexperienced king, and be appointed thus to deliver the Scots loyalists into English hands? He might be an efficient soldier, but was he to be trusted?

That was the consensus.

Glencairn was in two minds. He did not trust or respect Middleton either. But he felt bound to respect the king's commission, his own authority for acting as he had done. Even if Charles was foolish and deluded, he was still the king to whom he had sworn allegiance and obedience. He felt that he had to go to Middleton at Dornoch. Whether he would thereafter serve under him was another matter.

He was all but shouted down in that hall. The vast majority of the leadership was determined not to go with him, in that case. Let *him* go, if he must, but they and their men would not.

Out of much argument and declaration, Glencairn made his decision. His great force would temporarily disband. He would take a number of them with him to Dornoch, to test the situation there; and all the other chiefs and leaders be ready to reassemble at his call, if he was satisfied that this was the best course for the king's cause. Middleton might not be so bad as he seemed to them, prepared to share command. Matters might not be so grim. They would leave a moderate number of the more local Moray lairds and their men here, to hold Elgin, and the rest could disperse meantime, agreeing to re-muster at his summons.

That was, at length, accepted, if doubtfully. Most there had been away from their homes since August and would be thankful for the break. Late at night, the council broke up.

So, in the morning, all so unexpectedly, Jamie and the

Airlie contingent, with Glengyle and his MacGregors, found themselves on their way south again, thankfully, for their own Angus glens, however much they wondered about the future and their cause.

26

Great was the joy over seeing the brothers back home at Bamff House after their five-month absence, Tina's welcome to Jamie almost worth the waiting for. They did not let the very uncertain national situation spoil it all for them, though inevitably that was never far from their minds. Meantime it was warm satisfaction and delight – and relief on the part of the stay-at-homes, for of course they had been worried about the brothers' safety and had had little or no news as to what had been taking place in the north. Great therefore was the recounting of events.

Nothing of vital import fell to be reported as to life at Bamff in the interval. Tina had clearly settled in to be a valued member of the household, and indeed quietly, unobtrusively, was making her mark on the establishment, she and Jean great friends. In the absence of the two young men, as well as the party of their supporters, the girls had been taking over quite a proportion of their responsibilities on the property, riding afield, helping the other womenfolk to cope with the extra tasks which had fallen to them, assisting the older men to bring in the cattle and sheep to their winter pastures, aiding Sir Gilbert to superintend the fuel ingathering, the milling – this last complicated by the icy conditions – and the other necessary activities of the barony. They had kept in touch with all over at Airlie, and had no troubles to report from there, and the pleasing news that the Lady Margaret had become betrothed to David Falconer, heir to the Lord Halkerton.

Not knowing for how long he would be permitted to enjoy this remission from active service, Jamie threw himself into all the aspects of life which formerly had been so much taken for granted, although those concerned with Tina and her delectable person did not come into that category, and were exploited to the full nevertheless, and with no lack of co-operation on her part.

He felt in duty bound to go and report to the Earl of Airlie on his views of the military situation. Admittedly David would have given his father all necessary details and accounts; but Jamie had his own views of Glencairn's campaign; and he would also be very interested to hear the earl's reactions to events and his assessments as to the future.

So a week after their return, in early February, he, with his father, Thomas, Jean and Tina, made their icy journey to Airlie, dropping Jean at Lintrathen on the way, to exchange gossip with Mariota, and finding the loch there frozen over. Never before had they seen it wholly so.

The earl and the Ogilvy sisters welcomed them with their usual warmth and high spirits, Margaret's romance much discussed. Of less personal but more general import was Airlie's reception of Jamie's views on the royalist campaign to date, and his own assessments thereabout. The earl was greatly concerned, of course, over the appointment of Middleton as commander-in-chief, believing it to be a great folly which might well grievously hinder the royal cause in Scotland. If the man would allow Glencairn to act not so much as second-in-command but in concert with himself, a double leadership, it might serve to keep the king's supporters together and acting in unison; but from all accounts of Middleton's character so far, that seemed doubtful. If he and Glencairn did not co-operate then it meant a major split in the national effort, for nothing was more sure than that the great lords and clan chiefs would not take orders from a man of his standing and reputation. It would be interesting to know why Charles had appointed him, when Glencairn was doing adequately well, even if winning no great victories. It did not bode well for the future if the king could make such misjudgments. It made one wonder what his advisers with him in France had said, the Earl Marischal for instance? Airlie did not think that there could be any basis for the idea that Middleton was in fact working for Cromwell; surely even a man easy in his allegiances would not go so far against his own country? Yet it was very strange that he had managed to get out of London Tower, surely one of the most secure prisons in existence.

As to continued armed resistance to the occupying English, they could only wait and see what developed, how Glencairn and Middleton got on. Monck was reported to be coming back from Ireland shortly, having established Roundhead dominance there, and might well take a more vigorous role, even lead a major assault northwards. So they must try to be prepared for such. It was deplorable about Lorne and the Campbells. Troubled Scotland could have done without their defection. But, with the father he had!

So Jamie, with the others, went back to Bamff little reassured and wondering how long it would be before he got the summons to report again for action. Keen royalist as he was, he rather hoped the call might be delayed. And the lambing was almost upon them . . .

In fact, it was not long before they were called back to Airlie, not in a summons to arms but to hear and discuss extraordinary tidings emanating from the north. One of the Earl of Crawford's Lindsay kinsmen had apparently been executed on the orders of General Middleton, the Earl of Glencairn was said to be under arrest, and all was in disarray at Dornoch in Sutherland, with men deserting the colours fast.

Aghast, dismayed, scarcely crediting it all, the two earls – for Crawford had come to Airlie from Finavon with the word – were urgent for further information. Was it true? If so, what was to be done?

The Ramsays were no less upset and astonished. Had madness taken over? Surely this was mistaken, some wild story? There could be trouble and disharmony up in Sutherland, yes – but not to such an extent as this. Glencairn arrested!

Crawford said that it was a couple of his own Lindsay troopers who had fled the army and come to bring him the tale. Admittedly they were scarcely the most reliable of informants on matters of moment, mere men-at-arms; but they had been entirely definite about their master's execution, ordered by Middleton, and all the army commanded to watch

347

it, the Earl of Glencairn however not present and declared to be imprisoned in Dornoch Castle, a man called Sir George Munro in his place as second-in-command. Cross-questioned, the troopers had sworn that it was the truth. In a state of mixed disbelief, anger and all but despair, the two noblemen must have fuller and reliable information. The Lord Gray was always the best-informed man in the land, up in his Redcastle of Lunan, partly because of his sea-going vessel which could bring him news from near and far, partly because of his close links with Dundee and his spies in the English camp, and also because he was a Catholic and the wandering friars who visited him were still the best news-carriers extant. Jamie Ramsay knew and had worked with Gray. Would he go up to Lunan and try to discover the true situation for them?

That young man could not refuse. And horrified as he was by the entire story, he was as eager as anyone to learn the facts of it. Yes, he would go, and without delay.

Back at Bamff, when Tina heard the grim tale and Jamie's new mission, she announced that she was not going to be parted from him again so soon. She had gone with him to the Lord Gray's house before; she would go again. Her husband was not of a mind to say her nay.

The very next morning, then, they set out together, taking the same route as before, by Meigle, Glamis, Forfar and Frioch, to the Lunan Water. It was almost March and the days were lengthening a little, the frost lessening, but not sufficiently so as to produce flooding, which would come for sure. They reckoned that, with luck, they could cover the thirty-five-mile journey in one day's steady riding.

At their arrival at Lunan Bay, it was not so dark that they could not see Lord Gray's ship tied up there, so it was probable that he was in residence. They found him to be so, and were well received, Anne, Mistress of Gray, being especially pleased to see Tina, for she tended to lack feminine company in this isolated castle of her father's, with no other lairdly establishment for many a mile.

Gray proved to be indeed fairly fully informed as to the sorry events up in Sutherland, and dejected thereby, more unhappy than Jamie had ever seen him. It was no itinerant friar who had brought him account of it all but a Carnegie kinsman of the Earl of Southesk on his way home from the disbanded army to Kinnaird. Gray poured out a grim story.

Glencairn had marched north from Elgin with less than half of the force he had brought there. Avoiding Inverness town itself he had crossed the River Ness about eight miles westwards, near its emergence from the long loch of the same name. Here more of the west-coast clans had taken their departure, but apparently he had persuaded MacDonnell of Glengarry to remain with him meantime. They had had a skirmish or two with Roundhead parties sent out from Inverness, but no real battle, and had proceeded on northwards by Beauly, Dingwall and over the Struie pass to Tain and the Dornoch Firth, some seventy miles. There they found General Middleton with only a small retinue, mainly officers who had sailed with him from France and some local recruits, Munros and Mackays, for this was their country. Amongst them had come Sir George Munro of Obisdale, a colonel, as second-in-command.

Despite the grievous replacement of himself by Middleton, apparently Glencairn had behaved most magnanimously, greeting the other well, introducing his lieutenants and even conducting a banquet of sorts for his successor. It was at the end of this, when proposing the health of the King's Grace and that of his new commander in Scotland, coupled with hopes for the success of the royal forces, of which he had brought fifteen hundred horse and three thousand and five hundred foot, declaring them to be right worthy supporters of the king and having proven it, that this Sir George Munro, presumably drink-taken, had jumped up and declared that from what he had seen of them they were much otherwise, a rabble of Highland thieves and robbers, and that he would ensure a different sort of support for His Majesty's cause.

All but a riot had ensued then, Glengarry leading the fury, Munro and even Middleton endangered in their persons. It was Glencairn who eventually gained control and calmed the company somewhat. But he was not going to hear his people so decried before their new general, and had named Munro

349

as base liar so to speak of them. Further insults of a personal nature were then hurled at the earl by the colonel, resulting in him being challenged by the former to a duel, in the morning. Middleton had apparently made little attempt to restrain his henchman. The company had stormed out of Dornoch Castle, and there had been a night of next to mutiny.

In the morning the duel had indeed taken place, with swords, and Glencairn had won, wounding Munro, to the cheers of the onlookers.

But the cheers had turned almost to tears presently, when Middleton had had Glencairn arrested, stripped of his sword and declared no longer any sort of commander in the king's forces. He was thrown into a cell of the castle.

Thereafter there had been fighting between the two sets of officers, with some deaths, a Major Lindsay having slain a Major Livingstone. In revulsion and revolt, Glengarry had led off almost all the force Glencairn had brought north, to join those left at Loch Ness-side.

That was the position as far as Lord Gray knew it; Glencairn a prisoner and his army dispersed who knew where.

Shocked and all but speechless by this account, his hearers nearly wept for their native land. What was it with Scots that they should so often choose to fight each other rather than the common foe?

In the morning, however, Gray gave them news of a more pleasing and personal nature. He had had a visitor a few weeks before, a notable one, none other than Sir James Hope, a Lord of Session under the style of Lord Hopetoun, Master of the Mint and Commissioner of Public Accounts, a very prominent character who had managed to hold on to those positions despite the English occupation, not co-operating with Monck but seeking cleverly, with others, to maintain some continuing authority in national affairs. A lawyer and no soldier, he had done more for the country than many of the latter. He was a son of that other distinguished lawyer, Sir Thomas Hope of Craighall, former Lord Advocate, who with Sir Thomas Hamilton, Tam of the Coogate, Secretary of State, had all but ruled Scotland for James the Sixth when he went south to take over Queen Elizabeth's throne in London. This Lord Hopetoun was shrewd and personable, aged around forty, and trustworthy, Gray was assured. And he had come to see him about, of all things, the missing regalia.

It seemed that he was concerned largely because the Lady Anne Douglas, Countess Marischal, who had been a close friend of his late wife, she to whom James Grainger had written detailing the Honours position, had sought him to do something about it, she being unable still to join her husband in France. She felt that someone in authority should know the full situation and ensure the safety of the regalia. He had a private reason for accepting her charge: his father, when Lord High Commissioner to the General Assembly of the Scottish Kirk, had had the crown, sceptres and sword carried before him to the various sessions, as representing the king, and young James had been in the procession carrying them. He had known that Lord Gray had been involved in getting the Honours safely out of Edinburgh Castle up to these parts, and probably knew as much as anybody, so he had called on him for information.

Telling him all that he knew, he had sent him onward to Kinneff and Dunnottar.

And, unexpectedly, Hopetoun had come back to Lunan, not immediately but just four days ago, on his way north again, and passed the night. And in his talk had spoken frequently of the Lady Mary. Gray would be much surprised if there was not something of a romance brewing there.

His visitors were intrigued to hear of this, more than pleased if indeed it proved to be true, and the attraction on Mary's side as well as seemingly on this man Hope's. There and then Tina declared that they themselves should make the extra journey up to Dunnottar instead of returning south right away; almost she had suggested this anyway, while they were thus near, only some twenty-five miles after all. It would not greatly matter if they were a couple of days later in getting back to Airlie with their news, would it? Jamie did not take overmuch persuading. Gray nodded his head sagely.

So they rode on northwards again, on the now well-known

road, wondering what they were going to find at Dunnottar. The castle was less than twenty miles south of Aberdeen. Did General Morgan ever revisit it? Or did he shun the place, reminder of failure?

After the usual delay at the lowermost gatehouse, they were recognised by someone, and admitted. And halfway up to the rock-top, Mary Keith, informed, came running down to meet them, all exclamation and gladness. The hugs and kisses were generous for both of them.

She barely listened to their explanations about being so comparatively nearby at Lunan Bay, and so having to come and see them all here, when she came out with her announcement.

"There is a man here, a wonderful man!" she declared. "I rejoice that you can meet him. He is . . . most notable. Kind! Handsome! Of much spirit! Hope is his name. Some sort of judge. But not old. Older than we are, but . . " She shook her head. "Oh, you will like him, Jamie, Tina. He is a man to, to cherish!"

They both made appropriate noises.

The Keith household, acclaiming their visitors, were not long in producing this prodigy from Edinburgh. Lord Hopetoun of Session was a darkly good-looking, well-built man, his forty years sitting lightly upon him, with a sort of wryly genial expression and a confident bearing. Jamie's first reaction was that, if this was a high court judge and *he* had to be tried, he would not be averse to appearing before him. He greeted the newcomers amiably, declaring that he had heard much of them, and all very favourable, pronounced Tina as even fairer than he had been told, and expressed his admiration for Jamie's exploits, particularly in the matter of the endangered regalia. Altogether it was an auspicious meeting, with Mary becoming ever more delighted, and beaming with all but possessive satisfaction. Clearly she intended to become Lady Hopetoun; and the fact that Hope was here, so soon after his previous visit, and not in the best travelling conditions, surely indicated that he was of the same mind.

They all spent a pleasant evening, although unhappiness was expressed about the national situation and the unfortunate imposition of the man Middleton to lead resistance to the English, and its first consequences. The state of affairs in the north was not news to the Keiths, for of course Hopetoun had heard of it from Gray and had informed his hosts.

He said that he had called upon the Reverend Grainger, and had been shown where the Honours were hidden. He was well content that they should be left there meantime, until the hoped-for return to power of King Charles.

In the course of further conversation Tina and Jamie heard much of interest from their fellow-guest, on matters of governance under the occupation, learning surprisingly that, so far as the general behaviour of the Scots population was concerned, there was in fact actual improvement, the Cromwellian Puritan rule imposed being strict and stern, so that unruly conduct and petty crime had much decreased, and assault and robbery lessened. Also to be wondered at was the fact that the fiery Kirk Covenanting ministers were being kept subdued, for the Puritans, extreme religionists in their own way as they were, appeared to find these fanatics obnoxious, which clearly commended itself to Sir James Hope, Lord of Session and Commissioner of Public Accounts.

Another interesting subject he touched on was, of all things, mining, for coal, lead, ironstone and other minerals. Apparently he had become an expert on these matters because of his arranged marriage, as a young man, to the heiress daughter of Foulis of Leadhills, and his gaining the estate thereby, the greatest silver and lead mining area in Scotland. The exploitation of this underground wealth had become a major interest to him, of value to the nation as well as to himself. His hearers learned a lot which was entirely new to them. Here was a man who saw life from a very different angle from their own, a man for the future perhaps?

They spent the next day at Dunnottar enjoyably, visiting Fowlsheugh and reintroducing Tina and Hopetoun to the excitements of the cliffs and the birdlife. And at the evening meal thereafter, Mary made her announcement. She and James Hope were going to wed. She flourished her betrothal ring.

Great was the acclaim and congratulation, although none of them could have been surprised by the news.

In the morning, Jamie and Tina were off for the south again, leaving behind their warmest good wishes for all concerned. They were glad that they had come.

It was some weeks after their return to Bamff that they heard more dire tidings. Monck, on his return to Scotland, was not long in assembling further troops and heading north to join Morgan. Meantime, after a couple of weeks as prisoner at Dornoch, Glencairn had effected his escape and fled southwards, pursued but not caught. Then, with no very large force, Middleton marched, also southwards but avoiding Inverness and Aberdeenshire. He had sought to avoid Monck's superior forces, but eventually had been caught up with, in the Atholl area. And there, ironically, fates had been reversed, the Scots caught in a defile of the hills by the English, near Loch Garry, and therein completely defeated with great loss of life. Middleton himself had effected his escape, and was said to have returned to the Continent. So ended a sorry, inglorious chapter in Scotland's story.

The news was received unhappily but hardly with surprise by the Ramsays and Ogilvys; after the débâcle at Dornoch, little other could have been expected. What now, then?

Wait, the Airlie faction could only say, wait on developments. There was nothing else that they could do, there in their Angus glens. Monck's grip on the land was now complete, vehement, reinforced from England, and with much artillery reported to be landed at Dundee. Scotland would rise again undoubtedly, from these ashes, as she had done in the past, many a time. Glencairn might manage to rally support in the Lowlands; but it would have to be seen to be large-scale and vigorous, and with no more upjumped commanders sent from France to take it over, before the Highlanders would rise again, that was for sure. So it was waiting, heads down, lying low, in the interim. Heaven give King Charles and his advisers, George Villiers, Duke of Buckingham, in particular, some wisdom.

There was of course the other side of the coin to consider, at Bamff House. No more absence on military service likely for some considerable time, and not only to Tina's satisfaction. Life could be established on a more settled and personally rewarding pattern, there amongst their foothills of the mountains. The Ramsays had been there for four hundred years; they must continue to hold the Forest of Alyth, whoever temporarily held the nation at large; that was a parallel priority, even though it looked as though the Honours of Scotland would remain buried in Kinneff kirk for some time to come. Tina was strong on this conception of events. Jamie must not fret and feel guilt. He had done his bit, more than done it. Besides, there were duties and duties.

"My dear," she told him, the night of his return from Airlie Castle and a conference there which had decided on the programme of waiting in readiness. "You are, I am now sure, going to have to shoulder a new burden. I have anticipated this for a week or two. Now I have no doubts. You are going to become a father. Father of one more Ramsay to carry on the line, for the child will be a son. Somehow, of that I have no doubt. A son, Jamie! Can you bear this new load, my heart? As well that King Charles's cause slumbers meantime, since his so-loyal supporter is going to be otherwise committed. I . . ."

She got no further, as he took her in his arms and swept her off her feet, wordless as on other dramatic occasions until, suddenly putting her down, he found his voice.

"Oh, forgive me! I am sorry. This is not . . . endangering you. And, and him? Bad for you? Oh, Tina . . . !"

"Foolish one!" She laughed. "You are in too much of a hurry – as so often! You have months to wait, yet, before we need take such precautions! See, come you!" And she took his hand, to lead him to their waiting bed.

Continuum

The waiting for young John Ramsay – for it was indeed a son that they produced – was the least of the waiting which they, and others, were called upon to endure thereafter, six grim years of waiting in fact, until in 1660 King Charles was able to return to his joint kingdoms, summoned there at last – and of all men, principally by General George Monck.

If these six years were dire for Scotland, they were scarcely less so for England, not to mention Ireland and Wales, discontent with the Puritan rule ever growing there. One year after Middleton's defeat and flight, Cromwell set up what was called the Rule of Major-Generals, which more or less superseded the now seldom-meeting parliament. Two years after that he was actually offered the throne, however unconstitutionally, but refused it, a man troubled in mind and sickening in body. In another year he was dead, and the reins of government were taken over by his son Richard. But Richard Cromwell was not of the stature of his father, by no means the man to control four nations stirring against the harshness of puritanical rule. He called a new parliament, but could not gain its support, and resigned as Protector.

Scotland began to stir likewise. Monck, the pragmatist, saw the writing on the wall, made up his mind, and marched off southwards with his Roundhead army, leaving Morgan in tentative command, for Lambert, a more dedicated Puritan, had repaired to Richard Cromwell's side earlier. Outside London, Monck was actually held up by his former lieutenant; but militarily Lambert was no match for Monck, and he and his force were brushed aside, and the latter entered London town more or less as a triumphant saviour. There he urged a tumultuous session of parliament to call for the return of King

Charles to his kingdom to resume his throne, the parliament thereafter dissolving itself. On 5th May, 1660, Charles Stewart and his exiled court landed on English soil, without having to strike a blow. The Commonwealth was dead.

Six years of decisive activity in England, and practically no activity in Scotland.

In the common revulsion to puritanism, Charles the Second, loose-living, pleasure-seeking and the reverse of bigoted, found himself swept along on the crest of a wave of popularity, however unearned – in England, that is. In Scotland memories were longer, and tempers less volatile. The Scots were thankful to see the Roundheads gone, and approved of their king regaining his thrones; but he had not created any particularly good impression while he was there, and his priorities now did not seem to include concern for his more ancient kingdom; indeed he never again visited Scotland, his concerns otherwise. So, in the event, he never set eyes on the regalia so painstakingly saved for him, although it was in time duly dug up from its hiding place, and transported back to Edinburgh Castle. And there it remains to this day, although for long, with the Stewarts gone and the Union of Parliaments in 1707, it was all but lost and forgotten, until, in 1818, Sir Walter Scott instigated a search for it in the castle, and the Honours were found hidden away there, locked in an old chest. They were, at his urging, restored to prominence; and four years later were shown to George the Fourth, on the first visit to Scotland by a monarch thereafter. They are now proudly used at the Scottish enthronements of the monarchy and are admirably displayed in Edinburgh Castle.

It took some time to remind and convince Charles that some acknowledgment should be made of the services rendered by loyal subjects in the matter of the regalia; after all, he had other preoccupations to concern him, such as the creation of George Monck as Duke of Albemarle and the elevation of John Middleton to an earldom, and the entrusting to Buckingham of much of the rule of the kingdom. But eventually in 1677, Sir John Keith was created Earl of Kintore, and George Ogilvie of Barras given a baronetcy, while Mrs Christian Grainger was allotted two thousand merks, then equalling about one hundred pounds sterling. Such was royal gratitude.

Oddly, Jamie Ramsay in time gained royal recognition also, and in highly unusual fashion. In 1666, his gallantry at the Battle of the Pentland Hills won him the honour of knighthood. It would have been even better, a baronetcy, only it was considered unsuitable that a youngish man should be more loftily placed than his father and elder brother. So it was Sir Gilbert who was made the baronet, in that Jamie could succeed to it in due course, for his brother Thomas died without issue. Tina then became Lady Ramsay of Bamff, and their son, eventually, Sir John Ramsay, third baronet. The line happily still persists at Bamff.

Were the honours evened?